One Hundred Voices

Volume Two

Centum Press
Dover, NH

One Hundred Voices Volume Two
Copyright © 2017 Centum Press

For information contact :
Centum Press
http://www.centumpublishing.com
email: info@centumpublishing.com

ISBN: 978-1-945737107(paperback)
        978-1-945737114(hardcover)

Edited By Destiny Rose Editorial Services
Cover Design by J Asheley Brown Designs

First Edition: January 2017

10 9 8 7 6 5 4 3 2 1

EDITOR'S NOTE

Out of respect to those represented in our book who reside in Canada, the United Kingdom, Australia, Egypt, India, and other English speaking countries that do not use American English, we have not sought to impose American punctuation styles throughout the book.

TABLE OF CONTENTS

PINKIE

BY
RIHAM ADLY

It's so dark out there, the only thing I see is the electric fingers of thunder slicing through the sky. The power's been out for ages, and it's getting colder.

Pinkie here keeps me warm as I look outside my window. I know Emma would have loved Pinkie too. She would have held Pinkie tight to keep her warm, and wouldn't ever go to bed without it. She would have played with its furry ears and poked at its button-shaped eyes just like I used to when I was little. Pinkie would have been her favorite toy too. She would have invited it to her tea party. I can see her setting the pink tea cups neatly over their saucers, a napkin at the side, spooning imaginary sugar cubes in Pinkie's cup. She would have watched cartoons with Pinkie. She would have laughed so hard while watching "The Looney Tunes". She would have told Pinkie that it was a much prettier rabbit than the infamous Bugs Bunny, and she would have done made swooshing sounds and kicked stuff around while watching "The Powerpuff Girls" and pretending to be Blossom because she was the leader and wore pink. She would have worn lots of pink dresses that were the color of Pinkie's fur. Emma would have loved Pinkie very much. He was mine, and I would have passed him on to her.

Thunder roared outside still, but the lights were thankfully back.

"Hanna, what are you doing here all alone in the basement? I looked all over for you. I was about to call…oh come on, not that old stuffed rabbit again. Hanna, that thing is just dirty and creepy. You should give it away, or just get rid of it."

Larry grimaced, poking a finger at Pinkie, as if to check that it wasn't haunted by some evil force.

"But Larry, Pinkie's mine ever since I was little and…" I started, but he wouldn't let me finish.

"No buts. Look at this thing, It's even missing an eye, and there's that rip with the stuffing poking out. How can you keep such a thing?"

I swallowed hard. My throat started to hurt as I tried to keep my tears in check. "Emma would have loved Pinkie. I just know it, Larry."

"Emma who, darling?" Larry sounded baffled. "What are you talking about?"

"Emma, our daughter." I barely managed to say, turning my head away to the thunder-lit sky.

I felt his arms around me. I was relieved when he didn't try to put Pinkie away.

"Honey, I know you haven't been well since the miscarriage." He caressed my face, and for a moment the pain the memory left showed on his face. "Why are you so sure it was a girl?"

I didn't say anything, but I knew it was a girl.

He cupped my face with his hands, their warmth making me feel better. I loved it when he looked at me like this, like he genuinely loved me. I could tell when he was forcing it or pretending, but right now he wasn't.

"Come on, let's go make another baby."

Riham Adly is an emerging writer from Egypt, mother of two and a dentist. Riham teaches creative writing in Cairo and hosts her own book club "Rose's Cairo book club".

THE WONDERFUL LETTER A

BY

MILEVA ANASTASIADOU

Once I set my foot on this place, the weight on my chest disappeared, that weight I have been carrying deep in my heart since the day I lost her. Time travel does not allow feelings. This has been clear, since the first trials. It was predicted by the scientists theoretically, since otherwise the traveler would collapse under the intensity of feelings which he would have to experience for the second or third time. In the beginning, time trips were considered the best antidepressant therapy but due to high cost, they are not used for that purpose any more. Instead they can be bought only as vacation trips to the past or the future by the fortunate few who can afford them.

I do not feel the pain anymore and this is a relief. I wish I could stay here forever, yet I only have eleven minutes to execute my plan and return to the time where (or better; when) I belong. Under normal circumstances, interventions to the past are not permitted and once ascertained, they are severely punished. However, I am extremely determined to violate the rules. I do not care about the punishment, I only want to escape the pain. Unfortunately, there is no other way. I'd rather spend my life in jail, than continue living with that weight on my chest.

A trip in time does not erase memories. Basically, time continues to flow in the usual linear way, or so they say. It is the traveler who keeps moving back and forth collecting experience, instead of continuously moving towards the same direction. It is like when you are on a street

13

and you can move ahead, but if you wish, but you can go backwards as well. The same logic applies to time. The only difference is the change of direction is still rather expensive, in this case. Memories can theoretically be erased, only if something changes in the past.

I initially planned to use this trip to deter the accident. I imagined the way, calculated every little detail, to ensure her trip through the alphabet of life would not be abruptly interrupted. Some days before the trip, a thought crossed my mind that puzzled me. Even if my plan proved successful, I would only postpone the inevitable. I would come back to my time, I would have the chance to hold her in my arms a while longer, yet sooner or later, I would still lose her. Or even worse, I would die first and then she would be forced to experience the pain. It became apparent my plan did not ensure eradication of the pain I was desperately trying to escape. My thoughts went even further, to the relatively improbable case; I would return to my present time, only to be alone again, as she might have left in another time of my past, that I could not even imagine. Fate does not lack imagination, once determined to achieve her goal.

I spent all my fortune for these eleven minutes. The trips to "the convenient side of truth", as they are called, because they preserve the truth without the emotional baggage that usually accompanies it, are too expensive for me to risk a failure. At the last moment I decided to back down and redesign the destination. Instead of saving her, I decided to never meet her in the first place.

The time is counting down to my return and I should move on as fast as possible. The easiest thing would be to change my own past, which I know best. A dirty shirt, or even a false step, would be enough to delay my old self, so I would never meet her. This way, I would not catch the bus, I would not have time to get the coffee, I would not fall over her, I would not pick her things from the ground, we would not engage into small talk, I would not fall in love with her and I would not lose her in the end. I chose the hard way instead. I decided to intervene in her routine, more as an attempt to see her for a last time, before I forget all about her.

I am watching her getting out of the bus and I am walking, head down, towards her direction. My steps become faster and faster the closer I get to her. For a second, for a very short second, I am lifting my eyes in order to orientate, without even the intention to look her in the eye. But our eyes meet. The tension rises fast. My mind is getting messy, as memories, deliberately buried and forgotten, are now gathered on an accessible point on the roof of my consciousness, as if moving from the rear of a bus to the front, from the back seats of the classroom to the front seat, in order to be taught a lesson that has already been taught. My legs begin trembling as my brain seems too loaded to give the necessary orders. During this short second, I doubt my decision to see her again. The pain is absent, yet the mind stands still, immobilized by nostalgia, which is more about recollection than an actual feeling, without the melancholy that usually comes along, without the pain in the chest.

I accelerate the pace using all my strength, as I almost hear the clock ticking, counting down the seconds until my return, in order to step on her, supposedly in accident, and delay her. I have a few minutes left before I disappear completely and go back to my time, leaving a blurry memory in her mind of a stranger who apologetically smiled. Five more minutes are enough to escape the agony that will find me in my time, if I do not act fast.

I am not certain if it is the blowing wind that clears up my mind, or the lack of the excruciating pain with which I have been living with for so long, but at the last moment, just before our bodies collide, I step aside. She manages to move on after a slightly awkward maneuver. I stop walking, as it does not matter anymore, and look back at her. I watch her looking at me, as she keeps moving forward, a trace of curiosity in her eyes. The truth unveils in front of me, free from the heavy load of feelings, gentle like a summer breeze, colorful as a rainbow. I do not want to deprive it from my younger self. I do not have the right to deprive him of love, for as long as it may last. Life is like a trip though the alphabet, they say. You start from A and travel on to Z, hoping the journey will be pleasant enough to be considered worthwhile. I cannot allow myself to jump directly from letter A to letter Z, without having the chance to live through the whole alphabet. The trip might be painless, yet worthless at the same time. I may regret it, but at this very moment, free of feelings, based on pure logical assumptions, I truly believe all this pain is more than worth it.

She steps aside and decides to rest at the nearest bench. She feels agitated without being able to explain the reason. The stranger who just crossed her way reminded her of somebody. As if she has lived through this moment before, or as if she has just lived a moment of a predetermined future.

"If time is not linear, this could be somehow explained," she thought to herself. She went back to find him but he had disappeared. She spent the rest of her day in bed, reminiscing about the stranger's eyes. She spent the rest of her life in the memory of a blurry love that she was not certain she had lived.

He spent some years in jail, due to a time offense, which he did not remember committing. This is usual with time offenses, since you return to a different reality than the one you were used to, without recollection of the change.

"If time was linear, I should be able to remember the trip," he thought to himself from time to time. Most people think by escaping the experience of the most unpleasant letters of their own alphabet, they will always remain on the wonderful letter A. The clearest, most promising letter of all. They are wrong. They only move on, remaining empty. He was not sure how many letters he had left ahead of him, but he did not care either. He was sad but the pain in his chest had vanished. He was finally cured.

Mileva Anastasiadou, author of «The Wonderful Letter A», is a neurologist, living and working in Athens, Greece. Her work can be found or is forthcoming in many journals and anthologies, such as the Molotov Cocktail, Foliate Oak, Maudlin house, Menacing Hedge, Midnight Circus, AntipodeanSF, Big Echo:Critical SF, Jellyfish Review and others. https:// www.facebook.com/milevaanastasiadou/

IN THE GREY

BY

MEREDITH ANDERSON

The beach was small. It stretched out past the caves to the tip of the island, and there melded with the water. Samael was playing in the sand when the hooded figure arrived. Had he seen the man sooner, he could have run. As it was, he was trapped between the man and the water.

"Tell me, boy. What's your name?" The hooded figure leaned down as if to close the distance between them. His hooked nose and silver-blue eyes resulted in a fierceness that made Samael gasp.

Samael backed up a few steps, the water licking his ankles.

"There's no need to fear me. Now, tell me your name."

"It's... Sa-Samael," he said.

"And your age?"

"Ni-nine."

The hooded figure laughed. It was a hearty laugh that made him taller and more menacing. "Samael," he said. "It's nice to meet you, boy."

Samael looked at him, wide-eyed. "Who are you?"

"I could be your friend, if you wanted." The hooded figure let that idea hang between them for a moment. And then he added, "Or I could be your worst enemy."

"What's your name?"

"My name is of no consequence to you." Glancing around, the hooded figure—a man who looked like he could be the Reaper from the stories his mother told him—smiled. His lips curved at one corner and there was a glint in his eyes that could either be amusement or something far more sinister. "I need you to do something for me."

"I should go home. My mum will be waiting for me and—"

"QUIET!"

Samael stilled and let out a small whimper.

The figure's face was blank as he commanded, "If you do one thing for me, I'll let you be, and you'll never see me again."

Samael nodded.

Again, the man leaned in close. He was close enough Samael could smell rotten eggs on his breath. Samael scrunched up his nose.

"There's something I need you to find for me." He whispered the item to the boy, and then smiled. "Do not fail me; I know where you live and won't hesitate to pay you a visit. Once you have the item, bring it to me. Now, go!"

Samael nearly tripped over his own feet as he hurried off to do the Reaper's will.

*****

The item the Reaper requested was very specific. Samael found it within minutes of returning home. If he gave this one thing to him, the Reaper would be his friend and wouldn't cause him or his family any danger. As the man of the house now, Samael had to take care of his mother and sister.

He took the hairbrush from his little sister's room and slipped out of the house again to gift it to the Reaper.

*****

The next day, when Samael awoke, he found his mother frantically searching the house. He watched her for a few minutes before she even noticed he was there. When she saw him, she hurried over, took him by the shoulders and asked, "Where is your sister? Have you seen her?"

He shook his head. He hadn't, not since the previous night.

"Help me find her."

They searched all day, and even had the neighbours looking, but no one could find her. It wasn't until they were sitting at the dinner table, one spot empty, that Samael remembered his deal with the hooded figure.

"There was a man," he said. "He wanted Abby's hairbrush."

"What man? What did he look like?"

"He was scary and he wore a big, black hood. He said if I gave him Abby's hairbrush, he'd leave us alone. I think he was the Reaper."

His mother put her hand to her mouth and looked away.

"What is it?"

She took a moment to respond. "Lead me to him."

*****

Samael led his mother to the beach where he'd met the Reaper. He half-ran, half-stumbled across the cool sand toward the cave, his mother by his side. Though his mother was breathing hard by the time they reached the cave's mouth, she pushed on and refused to slow down.

"Samael. Is this it? Is this where the man was?"

He nodded.

His mother climbed into the cave, slowing for a moment a few steps inside and blinking a few times.

A question that had been bothering Samael came to the surface once more and he asked, "Is he a Reaper?"

No answer, only the pounding of footsteps on the rock floor.

The cave wasn't very deep; they followed the tunnel as far as they could before the light from outside was too muted to see by. There, they stopped.

"I didn't go into the cave last time," Samael said.

"We should."

A whimper. They exchanged looks, and then rushed blindly forward, into the all-encompassing darkness. Then they saw the Reaper.

"Such a lovely day for visitors."

"Give me back my daughter!"

"She's my child, too. Did you think of that fact, when you took her from me and moved to this place?"

Samael's eyes widened. "Mother?"

"Samael. It's okay. It's..."

"It's not okay, Samael. Your mother thought it was okay to take away my child and never let me see her."

Samael looked from the Reaper to his mother and back again. "But she's my sister. Does that mean—?"

The Reaper shook his head, something between a snarl and a sneer on his face.

"This man isn't your father, Samael," his mother said. "Nor is he Abby's, by anything but blood."

"Where's my sister?"

"She's right," the Reaper said, disappearing into the cave, and then reappeared with the unconscious girl in his arms, "here."

"Give her to me," begged Samael's mother, reaching for her daughter.

"We're not leaving without her," Samael added.

"That's okay." The Reaper smiled. "*We're* leaving." In a blink, the Reaper and Samael's sister disappeared into thin air.

His mother lunged forward, her arms outstretched. Her hands closed on empty air.

The Reaper and Samael's sister were gone. The cave stretched on, empty before them.

Meredith Anderson is a writer and editor. She has studied writing, editing, and screen production at three universities, and loves Firefly, gaming, and pineapples. She lives in Australia with her partner, Zach, and dog, Axton.

INSTINCT

BY
CLARISSA ANGUS

Dylan felt the plane glide reluctantly away from Honolulu. Through the window to his left, he stared down the island as it taunted him with its lush, pulsating foliage and volcanic humps. The sky was the blue of Photoshop brilliance. He leaned back into his seat and took a swig of his contraband can of gin and tonic.

The woman sitting beside him returned to her seat. It was difficult not to check her out. Still dressed in holiday gear, her dress hugged her in all of the right places. Hawaii's sun had made her ebony skin richer in tone, and he felt prouder of his tan.

She quickly glanced his way, and he flashed her a smile.

'You don't think this is one of those flights, do you?' she asked in a hushed voice.

The flight to Los Angeles was approximately five and a half hours long. The plane was an older model, complete with five screens that hung overhead at equal distances down the length of the aisle; each one was screaming with colourful infomercials.

'If you mean it's a bit boring, then yeah, probably,' Dylan joked.

The woman's eyes betrayed a worry he instantly tried to ignore. She giggled. He hoped that she wasn't one of those who would talk nonsensically to him for the entire flight, or until one of them faked falling asleep.

'I guess it is hard to imagine that it could be one of those flights,' she said.

He didn't know what she was talking about, but nodded absently.

The enthusiastic ping of an incoming cabin announcement rang out. They were officially allowed to remove their seatbelts. The woman relaxed into her seat, but didn't remove hers.

Dylan readjusted his legs, unclicked his seatbelt with a flourish and sank deeper into his chair.

'I'm Gayle,' the woman said.

Dylan offered her his hand. She took it and squeezed, hard. A quick and dirty vision of them sneaking to the loos and making the most of their time together came and went through his mind.

'Dylan,' he replied.

Gayle retrieved the glossy magazine stashed in the back of the seat before her.

Dylan placed the in-plane earphone buds into his ears.

Time passed. The sky fell away beneath them. Out of curiosity, he looked over at the article Gayle was avidly reading: 'Conspiracy theories: what would you do in an in-flight emergency?'

He closed his eyes.

When he woke up, Gayle wasn't beside him. He stretched, rose up in his seat and cast a quick look around at the other passengers.

Heads lolled left and right. Necks craned upwards, staring at their nearest hanging screen.

Across the aisle, to his right, a pregnant woman sat in a three-seater section on her own, stroking her stomach, her head down. The sun fought to be seen through white, voluminous clouds. He looked out of his window again and caught the glint of cliffs resting in the expanses of the ocean. How small he felt. How invincible.

The magazine Gayle was reading lay resting in her seat opened at where she'd left it: 'If you had the choice, what would you do – sacrifice others to save yourself, or yourself to save others?'

Gayle returned. Her knees met his eye line first. She threw him a smile. Her eyes were puffy.

'Good sleep?' she asked him distractedly.

'Think so. How long was I out?' he asked.

'A while. I was talking to that woman over there,' Gayle said, nodding to the pregnant lady. 'We were talking about this article'.

'It's rubbish. Pay it no mind,' he said.

'Yeah. Maybe.' She smiled at him again. It sent a tiny, irrational shiver of something hopeful through his bones.

The cabin pinged again.

'Ladies and gentlemen, this is your captain speaking. We've just received notification that we may need to make an emergency landing at Seattle due to oncoming turbulence. I'll let you know more when we do.'

Dylan looked out of the window. The skies were a postcard.

Gayle breathed in deeply, and then out again.

The pregnant lady was looking their way.

The plane shuddered and then was still.

Ping. 'This is your captain speaking...'

Dylan noticed how Gayle was sitting: poised, an ebony statue, ready to spring into action any second and do something. Gone were his initial thoughts and feelings about wanting to get to know her better. Now he wanted to get home.

Frantically, Gayle retrieved her handbag that was stashed under the seat in front of her. She grabbed a notepad and wrote something down.

'Everything OK?' Dylan asked. A nosey question, but born from a sense of urgency he couldn't help but suddenly feel.

Gayle wrote something again. 'No,' she said.

'Can...I help?' A pointless question, he knew.

She looked straight into his eyes and didn't hesitate in the delivery of her next words. 'I think this is one of those planes.'

Ping. 'This is your captain speaking...'

The announcement came and went. Dylan realised he hadn't listened to it. His mind started to race with scattered memories of the last few days. How easy it had been to forget everything there ever was, and is, on holiday. Idyllic beaches, trying his hand at surfing. A commercialised but enjoyable luau. Nothing but time on his hands. Homesickness, in dribs and drabs. Missing home. Wanting to get home. Elated that he would be home soon.

Across the way, the pregnant lady was surrounded by air hostesses. One was trying to reassure her. No, ma'am, there is nothing suspicious under your seat. Oh this? Surely something another passenger left behind. An error on the previous crew's part not to notice. Please don't worry.

Gayle shot Dylan a look.

Ping. 'Ladies and gentlemen, this is your captain...'

We know who you are already, Dylan thought.

'It appears that there is a situation at Seattle airport. There is nothing to be alarmed about.'

'Oh my God' Gayle brought her burgundy painted nails to her lips. 'We are one of those…'

'Nope.' Dylan bolted upright in his seat. This was stupid. A joke.

'So what's this?' The pregnant lady was demanding answers from the hostesses who still surrounded her like wraiths.

'A situation. Isn't that just a fancy way of saying an incident?' Gayle asked no one in particular.

Dylan's mind was an elastic band.

Gayle was on her feet, looking the pregnant woman's way.

She sat down again.

'What if we are one of those planes? What if we have to make some kind of decision?' she asked.

The question was out of Dylan's mouth before he could catch it.

Gayle's eyes were two dark pools of certainty. She clutched the magazine to her chest.

Around them, the other passengers had begun to stir. Someone pressed a button overhead to call more hostesses.

Ping. The captain was silent.

Dylan felt that logic was at stake. He knew this was impossible, and with that, everything was totally possible.

'No!' The pregnant lady screamed. Whatever she'd discovered under her seat flew over the heads of the stewardesses and landed at Gayle's feet.

She picked it up. Opened it.

Dylan felt as if he was watching a horror movie unfold.

A small, non-descript black case, containing a sheet of paper with instructions that may as well have been in Latin. Beneath the paper sat three orange buttons: 'Captain', 'Execute', 'Abort.'

'Dylan, what do I do?' Gayle was trembling.

He wanted to hold and push her away all at once. He looked to the window again and saw nothing but blue and white and sunlight sparks. He saw just himself tumbling furiously out of the sky to meet a beautiful, calm ocean.

The screens overhead went black and silent.

The buttons in the suitcase settled onto his psyche. The captain was just being a captain, his hands presumably tied to a fate ordered by air control. Execute sounded terribly finite and obvious. That left abort – whatever that meant, perhaps life.

'I want to live!' he screamed. He reached over, pushing Gayle out of the way, and thumped on the 'Abort' button.

It was over.

The stewardesses surrounding the pregnant lady dissipated. She reached under her skirt and pulled out the fake pregnant belly.

The other passengers immediately calmed down and returned to their seats.

Gayle turned to Dylan. Her face was calm and professional. She wrote once more on her notepad.

'Thank you for taking part in this social experiment,' she said. 'Would you like to know what the outcome of your choice is?

Dylan, his face covered in sweat and shame, and the instinct to survive, didn't answer right away.

Clarissa is based in London, UK and likes pretending to write. You can find out more about her pretending here, if you like: https://cangusblog. wordpress.com/ She is overjoyed to have her piece 'Instinct' form a part of the Centum Press family.

ROOM 14

BY

WALBURGA APPLESEED

The towels smelled of mildew and had pubic hair stuck to the soap. David pressed the yellow switch; the fan croaked, gave a feeble turn, and stopped.

"It used to work. Remember?" said David.

He glanced at Pat stretched out on the polyester cover of the single bed, his limbs pale and glistening in the heat.

"It's Truro after this," he said. "Nice that we can finally re-live the experience, isn't it, dear? I know you'd been looking forward to it."

Pat didn't answer. David shrugged and unpacked his belongings – corduroy trousers, a pair of khaki shorts, four t-shirts and a Bible. He tidied them away in the cleanest of three drawers. He filled the travel kettle and found a plug next to the fan switch. He set out two coasters, two mugs, and two tea bags. One Earl Grey, and one ordinary. One with a spoonful of each sugar and milk, one plain.

"Even the powdered milk is turning sour in this heat," he said.

"We'll have to get you cool again soon…Here's your tea, dear."

With a sigh, David installed himself on the remaining bed, sipping his plain tea.

"Remember 20 years ago? Room 14. Still smells of damp, doesn't it? But it never bothered us. Just married and not a cent in our pockets; we had a smashing time. The fan worked, back then."

David placed the empty mug on the coaster and picked up the Earl Grey. He slurped it despite the sour milk.

Pat's head lolled to one side and her arm dropped to the floor. Her body slipped off the polyester cover.

David grabbed Pat with a laugh.

"Caught you just in time," he said.

He carried Pat down the green carpeted stairs and past the unmanned reception, twirled her through the revolving door and set out towards the lonely campervan in the parking lot.

"Twenty years ago, I carried you the other way. Remember?" he said.

He opened the freezer compartment which took up most of the van, and slid Pat in, feet forward.

"I'm sorry. I'd much rather you stayed up in room 14 with me."

He kissed her hair.

"Anyway, dear. Night, night. Sleep tight," he said, and shut the freezer door.

David locked the van. He dragged himself into the hotel and up the stairs. His body seemed heavy now he didn't carry her, and when he reached room 14 which still smelled of twenty years ago, he fell onto his bed and wept.

Walburga Appleseed likes her chocolate dark, her wine rich and her fiction short. Her work has been published online and in print and, for some strange reason, seems to be particularly successful in small British towns beginning with a W.

THE DIRT ALWAYS FORGIVES

BY

DIANE ARRELLE

|Johnny Scarlett was a good-looking man. Everyone told him so enough times that he knew it to be true. He also knew he was a charming talker and could talk the rattle off a snake's tale.

But mostly he knew, with unfailing certainty, that he was not cut out to be a prairie dirt farmer saddled with only one horse, and a family.

Life being interesting, as his daddy always told him it was, led him to meet the dying man on the road, which of course led to his present circumstances here in town. He thought back to his daddy, a dirt farmer raising just enough crops to survive and happy to do so. Daddy always told him, that he needed to be content with his life, told him that he might try to go far on his looks and charm, but he'd leave everything of real value behind. Daddy told him that folks were fickle and would turn ugly in a heartbeat, and finally Daddy told him that the land, unlike people, would love and forgive him forever.

Johnny walked across the packed dirt street in the town he now called home. He stepped quickly out of the way of a horse and buggy and smiled at all the people around him, especially the womenfolk. All the females in town, well most of them, usually giggled behind their hands and lowered their gaze. After all, it could be considered disrespectful to flirt with the new minister. Although that didn't stop them from baking him cakes, inviting him in for dinner after service on Sundays, and quilting him a fine warm blanket.

Heading for the small wooden church the townsfolk had built for

28

him, actually for the real preacher who had died of the fever two months ago, he tried to think of a sermon for tomorrow. Remembering Daddy's good-sense sayings and Momma's constant bible quoting he always had a topic. He hadn't bothered to learn to read the few years he'd been sent to school, so he never actually spoke directly from the good-book. A fact that bothered sour, old Mrs. Quince every Sunday, but his charm won over the others.

He went into the small living quarters attached to the back of the church and made a pot of coffee when he heard someone behind him. He spun around and there she was, the last person on earth he wanted to see. "What are you doing here Darlene? Nobody saw you coming inside, did they?"

She waddled up to him and gave him a long kiss, her big belly rubbing against him. "I'm fine Johnny, how're you doing? You can see for yourself the baby's getting bigger every day and kicking now."

"Uh, …well… that's just fine Darlene. How's Little Johnny and Isabel?"

"They're fine too. We all miss you, Honey. The farm's fine, the cold is beating up the barn, but the cabin's nice and warm. I am so glad you found a job for the winter. So is Mr. Haskins. He's mighty glad you came here to help him out."

"Mr. Haskins? Reverend Haskins?" Johnny asked feeling confused. "He's dead."

Darlene poured herself a coffee, cupping her hands against the small porcelain cup. "Oh, so delicate, a china cup like the one my mother had. Don't miss much, but once in a while I wish we lived like town people."

Johnny snapped, "Reverend Haskins?"

"Remember when it looked like he was dying of that fever, how we couldn't wake him up? Well, three days later he opened his eyes. The man was weak as a kitten, but he finally feels well enough to come get his job back. He's mighty grateful for you coming here and explaining about him being so sick. He says you're welcome to keep all the salary you earned as a handyman while you were here helping him out."

Johnny stood there not knowing what to say. So, he just didn't say anything. He didn't want to have to explain to her how he came here and lied, pretending to be the Reverend. He couldn't tell her how he didn't want to go back to being a farmer and that he liked being the center of all this attention. And, although he never touched another woman, the thought did tantalize him.

Darlene stared at him for a moment and said. "Johnny you got that shamefaced look about you. What have you done?"

He stepped over to her still not knowing what to say, so he hugged her, kissing her forehead, then her cheek, then her mouth.

There was a knock on the door and it was pushed open by Mr. Quince, who stopped and stared open mouthed. Johnny quickly stepped back and Darlene stood there, her full pregnant belly in profile.

"Oh my Lord, Mr. Haskins! My wife was right about you all along!" The man gasped, turned and rushed to his horse to spread the news.

Darlene gave him a hard cold look.

Johnny gave an embarrassed and frightened grimace. "Guess we better get on back to the farm. No time to pack, let's just go. Now!"

He grabbed the beautiful quilt draping it over Darlene's shoulders and he shoved the china tea cup she'd been drinking from into her hands. Pushing her out the door, he gave a sad backwards look at his cozy home. As they climbed up on the buckboard for the seven hour ride home and Johnny sighed, "Hope Mr. Haskin's forgives me enough to send me my pay and clothes."

"Thank goodness this isn't a town we ever have to come back too," Darlene said, and suddenly laughing added. "Because I think they'd tar and feather you if you ever show your pretty face again."

He laughed as well, although his was tinged with regret. "Guess you're right. As my daddy always said, the dirt forgives you even when people don't. Yep, time to go back to the farm where we belong."

Diane Arrelle, the pen name of Dina Leacock, has sold more than 200 short stories and two books including Just A Drop In The Cup, *a collection of short-short stories. She recently retired from being director of a municipal senior citizen center and resides with her husband, sometimes her younger son and her cat on the edge of the Pine Barrens (home of the Jersey Devil).*

DIETRICH AND ME

BY

BARBRA HANA AUSTIN

Brooklyn 1943

Less than a half a block away, on the corner of our apartment house; the Kings Highway side; lived the Avalon theater. An illuminated "electric tiara" surrounded the movie title, *The Lady Is Willing*. We never let having no money keep us from whatever film was playing and on this Saturday Marie and I snuck in the back way again.

On the iron backdoor was printed FIRE EXIT. When it clicked after us, we knew we were safe. In the black of the theater, we snuggled down in the top row balcony. It stunk of cigarettes; "a small price to pay" I thought for enchantment. Miss Dietrich's face covered the screen as she smoldered and smiled at the same time. For me, it was her eyebrows that mesmerized. The face that housed them was as white as milk, and the line where her brows had been had not a hair. They lived provocatively painted on, higher up.

On the way home we talked about how unusual she was and how different from Rita Hayworth Marie's favorite. Silently I thought that if Miss D were a drink, she would be the champagne I sipped called "the bubbly" last week at Uncle Hy's wedding. In my mind, that would make Rita Hayworth an egg cream without the milk for fizzle. I did not share this.

Saturday evening, Mommy and Daddy would also go to the movies.

31

Mrs. Oldfield, the wife of the superintendent of our building, would look in on us every so often. I knew that if I needed her, I could dial, Dewey-9-4786. I never called her, not even once. Rhoda was three and, aside from being a fussy eater, she was a good sleeper. *Lassie Come Home* would soon be on TV that Daddy had left it on. I was told to press the off button after the show and most of the time I remembered.

ll

It was on this particular night just after they left that I opened Mommy's makeup drawer. I would "Marlene" myself; my heart beat out of my not yet budding chest. Marie's buds were more than buds, and her Aunt Tillie, aka "the moody monthly", had already come and gone. She said it was nothing to wish for, unlike boobs. I had neither. The mirror where I could see well was in the bathroom. I had to sit on the side of the sink and lean over a little. Once comfortable, Mommy's black pencil in hand I squeezed my eyes together envisioning just how Miss Dietrich looked.

Soon the realization came. Miss Dietrich's arches were half moons and high up, and my eyebrows were just above my eyes. This placement of my eyebrows would not do. Determined as I was star struck; my plan instantly came to mind. I opened the mirrored door for ideas and found myself with Daddy's Gillett safety razor in my hand. I smiled and screwed the shaver closed; a movie star smiled back approvingly. Soap in hand, I slathered my forehead with suds and proceeded to shave my eyebrows off. I wiped my face with my blouse, sure not to leave a trace on Mommy's initialed towels. I had to hurry and get ready for the hugs I would get when they came home. I would be kissed and applauded for letting them go to the movies, even though I didn't have a say in the matter.

It was her brows I would carefully draw that had me in its clutches. I drew and wiped and drew and wiped, all to no avail. My idea was quickly belly up. The black marks on my face looked like I was getting ready for Halloween. A lighter color just had to be somewhere, and I would find it! My voila moment happened when the word "Crayola" jumped into my head. That was it! Feeling relieved my breath easier, I opened the yellow and green box. Red, orange, yellow, green, blue, violet, brown, and black were my choices. I reached for the brown. It's serious now I thought. "This will work," I sang out.

Propped up again on the sink, crayon in hand, however soon realized that although I pressed hard and went over and over the ersatz half moon to create my bonafide brow, all the crayon did was to leave a smudge. It was as if a splotch of Fox's U-BET chocolate syrup magically jumped off the shelf and out of the bottle and aimed itself across the room to hit me. My crestfallen heart pounded, but as soon as I caught sight of Mother's little nail scissor on the window sill next to the bath sponge, I knew what I had to do.

lll

My newly cut bangs all but covered my eyes.

Soon the key turned to announce the arrival of my parents, I tiptoed into bed and covered my head with the blanket.

Barbra Hana Austin was born in Brooklyn on the kitchen table above her fathers linoleum store. A few minutes after graduation from high school, she married had two brilliant kids. She got divorced and married several more times. Barbra has been living her bucket list in Northern California ever since. She began writing at 81 years old.

KINDNESS OF
HIS ENEMY

BY

PATRICK S. BAKER

Jerry's patrol leader stepped on a landmine, disappearing in a bright flash and a powerful shockwave. The force of the blast turned otherwise harmless stones into deadly projectiles.

A rock the size of a human fist, smashed through Achmed's faceplate and into his forehead. The blow killed him outright. Three hit Jerry. One clipped his communication antenna neatly in two. The second one hit his only aerosol can of Quik-Heal and sent it flying into the trees, out of reach. The third stone, shaped very much like a spear-point, slipped between the thigh and knee armored plates on Jerry's right leg. The projectile cut his lateral and medial collateral ligaments; destroyed his meniscus and articular cartilage, leaving intact only the posterior cruciate ligament connecting his femur to his tibia.

Jerry didn't even have time to curse before the pain sent him deep into a dark well.

When the seventeen-year-old soldier came to, the pain in his leg was a dull, sickening throb. He reached for his can of Quik-Heal, but found the pouch torn, the can gone. He cried out in frustration. Jerry looked over at Achmed, his best friend in the army, but Jerry's helmet

Heads-Up-Display told him his teammate was dead and gone.

Pulling himself into a seated position nearly caused him to pass out again, but Jerry gritted his teeth and managed to stay conscious. He put his Mark-19 force rifle across his lap. Then, slowly, clenching his jaw, and breathing deeply with every move, he pushed himself backwards, scooting along the ground with his legs out in front of him, every action sent waves of horrible, nauseating, exquisite agony up his leg. After what felt like hours and kilometers of scooting, his back found a tree truck. He sighed in relief as he rested against it.

Jerry examined his injury. His combat suit, sensing the breach of integrity and the blood loss , had tightened down to create a tourniquet and immobilize the area as much as possible. 30 millimeters in any direction and the projectile would have bounced off his armor. He silently cursed his bad luck, but immediately thought of poor Achmed.

Jerry pushed the button on the left side of his combat helmet, trying to activate his communications. His HUD display showed a baleful red light next to "COMS". He disconnected the power leads and gingerly slipped the helmet off his head. For the first time with naked eyes, he looked at the forest he and his mates had been fighting for these last few days. Green-leafed Earth species mixed with blue-green native plants and yellow leafed Corvo varieties; here and there red, blue or purple flowering shrub was clearly visible under the double moonlight. While it was lovely to look at, it certainly didn't seem to be worth dying for.

The youngster examined his helmet as best he could in the light cast by Selene and Kaguya. It didn't take an electronics expert to see the antenna was cut. He put the helmet back on, reconnected the power and dialed up the vision enhancement. The woods now seemed brightly lit, but with the colors washed out.

He checked his chronograph. Jerry knew protocol called for reports every hour from any three-man scouting unit. When any patrol didn't report on time a platoon was sent to investigate. His chrono read that his patrol was long past time to call-in. He only had to wait until the quick-response platoon showed up. He leaned his head back and closed his eyes; exhausted.

The combat suit's proximity alarm beeped Jerry awake. He checked his chrono again, only ten minutes had passed.

The two Corvos padded quietly down the forest trail on their four feet. Vaguely centauroid, the Corvos were about the size of small earth horses. Their four legs ended in camel-like split-toed feet covered by soft cloth boots. They had two double-elbowed arms, with hands that had two middle fingers and two thumbs. The Corvos had surprisingly human faces with distinct noses and mouths, their cat-like eyes were on short stalks. Plain metal pot helmets, with cheek pieces covered most of their heads and faces. The species had blue hairless hides that darkened to purple as they grew older.

The two Jerry spotted were soldiers. They wore camouflaged suits covering their bodies from neck to ankles. It changed patterns to blend in with the surroundings. Each had a vest with lots of pouches and pockets, and each carried a force rifle, very much like Jerry's weapon. These two were young; their hides almost Earth-sky blue.

The Corvos spotted Jerry and quickly turned their rifles on him. Jerry slowly put his hands up. Then, for some unknown reason removed his helmet, showing his bare face to the enemy. He slowly pointed to his injured knee.

The larger of the two centauriods kept his rifle aimed at the human, while the other one slowly approached Jerry. He was too tired and hurt to be scared. The approaching Corvo turned its eye-stalks, looking at Jerry's wounded leg. The smaller Corvo grabbed an aerosol spray of human Quik-Heal out of a pocket, gingerly handed the can to Jerry, then hastily walked backward, rejoining its companion.

The human soldier sprayed the chemical on his knee. The throbbing ache faded to nothing, the slow bleeding stopped as the Quik-Heal covered Jerry's wound. Looking at his enemy, he nodded his thanks. The Corvo dipped his eye-stalks, perhaps in response.

Jerry then heard the distinct whine-pop of human force rifles. The Corvos turned and ran, the larger one following closely the smaller one, as they both fled the area.

In a moment ten human soldiers came quick-walking toward Jerry. He waved to show he was still alive and friendly. The squad sergeant gave the wounded man the once over and ordered two of his men to carry him back to base, while two more recovered Achmed's body.

"Come on, soldier. We'll get you home," the squad sergeant said as the two soldiers pulled Jerry up.

Patrick S. Baker is a former US Army Officer, currently a Department of Defense employee. His work has appeared in the Sci Phi Journal, Flash Fiction Press and in King of Ages anthology

ROSES FOR SYLVANA

BY
CATH BARTON

It didn't seem right that it should be a day of high summer, the scent of honeysuckle in our nostrils as we came through the big wrought-iron gates. Summer is not the time for death. Neither did it seem right that my mother and Sophia were wearing black. Their sister Sylvana never wore black. I could see her only in the reds and purples of her costumes, always with shoes dyed to match. And I had dressed in these colours to celebrate her memory.

I had brought a bunch of blowsy old roses from the garden, and put one in my hair as Sylvana would have done. I walked, eyes down, towards the gaggle of people standing by the green baize. I smothered a giggle at a mental picture of Sylvana astride a snooker table and pulled my face into neutral, shocked at myself. Out of the corner of my eye I saw Mummy give me one of her looks.

The mound of earth was disconcertingly high. My sisters were there ahead of me, heads close, curls tumbling. My brother Charlie was, as ever, late. He came running in, jacket flapping, feet crunching the gravel as the vicar began to intone. I kept my eyes lowered as the voice droned, mingled with a nearby buzz of feeding bees. One of the roses was dropping petals, bloody teardrops smeared on the grey stones in the heat of the afternoon.

When the moment came I stepped forward with my roses. I gave one to Mummy, another to Sophia. There was one for each member of the family, my sisters, Charlie, even the distant cousins. I was pleased I had thought of doing this for Sylvana, for all of us. I watched as one by one the roses fell on the coffin and one by one my family stepped back into their separateness. So much for me thinking I could bring us all together again. For a moment everything was still, the hot air thick and sticky with the emotions of the day. Then I put my gaudy arm through my mother's sombre one and gently turned her away from the grave.

As we started moving back towards the gates, behind us the regular thud, thud, thudding as clods of earth hit the coffin seemed obscenely loud. For a split second I froze at the thought of the scarlet rose petals, the wood, the pink satin between them and Sylvana's waxen face. Then I turned to my mother and started talking about sandwiches. Tuna, egg and cress, chicken. There would be all of these at the wake, and a secret bottle of whisky so that I could lace my tea, and Mummy's, to make the time bearable when it actually wasn't.

Suddenly, at my elbow, a stranger. In my nostrils a strange scent, expensive perfume. In my ears, a different accent. French? Russian? Something more exotic?

"You're... Sylvana...?" The woman's voice was clipped, urgent.

"Sylvana is dead." I hadn't meant it to sound so harsh, so abrupt, but this person's arrival from nowhere had jolted me into it.

"I have heard. I am..."

I knew who she was. So did Mummy. But we both gazed at her in disbelief. In my stomach was a clutching knot of fear. I had convinced myself this was not possible, that she would not, could not, come.

"Why are you here, Magdalena?" I said, putting a hand out to stop her trying to embrace me. But I knew why. I knew she would have wanted to be near Sylvana, at the end. I also knew no-one in our family wanted her to be here.

Mummy pulled her arm from mine and moved away towards Sophia, the sobs so long suppressed pulsing out of her now.

I tugged at the stranger's arm. I had never met her, but I had heard enough to know for certain this was Magdalena, the lover who my aunt Sylvana had pursued across Europe in their circus world. The lover who used and abused her until, after years away, Sylvana had returned broken and ill to the heart of her family, to her sisters. My mother and Sophia had cared for her at the end, but they were unable to nurse her back to health. Some believe Sylvana died of a broken heart.

"You broke her heart, Magdalena," I hissed. "You should have stayed away."

But she hadn't, and she came back with us to the house for the sandwiches and the tea. No-one invited her, but she still came.

I even gave her whisky. And when Sylvana's will was read, we heard she had left everything to Magdalena. We were all shocked. When she started to speak, we took our cups with tea left in them, and our plates still holding abandoned sandwich crusts, and we lifted the china as one, we threw them at this woman who had burrowed into the heart of our family like a worm. Then we made her leave.

And then, Sylvana gone, Magdalena gone and all that money was lost and gone. We turned one to another in the fading heat of the day, beginning to speak of things so long hidden and unspoken. We gathered up the fallen things, all mercifully unbroken, and brought out more tea and more whisky. Someone found food and put lights in the trees. We carried on talking in low tones in the garden as the scent of the roses was released into the evening air. "At last the good memories were restored." someone called out

"To Sylvana!"

At the sound of that voice a dove flew up, white against the darkening sky and we all raised our glasses with an answering susurration

"To Sylvana!"

Then we all looked towards the reds and purples of that unrepeatable sunset, and I knew that we shared the sense of an ending.

Cath Barton is an English writer who lives in Wales. As well as writing short stories she is a regular contributor to Wales Arts Review www. walesartsreview.org

PURSUIT

BY

GARY BECK

"There he is. Let's get 'im," cried an impatient voice, as I hesitantly opened the main door. The other boys, more experienced in the chase, waited to see which exit I would risk today.

I left my 6th grade class as soon as the 3:00 bell rang, but as on almost every other day in the past few weeks, they were already waiting for me when I got downstairs. I muttered to myself: "If it wasn't for that lousy Mrs. Borgman stopping me from running, I would have gotten out before any of them." I dashed for the side exit that would force me to take the long way home. What made it even worse, was many of the boys lived that way and could chase me further than if I went by Albany Avenue.

I slunk out the door, trying to conceal myself in a crowd of laughing, unpersecuted kids and warily looked around. I cautiously started down Farragut Road. I began thinking I escaped for a change, when Joanie Collins waved to Artie, getting his attention and pointing to me. Artie was the biggest and oldest boy in the class. He was also the most favored by Joanie in the fumblings in the cloakroom when the teacher was late. I started running, cursing Joanie, finally accepting that she'd never go into the cloakroom with me. I still couldn't help wondering why they picked on me.

My vicious classmates ran after me, a mindless pack pursuing its prey. Artie was leading and the almost moronic Bobby Bryan was close behind. I saw Artie's long legs churning, as he slowly drew closer. I heard him holler in his deep voice that always ended in an evil laugh: "Where ya' going, Billy? Don't ya want to talk to yer old friend Artie?"

"Why dontcha leave me alone?" I called over my shoulder.

I saw the railroad embankment ahead and decided to risk slowing down for the railroad crossing, instead of running further and using the underpass. I vaulted the low concrete wall and started up the weed-infested slope. I only needed to cross the rock-filled tracks and they'd stop chasing me. I just reached the first track, when short, fat Milton Glasner, who was only brave when he was with the others, picked up a rock and threw it at me. The pack was disappointed that he missed. "See ya tomorrow, Billy," Artie called in a taunting voice. But I had escaped again, and there was always hope that plague or lightning might strike my persecutors. In the meantime, I could relax until tomorrow.

Gary Beck has published 12 poetic works and 3 novels and will have 5 new books out in 20017. He lives in New York City.

SNATCHED

BY

EMILY BILMAN

Like primeval fern forests, shanty towns sprawled around the city's periphery. The maps I studied on the flight to Praguzi were marked with void spaces on the margins of the city. They were spots of a no-man's land where refugees from the recent ethnic war had been gathered. I had to investigate and report on the corruption hidden on these Hades-spots.

In the hotel, I changed into my jeans and put on my panama hat, after shaving in front of the mirror. I hired a car and drove to Murti shanty town. Children ran out to my car, banging on the windows, trying to stop it. In the coffee house men drank tea and were smoking. Two adolescents were boxing near the fountain, both covered in thick mud. "This way, Mister. Come our way!" they cried.

"What brings you to Murti?" one of the elderly men asked.

I hid my game, so I said: "I'm looking for my nephew who escaped the civil war as a refugee. He has a wound on his left cheek."

"Oh! That's Anton," he said. "Funny, you're looking for him and he is looking for a missing girl."

The children shouted: "Come, we'll take you to him. He lives in a small shack on the top of the hill."

The door and the windows were shut. I camped by the ash tree in front of the shack. The children began playing. One of them fell and hurt his knee. I bandaged his leg with my scarf. After an hour's wait,

Anton appeared. I greeted him and he recognized me immediately.

I explained I was on a mission to track down Carla Jason who was snatched from the supermarket while shopping with her mother. Her mother had been looking for an exotic ingredient for her cake. When she returned to the counter, Carla was gone. Anton said that he cooperated with local detectives who were looking for her, too.

Suddenly, my cell-phone rang with a strident noise. In the message, the chief detective ordered me to return to headquarters as soon as possible. The police had succeeded in tracing a suspect's car in the city. We were going to follow him until his arrest.

Anton joined the challenge. As we were leaving Murti town, the children who had felt our excitement, cried out to us: "Take us with you, Mister! We want to help!" But we left without them. Training children to track down their own predators would be a future feat.

The car chase was rough. We swirled around the twisting labyrinths of the shanty town and the winding streets of the suburbs until, with the help of the local police, we stopped the suspect's car on a curve on the outskirts of the city. Back in the police station, the chief detective questioned him. He shook, sweated heavily, and panted for breath. Finally, under the strain of the stress, he confessed.

Anton asked the detainee when the girl had been kidnapped. "A year ago." The suspect said. The time fit the abduction from the supermarket. Then, the suspect who was suffocating for breath, revealed where she was taken and why.

Children were sold to rich people who used them as slaves. The money was used for guns and ammunition for Tumalo terrorists. Carla was bought by the gang's head who purchased his villa on the outkirts of town with terror money. The gang's territory in town was known to the police who found their chief's villa through the suspects' addresses in their files.

We got into the car and reached the lit villa. In the kitchen I found Carla, propped up on a wooden stool, washing the dishes. She looked thin, tired, and too excited to speak. Her fair hair was disheveled. She gazed at me with astonished anticipation.

"How would you like to go back home, young lady?" I asked.

She burst into tears, "I love my Mom and Dad."

The detectives arrested the couple. They had held Carla captive for a whole year and abused her as a maid. The computers were confiscated and the hard drives removed to track down other predators.

Before leaving the villa, I took a last look at the kitchen where I had found Carla. There were dirty dishes everywhere, the coffee machine burst with stale coffee, empty whisky glasses littered the table, and the ashtrays were filled with cigarette butts diffusing a stench of acrid tar. The kitchen-mess was the microcosm of our misfit world which, in the future, we would have to clean up for our children with the help of our children.

Emily Bilman is an academic writer and a poet with three poetry books: La rivière de soi (Slatkine, 2000), A Woman By A Well, and Resilience (both from Matador, UK).

THE TETHER

BY

MATTHEW BIN

The winds swirled pink and black around our tiny pod, eleven thousand metres above the surface. The *Sisu* was barely visible among the colours, her dull grey hull only a smudge against the roiling clouds.

Javac took his place in his seat beside me. "You haven't deployed the tether yet?"

"They're still pretty far out."

"Were you able to raise them?"

I wasn't an idiot, but Javac always assumed I was. "Yes. They've locked onto the beacon. I don't know why they aren't approaching."

Javac opened the scanner window and the *Sisu's* hull came into view, long slim lines widening out towards the stern. Nice-looking ship. "I wonder what *Sisu* means," I said. The names of these ships tethered with us was fascinating, coming from all over the solar system, every possible combination of letters and languages and codes and in-jokes and dreams. This was a big ship, an important ship from the look of it, but the name was strangely obscure.

"It's Suomi," Javac said, his voice barely audible. "It means strength. Grit."

"They're going to need more of that," I said. "They're barely moving."

"Look, there." Javac slid the view on the screen into a closer zoom, and moved his cursor to the middle of the ship. "They're hurt."

It was difficult to see on the wider scan, but now it was clear. Javac

46

was right: something had belted the *Sisu* good and hard. Ragged, frayed ends of the hull were bent outward, and there was a hole in her side. "Meteor?" I asked.

"Looks like a torpedo to me," he answered.

How could he tell? Javac had been on this job for many years, far longer than me, but he wasn't much of a mentor. I often got the feeling he was deliberately keeping secrets from me, hiding the tricks of the trade he learned long ago. Mostly I didn't care—I was competent enough, thank you, and I wasn't here by accident—but sometimes it would have been nice to know why he said these things.

"I'll try to raise her again," I sent out the hail.

Javac zoomed in again, panned over the *Sisu*'s hull from top to bottom and from bow to stern. It didn't look like much, no reserve tanks, no defensive systems, no armour. Just a light transport, maybe a pleasure craft.

"I've been on her before," Javac's voice was another whisper of wind in the muffled howling all around us.

"Oh, really?" I tried to be polite with Javac about these things, but sometimes his war stories were a little boring, and I didn't like to invite him to tell them every time.

"I did a rotation on her," he said. "They don't have a high turnover. They were a good crew, though."

I had never done any serious time on ships; I came out of the academy as a docking specialist, and spent the last two years sitting in these little pods at the top of tether towers, guiding ships in through the high-atmosphere storms.

"She's a nice ship," Javac said. "Smart. Well-made."

"Well, she should approach and grab the tether, then," I said. "Or maybe answer my hail. She's barely moved since you came in."

I pointed to the readout, which showed her distance steady at thirty-eight hundred metres. I hailed her again, and waited.

"She's really hurt," Javac said.

I looked at the comms screen, the unanswered hails. "Why aren't they sending a distress, then?" I asked. It wasn't as though we could do anything—we were a tether tower, and didn't have much rescue equipment. It would have been nice to know, though.

Javac didn't answer, just stared at the screen, his brow furrowed.

"What is she? Transport?" I asked.

"Yes. Freelance."

"Big ship, for a freelancer."

"She's a good ship," Javac said.

That wasn't helpful. I started an energy scan, just to see what she was doing, and suddenly the picture was clear.

The torpedo hit—and I hadn't believed him when he said it before, because who would torpedo a ship like that?—had ruptured something deep inside her. Heat and light poured out of her, lifeblood seeping into the empty winds swirling around her. "She's not going to make it," I said.

"Hold on."

Was he saying it to me, or to the *Sisu*? I hit the hail three times in quick succession. I didn't want to strike the emergency without hearing from her. From this distance, you could see what was happening with a ship, but you couldn't know what was going on inside.

"*Sisu*," a strong female voice stated.

"*Sisu*, this is Alpha Alpha Kilo Tower," I said. "Sitrep, please."

"We're working on it," she answered. The speaker went silent; impossible to know if their comms were shaky, or the winds were whipping the antenna array, or she had just stopped talking.

"The winds tend to come at two seventy-five," Javac said into his mic. "Try to steer above that and let them carry you in a little bit."

"I know."

The strain in her voice was clear, even under the metallic ring that seemed to accompany the comms. "We can deploy the tether on your mark," Javac said. "Let us know what you need."

"We're—"

The speaker was silent for many long moments.

"I've got to get back and help." The woman spoke quickly, and static clipped the ends of her words. "If we need you, we'll hail you. Out."

They had fought their way another hundred metres or so closer to us. "Please," Javac said.

I looked at him; his eyes were on the scan, still, watching her hull slowly twist as they tried to make their way through another buffeting wind.

"They'll get here," I assured him.

Thirty-five hundred metres. They were making progress.

Javac's hand stood by the tether release, which was ridiculous. It was an eight hundred metre tether, and the strain on it at half that distance was enormous; he'd wreck the tower if he put it out and waited for the *Sisu* to arrive at this point.

"She'll be okay," I said.

"She's a good ship," he answered, which sounded like agreement.

I glanced at the energy scan again, watched the blue halo behind her intensify as she burned her engines harder. How much fuel did she have?

Thirty-five hundred metres. So far away.

"I hope she has the fuel," I commented.

"She's a good ship," Javac said one more time.

I looked over at him, the deep lines around his eyes, the tightly-held mouth, the soft, pockmarked cheeks.

"I'm sure she'll make it," I said. Thirty-five hundred metres.

Javac's head sunk lower, almost down to the console, and I hit hail again, waiting, hoping, for someone to reply.

Matthew Bin is an author and consultant living in Oakville, Ontario, Canada. His upcoming book, Brendan's Way, will be released in the spring of 2017.

UNSEEN

BY

JESSE BOOTH

Sometimes being unseen has its advantages. I can listen in on conversations that probably wouldn't take place if others knew I was there. Having people walk right through me is a surprisingly exhilarating experience. You know that whooshing feeling a cloud gets when an airplane soars through it? Yeah, it feels like that. If clouds could feel, that is. And yes, I feel.

But when your best friend begins to un-see you, it's the worst thing in the world. You know that sinking feeling a ship on the ocean feels when it begins to capsize? The sense of inevitably. The sense of imminent doom. The unavoidable promise of death. Yeah, that's what I feel right now.

My earliest memory occurred when Howard was very little. I think he was three or four years old, but since I began fading in and out things are starting to get a little hazy, so I can't say precisely when it happened. But I do remember he sat crying in his bedroom, curled up on his bed with crocodile tears pooling in his sea-blue eyes. His uncut white-blond hair was disheveled and his lips quivered as he whimpered softly. Howard appeared to be on the verge of wailing, but he somehow stifled it.

"Little boy," I said. "What is wrong?"

A light came to his eyes as he noticed me for the first time.

He rubbed at them, smearing the built-up tears around his eyelids.

"Who are you?" he asked in a high pitched, quaking voice.

The question caught me quite off-guard. I had no name.

I shrugged as I said, "I don't know." Something stirred within me. The next thing I said felt natural. "I think you're supposed to tell me that."

He sniffed, but the redness of his eyes was starting to diminish. "Are you my friend?"

I knew the answer to this question. "Yes," I said simply.

"And you're not mad at me, too?"

I shook my head, giving him an encouraging smile. He shifted to the edge of the bed, drawing closer to where I stood. We were about the same height. "Mom is mad at me," he said, looking down at his dangling feet.

"Why?" I asked with concern.

"I broke something," he said. "A cup with flowers in it."

"Did you mean to?" I asked.

After wiping his nose on his arm, he shook his head. "I bumped into the table and it fell. It broke into lots of pieces. Then Mom pulled my ear, dragging me all the way here and yelled at me. Then she left me by myself."

"But I'm here now, aren't I?" I said with a smile.

He returned a slight grin. "You really don't know your own name?"

"I've never had one," I replied. "What is your name?"

"Howard."

"That's a nice name," I said. "Will you give me one?"

Howard nodded eagerly. "Your name is Martin."

I instantly liked it. Martin has been my name ever since.

***

Years passed. Together, Howard and I slew hundreds of dragons. We saved multiple fairylands. We escaped pirates who chased us in big black ships on the open seas. We became firefighters with squirt guns putting out giant flames scorching building after building. We traveled through space and time, encountering dangers and situations nobody else in the whole world ever had.

I was there for Howard whenever he was sad or angry or lonely. I could quickly turn his frown upside down, helping him forget his problems.

He didn't know it, but I needed him just as much as he needed me. And now I need him more than ever.

Howard is shutting me out. He ignores me when I shout his name. In the brief moments of communication, he tells me I'm not real, that he's grown up and that I need to go away. Every moment I feel more unseen. I am now the lonely child curled up on a bed, with crocodile tears built-up, ready to start wailing. But he won't care. He will pretend I'm not here.

Where is here? I see a growing blackness encompass me – an abyss rising swiftly, reaching for me.

I've been replaced. Replaced with *real* friends. Not imaginary. Does Howard not realize what he will lose when I'm gone? I was more real to him than anything he will look for in this world. I was his.

Where do unreal friends go when their best friends are done with them? To the blackness?

I only see blackness. It is so dark. I can't even see my own hands. I can't keep my thoughts focused. There is no sense. There is no world. Just darkness. I am empty.

***

Blackness. Blackness. Blackness. Blackness.

Emptiness. Emptiness. Emptiness. Emptiness.

A whisper.

"Martin."

Who is Martin?

"Martin." The whisper grows louder.

"Martin! I need you!"

The voice is desperate! A light turns on and I breathe deeply. Memories come streaming back to me, of a life shared with a small boy.

"Howard!" I exclaim. "What's wrong?" I look about for him.

And there he is lying in a bed, in a room all by himself. His hair is white with no tinge of blondness. His face is lined with wrinkles, framing eyes that look exactly the same. Big crocodile tears are pooled there. But the emotion on his face is not that of sadness, but of joy.

"You came back, Martin," Howard says, reaching a weak arm my way. A tube is attached to it.

For the first time I notice he is surrounded by machines with odd numbers and dials. Some make odd noises. I don't know what they mean.

"I never left you," I reply, walking to his side to hold his shaking hand.

The built up tears begin to stream down the corners of his eyes.

"I know," he manages through sniffles. "I left you. But you still came back. I'm alone, and you came back."

"You are my best friend, Howard. I will stay by your side as long as you want me to."

His eyes burn with gratitude, but quickly shift to pain, and then fear.

"I am dying, Martin," he cries out.

I know what that feels like. It happened to me when Howard shut me out. It was hell. But I don't tell him that.

"Do you see the darkness?" I ask.

He nods with terror.

"Do not be afraid. I will come with you, Howard. Together, we'll face the darkness, and defeat it. Just like we did with all of the dragons and pirates and fires all those many years ago."

I watch as the terror evaporates from his face, replaced with renewed adventure. His rapid breathing slows. And then it stops.

Hand in hand, we enter the darkness, ready for whatever it brings.

Jesse Booth is an IT professional, a husband, father, and a musician.

MEANT FOR DRAGONS

BY

KATARINA BOUDREAUX

"It's a fine day for a meow."

Margaret looks up from her book. An older man with a long ostrich feather in his animal print hat rolls to a stop next to her.

"A fine day," the man repeats.

"I wouldn't know," Margaret holds up her book.

"Of course you would," the man takes paper and a tobacco pouch from his pocket and begins to roll a cigarette. "You aren't really reading."

Margaret doesn't like the smell of tobacco or the man's words. His hair is greasy and his clothes are outlandish. "I'm sure I would not know."

The man lights his cigarette and smiles. "Don't you want to be introduced? I'm a legend."

Margaret looks back at her book. She hopes her ride will pick her up sooner rather than later. She's planned this day for so long, she isn't going to move because a man in a funny hat has encroached into her space.

"I'm the Preacher," the man says and twirls his cigarette in his hand. "I specialize in cats."

Margaret ignores him. The words on the page are jumbled up, but she pretends to read them anyway.

"I've been preaching the Meow for fifty years," the Preacher continues. "I've had many disciples, but none come to mind at the moment."

Margaret turns the page of her book. When Giselle arrives, she will finally be free. Four wheels and enough money to get out of the hole she is in, and open road as far as Canada, with someone she doesn't know and doesn't want to know.

"But you, now you are on a quest, aren't you?" the Preacher says.

Margaret looks up sharply. Could her boyfriend have told someone that she had left early? Called the police?

"I'm just waiting for my ride," Margaret says.

"A ticket out," the Preacher says. He takes a drag from his cigarette. "There's out, then there's in. And your hair is rather beautiful."

Margaret returns to her book. Her hair was blue at the moment, but the top was already washing out to the white blonde she was born with. She doesn't like compliments, especially from old men in wheelchairs, and she hasn't been able to dye her hair in months because of her circumstances.

"But perhaps not quite you," the Preacher says. "There are worse things, though. It could be short. Then I would know for sure you were in mourning."

"Mourning?" Margaret asks.

"For loss of something," the Preacher says. "The old ways of Meow. But, maybe you just haven't found the right shears yet."

Margaret closes her book. "I don't need shears. I need to be alone right now, if you don't mind."

"Oh, but I do," the Preacher says. He points to the building behind him and the street. "This is my corner. I receive my morning Meow at this establishment, then smoke my morning Meow right here after breaking my fast."

Margaret watches the Preacher carefully. He doesn't seem harmful, especially in the wheel chair, but she's seen shows where murderers pretend to be handicapped when they aren't. It's sickening.

"Look, I'm going to move," Margaret says.

"That would be prudent," the Preacher says. "The Meow is a powerful force once it gets a hold of you."

Margaret puts her book in her duffle bag and stands up. There is a bench on the other side of the street, but Giselle may not recognize her. And then the plan would fail. She sits back down.

"Is it a woman or a man?" the Preacher asks. "That's what I want to know."

"Neither," Margaret says. The sun is hot today, and she feels her skin starting to cook. She hopes Giselle hurries.

"Then it must be the *in between* that has you running," the Preacher says. He puts out his cigarette in the plant beside the bench and stretches. "The *in between* is no place to have a Meow. Not when someone's been lost."

"What is this Meow you keep talking about?" Margaret asks. She can't move, and the Preacher seems not to want to.

"Only the best philosophy on Earth," the Preacher says. He wheels himself to face Margaret. "It's the adoption of the behavior of the feral cat."

Margaret looks at the Preacher blankly. "I have no experience with cats."

"That may be the root of your problem," the Preacher says. "For life rolls across us, and the feral cats Meow."

Margaret looks toward the street. The red 4 Runner has yet to appear, and she clears her throat. "So, I should Meow?"

"Always," the Preacher says. "Let's practice now. MEEEEE-OOOOWWWW."

Margaret looks away from the Preacher. She has never meowed out loud, and she isn't going to start now. "No, thank you."

"It will heal the constitution," the Preacher says. "It makes the wait more bearable. And I have waited for a long, long time."

"For what?" Margaret asks.

"Why for the Great Meow," the Preacher says. "Complete enlightenment."

Margaret winces. "Right. Like the Great Pumpkin?"

"I am not aware of great pumpkins," the Preacher says. "Only great Meows. And gravy. Gravy is the second great religion of this world."

Margaret scans the street. If Giselle doesn't appear soon, she will have to go home in defeat. She paid the money for transportation up front like the Craig's list ad had indicated, but if Giselle doesn't show...

"The real question is what you will do if left here to die," the Preacher says. "It's a sobering thought. I would suggest Meowing."

Margaret freezes. "What do you mean?"

"We either lay down like cats, or lay down with dragons," the Preacher says. "I know you will choose wisely."

"Lay or lie?" Margaret says sharply.

"Is there a difference?" the Preacher asks. He meows and turns his wheelchair around. She watches him wheel himself down the street. He meows at everyone who passes him in a loud, long voice.

Margaret opens her duffle bag and takes out her book. She opens it, but shuts it and take out a sealed vase instead. She cradles it in her arms and rocks herself. A woman passes by with a stroller, and her breasts hurt.

Her skin is cooking, blistering like the surface of an unknown planet beneath twenty suns, and she wonders if she is meant for dragons.

Katarina Boudreaux is a New Orleans writer, musician, composer, tango dancer, and teacher -- a shaper of word, sound, and mind. Her play "Awake at 4:30" is a finalist in the 2016 Tennessee Williams Festival and her novel "Still Tides" is a semi-finalist in the 2016 Faulkner-Wisdom competition. www.katarinaboudreaux.com

BOTTLE PEOPLE

BY
FRANCES SUSANNE BROWN

Nobody knows where she came from, or how she got there. A few days or weeks passed, maybe a month before anyone in town noticed, even though she was special. She was The First. Small towns didn't usually have Bottle People.

In small towns, everybody knows everybody else. People passing on the street once smiled at one another. There was a time when the druggist on the corner greeted every tinkle of his belled, glass door by name.

The drugstore has gone out of business since then.

She sat right in the middle of the town, in the center of the wide intersection of Main Street and Countryville Boulevard. Her bottle's glass was crystal clear, though there were rough places on its surface where sunbeams caught and flashed on less cloudy days. Passersby would squint, shield their eyes and turn away. She was right under the town's only traffic light, which is why, perhaps, nobody noticed her right away. Their line of vision rose higher.

At the top her bottle narrowed and was stoppered with a candle. The flame, though flickering, continued stubbornly to burn.

Although it was impossible to estimate her age, no one looked long enough to ponder. The dark hair fell on her shoulders, streaked with silver, separated into tacky strands. Her tattered clothes didn't fit right. Her baggy sweatshirt was torn, and her socks didn't match. Sometimes, on cold days, she wore another pair on her hands. They didn't match either. She wasn't so thin at first, but after awhile you could see hollows under cheekbones, dark patches under eyes that stayed closed most of the time. But nobody noticed her. There was no point in her noticing them.

Even after the drugstore closed, the little town still buzzed on weekdays and Saturdays with intermittent flurries of people and traffic. The doctor upstairs from the drugstore still practiced. Lawyers still reigned in the fancy new office on the southeast corner of the square. Halfway down the block on Main, the Quick Stop still sold milk and newspapers and cigarettes. The tiny bookstore, *Life's Pages*, still offered new and used volumes, although not with the same rigor as once upon a time.

The townspeople never talked about her to each other. Sometimes a stranger came to town. They'd cast a fleeting glance, shake their heads, and quicken their pace. Even on Sundays, when the tall-spired church on the southwest corner of the square gathered its shrinking fold, nobody discussed the Bottle Person. Nobody even looked her way, except sometimes a small child who lagged at the entrance, craning to stare and wonder. A tiny hand was quickly grasped. The child stumbled up the steps.

Bottle People didn't come to small towns. Country folk knew *of* them, heard stories that they could be found on every street corner in the big cities. She was the first Bottle Person to come to Countryville. The townspeople didn't understand at first, and were afraid to think about the meaning. For a long time, she was the only one and they were glad.

When the drugstore closed, people wondered for a time, but Mr. Druggist didn't join her. Talk was he'd done okay with his business, had family and some money squirreled away.

And so the townspeople walked quickly past the Bottle Person, and swerved around her in their automobiles. It became easy to pretend she wasn't there. Days or weeks or months went by.

One day, her candle went out. For a day or two, nobody noticed. Then, a big black car came. Two men wearing garish blue, neoprene gloves with their black suits, lifted her, averting their eyes and setting grim lips. They slid her inside the black car, bottle and all. They moved quickly with bowed heads. Quietly, the Bottle Person disappeared.

Nobody knows what happened to her. There was no notice in the newspaper, no line of mourners outside the big white Parlor on Countryville Boulevard. She just vanished, as though she'd never existed.

People talked about the Bottle Person after she was gone. She was less threatening when no longer an undeniable presence; only a grim reminder, an unpleasant memory. They asked what it meant, this appearance of the First Bottle Person in Countryville. That was before the doctor moved his office to the big new Medical Arts Building, and the Quick Stop went out of business.

There's been a "For Rent" sign in the window of the attorney's suites for six months. But nobody will see the sign anymore, because today the bookstore, *Life's Pages*, is having their last sidewalk sale in Countryville.

Frances Susanne Brown is an award winning author of both fiction and nonfiction who also writes under the pseudonym Claire Gem. A graduate of Lesley University's MFA in creative writing program, she is a native of New York who now resides in Massachusetts.

STARBUCKS NATION

BY
MARCIA BUTLER

We were on the rise — shooting super stars of the future. That's what our teachers told us when they handed over our diplomas at high school graduation. We felt we could finally believe them because we'd been accepted to Harvard. In just two months we'd be moving into storied dorms and begin taking on the elite Boston accent of the likes of the Kennedys – "paaak the caaar in Haaavard yaaad." We knew who John Kennedy was. We didn't even have to Google him. We'd learned all about the book depository and the grassy knoll and Jackie with her big black sunglasses in the plane while LBJ took the oath. Our parents made sure we'd seen the black and white TV clips before the start of our freshman semester.

But now it was June and we came to Dallas to begin a two-week retreat to prepare for our upcoming summer internships at the Starbucks on the corner of Lamar Street and 5th Avenue. (Not to be confused with the Starbucks on 4th and 3rd and 2nd and 1st.) Of course, we were okay with an unpaid internship. That was fine because, after all, we were lucky to have a job. In Dallas. Even though we all lived in Caribou, Maine about five miles from Canada. But we had to go where the internships were. Besides, Harvard was waiting.

The retreat was simply fantastic. We learned about milk: soymilk, 2% milk, skim milk, powdered milk, breast milk, half and half, cream. And foam: plain foam, foam with bunnies, foam with starbursts, foam with fractals and rhombuses. And sink drains. Because it was easy to clog up the pipes with wet coffee grinds and we soon saw how was useful it was to know the basics of plumbing. Plungers, Drano, Liquid Plumber, pure lye acid and the phone number of the local handy man. And of course, we learned about all the coffees: Argentinian, Australian, Alaskan, Altoonan — and those were just some of the "A's". The alphabet went on and on.

But the most important lecture was about how to pace our *own* consumption of coffees and lattes and grandes and espressos. This was important, we were warned, because we might get too jittery, causing problems down the road. Like ulcers. Or psoriasis. Or crotch rot. Or eventually, they cautioned, even impotence. So, we paid attention. At the very end of the retreat, just when we thought we couldn't retain one more iota of information (or coffee), we took stock and learned how to print neatly because most of us didn't use pens or pencils anymore. We could barely sign our names.

After the retreat, we settled into our apartment clear across town from the store and began negotiating how we'd all take showers and still get to work on time. Our twelve-hour shifts began at 6am, so we calculated that we'd each have five minutes from the time the bathroom door shut to shower and towel off, and then hand off the bathroom to the next bather. With twenty people needing to bathe every morning, a tight schedule must be strictly enforced, which caused some anxiety because we weren't used to getting up at 3am in the pitch dark. We called our mothers for advice and once they calmed us down, we understood that nighttime is the same as daytime, it's just kind of black, and that's how we'd have to think about it while we all showered and shaved and flossed and dressed in our five-minute allotment and then travel on the bus for 45 minutes – all before the sun came up. We heard our fathers screaming in the background about having to pay a $2,000 fee for the retreat and then our not getting any pay for the actual work. We heard our fathers wondering at the top of their lungs just what kind of racket Starbucks was running, anyway? But that's just what our fathers did. They wondered out loud, and then ended up screaming. We knew to listen to our mothers.

Throughout the first week of work we gradually met the rest of the employees (the ones who were actually getting paid), and our nerves settled down nicely. The retreat had actually prepared us well for the work at hand. We could make those coffees and spritz that foam and unclog the drains and actually write customer's names on the cups. The staff was fantastic. They had so much wisdom to offer us — kind of like our mothers — because they'd also gone to the Ivy League schools like

Yale and Princeton and Duke and Penn State and Georgetown. And Galveston Community Collage. Two guys, both in their 60's, had even gone to Harvard.

On the two-minute breaks we were given every four hours, the staff took the time to gently offer council on our futures. It was reassuring to speak with adults who had been right where we were – at the cusp of a life that seemed endless, frightening, and shockingly depressing. They told us to keep our heads down, study hard, not to take too many drugs and to ultimately try to get a job that allowed for regular sleep at night. They warned not to get any girl pregnant like they had, and even abstain from sex if absolutely necessary. And then they assured us that we *would* get jobs and that, actually, Dallas was a great place to eventually settle down and raise a family. Starbuck's offered health benefits and 401-K's and even profit sharing. We soon saw how very lucky we were. We could see the top of the curve. Because we were going to Harvard.

Marcia Butler was a professional oboist for over 25 years in New York City. She has published a memoir, The Skin Above My Knee (Little, Brown), and is at work on a memoir.

WELCOME TO THE UNITED STATES

BY

TONY CARLIN

It was all his own fault. If he hadn't lost his temper on the telephone with that arrogant agent, he would not now be about to vomit over the Immigration desk at Kennedy Airport.

Peter Martin was a mild, easy-going man, but that agent would have tested the patience of St Francis.

"Hello, Mr. Martin? This is Harold DeVries-Jordan."

That was meant to impress. He owned the DeVries-Jordan Passport Agency in Dublin, Ireland.

"What is your address, Mr. Martin?"

"I've just given your secretary all the information."

"Yes, sir, and now you'll give it to me."

That's what did it: the high-handed demand delivered in a haughty, upper-class accent.

Peter said nothing, counting to ten.

"Mr. Martin, did you hear me, sir?"

It was the "sir" that grated: not a term of respect, but rather Mr. Bumble addressing Oliver inside the coffin.

"Mr. Martin, you will answer me now or I shall terminate this phone call and you can find your own way into America!"

Peter hung up.

What was the big deal? He had a teaching job waiting for him in Tarrytown, New York, thanks to that little Irish nun. She had been so enraptured last year by his piano-playing for a touring choir that she just had to have him on her faculty.

"How did you get on?" called his wife from the living-room.

When Peter explained the breakdown in negotiations, Maria wound herself up for her customary condemnation of his incompetence: she would make the initial accusation in her opening remarks and continue to say the same thing in so many different and colorful ways that Peter, despite himself, ended up admiring her apparently infinite fund of invective. He stoically ran his hand through his thinning hair before remembering his trump card: his Irish passport with a United States visitor's visa stamped "Indefinitely".

At Maria's first pause for oxygen, he jumped in: "Who needs agencies? We can enter the country on my visitor's visa and pick up the work permit at St Patrick's School."

"Whatever you say. You know it all," shrugged Maria, switching her attention back to "Dallas" and "Jesus, I'd give anything for that kitchen!"

The Martin family's arrival at Kennedy was quite a spectacle. Each of the four members, including eleven-year-old Ciaran and nine-year-old Brendan, was pushing a cart overloaded with six suitcases. Exhausted after the flight from London, the four huddled masses inched towards the Immigration desks.

Peter was beginning to feel less cavalier about his visa situation. His queasiness began when he filled in the Customs forms on the plane. "Purpose of Visit" posed a dilemma: "Pleasure" was not true; "Business" was true, but on a visitor's visa? Maria derided his scruples, scornfully insisting that "Pleasure" would get them through without any questions.

Questions, however, were fired by the incredulous Immigration official faced with a family of four pushing their entire worldly belongings on carts, with no return tickets and no work visa. Peter was now the color of a corpse and his attempted replies to the increasingly suspicious official emerged as stuttering gibberish.

Maria took over, blithely stating that they had no return tickets because they were going to tour Canada afterwards.

"With twenty-four suitcases?"

The official's sarcasm reflected his conviction that he had foiled an attempt at illegal entry.

Maria was undeterred:

"Oh, those are presents for all our friends in New York."

Eventually the official, failing to cope with Maria's unflinching fiction, directed the Martin family to follow the red line. Peter breathed again. Prematurely, though, since the red line led to a more thorough investigation involving luggage inspection.

As they joined the line of other suspect travelers, Peter glanced at his two boys, wincing at Ciaran's sad bewilderment and Brendan's sullen resignation. He reproached himself yet again, his American Dream eclipsed by the misery he was inflicting on his uprooted children who had wept their way across the Atlantic.

"You liar! That's a $25 fine for lying to an Immigration official! Open the other bags!"

All heads turned towards the commotion. A turbaned Indian had been caught with some sort of plant in his suitcase. It might have been simply tea from Darjeeling, thought Peter, but the official who discovered it, a muscle-bound Cagney lookalike, smelt a bonus for himself.

As the turmoil increased, a lady official approached the forlorn Martin family:

"Are you being seen to?"

Maria, Lady Macbeth to Peter's Hamlet, sweetly replied:

"Yes, we were told to go on through."

Smiling, the official led the illegal immigrants around the sweating swami and the cocky Cagney, towards the exit:

"Welcome to the United States!"

Born 1948 in Derry, Northern Ireland, Tony Carlin is the 2nd of 6 children who inherited a modest talent for music and writing from both parents. Now a widower of 6 years, he lives in California, trying to play golf.

A DECENT MAN

BY
STEVE CARR

Gary considered he had led the life of a decent man; in fact, he was certain of it. He was decent to his wife and two children, to his friends, and to his parents; especially when they grew old and needed lookin after. Gary believed he was decent to his country, having joined the Army when he was young, putting himself at great risk of being killed in some jungle in a foreign country, and never asking anything in return except if he were killed in combat he wished to be buried in his uniform. Gary never wavered in his belief that he may quite possibly be the most decent person anyone had ever encountered.

He came to regard his own superior decency quite early. As a young boy in school his teachers always called on him first to do small tasks; clean the blackboards, pick up test papers, tattle on other children who misbehaved in the school hallways or on the playground. He was always the first praised for neatness in both his appearance and his schoolwork, and was never scolded for talking, and always raised his hand first to answer questions. He helped trouble students with writing, reading or arithmetic, and when new students arrived at school, Gary was always willing and eager to offer assistance.

It's not that he thought he could do no wrong. He was taught early by his father that life included making the occasional mistake.

"But a mistake can always be forgiven," his father told him.

To test this idea, at the age of eight Gary poured some lighter fluid on the family cat, Spock, lit a match and set Spock on fire. He stood by and watched as the cat's fur burned until his mother ran into the back yard and doused the burning cat with water, saving it before it ran off never to return. She asked Gary what happened.

"It was a mistake," he told her.

She forgave him.

From that point forward Gary vowed to always be a decent person, but to allow for mistakes. If he created a problem he was certain it could be easily undone, and lived his life unencumbered by anxiety he might commit acts that were not decent, free of guilt that his wrongdoing may have any lasting consequences. Life moved along fairly rapidly for Gary, with the typical landmarks of maturity and aging. He made commitments, formed relationships, tended to his duties, and forged a life that provided comfort and security for himself and those around him.

One morning Gary woke up and showered, shaved and dressed to go to the college where he taught psychology. At age fifty-five he never intentionally committed an indecent act since he set Spock on fire. He ate his breakfast listening to his wife talk about her charity work at the local homeless shelter, kissed her cheek, went out to his car and drove to work. Along the way, he noticed the flowers were more vibrant, the grass greener, and the paint on the houses brighter. It was that morning, feeling more alive than he had for years, he intentionally did the thing he deprived himself of doing for so many years.

He arrived at school late, something practically unheard of happening regarding Gary. He was punctual, reliable and deeply dedicated to his job. He arrived to each class eager to teach, always prepared, and was considered a shining example of what a tenured professor should be. He completed his doctoral thesis on the psychodynamic works of Irvin Yalom, and he was a respected scholar regarding group psychodynamics. Entering the classroom and seeing the surprised looks on his student's faces, he quickly apologized.

"I hope you will forgive me," he said as he placed his briefcase on his desk and began his lecture.

By the end of the day he'd taught two classes, attended a department meeting, and saw three students who were doing internships. No one seemed any different toward him than any other day. His lateness that morning was not mentioned. He realized he was forgiven. He went home, stopping along the way when an opportunity arose for him to repeat the morning events, then arrived at his door whistling. Inside his wife was setting the table for dinner and reminded him the Burleson's were joining them. They were two of Gary's favorite people. Although he had forgotten the dinner, he considered it a perfect way to top an exceptional day.

Throughout dinner Gary was very attentive to the two guests. Afterward they sat in the living room enjoying drinks and reminisced about trips they had taken together, making plans to take a cruise next summer to Cancun or the Bahamas. The Burlesons left with hugs and handshakes all around. Gary and his wife shut off the lights and went to bed. That night Gary had dreams unlike any he ever experienced, strange, exotic dreams, almost fairy tales, narrated from a haunting benevolent voice. He awoke the next morning looking forward to another wonderful day.

He rushed through his morning routine, hastily ate breakfast, said goodbye to his wife, and drove in direction of the college, but took several side streets looking for just the right thing to start his day. Finding a place in the local park to perform his ritual, he completed it quickly, covered it up, and then went to work, arriving exactly in time for the first class of his day.

What began at first as a morning and after work activity, Gary continued, taking evening drives when the streets were dark and he was less fearful of being caught and could pursue his new obsession more leisurely. His wife asked about the late night drives and Gary would simply say, "I'm just restless, I hope you can forgive me?"

"Of course, dear," she would say.

Arriving home late one night after one of his drives, he found his wife sitting on the sofa watching the news. "This is horrible," she exclaimed as he sat down beside her. "Someone has been setting cats on fire and leaving their burned bodies all over town."

"Is that so?" Gary nonchalantly put his arm around her.

"I hope they catch him and lock him away," his wife clutched Gary's hand, seeking reassurance. "What that person is doing is unforgivable."

"It is?" He asked surprised, but not expecting an answer, because he already knew when he was caught, and he was certain that eventually he would be, but in the end he would be forgiven, because after all, he reasoned, he was a decent man.

Steve Carr began his writing career as a military journalist and is a frequently published author of short stories in magazines and anthologies worldwide and is a 2017 Pushcart Prize nominee. He has had his plays produced in several US States and now lives in Richmond, Virginia, after spending many years traveling.

DIANA FROM ANDERSON AVENUE

BY

PATRICIA CARRAGON

Diana and her imagination lived on Anderson Avenue. Pseudo coat-of-arms embellished the entrance and long vestibule. In her head, she was royalty. At school, she was the designated pariah.

She loved to walk on weekends. Her penny loafers could testify to that. After her walk she would jot down what she saw in a notebook. Improvised theater was everywhere. Changes in the wind and sky, laughter from children playing "Hit the Penny," and the noise from the Polo Grounds shuttle turning at Jerome Avenue. A solitary leafless tree near the broken Coca-Cola bottles held a tale. She strung these images into fiction. Reading books didn't stir her imagination like her walks. For assignments she used tidbits from her notebook. She read a few of them to her mom. Her mom would say, "Show them to your brother." The teacher wasn't impressed and made red notations across the pages. Diana figured she wasn't good enough. She stopped writing and tossed the notebook into her closet.

Art was considered her forte. Brush strokes painted scenes or still life. Penciled lines took human form. Yet her work lacked the connection between art and artist. It was her downfall at Music and Art High School. She hated drawing. Her hand would always stiffen. The kneaded eraser did its best to remove unwanted lines, but could not heal the scars of indentation. Oil and tempera paint did a better job in camouflaging errors.

For four years, her academic achievement paralleled with her artistic struggle. She couldn't compete with the Artista kings and queens at the "Castle on the Hill." She sat by herself in the lunchroom, listening to her neighbors' boisterous conversations. Her Highbridge schooling and family never trained her to develop people skills. She was a dumb loner, and it was her fault. Her nights were spent doing assignments, between blank stares and coffee sips. Her walking days terminated. Her brother was graduating from Columbia University. Diana wanted to get out of Highbridge and walk.

She retired her worn-out penny loafers for pumps. Immune to the July heat and foot pain, she went from one interview to another. Her mediocre appearance and lack of experience backfired. After a few weeks of "sorry the job was filled" or "come back in a few months," she struck fool's gold—a receptionist /file clerk position at a small ad agency on Seventh Avenue. The place was dingy and had a staff of three. Throughout the interview, Mr. Janovich eyed her up and down, even though he was old enough to be her father. Diana needed a job and to get away from her parents. She accepted the job, until a better one came a month later.

She missed her weekend walks. She bought a new pair of penny loafers at Alexander's. She rented a studio apartment on Walton Avenue, west of the Concourse. Her loafers traversed the Art Deco strip up to Fordham Road. Plymouth Shops had a sale, but she stopped by Gorman's for a hot dog and Nedick's orange soda. As she bit into her hot dog, an elbow jabbed her side. Her soda dropped and stained her cotton skirt. Diana snapped.

The man apologized and offered his napkin. His brown eyes softened her mood. From his accent, she surmised he wasn't from the area. Perhaps a Fordham student from Westchester? The man asked the clerk to give her a glass of seltzer and extra napkins. She did the best she could with the cleaning. Lucky thing the skirt was a salmon color. Most of the orange soda stain came out.

The tension subsided. The sale at Plymouth Shops would wait another day. The man ordered another hot dog for Diana and bought one for himself. As she ate, she learned he came from Bedford. He was an assistant professor of English at the University Heights campus of NYU and lived near Van Cortlandt Park. She spoke about her love for walking and how it stimulated her thoughts. He asked if she ever wrote them down. Embarrassed, she confessed she did; however, her stories were juvenile. She honestly revealed she wasn't smart enough for college. Her vocabulary was limited, and she was bored at school. He inquired if she showed her stories to her parents. She replied that they weren't interested. Her brother was the main focus. She was meant to go to high school, then get a job, and marry. He questioned if she kept those stories. She nodded yes. Perspiration enhanced her white lilac scent.

He asked if she was wearing Mary Chess. Diana nodded again. He commented on how he loved floral eau de toilette. She said, "You mean toilet water?" He smiled and explained the correct name was in French, not to be confused with the water inside the toilet bowl. Her faux pas stained her cheeks, matching the one on her skirt.

They spent a half an hour talking. His name was Edward, a king's name. He came from a well-off family. His future was beginning. Hers was on hold, filing résumés for potential candidates. She never answered his question about pursuing a career in the arts. She hated Music and Art, and buried her pencils and brushes in the closet. Reality taught Diana from Anderson Avenue that she wasn't royal. Her education and talents were limited. Torn pages from her notebook sat in an old Stride Rite shoebox on her closet's top shelf next to her art supplies.

She scribbled her name and telephone number on a clean napkin. Although he didn't give her his, Edward promised to keep in touch. As he made his exit, the radio behind the counter played "Goodnite, Sweetheart, Goodnite."

Patricia Carragon has two forthcoming books: Cupcake Chronicles (Poets Wear Prada) and Innocence (Finishing Line Press). She hosts the Brooklyn-based Brownstone Poets and is the editor-in-chief of its annual anthology, and is an Executive Editor for Home Planet

THE GAUDY SUNGLASSES

BY

MELINDA K. CHERRY

The fundraiser was a success, exceeding their expectations by $2000, according to the figures. Lauren blew the stray wisp of frizzy hair from her damp forehead. My, it was hot. The sun was demanding, even for a late July day. A sharp contrast from several months ago when she and the rest of her co- workers volunteered to sponsor a downtown carnival to raise money for The Youth Group. The funds would help sponsor some of the town's underprivileged children a trip to Disney World. On that chilly rainy day back in March, it was my idea to organize a street fair. But not to be outdone Darla would run with her idea. She would suggest a 1970's theme, complete with mood rings and pinball machines. A dance contest would feature popular oldies like "the bump", "the roebuck, and "the hustle". She even went so far as to dress as disco diva Donna Summer in a gold lame, halter jumpsuit and a curly black wig. A makeshift podium was designed for her and she captivated the crowd with her rendition of "Bad Girl", her svelte body gyrating to the beat. No doubt, she had the undivided attention of Ryan Callier, the new art director. Quick and arresting, if not exactly handsome in the pretty boy way, you could tell he worked out; he was well-built. He was certainly proving his worth at the firm. He had worked for a much larger advertising firm on the west coast, but felt he gained better opportunities in a smaller firm in a growing town like Charlotte. Most important of all, he was single. An even greater asset, not that Lauren cared. After her break up with Frank, she was immune to dating. Still she couldn't help but overhear snatches of gossip among the other women in the office. Darla Woods, the beautiful account manager, who always got what she wanted, was calmly biding her time. A tall good looking blonde, she was successful in all her conquests. Though not surprised, it was still a blow to Lauren when she was passed over for a promotion in favor of Darla, who often took center stage for other people's work.

Lauren pushed her pink sunglasses farther up her nose, took a sip of bottled water and sighed. It had been a long day and she had agreed to work the concession stand, which by midday received the brunt of the sun. She made a killing on those soft drinks. By that afternoon they had to restock their supply.

She glanced around, everyone was packing up. She noticed Ryan across the way putting away his art supplies. All day long, customers flocked around him, anxious to have themselves sketched. Lauren passed out leftover bags of popcorn and the remaining cans of soda pop to the children nearby. As she pulled off her sunglasses and wiped them on her shirttail, she noticed Darla sashay past and stop in front of Ryan. She threw her head back, laughed and uttered something Lauren didn't catch nor cared to, and walk off partway. Poised with one hand on her hip, she looked over her shoulder and silently mouthed "call me".

Lauren put her sunglasses back on; she always bought el cheapo sunglasses because she was forever losing them. After she finished cleaning up and turned in her money, she returned to her stand to double check everything. All and all it had been a good day. To her surprise, she found Ryan leaning against the counter. "If you want something to drink, I'm closed." she coolly stated. About to leave, she collected her car keys and water bottle.

"I didn't come over for a soft drink," he replied. "I thought you might like these." She noticed for the first time the sketches he was holding. Taking them from him, she gasped. They were various charcoal sketches of her during the day. In one sketch, she was hurriedly popping popcorn. In another, she was making cotton candy, and in the last one the theme clearly revealed that she let the little boy have his candy apple for free and she paid for it herself. "I didn't think I would get chance to capture you, but I managed."

Lauren was speechless. "These are captivating." She finally managed to say.

Ryan grinned, "I have to admit, I hate those tacky shades."

Lauren was startled; he had a lot of nerve. Before she could retort, he leaned forward and removed them, then gently lifted her chin. "They cover up your beautiful amber eyes with the green flecks. I get lost in them."

Ms. Cherry is a clerk for a utility company in S.C. She recently received her degree in liberal studies from USC. She has published several short stories in True Renditions.

A WINTER WEDDING

BY

STEPHEN CONNOLLY

The snow is gone. When I open my eyes, the snow is gone and all I can see is grass, beautiful green grass everywhere I look. Blackbirds sing, spectators murmur in the grandstand. Beyond lies the city, hazy and beautiful.

*

We should have stayed with the ship. She might yet be freed from the ice, help might still find us, a ship from home even. We have been gone so many years, surely they have missed us? 'One more ridge,' the lieutenant calls with as much encouragement as he can muster. 'Just one more ridge.' We have been dragging the boats across the ice for weeks now, an act of madness. It has ruined our health. We shall be scattered and lost. Nobody will ever learn our fate. We should have stayed with the ship.

*

I laugh to see the city, its towers and buildings so familiar, the sun so warm. It is so good to be home. My friend the bear pants in the heat, his fur white gleaming in the sun. 'You'll like it here,' I tell him, patting his mighty shoulder. A flock of sheep graze the wicket, but nobody minds. The players chat, throwing a ball around as red as a Cox's Pippin. I wait at Mid-on, patting my pockets, but my friend the bear has the ring. He holds it aloft, immense and studded with diamonds of light, so large it encircles the Sun.

Your father escorts you onto the wicket as the spectators applaud. I know it's you, despite the veil, despite the dandelion blossom in my face, in my eyes, blown by the wind. Your father glares at me, or is it my friend the bear? The sunlight glints off the blade of the dirty knife.

*

The fierce little men rushed around us in their rough fur coats, the first human beings we encountered since leaving the ship. But they would not come close, shouting at us from a distance, words we could not understand. They looked strangely Oriental, comic yet formidable. Do they perhaps change into terrible white Bears when the moon is full? Or become like Doctor Jekyll in Mr. Stevenson's terrifying story? They threw stones at us before fleeing the lieutenant's pistol shot, speeding off on their wonderful sledges, pulled by packs of hounds. Dogs like wolves, fierce and beautiful.

If only we could travel so quickly, so easily. If only they would come back, and throw more lumps of dried meat at us.

*

Your bridesmaids line up behind us and argue over the loads, complain their boat is too heavy. I take your hand as Queen Victoria recites the wedding service. Prince Albert whispers a joke to Mr. Dickens who writes it down in his notebook, or is it my friend the bear? The fielders line up behind her Majesty, fascinated by the tiny crown bobbing on her head. I try to kiss you, but you move away as I reach for your veil.

You wait for me on the bridge. Beyond, sails lean into the wind on Coniston Water. Although it's hard to see, the wind drives hawthorn blossoms into my face, my eyes. The moon glares down on us as my friend the bear wanders off in search of refreshments. I hear the crack of blade through bone or is it a tree branch, snapping in the wind?

*

They look at me, my fellow explorers. Considering. Calculating. I am the weakest of the party, there is no denying it. They stare around for the things I describe, the things only I can see, wishing I would shut up.

They listen to my constant racking coughs, each time producing more blood on my frozen gear, on the snow around us. I have almost no strength left to pull on the rope. Our poor fire gives little warmth, barely enough to heat our terrible supper.

*

We walk through the Snowdrops to the Green Chapel. My friend the bear loads our plates with meringues and pours cream on the strawberries. Bubbles froth on a glass of champagne, steam rises from a bowl of soup. The cold has taken all my teeth, I smile with mouth shut as sunlight gleams off the dirty knife. The wind blows sugar into my face and eyes. When I can see again the room is deserted. Outside I hear music and the bridesmaids' laughter as they dance.

*

From the top of the ridge I look South. Only more ice awaits us.

Does her Majesty still reign? Does Prince Albert still plan great things for the city? I remember schemes for a great palace of crystal, how I should have loved to visit it with you.

*

You beckon from the top of the stairs, I know it's you although your face is in shadow. A grim Aunt glares down at me from a picture frame, or is it my friend the bear? In the bedroom, you remove my icy gear. The wind blows talcum into my face and eyes. When I can see again, the chaps have scratched 'Just Married!' onto my harness.

My friend the bear settles on the floor, rests his head on his paws. You pull sheets and blankets over me, yet I still can't get warm.

*

No strength remains for writing, and neither pen nor paper. Nothing flammable may be kept from the common store.

I have one more purpose to fulfil. The others stare as my coughing becoes uncontrollable, as I become ever weaker; as they become ever hungrier. Think well of me. I had no wish for exploring, no hunger to see a Northwest Passage. Only to make your father smile upon me and give his blessing.

A great cough builds within my chest, it cannot be denied.

*

The bridesmaids help me lie down, taking positions around me. An honour guard, each bearing the dirty knife like a sword, each now with a scarlet cross splashed across his chest. You lie down beside me and I take your hand as my sight begins to fade.

An eiderdown has split. Its feathers rain down upon us, a pleasant tickling, covering my eyes until I can see nothing. Why should I want to get up when I am finally beginning to get warm?

Stephen's short play The Garden of Earthly Delights was performed at the New Venture Theatre, Brighton in July 2015, his short play The Gasman Cometh was performed at the Salisbury Fringe, August 2016. He is currently recording radio plays for local radio and writing a novel about Magic.

MEANT TO SAY

BY
DEVO CUTLER-RUBENSTEIN

Meant to say "smell the roses" instead it came out as "watch the cracks," which you have to admit have many interesting things going on in them... like small grass coming up out of holes, sow bugs looking for a place to curl up and fragrant droppings of invisible insects too small to see. You can smell them if you get on your knees and put your nose in the crack.

Meant to say "enjoy the hummingbirds" that float into the face of the bird of paradise searching for nectar, which if you see them means good luck in some cultures... like finding a penny, or seeing the first star in the sky at dusk, or breaking a glass at a wedding in front of Uncle Maury who smiles knowing what that night will look like remembering. Years later you'll remember, visiting the hotel ballroom, when you step on a glass shard hidden in the crack between the ceramic tiles.

Meant to say "taste the air not look out for trouble, even though trouble finds us where we are - or are not - looking. Fact of life, like clichés about love and hate, and friends that bore holes in your brains with endless stories of their fates - good and bad - from their POV, even if you turn their fate around in your hand like a tiny gyroscope, or kid's kaleidoscope and show them a new way to throw the yo-yo. They are stuck in mind the cracks.

Sometimes it feels like there are different species of saliva, the kind that is all sinewy and stringy, and the kind that is smooth like vodka, maybe it happens at different times of the day.

I'd rather not have this discussion again, so hopefully you have been listening.

Devo Cutler-Rubenstein is a writer, teacher, and the Director & CEO of The Script Broker, which provides coaching and brokering services for writers and actors.

RED LETTER DAY

BY

PAT JEANNE DAVIS

Each year that flew by, Debbie fell more deeply in love with Charlie. They'd been married twenty-three years, but never had a real honeymoon. Charlie promised Debbie they would go as soon as they could afford one. She knew her husband had good intentions.

As the size of their family grew, a honeymoon seemed unlikely. Vacations were wonderful, and they had plenty of those with their four children; still, it was difficult to be romantic with toddlers under foot. Debbie never abandoned her dream of one with Charlie—just the two of them.

When the twins left home for college, Debbie knew her dream could finally become reality. She collected and pored over glossy brochures, eager to plan a romantic get-away.

"To think we've waited all this time," Charlie said, surfing the web, looking for the ideal spot. "How does this sound? Two all-inclusive weeks at a resort. Nothing to do but soak up the sun and be together."

"I thought it would never happen," Debbie agreed. "Let's go right away."

"I have another idea. Why don't we wait until our wedding anniversary?" His arms draped around her shoulders, and his eyes gazed into hers. "That'll make it even more special."

Debbie leaned forward and kissed him. What was a few months more?

She smiled as her husband drew a large red circle around October 10 on the calendar. A red-letter day. She could hardly contain her excitement.

"It'll be worth the wait." He gave a low chuckle. "Just you see, sweetheart." He kissed the back of her neck. "We'll have the best honeymoon ever."

A week passed, Debbie was sure she couldn't put it off any longer. When Charlie came home from work, she pulled him over to his favorite chair and made him sit.

She placed her hand over his. "I need to tell you something."

Charlie sat upright. "What's wrong?"

"I'm sorry, but we may have to cancel our honeymoon."

He caressed her arm. "What is it? Are you okay? Are the kids?"

Debbie nodded, then walked to the window and looked at the springtime buds forming on the trees. "It's nothing like that." She took a deep breath, praying that he'd take the news well. "I don't know how to tell you this."

Charlie jumped up from his seat. "Tell me what?"

She turned to face him. "We're going to be parents again."

His eyes widened. "B—but you're . . . That incredible."

Debbie choked and her pulse quickened. What if he wasn't happy?

Her worries vanished in a second. He swept her up in his arms and danced her around the room. "I'm going to be a dad again. I can hardly believe it."

Debbie gazed into his blue eyes, sparkling with tears. "Neither can I."

"Are you sure you're not upset?" He frowned. "I know how much you've been looking forward to just the two of us and a real honeymoon at last."

She rested her head on his chest. "Of course not. Ever since the boys left for college, the house has been too quiet."

"I miss the noise the children made too. It'll be wonderful with a baby in the house again."

Debbie laughed. "We're obviously not meant to have a honeymoon."

He held her at arms' length. "Why not?"

"Well, we have a baby to get ready for."

"Not so fast." He pulled her back into his arms. "Just yesterday I spotted another terrific spot while I was online."

He led her to the computer. "It's last minute. What do you say? This might be our last chance."

Debbie reached up and placed her arms around his neck. "Why not?"

"I'll book it now."

She watched as he entered their information into the computer.

Then Charlie pushed back his chair from the keyboard and drew her into his lap. "Soon we'll be sunning ourselves at the seaside." He brushed a soft kiss on her cheek.

Debbie studied his handsome face with the irresistible laugh lines at the corner of his eyes. "As long as we're together." She ran her fingers through his light brown hair. "You're really happy about the baby, aren't you?"

"You bet." He grabbed the red pen from the desk drawer, marched over to the calendar hanging on the wall, and drew a large circle around May 30. He grinned at her. "Might as well cross out October tenth."

As he turned the calendar pages, Debbie took his arm. "You haven't asked when the baby is due."

He rubbed his chin and a ghost of a smile swept over his face. "Not October tenth—our anniversary!"

Debbie met his gaze and winked. "A red-letter day after all."

Pat's work appeared in Guideposts, The Lookout, Bible Advocate, Faith & Family, GRIT Magazine, Splickety Magazine, Ruby For Women Magazine, Woman Alive and Chicken Soup for the Soul books. Visit her at www.patjeannedavis.com

GRAVEYARD

BY

BLACKIE DETH

One of life's rare thrills was when one did something forbidden. Tonight Wiley whistled past the graveyard. His hubris was conjured by liquid courage from *The Pour House*. With Halloween around the corner, the chilly night made him quiver. A wiry, angular man, he'd been lucky to escape the watering hole without getting his butt handed to him. Stupid bullies.

But when the heads of the statues of angels turned to look at him, his heart crawled into his throat. He rubbed his eyes and shook his head, but they still pierced him with their marble eyes. They pointed to the sepulcher of Aelfwine the Dark, a sorcerer who'd made a sizeable amount of money after promising his customers absolute power. It had paid dividends. The businesses in the area were run by those who'd joined the coven of the old magician. They didn't keep quiet about it, either. To the contrary, they were proud of absolute power corrupting absolutely.

Wiley had never thought much of riches, content with barely getting by, washing dishes at *TGI Fridays*. To him, people were important, not possessions. Being a young, handsome man, he had no problem getting laid.

So why did he feel the pull on his mind toward the creepy warlock's sepulcher?

And how had he found himself standing before it?

Insanely, the door slid open.

Come, young Wiley. I have much to show you.

On shaky legs, he walked inside the tomb. How'd he get himself into this mess? He'd never been a crazed adventurer. His heartbeat drummed in his ears; butterflies erupted in his stomach. He hoped he wouldn't fall victim to death by misadventure. But what could harm him? Just dead people, who'd already done their full of damage.

Yet the locks fell off the stone coffin, and the creaky door slid open. Wiley covered his eyes. In shock, he could barely move. He also couldn't help peeking through his fingers.

Aelfwine the Dark sat up, his face eaten by maggots, his teeth forced into a rictus grin, his empty eye sockets—flashing lightning—staring deep in to his dark soul.

Wiley fainted.

#

No longer at the wheel, his head full of evil fantasies never before dreamt up, Wiley walked up to the most vivacious girl at *Thrills*, the local club. Ankle-bracelet clad, olive-skinned, generously breasted, with long blond hair like silk, she wore prissy high-heels that amped up her siren power. She met his stare with enchanting hazel eyes that bewitched him.

"What's a gorgeous, young girl like you doing here alone?"

Why had he called her young? They were the same generation.

She pointed behind her. "My friends are either getting more drinks or in the bathroom."

"I'm Wiley."

She stuck her hand out. "Heighley."

He kissed her hand. The soft, warm skin was tantalizing.

"Just to let you know," she added, "our boyfriends are working. You might not wanna be around when they get off."

"Does he treat you right?" He was having a feast of her with his eyes.

"He's an asshole. I'm about to marry someone just like my dad."

"Why? You're perfect. He should love you for who you are, and worship you, as well."

She smiled, practically ear-to-ear, flashing those square-shaped pearly whites. Then he and Heighley—plus her lovely friends, a stunning redhead and an enchanting brunette—danced the night away.

"You girls wanna get out of here?" Wiley asked. "I'm buying $100 worth of booze."

He was met with the chant of, "Hell yeah!"

The party was on.

#

After a week of Sapphic sex that set Wiley's loins afire—why he hadn't thought of going to bed with more than one woman before was beyond him; this was so much better than the missionary position—once again, they were at it. Their soft, warm flesh made him quiver in his rapture. Perspiration poured. Wiley thought he'd died and gone to heaven.

Or hell, as the case might've been.

After dressing, Heighley found Wiley's laptop open.

"Ooh! Add me on Facebook! My handle's Facebook.com/HeighleyTisdale, H-e-i-g-h-l-e-y."

Still sizzling with passion, Wiley rushed over to the computer.

Voyeur time.

#

On Halloween, Wiley used the iPad Mini his parents gave him to check Facebook. Heighley had approved the add. He sent her a message. "Hey, baby girl. Thanks for the follow."

The answer: "Please quit messaging my girlfriend."

Now, that might have frightened him before, but not after the trip to the graveyard.

"Screw you," he typed. "Quit stealing her account or I'll report you."

It took a quite a spell for a message to come back.

"That's it. I'm gettin' my homies together and beatin' you bloody. Where do you live?"

Enraged, he gave him the address. He also typed, "Don't chicken out, you Internet troll."

#

Wiley was rapt when the gang showed up at his house. They pounded on the door so vehemently, he thought they'd crush it to splinters.

"Let us in, you woman-stealing jerk," one of the guys said.

Wiley gesticulated toward the door and it swung open.

A muscular young man with short, light-brown hair and glasses stood there furrowing his beetle-brow at him. "How'd you open the door from way over there?"

"You must be Jack. Heighley spoke lowly of you."

"She's my *girlfriend,* you moron!"

"Then why are you a virgin?"

Jack blanched. "What . . . how . . . I am *not!*"

"I know things." Wiley snorted.

"Well, know *this*," Jack answered, "we're not leavin' till you're dead."

With Jack was a young, short man, a spook with his black goatee that matched the short-cropped raven hair on his head. A guy with an average build, a buzzcut and glasses stood on the other side of Jack, next to a long-haired young man, who produced a switchblade.

"Your ass is mine, said the spider to the fly," Jack said.

"You sure you're the spider?" Wiley snickered.

"Heh." Jack nodded. "All right, fellas, let's teach him a lesson about stealing girlfriends."

"Yeah, you took ours, too—the other girls you met at the club," he of the Samson hair added. "We talked to 'em on the phone, and they said you had them doing some lesbo pervert crap, you sicko."

Jack smiled an evil grin. "You tell him, Fabio."

Wiley stood. "I'd hate to see you men get hurt," he lied. "Why don't you leave."

"Chickening out?" Jack asked.

"Don't look for trouble. You might find it."

The young men laughed.

"Do not mock a man of my power!" Wiley warned.

Again, they snickered.

Jack said, "You ready for your beatdown?"

"Fools! Do your damndest."

They ran for him. Wiley stuck out both hands. He moved his arms one way, and two of them flew into the air and crashed against the wall. He moved his arms the other way, and long-hair bashed into the other wall. He pulled up with his arms and sent Jack soaring through the air. He crashed against the front door and slid down it. With the others, Wiley made a twisting gesture with his hands, and their necks whipped around and snapped.

Still sitting on the floor, Jack touched the back of his head, and his hand came away bloody. "What the *hell?* You killed my *friends.*"

Wiley snorted. "It's worth it for what I'm getting from your girl, every night."

"All right, you won! Now let me go!"

Wiley bent over him and slapped his face, hard. Jack's head flew to the side and a tooth came out. He wept like the wuss he was.

"I've got something different planned for *you.* Something . . . *special.* Come now, we mustn't leave my coven waiting."

"Your *what?*" Jack asked.

Wiley grabbed him by the hair and bashed his head into the wall until he was unconscious. He dragged him to the graveyard, then into his room of doom.

#

Wiley laughed when Jack woke, in a cage where only his head stuck out of a hole in the middle of a black table with runes written on it. It stood in place of Aelfwine's casket in his cold tomb.

Talk about a rude awakening for the punk.

Jack yelled, "What are you nutbags doing?"

Wiley could see his enemy's breath. "Unlucky with your girlfriend, you've been alone at home masturbating like a monkey at the zoo performing auto-erotic activities. So I'll treat you like one."

The others, wearing black cowls like Wiley, said, "Welcome back, Aelfwine." Following the actions of their high priest, they took their hammers from their laps, along with serrated, grapefruit spoons.

"In Singapore, they crush a monkey's skull with hammers, then spoon out the brains and consume them." Wiley fixed Jack with his eyes. "Coming after me will be the last thing you ever do."

"Oh God!" Jack said. "Somebody help me!"

But nobody would hear him at night, especially in the graveyard.

"No God here," Wiley added, "virgin sacrifice."

The hammering started.

Jack's world faded to darkness.

BLACKIE DETH is a death-metal musician and a new writer who pens terrible things. You can find his free novella, "In The Closet, Under The Bed, Dread," on Wattpad.com, where he's listed as Blackie_Deth. He also blogs at blackiedeth.livejournal.com and is on Twitter as @BlackieDeth Blackie encourages you to whistle past the graveyard . . . NOT!

AFTERNOON AT VERSAILLES

BY

KRIS DIKEMAN

Baron de Besanval squinted down at the courtyard through a gap in the boarded-over windows. Usually at this hour the gates stood open, offering a splendid, sun-dappled view of the Tuileries and the orange grove beyond. Now the gates were barred; musket fire rang out as the Baron's Swiss Guard fought the undead mob.

I wonder if the King is among them, he thought.

True equality and fraternity at last. Courtiers, soldiers and peasants standing shoulder to shoulder with the King himself, all baying like wild beasts for blood.

"Baron?" came a soft voice behind him, "they are still here?"

"They are, Highness," he said, turning as the Queen entered.

She shimmered in the light like an angel, in a gown of pale cream silk studded with pearls. Abandoned by her ladies in waiting she had arranged her blonde hair in a simple plait, tied at the end with a ribbon. He bent low over her hand, his lips coming close but not touching her fingers, as royal protocol demanded.

"What do they desire?" she asked.

"They hunger, Majesty."

Another volley of musket fire. A roar of fury from the mob. The sickening *crack* as the gates were breached. Their stench of blood, rot and gunpowder filled the air as they beat against the door leading up to the Queen's chamber. He recognized the torn red coats of his own men among them.

The Queen's wondrous blue eyes were bright with tears. Her lips trembled.

"But if they are hungry, can they not eat..." and with a graceful motion she gestured to the plates of petit fours and *gateau* upon the table.

The Baron placed his hand on the hilt of his saber and again gave his deepest gentleman's bow. The Queen, from force of habit, curtsied in return, offering him her hand once more. And for the first time in all his years of service, Baron de Besanval dared touch his lips to those pale and perfect fingers.

Still holding her hand, he straightened.

"They hunger, my Queen, for sustenance far more rare and sweet," he said.

With a splintering crash the courtyard door gave way. The mob, baying wordlessly, moved up the stairs as one.

He drew his saber. Her eyes widencd. With one quick motion he saved her from the mob, as he had vowed to at the start of the hideous plague. He had enough time to compose her body upon the couch before the door gave way.

Later, after the mob had finished, the Baron rose. Stumbling on a tangle of his own intestines, he was distracted for an instant by the afternoon sun, shimmering across peals stitched into crimson silk. Then he shuffled out to join the mob, in search of living flesh to assuage his ravenous hunger.

SAMANTHA

BY

EMILY DILL

The little girl had stopped her bicycle right in front of Father Buchanan.

He smiled at her, then continued the yard work in front of his house.

"Are you a cop?" she asked, rocking her bicycle back and forth. Pedaling forward, then pedaling backward.

Father Buchanan laughed. "No, I'm not. Why would you ask that?"

"Because you're dressed all in black."

"Oh." He glanced down at his clothes. "This is how I dress. I just took off clerical collar because it's really hot out here."

The girl tilted her head to the side. "Your what collar?"

"My clerical collar. It's a priest collar." He bent down to pull some weeds. "I'm a priest. Do you know what that is?"

She shook her head, blond bangs falling into her eyes.

"Well, I'm like a preacher." Her face was still blank, so he tried again. "Sort of like...I don't know, the Pope?"

Her face lit up. "Oh, the Pope!" She bit her lip, then spoke again. "So, you're a good guy?"

He chuckled, then stood up, wiping his hands on his pants. "I like to think so."

She put down the kickstand on her bike, then hopped off. She walked over to him and watched him pull weeds for a while, then spoke, but more quietly this time. "So if something bad was going to happen, I should tell you."

Father Buchanan knit his eyebrows together and glanced at her. "Like what?"

"Well, sometimes I know when something bad is coming. You know, before it happens."

He wiped some sweat off of his forehead with the back of his hand and tried to think of the right thing to say. He finally said, "Do you have visions?"

She wrinkled her nose. "Do I have vision?"

He grinned. "No, visions. Do you have weird dreams that tell you things?"

She shook her head.

"Then how do you know what's going to happen?"

She stared at the ground for several minutes. When she spoke, she didn't meet his eyes. "Things talk to me."

Father Buchanan was taken aback. He didn't know if she meant demons or ghosts or something else, and he was unsure how to proceed, but he wanted her to know that she could confide in him.

He crouched down to her level and put his hand under her chin. "What's your name?"

"Samantha," she replied, still looking at the ground.

"Well, Samantha, you can tell me anything. Okay? And you can also tell the other adults in your life. Have you talked to your parents about this?"

Even though her eyes were still on the ground, he saw something flash there. It only lasted for a second, and he wasn't sure if it was anger or fear or sadness. It was gone almost immediately.

"No," she said.

Father Buchanan sat cross-legged on the sidewalk and looked up into her face. "What do these things tell you, Samantha?"

"When someone's going to die," she said right away. "When a house is going to catch fire, or a car is going to crash. I know a lot of bad stuff before it happens."

Father Buchanan looked away from her. He sat for a minute, staring down the quiet street, deciding how to proceed.

"Do you believe me?" she asked.

"Samantha, I believe you. I don't think you're a liar. But how do you know these things come true?"

"I hear about them. At home or at school. I look at my dad's newspaper, or hear it on the news that my mom listens to."

"And do you want to stop these events before they happen?"

"Maybe," she said quietly.

He grabbed her hands and pulled her to stand directly in front of him. He looked up into her blue eyes and spoke as kindly as he could. "Then I can help you do that. I don't know how, but I can help you. We'll figure something out. Okay?"

"Okay," she grinned, not breaking eye contact. "What's your name?"

"Father Buchanan," he replied.

"No, your real name."

"Oh," he said. "Well, it's Frank."

Samantha smiled. "Do you know why these things talk to me, Frank?"

He paused, not liking the way she was smiling or the way she said his name. "Umm, no. Why?"

"Because I'm one of them." The flash was back in her eyes, but this time, from only a foot away, Father Buchanan knew that her expression wasn't due to a human emotion. It was from something supernatural.

"I'm glad you're not wearing your collar," she giggled, as he stared in shock. "It makes it easier to go for your neck."

Emily Dill has appeared in Writer's Digest and recently completed her first novel. She lives in Owensboro, Kentucky with her husband Jason and their crazy cats.

ZIRCONNIA BENNETT IS GOING DOWN

BY

GLEN DONALDSON

On the table the super-skinny soy moccacino latte lays cold, a film formed over the top. I'd been truly preoccupied clicking on law firms believing I could put the frighteners on troublesome Zirconnia Bennett and offer 'go away' money, I forgot what was right in front of me. Now as usual, first world problems were beginning to pile up all around me.

Latte art may have been a pleasant distraction, but now I had the name of the city's top 'Philly' lawyer Rushmore Knight lighting up my phone screen and I truly hoped breakfast was about to go all prima facie. "She's a stone in your shoe that we'll be able to take care of nice 'n good," promised Knight in his best non-conciliatory crisp suit, thousand dollar-an-hour voice, turning my eyes wide with what I was fairly certain had the accompanying grace of a wrecking ball.

Ok, so I'll soon be free of Zirconnia, but there's one little problem. Before she is disposed of, I need to find those files. She says she doesn't have them, that she destroyed them, but I don't believe that for a second. Covert remote computer hacking has never really been a quiver in my bow, making me imagine how a one-armed chef in charge of a twenty burner stove might feel, but those precious files must be retrieved.

I approached this task with all the urgency of someone fighting for breath. I got up, leaving a generous tip on check tablecloth.

With a quick wave of a hand I found myself in the back of a cab and en route to a face to face with the underground computer whiz they called *The Dreamweaver*. I didn't know much about *Dreamweaver* except that he was young, expensive and what I needed most, sure fire.

I found him secreted within his security camera-protected backstreet lair, bizarrely propped up in a coin operated, over-sized leather massage chair surrounded by banks of flickering computer terminals even NASA would envy. With the blue of his veins showing beneath pale skin and his watery, unblinking stare, *Dreamweaver* looked distinctly alien. Eyes as black as a mirror at night locked on to mine and a faintly charitable expression anointed his face to acknowledge my presence, though I'd seen happier smiles on a school bus going over a cliff.

After the initial quickly exchanged pleasantries, talk turned to the less than charming possibilities afforded by malevolent Trogan e-worms. Zirconnia was going down big time because of a tasty virus I selected that would do something very strange to her own files and to those belonging to anyone who had liked her on social media.

Once the celebration party I envisioned died down I began to luxuriate in thinking about the object lesson this would serve to Ms Bennett and anyone else contemplating frivolous litigation aimed at the commercial airline industry. "Stand back everyone," I thought to myself, "this is about to get squishy". Even blind Freddy, his half-brother one eyed Burl and their second cousin twice removed Myopic Mary could see, figuratively speaking, all the tumblers were indeed beginning to fall into place.

Glen Donaldson is a cliff-edged Brisbane-Australia writer with a nutty aftertaste. He has been known to lavish himself with his favourite 'baby's breath' cologne and on occasion writes under the pseudonym Stephen King.

PARTY ANIMALS

BY

BILL ENGLESON

The invitation was not unexpected. Whipple Parsons had been putting out signals for quite a while that something untoward, something peculiarly unusual was in the wind. Weeks earlier, we had walked down to the sea just before midnight, sauntering out on the public dock that stretched a couple of hundred yards into the bay; the moon was full, the sky sparkled with an explosion of sprinkled stars.

The night, as usual, was mightily abuzz. Sea lions, slipping and sliding on rocks across the bay, were testing their choral range, grouching and gargling a saltwater serenade.

"Look up, Sam. There!"

Whip pointed to a distant light. "Do you ever wonder what's out there?"

Whip knew I had little interest in space. I am a reporter. I deal in the real world; crime, politics, love, hate; the peccadilloes of mankind. That is what anchors me. His mind, his heart, on the other hand, are afloat in the heavens.

"You *know* I am spellbound by extraterrestrials, Whip," I tweaked him gently. "Space visitors, turnip recipes, all grist for *my* mill, buddy."

"You are such a know-nothing, Sam. Open your mind! Soon, I don't know when, but soon, I'm going to call you up and insist you come to my place lickety split. I expect your compliance."

I reassured him that, should he call, I would get off my high horse and gallop to his door. That seemed to placate him.

Late one afternoon, he made THE promised call. "Come," he ordered. "Bring Kate."

Kate resisted. We had been over to Whip and Arlene's a few weeks earlier for an excruciating Canasta party. Cards and Singapore Slings. It all got a bit much. She wanted nothing more than a night in front of the tube.

"Do we have to attend another Canasta party, Samuel?"

"Whip didn't mention Canasta. I think he has something else up his sleeve."

We seesawed back and forth. Finally she agreed to tag along.

We arrived just after 7:00. Whip came out on the veranda and greeted us.

"This is so great. You are going to have to brace yourself, guys."

"I think we are prepared for anything," Kate advised our excited friend.

"Good. Okay, come on in...."

I'm not sure what *I* expected. Kate was probably anticipating a couple of card tables and two other couples.

There was only one other...couple. Or whatever they were.

My family had never produced any arachnologists but I immediately saw, before my eyes, two humongous spiders.

"Great, eh?" Whip effused. "I know! I know just how you feel. Arlene almost feels the same way...except she's locked herself in the john."

As I too had been considering flight, or the locked security of the bathroom, I could well appreciate Arlene's choice of sanctuary.

"I looked them up," continued Whip. "Peacock spiders! From space! And do these two garish fellows love the ladies!"

With that, Whip's multi-coloured eight-legged guests did a bit of a jig and pounced on Kate.

She screamed.

I fainted.

The last thing I heard was Whip hollering gleefully, "Isn't this incredible?"

Bill Engleson is a retired social worker, novelist, flash fiction (aka short story) writer, essayist, poet and procrastinator. Feel free to visit his website/ blog, www.engleson.ca

GENESIS

BY

LAURIE FELDMAN

The sun is hot on my shoulders and dust rises around me from the ground where I just landed. My chin and palms sting. I probably skinned them as I dove for first base. But I got here seconds before the ball *thunked* into Jackie Goldwater's glove. I feel triumphant.

"Bob-bee! Bob-bee! Bob-bee!"

My raggedy group of friends and teammates jump to their feet and chant from the bench. The chain link fence separating the bench from the field rattles, shaken by the appreciative team. They celebrate my fete and my presence, after a four month absence from joining the afternoon softball game. I have missed them. It seems, they have missed me too.

From first base I yell, "go Maccabees!" Raising my right fingers in a "V", for victory sign, I pump my hand in the air three times.

"All right, thanks guys. Now let's focus on the game," says Mr. Mironov, our softball coach. He is smiling and I know he is happy to see me too.

"Batter up!"

I squint toward home plate and see Jake Weiner flourishing the bat. As I step out from the plate, toward second, Brian Finklestein touches my butt with his glove.

"Hey! Watch your hands!" I say, even though I know that's just the way it's done, Jackie Robinson style.

Noah Schum is on the mound, the best pitcher the Israelites have on their team. I hold my breath, waiting for him to wind up and throw.

Into the quiet of the afternoon the bell tower atop the church chimes, marking the hour. Absently, I listen as it tolls, one chime peals then the second. I expect the third and then silence but into the quiet comes a fourth clang.

"Oh, my God!" My heart races as I run toward the sidelines.

"Where are you going, Bobby? We've got the bases loaded!"

"I have to go!" I wheeze from lungs constricted by fear. "My dad is going to be waiting at the shul!"

The clamor of my teammates is instantly silenced. They know what this means and that it is serious.

"I thought it was three o'clock, not four! I gotta go!"

"Sure Bobby, take off!" Lenny grabs my backpack, runs and flings it at me. "Hurry up!"

I take off, it's only eight blocks. I'll be a little late but hopefully my dad won't notice. I know I wasn't supposed to go to the ball field, but I couldn't resist. I've missed my friends, missed being able to play after school, I didn't mean to stay so long.

My lungs are on fire. Every breath I take feels like sandpaper rubs inside my air passages.

"Bobby, where are you running to?" calls Ms. Edelman as I sprint past her delicatessen.

"No… time… to… talk… now…" I gasp, sprinting toward my target.

At the corner I reach out to grab the lamp post, swinging myself around, adding some propulsion as I turn down the last street. Almost there.

My head hangs down, to save effort and oxygen, but as I approach, I force myself to look up. There it is, looming ahead. The doors are tightly shut and the dark wood reflects nothing but mystery. It chills me to look at it, as it always has. I feel only anxiety as I near my destination, there is no comfort there.

"Watch it, young man!" says the orange vendor as I almost crash into his cart.

"Sorry… Mr. Rothman…"

The doors are heavy as I weakly pull at them, working to get them open. I'm panting and sweating but in spite of the heat generated by my run, I'm in a cold sweat of panic.

Finally, the door squeaks open twelve inches allowing me to squeeze through into the building. Without waiting for the doors to close, I try to straighten my clothes and my spine as I walk toward the bimah.

"Bobby. How could you? Where have you been?"

"We've been waiting for you to daven, without you there's no minyan."

"Bobby, if your mother was still alive she would be ashamed." This last said by my father who is flanked by my two uncles, my mother's brothers.

Behind me, I hear the doors of the synagogue clang shut, testimony to my failure and my misery.

My shoulders sag and I look at the floor. This is it. I've really done it now. How could I have done this to my mother? Without my prayers, they tell me, she's going to hell.

Laurie Feldman is a writer and psychiatric nurse practitioner specializing in post traumatic stress disorder. She lives in Los Angeles and enjoys spending her time formulating theories about dog behavior.

THESE HANDS

BY

ANN FIELD

The hands before me lie gnarled with risen blue veins on mottled skin. Once they were tiny fists of pink flesh, angry with their new environment, grasping for survival. Holding food, toys and pencils along the path of childhood. Nimble fingers master complicated machinery and become adept at producing automobiles for the wealthy. Work is tough and play even harder. Age brings the skirmishes that only young men endure.

The pain of split knuckles connecting with an open jawline is put aside as my opponent pummels my face. My next swipe makes contact with an eye and blood from his wound is sticky on my hand. No time to rest on any laurels as my other fist follows up and under to finish the job. He falls to the stained concrete with a satisfying thump. Cheers erupt from the paying crowd. Although I hurt, a smile accompanies my arm rising high to shake a winning fist. His blood mingles with mine diluting with the sweat dripping down my bare chest. The forty guineas are held tight, a prize worth fighting for. At last I have a title. Champion of Yorkshire 1934 settles comfortably on my shoulders.

Victoriously I lift a ready pint between split lips. I down it in one go letting the contents flow cold against the back of my throat. Fans cheer as the empty glass is placed on the counter. Later I lean against the slimy wall and watch my stomach contents fall into the unclean toilet bowl. Holding back my hair I wipe my mouth across the back of my hand, my lips sting and my eyes are swollen to slits. I return to the well-wishers who chant my name. Celebrations are underway as drinks line the mahogany bar. Oblivion engulfs me, aided by the flow of free alcohol. Amid pats and claps, the revellers carry the dead weight of my inebriated body home. Yet drink cannot heal these blood-stained hands of the night's events. Visions of the beaten and battered man arrive uninvited. Two throbbing fists lie beneath my bedclothes. Sleep doesn't come to take hold of me. A man must do what he has to as there is no backing out of a contract. Not with my pride at stake and successful businessmen's money riding on my back.

A new different world of experience now lies at my fingertips. Healed of scabs, my scarred hands feel their way around the woman's body. I caress her curves. Her soft buttocks move in rhythm against mine and bring unimagined pleasure. She lies in my bed until the next willing woman takes her place. How many more I hold is lost to me as the parties are never-ending. Success brings bonuses in different guises. A parade of blondes, brunettes and everything in-between vie to enter this champion's bedroom.

The fast car I purchase oozes power as it speeds along with comfortable ease. Its sleek body brings admiring glances from men as well as women. Leather seats and trimmings in walnut compliment my expensive suit, crocodile shoes and tanned face. Good looks and success attract the attention of the press as I become a household name.

Mary feels special from the start. The feel of her skin sends tingles into my bloodstream as I let my fingers trace over her. This woman brings something new to my life, never experienced before. I wish to protect her and keep her with me. The gold band slides along her manicured finger. We make a pledge to each other in the ceremony of marriage and I commit myself to her side forever.

Inevitable sparks arrive as we settle into the rhythm of living together. Accounting for my whereabouts does not come naturally. Disagreements evolve into arguments. Words, never my strong virtue, mean I lose every shouting match. I am constantly on the back-foot. My fingers curl into balls, as the fists form by themselves. Unbidden, they lash out. At first hitting walls until they find another, softer target. Remorse and guilt force me to master my frustration. Exasperated, I struggle to keep these weapons in my pockets or clenched behind my back. I head for the playing field. Freezing air numbs them as I run rings around the circuit to disperse my anger and keep her safe.

Forgiven once again, the second chance holds and disputes settle without resorting to violence. I am healed and commit with promises and enough love to provide a safe nest for us. Holding my new born son makes my fingers tremble and fasten protectively around the precious bundle. Secure in my strong calloused embrace, he sleeps contentedly as love softens my heart.

The conflict is unexpected when it comes. Overseas a battle rages and able-bodied men enlist to fight for their country, for their family. The training is tough with discipline being the hardest to contend with. Waving to the good-looking woman with the little boy at her side, my ship sails. The struggle to survive as war engulfs Europe doesn't come without a cost. Friends fall at my feet. Acrid smoke fills the air making headway both terrifying and treacherous. I cross the quagmire stepping on soft body parts lying in pools of blood as my comrades' bodies lie in muddy fields. Red poppies droop into puddles coloured by blood. Using nightfall as cover, time and again, my strong hands lift the fallen; the dying and the dead. One by one I carry them on my back. I have found my coping method as well as my atonement.

Moving onward, our small battalion arrive at the outskirts of a town overrun by the enemy. A band of five men accompany me toward the farmhouse. Voices speaking in a language not known to us, drift from open windows. Lit from inside, their shadows are visible targets. Our shots ring through the darkness and the silhouettes freeze then fall out of sight. Going forward we are surprised by a man in enemy uniform staring down the sights of a rifle aiming in our direction. Diving for cover we return fire. Crouching thirty feet away he plugs my colleague. The old anger resurfaces as the young body lies in my hands, baby-faced and dead at twenty. The enemy soldier advances with the onslaught of bullets. I crawl through the undergrowth to my left. Silence falls as he reloads his weapon. Chances are few in war and immediately I force him to his knees with the strength of my hands around his neck. His rifle explodes a final time. Sinews and muscles send sparks of pain along my arms to a disengaged brain. I hold fast. No matter how he struggles, I hold my grip, choking his life away until he lies limp on the sodden ground. Staring at my bloody shaking hands, I control the anger and re-group the men. We leave with the body of our colleague weighing heavy on my shoulder.

The damage to my hand is beyond the basic capabilities of the battle-field hospital. I arrive home with bandages covering the gunshot wound. Mary is unable to hold these hands or comfort me as I relate my ordeals of combat. No longer with my love beside me, I feel overwhelmed by sorrow as she chooses to leave. While away fighting for us, she found a love that holds no underlying threat. My benevolence surprises me as I understand her decision.

Undoing the bandages for the last time, the nurse lets them fall into the waste bin. Distorted, my hands lie one on each knee, not sure what to do for the first time in their existence. Life with struggles is better than no life at all. I learned that much from those battlefields. I become used to my mutilated hand. During the months and years that follow, the war fades into memory until only the dreams bring back all the horrors in stark clarity. I chase the vivid images of long dead faces that enter my sleeping mind. These nights wake me in terror. I am glad there is no one lying beside me to explain away my tears.

As my son holds his baby on the altar, our eyes meet from above the holy water font. These withered hands with raised blue veins against mottled skin, lie trembling by my sides. Unable to take the risk and embarrassed now, I shake my head as my son offers my newly-christened grandson. Instead I sit on the wooden pew, my head bent in shame, filled with old memories. He comes me and lays the bundle of blue blankets onto my lap. My calloused finger traces the skin of the tiny fist. It waves as though it wants to fight the world. I hold it steady, wishing it to remain soft and harmless.

Ann Field lives in the small town of Leixlip, County Kildare in Ireland, where many of her short stories have been published. She enjoys reading fiction, especially crime thrillers and stories with a twist.

SLEEPING PORCH

BY

SHARYL FULLER

It was just before 6am when Georgia stepped outside. The pale early morning sky still had enough night to look more grey than black. A fresh wind blew from the southwest causing the treetops to dance. There was a hint of chill in the early July air and this thought ran through her mind, "*sleeping porch weather*". This brought back childhood memories of sleeping on the breezeway that connected their house to the garage. Not a true 'sleeping porch' in old South standards, but a screened in area that was the next best thing.

The cement floor of the breezeway was cool underfoot and at this hour, outside air was cooler than inside. There was something about using the AC that could never really equalize temps between inside and outside at this time of early morning. The humidity had not set in for the day and the night air was cool. Georgia felt her damp hair stick to the back of her neck and her lightweight cotton gown clung to hips, thighs, and other moist places. She shivered as the cool morning air-dried her sleep-dampened skin. Soon the humidity level would equal the air temp and this moment of pleasure would disappear with the coming dawn.

At this moment, Georgia decided the screened in sun room at the back of the house would become her sleeping porch. Being on the southwest corner, it caught the perfect nighttime breeze. This would be her sacred space and an option when sleep eluded her in the house. The bedroom was a torture chamber most of the time. Too many memories—too many ghosts hiding in the corners, lurking in the shadows. Ghosts who came out and danced on the inside of her eyelids keeping sleep at bay. At times they didn't show themselves, yet came flooding into her brain after midnight, making sleep impossible for the rest of the night.

A sleeping porch would be Georgia's ghost catcher; ghost chaser. No walls to cower in the corners and creep out to ruin her sleep. Screens would filter out the ghosts when they tried to enter her thoughts. Screen walls allowed cool breezes to blow away the bad things trying to catch her. Her memories, her life. Screen walls; her safety net.

With that decision made, she went inside and decided today would be a full Southern breakfast morning; a country breakfast from her childhood, rather than the granola and yogurt she usually ate most mornings. During the summer everyone woke at different times and fended for themselves.

Not wanting to wake anyone just yet, she quietly started coffee brewing, bacon frying and hand cut thick slices of bread ready to pan toast in a combination of bacon drippings and sweet cream butter. As she worked, her stomach grumbled appreciatively and in anticipation of breakfast. She knew bacon would wake the sleepy heads. They could let her know how they wanted their eggs, or no eggs, when they stumbled in looking for bacon.

Georgia sensed his presence before she felt the feather light kiss on the back of her neck. He pulled her close and asked if there was a special occasion for a big breakfast in the middle of the week. She smiled and turned to kiss him full on the mouth saying, "Nope!"

"You know," Scott said, "I think we need to turn the sun room into a sleeping porch."

Snuggling close under his chin, Georgia replied, "You have been sleep walking in my mind again." No further discussion was needed.

Sharyl is a retired teacher living in the beautiful Texas Hill Country. Currently she is the Senior Managing Editor for Downtown LA Life International Online Magazine ... downtownlalife.com

THE FUSE BOX

BY

JONI GARDNER

One seventy-five, the numbers read above a doorway between a Chinese Restaurant and Laundromat. I pulled on the handle and stepped inside. The only way you could go was up. As I grabbed the handrail on the wall, it yanked out the screws that held it. I went crashing into the opposite wall, banging my tool box into my knee. I swore and limped up the steps.

I can't believe Janice couldn't have afforded to live in a better place than this! When I reached the top of the stairs, which were almost straight up, there was another door and to my surprise, a shiny gold keyless entry plate. Now I remember, her birthdate was the code. I punched in 5-28-83 and the knob turned. I stepped inside and a white ball of fur came rolling over to me. This must be Ralph, I thought, as I reached down to pet the loud purring cat.

"Where is the fuse box?" I asked Ralph, as I threw my jacket on a navy blue upholstered chair covered in white fur. It was a nice apartment I had to admit, but wasn't convinced it was a safe neighborhood.

I found the fuse box in the hall outside a bedroom. When I opened the old metal door, I cringed as I saw damage from an arching and sparking history leading back to 1928, which is when Janice told me the apartment was built. I took a deep breath, relaxed, and opened my tool box.

I only worked for a short time, when I heard a knock on the door. Walking over to it, I stopped and asked, "Who's there?"

"Dale Yees, carry out, please?"

I opened the door and an old Chinese man handed me a white bag that was stapled shut.

"Janice say her father like sweet n' sour pork."

"I do, but I didn't order any."

"Janice order for you, and I deliver. Your nice daughter helped my wife when she is sick." The Chinese man's face melted into a warm smile.

"Thank you. I'm very proud of her myself. What do I owe you?"

"No charge! No charge!"

"But I can't just take…."

"Yes, take, eat, must go."

I thanked him, closed the door, and saw Ralph standing on his back feet licking the savory juices leaking through the bag. I smiled and felt so proud that Janice had turned out to be such a caring person. I never felt confident that I gave her what she needed, being a single parent her entire childhood. I chose to err on the side of being too lenient, and encouraged her to make her own choices, but to accept the possible consequences. I knew she was strong willed by the time she was two. It was probably just easier to trust her judgement. When she moved to New York right after she graduated nursing school, I only saw her once or twice a year for too many years. Now that I moved to New Jersey, it was possible to see her much more often, if she wanted. I would wait and see.

Sitting down at Janice's kitchen table, I tore the carry-out open. It was as good as it smelled. I wondered what she had done for the Chinese man's wife. Certainly more than he expected.

After another hour had passed and I got the old fuse box out of the wall, I went back down the stairs to my car to get the new fuse box. On my way back to the door, a young woman approached me with a clear bag of what looked like laundry.

"Hi! I'm Janice's neighbor, Kelly. I work at my parent's Laundromat right there," she pointed at the old building next door. They pay me $12 an hour, and $14 dollars an hour on Saturdays. You must be her Dad? I have limitations but I can work hard and I do work hard. I help Janice when she needs me to wash her scrubs for work. You know she's a nurse? She came in one day, and I was on the floor. You know I have epilepsy? Well, anyway, she called 911. That's an emergency number you can call to get help. They came and took me to the hospital and Janice went in the ambulance with me. I woke up and she told me to stay calm and I would be alright. Then she took a cab home and told my parents what happened. Then she came back to the hospital with them, and when I came home the next day and I was alright, Janice said, *We should go to Starbucks down on the corner for breakfast on Sunday mornings.* Well, guess what?"

"I don't know, but I'm sure you'll tell me, Kelly."

"This Sunday will be our 5th breakfast together since Janice moved in!"

"I'm so glad you're friends. It's good to meet you, Kelly."

"And guess what else, Janice's father? We take turns treating each other to breakfast. She started on the 1st Sunday, then I treated on the 2nd Sunday, and Janice says it's EOW. Do you know what that is? Every Other Week! Cool, huh?"

Kelly handed over the large bag, "Janice and I are good friends, and I'm glad she moved next door. Here's her laundry, right when I told her it would be ready!"

I took the large bag and smiled at Kelly. "Thank you for helping my daughter. I bet she appreciates your friendship.

"Oh, usually I use the code on the door and bring it in, but I didn't want to surprise you. She told me you were going to put a new fuse box in today. My dad says we need a new one too, but now is not a good time to spend the money."

"Yes, and I've still got more work to do up there before Janice gets home."

"You go ahead. I'll watch for the blue taxi with the white stripe on the side. She always uses that company. It was nice meeting you, Janice's father."

"Please call me Ralph, Kelly."

"Like Janice's cat?" Kelly covered her giggle.

"Yes." It finally occurred to me my daughter gave her cat my name.

I opened the door, stepped inside, grabbed the broken handrail again, and crashed into the other wall for the second time. I sobbed as I tried to straighten up, but not from physical pain. All those years I worried about being a good dad and only today do I realize that I couldn't have made too many mistakes because my daughter, Janice, had turned out better than I could have imagined. I climbed back up the stairs, put the code in, and entered her apartment again. This time it seemed even nicer.

Actually pretty, and homey.

Janice's father smiled as he took the new fuse box over to the old hole in the wall, and saw Ralph had curled up on his jacket, fast asleep.

Joni Gardner has been a writer for over half a century. Joni's many careers as special education teacher, cosmetologist, and veterinary technician provide a wealth of resources for her short stories and poetry incorporating irony and humor.

HOW I LEARNED TO STOP WORRYING AND LOVE THE PROM

BY
T. C. GARDSTEIN

After posting a photo of Max on Instagram for #meowgamondays, I scrolled down to see who else had just posted cat photos. I had barely been on Instagram for the past week, but now that the proofreading project was officially off my desk, I could safely fall into a cyber black hole and do some catching up while hustling for my next freelance gig.

It was then that I discovered there was a pet prom going on that very night: staring me in the face was a large tuxedo cat wearing a stop-sign red bowtie and matching cummerbund, alongside a photo of a fluffy white kitty wearing a bejeweled tiara that was clearly Photoshopped. "So excited about tonight's date with @the_doodle!" sweet_tabitha had written. "I was thrilled that this handsome boy from St. Louis, Meowssouri asked me to the IG event of the year: #petprom2016. We hope to be crowned #kingandqueenoftheprom!" I clicked on the heart to indicate that little_max_ liked this post before looking at posts from my favorite cat pages, where I found several more photos of cyber couples getting ready for the pet prom. There did not seem to be a set time, which made sense because of the different time zones in "Ameowica" (this was definitely a red-white-and-blue thing), but the pet prom was definitely on for whenever evening happened in your location. I spotted some other cats in real bow ties, others in Photoshopped finery including corsages, garlands, and boutonnieres. A few shots depicted cat heads atop human bodies in formalwear. A handful of photos even had a limousine waiting in the background.

112

Max's motto—well, one of them, anyway—was "Always leave them wanting more." I respected that by posting just one photo a day on his IG account. But my customary restraint died as the memory of my own prom night, which I had placed in a coffin long ago and buried in my brainpan's bone yard, heaved and rose up through mental topsoil. Breaking free, this ghoul overturned the cartoonish gravestone with the inscribed date JUNE 16, 1988, and forced me to inhale its foul scent. Next thing I knew, I was opening the Layout App to place a pensive-looking shot of Max sitting on my desk next to a photo I had recently taken of a gargantuan sunflower so droopy from the August heat that its head resembled a showerhead. Once I transferred the diptych to Instagram, my fingers flew over my smartphone's keyboard. Four months ago Max took pity on my extended case of writer's block and gave me the keys to his voice, as well as to his unique spelling. Here is what I channeled:

> **little_max_** Sew eye jest found doubt ah bout dis #petprom2016. R dare Annie luv Lee lay D Katz out dare still look kin fur a date? Eye have dis mass sieve son flour core saj two aw furr two a lay D kittea red E two putt on her dance sin shooz & throw down at dis prom with mee. Eye dew knot dew Bo ties, cents eye M a knew dust, butt eye yam well groomed, smell grate, & will re specked ewe because mi mom razed mee write. #tabbycatsrule #tabbytown #lookingforlove #romance #emeraldeyes #igcats #catscircus #gato #chat #katz

Almost immediately, Max received this piece of advice from one of his IG cat friends: "I'm sure there will be some lovely lady cats on their own at the prom," ginger_man counseled. "Why not go and meet them there? You can impress them with your pawsome dancing!"

To which little_max_ replied, "May bee eye shud go stag, but eye yam shi, & hoe pin a lay D kat will axe sept mi son flour & go two the prom with mee."

An endless hour passed, during which time the humiliating details of my prom night taunted me, refusing to go back underground. Here is what happened: my boyfriend of six months, who had also been my first lover, had suddenly dropped me for another girl after my parents had dropped considerable coin on a pale pink Betsey Johnson gown that made me look like a Degas ballerina. Of course I had already snipped off the tags, so the dress couldn't be returned. (At least I was able to wear it to the Beaux Arts Ball at my college the following spring.) Then, on the day of the prom, a guy who had intermittently flirted with me since our sophomore year called to invite me over to his house that evening.

He told me his folks would be out until very late, that we could watch Woody Allen movies in peace. We were both big Woody Allen fans— no surprise, since we were both neurotic and thought classmates who favored malls over Manhattan were pathetic. When I showed up, the guy reported that he had just gotten back from his best friend's and how cool it had been to watch him and his date, plus two other couples dressed to the nines, pile into a rented limo. "That's nice," I replied, putting more than enough sarcasm into those two words for him to notice.

"Oh, did you still want to go the prom, even after your dude dumped you for Courtney?"

"I'm going to pretend I didn't hear that question," I said. "Just fire up the VCR."

One and a half movies (*Annie Hall* and *Hannah and Her Sisters*), two bags of microwave popcorn, and an indeterminate number of sloppy kisses later, he abruptly pulled away to inform me that he loved someone else, a girl in our Advanced Placement English class he hadn't had the nerve to ask to the prom because she was out of his league. Stunned, I said nothing, just stumbled out of his house and drove down to the park, where I swung on a swing till I was chased out of there by the cops. I was too shaken up to drive into the city and could not bear to go back home where I would have to face my parents, so I kept slowly driving around the dark, quiet cul-de-sac until I figured they had turned in for the night.

I realize that saying this may make me sound like a drama queen, because my life is not so bad (#firstworldproblems, as IG users put it), but I am still mindlessly swinging, aimlessly circling. Nothing has really gelled. My series of progressively smaller apartments in semi-gentrified Brooklyn neighborhoods have felt more like way stations than homes. I drifted into freelancing because when the recession hit and office staffs were decimated, I was an inessential, undistinguished employee within hailing distance of forty. After my first novel was rejected by scores of literary agencies, I began and abandoned three more novels when they were each fifty pages in. I ostensibly had a few friends but only saw them if I was proactive; they never invited me anywhere. None of my romances had lasted. The closest thing I had to a child was Max, who was taking a catnap on my bed.

I was beginning to contemplate joining him when an IG comment landed from trudi_miezekatze. "Greetings from Vera, Trudi's human mother in Germany," the comment read. "If we were in America, I would let my girl go to this pet prom with you, Little Max. But as we are so far away, Trudi can send you only kittykisses and a big heart."

My own heart creaked open. "Know wo Reese, Vera, dis prom iz in sigh burr space," I wrote as Max stirred and made little pigeon sounds in his sleep. "Eye would l'ike two aw furr Trudi dis son flour. F she axe seps, pleez emale sum faux toes of Trudi to mi mom at RamonaClef@ hotmail.com sew shee kin p'oast up dates two knight."

(Yes, my name is Ramona, and punning is one of my least guilty pleasures.)

Vera wrote back, "Little Max, have your mom check her email...you have a date."

And that is how I learned to stop worrying and love the prom: by creating photo narratives of two petite brown tabbies having the kind of night I had been denied as a heartbroken seventeen-year-old at the tail end of the Reagan administration. The bed sheets Max and Trudi were separately stretched out on in uncanny attitudes of dance were the same shade of ivory, so it really looked like they were cavorting together; my disco ball also helped. Afterward, my boy escorted Trudi to the world-famous Katz's Delicatessen where they shared a bowl of meowtzo-ball soup and a pawstrami sandwich and made goo-goo eyes while licking blobs of mustard off each other's chins. Max picked up ten new followers, Trudi wants to "see" him again, and I have officially reached the point of no return in my evolution as a Crazy Cat Lady, but so be it. At least I am going somewhere.

T.C. Gardstein is a writer, artist, astrologer, performance poet, copyeditrix, and love child of Henry Miller & Anais Nin.

THE DIOGENES MIRROR

BY

PETER GLASSMAN

Paul Sennett hated New Year's Eve more than he hated New Year's Day. He began thinking about New Year's the day after Thanksgiving. Sennett decided to go into the antique store again and see if the mirror was still there. Maybe it would be on sale today–Black Friday.

The door activated a barely audible tinkle from the overhead bells, alerting the proprietor of the Antiques and Antiquities Emporium. It had a single door and a small windowed front, but inside appeared crowded, a single floor the size of a 6-car garage. The place smelled of ginger and a lemon-tinged spice.

"Back again Mr. Sennett?" Mr. D. Synopios asked.

"Yes Mr. Synopios. Do you still have the mirror?" Sennett scanned the clutter of disorganized framed art and dust-free furniture.

"Of course..." Synopios tented his fingers. "...and today it's on sale."

"Down from $11,000? May I inspect it again please?"

Synopios uncovered the full length square mirror set on two polished mahogany legs, like two lion's paws clutching shiny brass balls. The mahogany frame to the mirror was carved in a Grecian-Line with a fine gold wire outlining the up-and-down squares of the Greek pattern. "Before I tell you today's price let me remind you the Grecian-Line relief is outlined by an original gold wire. The dating goes back to the time of Doric Greek Architecture and many centuries B.C."

116

Sennett looked at the front of the mirror and then swiveled its full length around a central pivot to check its other side. "I really didn't think the Greeks had the technology to make a double-sided mirror. And the silvering hasn't aged at all. It's in perfect reflecting condition."

"Yes, indeed Mr. Sennett. This mirror is very special. The price today is only $2,000. It goes back to its original price tomorrow."

"What? I'll not ask your reason. I wish to buy it."

"Certainly Mr. Sennett. I knew you wanted it and that you were the right person for it."

"Right person for it? What do you mean?"

"This item has withstood the test of the ages because it has passed from one meticulous owner to another. There are certain conditions for its sale." Synopios smiled.

"I knew there had to be a catch to such a price reduction."

"You are indeed a true cynic, Mr. Sennett, but that is precisely the kind of person the mirror needs." Synopios swung the mirror back to its original position. "The condition of sale is that I personally crate, transport and re-assemble the mirror at its destination. And…" Synopios put his hand on Sennett's broad shoulder. "…it must be delivered on New Year's Eve and set up precisely at midnight–the exact transition into the New Year."

"I never heard of such a term of sale."

Synopios's smile faded. "Let me add that not only will the original price return tomorrow but it will also go to another buyer."

And now it was New Year's Eve with 3-hours to go before the year 2015 arrived. Sennett had accepted the terms without further discussion. He actually relished the delivery of the mirror on New Year's Eve. It would add significance to an otherwise meaningless human invention of a holiday. The buzzer sounded in his posh 5th story, 70th street, New York City apartment. The doorman had been informed of his visitors and the large piece of furniture.

"Good evening Mr. Sennett, and I will not wish you Happy New Year since you do not acknowledge such calendar events as being celebratory." Three burly men brought the disassembled mirror and its base into the apartment and began uncrating it. They left an hour later with the packing materials, leaving Synopios and Sennett alone.

"Will you need my help putting the mirror together?" Sennett looked at the components and sensed Synopios wanted him to participate.

"Yes it's important that you do." Synopios withdrew three wooden tools from his coat and then hung the coat up in the entry closet.

"Important? I don't see how."

"Mr. Sennett, may I ask you again why you dislike or rather do not acknowledge New Year's Eve or Day?"

"What's the sense of it? Each year is worse than the next. It's just hypocritical to celebrate it. When this country is not at war, there are terrorists poised to destroy people, places and things which are symbolic of our reason to exist. And today we are both at war and wary of terrorist action at any moment."

"Do you have specific reference to your stance on this attitude, may I ask?" Synopios handed Sennett a wooden screw driver. The handle and the screwdriver tip were both made of hard wood–not metal. Synopios used a wooden pliers and leather topped hammer.

Paul Sennett replied, "The United States is at war in Iraq and Afghanistan. ISIS is beheading innocent journalists and killing non-Muslim civilians for being just that–non-Muslims. The Taliban in Pakistan murdered over 140 children. Computer hackers threaten death and destruction as in 9/11, just for showing a movie parodying North Korea's President." Sennett paused. "Do you want me to go on?"

"No, your cynicism is well-defined. Tell me Mr. Sennett, what kind of world and time would you like to be in, if not in 2014 or 2015?"

"I would like to be in this country at a time when everyone talked of peace and practiced peace–a time when even the President outwardly proclaimed we would not be involved in other countries' violent ways of living." Sennett stepped back from the assembled mirror. He looked for Mr. Synopios to reply but couldn't find him. It was now 15-minutes to midnight and 2015 would soon be here.

"Mr. Synopios? Mr. Synopios? Where are you?"

"I am here Mr. Sennett and I know I can grant your wish." Synopios's voice sounded like he was right next to him.

"Where? I can't see you. Mr. Synopios?"

"Here. Turn around. Face the mirror."

Paul Sennett felt his pulse pound and race. "In the mirror? How? What's going on?"

"If you step into the mirror Mr. Sennett, your wish to live in the peaceful conditions you desire, will happen."

"What? Who and what are you Mr. Synopios?"

"My name is D. Synopios–Diogenes of Synope. I have been relegated to seek out true cynics such as myself. Long ago I gave up seeking an honest man. My banishment from society is to roam the earth with this mirror and to find people like you, Mr. Paul Sennett. Come. Step into the mirror. The time in America you seek is here. Come, the clock is striking midnight. This will only work at this precise time alignment."

Sennett's fear changed to excitement. His prayers had been answered. He extended his hand to touch the hand Diogenes offered and entered the mirror as the clock struck twelve.

As 2015 arrived there was a change on a small storefront amidst a throng of New Year's Eve revelers. A sign that once read Antiques and Antiquities Emporium faded to non-existence. The store window became devoid of framed art and ancient relics.

Paul Sennett stood beside Diogenes and saw vehicles he had only seen in old photographs. Throngs of people were shouting "Happy New Year."

"Where are we Mr. Synopios?"

"We're outside your apartment building–midnight New Year's Eve. It's now January 1, 1941."

Retired MD and former Navy medical officer, Dr. Glassman has written 13 medical & military novels including his wartime memoirs in US NAVAL HOSPITAL. He lives with his wife, daughter & 4 grandchildren in San Antonio, Texas and is an active San Antonio Writer's Club member.

MIRRORS

BY

JULIE M. GOLDEN

I slide one of my best friend's hair clips into my short chestnut hair. The blue and silver glittery barrette is my favorite. Paige owns every cool girl thing ever made. A table full of girly things my mom refuses to buy for me, is the highlight of her room. She gets me and so do her parents. Heck, everyone seems to accept me, except for the people who created me.

My mom regularly searches my room and confiscates everything deemed inappropriate. She destroys these small tokens. Lighting a candle, she says a prayer for my soul. My parents don't understand me; they don't even try. They beg me to be what God made me to be. The thing is, that is what I'm trying to do.

Paige lays on her bed, chin propped on her hands, flipping through a teen magazine. "Where are you supposed to be anyway?"

"Church youth group." Leaning into the mirror on her table, I apply a coat of Shocktastic Pink. "What do you think about this one?" I pucker up my lips, now coated with shimmery lip gloss.

Paige pops her head up, squints, and then scrunches up her nose. "No, try the Cotton Candy one. That one's not your color." Her feet, crossed at the ankles, swing back and forth as she returns to the quiz about how to determine your personality type.

I wipe the thick gloss off and sort through the collection of shiny tubes and sticks looking for Cotton Candy. "What do you think about Matt?" I say smiling, "Found it!" I hold up the thin tube of baby pink lip gloss. "I have such a major crush on him."

"Who doesn't? He's super cute!" Paige twirls her blond hair with her fingers and marks down another answer.

"Better?" I stand and strike a pose with pouty lips.

"Much." She jumps up from her bed, "Selfie time!" A moment of happiness is captured on her phone, but there is where it'll stay. An image my parents can never see. They forbid me from wearing makeup, even pink tinted lip balm is off limits. Paige owns nearly all of my happy moments. There isn't a chance I would've survived junior high school without her.

"Do you have any nail polish to match?" I ask, pulling out her bin of nail polish in every color imaginable.

"Probably," she returns to the magazine. "Hey, did you know I'm an extrovert who is exceptionally caring, yet stubborn?"

"You left off totally fab."

She giggles. "That goes without saying." Tossing the magazine aside, she flips through the songs on her phone and stops on a song by Katy Perry. "What happens when your parents find out you ditched church group?"

The polish bottles clank against each other as I search for a color that screams *pick me!* "Who knows. Maybe they'll follow through on their threat to send me away to some island for confused kids." The problem is, I'm not confused and no amount of praying will change who I am.

"No way. They won't ship you off." She holds her hand up as if telling me a secret and says, "What would the neighbors think?" Paige winks at me. "They can't control and contain you if you're not under their roof."

"Good point. Maybe I'll get lucky and they won't find out for a few days." Settling on a color, I plop down on her bed and pull my socks off.

"Instead of waiting for Matt to ask you out, why not make the first move? Be bold and ask him out."

"Paint my toes." I plunk my feet in her lap and wiggle my toes. "I can't, what if he—you know, says no or laughs at me?" The purple glitter polish I picked is amazing. I want to walk around in flip flops for everyone to see, but by the time I go home, I'll have to put on my socks and gym shoes.

"You are totally his type. Girl, you'll never know if you don't try." She gives me a coy smile. "Plus, I know for a fact he's not seeing anyone."

The very idea of dating Matt brings butterflies to my stomach and a toothy smile to my face. I smack my glossy lips together and bat my eyes. This is an area of my life I long to explore, like every girl my age. I'm sure my parents would approve of Matt, but they would never approve of me dating him. Never.

"Your hair is getting long, I like it." Paige pauses and inspects my toes. "Any chance your parents will let you grow it a little longer?" The sweet sound of hope in her voice fills my heart like a balloon. I raise a hand to the clip in my hair; with my pixie cut, it does nothing more than hold my bangs to the side.

"Doubt it." Paige's hair is long, blonde, and curly. I'd give anything to be able to pull my hair up into a pony tail or wear it down and let it drape over my shoulders. "They threaten to shave my head weekly, you know, to teach me a lesson." I admire my Firework Purple toes.

"Are we talking military buzz cut or straight up bald?"

"I'm guessing bald as a baby's butt."

"Well, if anyone can pull off baby butt bald, it's you." We burst into a fit of giggles. "My turn," She tosses Rose Blush Red at me and I start on her toes.

As I move from her big toe towards her pinky, a low rumbling from the first floor has me pause with one toe half painted. Time slows. My senses absorb the song playing, the blue numbers on her clock, and the smell of the nail polish. As if someone hit the volume button, the yelling grows louder. A door slams, jolting Paige and I upright. My wide eyes meet hers. This is it. Paige's parents plead for calm as the fury in their front hall grows.

Heavy feet stomp up the stairs. My mouth hangs open. My heart thumps hard and beats fast. The nail polish brush in my hand shakes in my rattled hand.

"No," I say in a whisper.

As the yelling grows to a roar, Paige jumps into action, grabbing the polish with one hand and throwing my socks at me with the other.

"Fast!"

"Shit!" Fearful tears well in my eyes for the wrath searching for me. I pull my socks on and jam my feet into my gym shoes. As my fingers reach for glittery barrette in my hair, the door flies open.

We freeze. I hear nothing as I fall down the rabbit hole. Paige and her parents beg for understanding and mercy. The red rage on my dad's face tells me there will be neither as he and mom drag me from my safe haven.

In the back of the Buick sedan, shame, my constant companion, sits next to me scowling in my direction. I wipe the soft pink gloss from my mouth with the back of my hand. Even on my hand, it's pretty. Why can't they understand, I just want to be me.

Why don't they love me?

No words are said during the short drive. I shuffle into the house behind them, my hands deep in my jeans pockets and head hung low. I walk past the mirror in the hall. The clip hangs from a short clump of hair, until my father's fat fingers wrap around it and rip it out. Still, in the mirror, I see a beautiful girl, longing to be understood. The night is filled with cruel words, confiscation of forbidden items, and threats of banishment. Then, comes my just punishment.

#

The next morning, as I walk past the mirror and run my hand over my now bare head, I can still see a beautiful girl, trying to survive.

Paige is at my locker waiting for me. With puffy red eyes, I know she was up crying and blaming herself. Her shoulders slump when she sees me.

"I brought this, just in case." She reaches into her bag and pulls out pink skull cap and hands it to me. With a weak smile, I slide it on. She pulls a mirror from her purse, framed in the words "girls rule". In that mirror I see a beautiful girl, trying to heal.

"Thank you."

We walk together, arm in arm to PE. As we stand in front of the locker rooms doors, she gives me a big hug. She whispers in ear, "I love you just as you are, Max. See you in class."

She spins and enters the girls' locker room and I go into the boys'. Passing the mirror, I see a beautiful girl full of hope.

Before starting a career in law enforcement, Julie studied psychology at Concordia University. She lives in the Chicagoland area with her husband and three children.

FRAGMENT

BY

NICHOLAS JOHN GREENFIELD

The first time I saw him was on the steps of a church.

The last was on those same steps, yet only from a distance, their arms around me as I struggled to reach him.

A child of pride, he had grown into a man of stubborn vision, one who dreamt of change and his place before it.

Once he bought me seeds in place of flowers, saying he would be there to nurture them to life, to give them water when they wilt, to remove the dead leaves and collect the fallen petals. He promised I would always be at his side, the flowers would grow for me and me alone. Yet I wanted him to see himself in their growth, to know it was not a case of he and I, but I and I.

We, two together, never apart.

There are times when I wish we never met, when I look at the steps of a church and feel only a deep sense of helplessness, an echo of the love I had for a man who saw something beyond me.

He swore he would never leave, but I knew one day everything he built would collapse upon him, abandoning me to carry a flame that had never shone bright enough to find everything he had lost.

"We can unite the world," he once whispered as we lay within the only space that was truly ours, the others banished from our bed while they lingered in our heads. To them he was a beacon, a pyre upon which to throw the world they wanted to burn.

"They don't understand you," I replied, the pronouns hidden in my heart.

He knew it to be true, yet they held him higher than I ever could, higher than I wished, for I wanted him to be mine like a crowd that drinks from the rain, a selfish love driven by the fact that I had always known he was going to die before we could grow old together, before we had a chance to see the world change, not from our actions, but from our age, seeing everything from the eyes of the children who would accept that which we gave them in a way he believed no one ever could.

Sometimes I picture those children having his brown hair, his tall stature and misshapen ears, a future finally cast in his image.

The building where we lived was a hollow of brick and exposed wiring, our place inside little more than a mattress around which I had hung some sheets to allow the privacy he thought to be my weakness.

The others slept around us, an honour guard to ensure he stayed by their side and brought them everything he promised: an end to the inequality they saw as the cause of their suffering.

We had been a collective for six months before someone finally gained the means to make us more than just an exercise in theory.

The explosive was in essence something simple, yet the devastation it was capable of verged on the poetic, a vision of violence in line with the modern age.

The one who brought it was the last to join, a girl whose quiet temperament made me think of myself, for she seemed more in search of companionship than social change.

"It has to be worn," she explained, the device laid out on one of our privacy sheets, that world forgotten now he had the gateway to another.

It looked like a sleeveless jacket, the pockets stuffed with wires and metal.

"When it detonates, the nails will spread in each direction, maximising the impact." She looked at me, although she spoke only to him. "As long as you are surrounded, then the damage will be extreme. If not, then it will be minimal."

He nodded as he listened, his eyes on the device.

"What are you thinking?" he asked her, the others a faceless mass happy to drown in his words yet reluctant to distinguish the surface from the depths.

The girl kept her eyes on mine. "It has to be somewhere unexpected."

"Yet no innocents," I declared, he reaching out to take my hand, his eyes remaining on the device.

"There are no innocents," he replied.

Beneath his coat you couldn't see it. Yet I could see death in his eyes, feel pain in his hands as he held mine and felt their presence around us, the sheets torn away from a world which had only been ours for a moment.

I thought of the future we would have had, the grey hair appearing at his temples, the aches filling our bones as they settled into the familiar position of holding each other, our bodies like rocks shaped by the sea. Our children would have been ours and then the world's. Our fingers entwined until the end.

Watching him push through the crowd toward the steps of the church, I willed him to turn, to see the white dress I wore and remember there was a different world at the summit of those steps.

The seeds he had given me had grown into flowers, nurtured at his hands to bloom and fill my life with fragrance.

He turned, his eyes seeking out mine.

Then the flowers died, their leaves turning from green to brown to black.

He turned away, our love forever destined to fragment.

Born in England then later shipped off to Australia, N. J. Greenfield has spent half his life exploring the world. After living in a tiny apartment in Paris, braving life in Mexico's chaotic capital, and eating his way through Rome, Nicholas currently resides in Germany.

SURVIVING YOU

BY

ERIN HAYES

I let them escape. My lips parted and the sounds flew out faster than my bent fingers were able to grab hold of them, like a toddler chasing a butterfly. An absentminded attempt to return words to the inner-sanctum they had grown accustomed to.

Your lifeless body lay on top of the crumpled and soiled sheets. Your chest heaved in and out; raspy breaths leaving a trail of ruffled snorts in their wake. You hadn't heard.

I caught a glimpse of myself in the mirror resting on your dresser. The ugly purple and blue welts on my neck glared back at me, angry and loud. Instinctively, I splayed my fingers over the wounds, a feeble attempt to hide them from view. My fists clenched as the bile rose again and I yelled louder.

Rolling your head to the left, an errant curl fell across your forehead, silencing my screams. The corners of your mouth turned up enough to awaken your dimple. Then I remembered.

We were nose to nose under the pregnant moon. Our toes flexed in the cool gritty sand, barefoot and eager. Your hands pinned tightly to mine as promises filled my ears in the space between stolen kisses.

We danced.

So steady and sure, your words were like fire, melting my defenses. We would rise above; escape. You knew the way out.

I followed you without question, an obedient and deferential soldier, hanging on every ideal painted perfect in my mind.

Attention waned and summer surrendered while the wind howled, blowing frigid into our rooms and spirits. I struggled to fill my empty days, longing for lost touches and running out of corners to scour.

I learned to measure your temperament by the way your truck door closed. Rigid and alert, I would wait. A click and we were fine, a slam and I knew. I had no defense.

Salty trails stung my cheeks, staining my sleeves. What did I have to cry about, you asked. After all, you led me out. Imagine where I would be. No, I would tell them. No concerns. I just tripped.

I watched in horror as the final threads of my dreams slithered into the dark abyss between my calloused fingers. You broke me.

Months turned into years as I drowned and resurfaced, gasping for air between fists and apologies. Each time leaving another piece, lost in the current of you.

Until today.

The print on the box said to wait thirty seconds. But I knew right away. Two pink lines appeared on the plastic stick and something warm fluttered inside. A single ember remained, glowing hopeful in the ruins.

My plan, my purpose, turned inside out. A steady resolve surged through my veins; foreign and welcome. My role instantly changed. I was now the protector.

Your lids, heavy and dark, eased open as you wiped the drool from your unshaven cheek.

One, two, three blinks as the light crept in and your focus cleared.

"Hey, doll," you said. The fight forgotten, unabashedly suppressed beneath a liquid haze.

I slid open the drawer, searching blindly for the cold hard steel. Finally, I am determined and sure.

There was no other choice.

"What's going on? You ok?" The gravel in your words hung heavily between us as you reached toward the stand, fumbling for the diluted cup.

I lifted my arm from beneath the scattered collection of mismatched socks, raising my hand pointedly towards you.

"Never better," I said and clicked off the safety.

Erin Hayes has written several flash flash fiction pieces and recently completed her first novel. She lives in New York with her husband and children.

TUGSHIP

BY

RUSSELL HEMMELL

"You're approaching, Ace. Mentally prepared?"

"No."

"Well, you'd better be. If you can't get it right the first time, rocket-assisted orbital mechanics ain't for you!"

"Nice." He replied acidly. "Is it the Agency's way of encouraging its elite officers, or just your sweet feminine self taking over?"

What a smug chauvinist you are, Ellen would have said, as she always did anytime he looked down on his female co-workers. But his sister, with her inimitable spirit, her cold, logical mind, her unfaltering determination, was no longer there. God, how he missed her.

Raj remained imperturbable like a Theravada monk, the screen blurring the contour of her big brown eyes. "Captain, it's one hundred years, give or take, that mankind is preparing for similar cases. The mission has been planned down to the smallest detail." She smiled, her tone becoming less flippant. "Nobody has been involved in its design more than you. You've gone through more space simulations than hangovers in your life. Just do it. That's what you're programmed for."

"You're talking to the wrong sibling, First Engineer. It's Ellen who wrote all the specs, not me."

"I see. Let's damn well hope that accuracy runs in the family then."

Accuracy does, not so the genius. Ellen had been the mind and driving force behind the mission. Ellen the visionary who devised how to

130

transform what had been just a stash of useless notes from state bureaucrats, transforming the ideas into an operational plan. With a Gantt chart, a deadline and several hundred equations, she lay it down, run simulations, and put together the budget and the crews who delivered it. His sister hired Raj as the new Station's Chief Engineer, trusting her guts and fighting against Agency's prejudices. She had also died before being able to see the actual deployment, leaving the responsibility of Mission Commander on his shoulders.

He adjusted his visor, magnifying the images on the main screen. The fat, crater-ridden body of SV-I-232 was quietly hovering in front of him, plunged into a green, glowing light. Difficult to believe this seemingly inoffensive rock could wreak such havoc. So far, things had proceeded according to plan. The primary slingshot over Mars had made SV-I-232 slow down on its voyage toward Earth. That had been a success. Raj and her team had perfectly executed that leg of the mission from the Orion Station on the Earth-Moon Lagrange point 2. The last terrestrial outpost in space, an Ellen Asher's brainchild, along with many others.

Now it was his turn. His tugship had to intercept, harpoon the asteroid and thrust it slowly until the position could allow gravity tractors to finally capture SV-I-232 into a stable Earth orbit. Transforming a mortal threat into an asset; even better, into a great opportunity for the whole humanity. All of it depended on the precision he was able to deliver. In a scenario with a set of constraints, multiple incognite and scarce energy, accuracy was essential. Double the mission time and you halve the delta-V, lowering the overall risk, but you also increase the fuel consumption up to a dangerous factor. And the asteroid was rotating, meaning he would be able to apply the required thrust only for a fraction of time. *Provided I can match the ship's rotation with the asteroid's spin axis first.* He sighed. Only one shot, that was all he got. He had to dock at the right time, into the right place, no margin of error allowed.

"Starting countdown in 2 minutes. Stand-by."

"Summers and Hart are in position?"

"Already on the lower deck. Tractors are ready to deploy after docking is completed and harpoons are in place."

"What are you going to do once you're back to Earth, Asher the Hero? I mean…provided you have a planet to come back to. If you screw up, you people might well remain out there until your life support lasts."

"Thank you for relieving the pressure on me, Raj. I understand better now why nobody dates you."

"Why, have you actually given it a thought?"

"Six months in outer space do work miracles."

Rendezvous point ahead. Time for some music. Space music, of course. He smiled. *Who ever said you can't hear a sound in space? Oh yes, you can, provided you know how to listen.* Wasn't that the reason why he chose to be there? Seeing what the others weren't able to see, observing Earth from a vantage point. Hear it breathing. He switched on, and an eerie plasma-wave generated music from Saturn's hexagon radio waves, sweeter to his ears than any classical melody and Ellen's favourite sound, slowly invaded the cockpit.

"Asher, what's this sound? Problems?"

"Negative. Initiating countdown."

Ellen, I'm doing this for you, Mugface. You who loved this planet and its dumb people so much you were willing to die for them. Hope you enjoy what you're seeing now.

He activated the SCM rendezvous procedure, and left the ship computer taking care of the intercept trajectory. At the scheduled time, he positioned the nimble ship just above Crater Theia and released the harpoons. The tugship made a complete turn around the asteroid, wrapping it into a shining, lithe cage. Its prey secured, it started travelling back to the Orion Station. SV-I-232 slowly moved out of its orbit, gently tugged away by the tiny vessel, leaving behind green gases and a derelict moonlet.

Russell Hemmell is a statistician and social scientist from the U.K, passionate about astrophysics and speculative fiction. Recent stories in Gone Lawn, Not One of Us, Strangelet, and elsewhere. Blog: Earthianhivemind. net. Twitter: @SPBianchini

TEMPLE CURTAIN ANALOG

BY

N K HENRY

the sky is silk and the birds in it are near-pictures that pulse slow. the mechanics of an appendage's single pump, see it; every nuance naked to the eons unfolded there. the seconds are god hours kept in their wings

A set of squinting eyes to catch it all. Eyes black, impregnable and deep set. Eyes that trace from those borne birds hung like clocks against space; a look that traces from them to your own, as if those sliding eyes alone could move in that sludge moment. Down a wall-less corridor they glare and at sixty feet they yet camp but from an inch off your nose. Eyes that indurate from under a brow obsidian, all shadowed and capped under the colour of an out-of-town team, or, more accurately, the *other* town team, and yet their rented bus smolders all the same like it bussed in from the outer realms just to clog the parking lot with its wreaking gears and alien team stripes. Bussed in just so this figure could stand up on a mound and peel adjectives at you making you general, as in unspecified, while yet he stares on exclusively; raw and recalcitrant; and they told you he would look at you this way.

They the Chorus told you this was his science, and to resist it; to cross those interstitial feet with a likewise glare, your own psychology; He's a bum, they say, and you ought let him know it too. He's a demagogue, a goddamn showman, he ain't even white. But of it, those so-sayers couldn't stretch to touch a toe, and singing the way they do says they don't got much other than what swings high and inside—this is what you think when the Chorus bleat their advice, their false equivalences. Meanwhile he's telling you else wise: I throw with sarcasm, he says, I'll tear out your flesh with every red stitch. The words have no grin, even if one is stretched across his face while he says it, even if when he says it he gets a laugh.

Yes sir, he'll metabolize you—so had said the batter before you, a man himself left swinging at the flies. He'll leave you in decimals, said another player from the flap of his collar, I seen it and I seen it and I seen it. And if he can't huck for a damn from here on out, his mouth'll run ibidem to every nasty tint his eyes ever composed. And his mouth'll run parallel and ibidem to every intention of his glare.

But that was the dugout, and now the figure on the mound is having his own say: Just you and me, kid. This is Dadaism down a gullet; now how much critique can you give, he says. And he says it again while his toe draws clear scars in the dirt.

And then without a cue he looks away; and this is formal, ritualistic caesura. And you might just hate it more than the impregnable eyes for there is no telling anything at all without the stare.

So now his nose jets with a single exhale. Your temples grind against the cap, you can hear them thump. The smell of grass, it should be in your nostrils, but you are cut from all that, all taste of chaw, gone, there is only the beating temples. Then he kicks high, winds like a coil and in one pyrrhic flash all that distance contracts at the physics of a pitch; and yet all that space expands just the same; by metaphysics is decorum torn; and separate worlds fuse by every yard the topspin sends. Red threads, the actual stitches pulling along the past, or pushing it or splitting it—yes, a temple curtain analog, but one a veil thicker than half a millennial's stretch, and broader than a continent goes, and you got to hit it on back as if that might undo what he's already done, as if it's supposed to mean more than you just trying to get at least a base hit, because that's the only reason you ever swung. But here you are trying to knock every Logos from the bat, and how'd they get there anyway?

In every work n k henry looks to stitch together the mythical and mechanical, the ephemeral and the dirt. And somewhere in the gulps of coffee and notes he's abandoned a story begins to breathe.

ALONE IN THE DARK

BY
JOSHUA HIDER

The wicked wind whispers "death" through the ragged and jagged oaks that hang like a gallows across the waxing moon as Ela pulls her buckskin shawl about her shoulders, moving headlong into the uncertain darkness beyond. The fact that the witching hour had come and gone some time ago worries her very little. She fears nothing the night has to offer. The real danger lies ahead and the realization of it almost takes her breath away as the raven haired girl steels her nerve with every silent step. The hunting knife no doubt would gleam wildly against the moon above were she to pull it from underneath her covering and brandish it for courage, but there is little hope in the protection that it offers. They could be upon her before the first stroke fell in defense, and the innocent maiden knows all too well that she is at their mercy.

It was never her intention to be in this situation, but life sometimes twists and turns. The blameless sometimes bear the brunt of fate. The night the first of their kind became brave enough to burrow beneath the barrier and creep in for a closer look at what would become their favorite quarry was monumental. It marked the beginning of the end. From that time forward, they knew nothing of fear and cared even less for reprisal. Their lust for flesh ran wild inside with no end to their thirst for the blood that ran warm just below the surface of her people's bronze

135

skin. They would easily replace those vanquished by revenge and cared nothing for those lost. They are the beasts of legend that the old folks sang of around the fire, and their tales of certain death had come to fruition.

Ela whispers under her breath the incantation that the medicine man gave her. She hopes those magical words will have some effect, if she is able to utter them before her evisceration. As the path becomes smoother at the crest of the hill, a distinctive stench meets the girl. The death and decay of her people emanate from the caves below. Her tribe once called these same outcroppings home. A flash of courage races through the determined young woman as her surroundings become more familiar. Not only has she come here to exterminate the vermin, but also to reclaim her home for those living in exile.

The rosiness of dawn will soon be creeping into the canyons above. The time is right to act as the first pair of beady red eyes flashes to life ahead like a pair of torches suddenly set ablaze. Ela grips the blade as her teeth grind and her mind suddenly goes blank. More torch-like sets of eyes move in the darkness. She can hear their labored, raspy breathing coming near her. "Selu, help me," she whispers under her breath, her brain racing to remember those sacred death words, and although she opens her mouth to speak them, nothing comes forth.

Certain death is slipping forward and any second she will feel their razor teeth rip her to pieces, but at least her death will be quick, although extremely painful. Determined to put up a fight and take a few with her, the courageous girl pushes her shawl from her shoulders and holds the blade in her strong right hand. U'du'du taught her long ago how to wield the short blade. Among her people few could best her at its use, but now she is outnumbered and death will come sooner than later.

A roar and a sudden rush of wind warns of the enemy just feet away. With blind luck the blade strikes home and the beast falls heavily upon her, its warm blood spewing upon her chest. Ela struggles to push the beast away and slithers out from underneath it, feeling for the knife that is sticking hilt deep in the soft fur, just underneath its ribcage. A bit sickened by her blood bath, she rips the knife from its purchase and whirls around, struggling to find a bearing in the dark. The girl feels the air in front of her part as another charges. That split second of warning saves her life. Now it is her turn to bleed as a large gap opens in her right thigh and the fluid of life oozes quickly down to pool in her moccasin. Fortunately, her quick backhanded stab finds a home between the shoulders blades of her attacker. It trips and careens headlong into an unseen boulder, knocking it senseless.

Ela grabs the cut in her leg, realizing it was not nearly as mortal as she first believed it to be. The warrior is determined to battle on, but realizes she must get to higher ground. Some of the creatures are circling around behind to flank her. She knows the perfect place to make her stand, turns, and races to a small shelf of sheer rock where she will have more of a fighting chance. The retreat sends the animals into a frenzy as their chase instinct kicks in and they charge forward as one savage group.

Out of breath and surely now out of time, Ela tries hard to get her wind back and mount one last sortie. U'du'du would have been proud if he could have seen her at that moment, her proud black hair fluttering in the wind and her bronzed body flush with battle. He would have seen a warrior princess of the highest order and felt proud she was birthed as his granddaughter, instead of the grandson he had hoped for. She knew he would join her someday in the land beyond, but a big part of her fears that place. She knows in her heart she would rather not make that journey today.

It appears she has no choice as the snarling eyes close in upon her. At that very moment, a peace settles within like she has never felt before, and instead of feeling tense and fearful, Ela feels extremely calm. The young girl even sits down upon the smooth stone, closes her eyes, and seems to go into a trance. The world around her peels back as each day of her life plays out before her as though she is living it all over again, but at a much faster speed. Time stands still and the days race into night, and then back into day again. Suddenly the pictures stop and the young girl's eyes snap wide open. She jumps to her feet and screams shrilly at the beasts just steps from her, "Great U'ne La'nu'hi, give your daughter the power of light." Instantly, a great flash illuminates the world around her.

Ela is blinded by the brightness momentarily, but soon regains her sight. Her foes are not as fortunate. A large group staggers around with hands cupped over their eyes, howling mournfully. The horrified girl then realizes these savage creatures are partly human. The thought sickens her. Such barbarity deserves no mercy, and as the damaged demi-humans writhe around on the ground in their agony, one by one her blade strikes home. As the last dies in misery, the piercing light snaps off, and the world again goes dark.

Exhausted, Ela sits down in the soft grass and watches the rosy peach of the sunrise come up over her home. Later, after a good long nap, she will return to her people and lead them back here. They will change her name to Us'di Nv'do'i'ga'e'hi, or Little Sun, for the courage shown that black night. U'du'du, her grandfather, will be the first to meet her, with tears streaming from his deep brown eyes upon her return.

Josh has always been a writer. He currently resides in North Carolina with his family.

THE SLAMMER

BY

JUSTIN HUNTER

"You know they call him *The Slammer* now, right?" The girl asked the question with hesitation, as if she were looking over her shoulder and expecting to see *The Slammer* there. She knelt on the white-hot cement sidewalk. The sun climbing, her classmates playing. The boy was across from her, bouncing on his toes.

"Yeah, duh," he said. "They've been calling him that for a while. Let's play."

The boy had a tube. In that slender plastic tube were caps, small circular collector's playing disks, colorful cardboard used for playing games. His favorites were the commercialized faces of television characters hawking a product. Leonardo selling chocolate milk or Sonic telling kids that McDonald's fries were the best.

The girl wanted to talk about *The Slammer*. He'd been at the school all along, but it seemed to her like he was new—a transfer student, maybe—after he earned the nickname. "He hits the pile so hard that you have to crawl around all over the place just to find the Pogs."

"Yep."

The girl had a tube of her own, capped off. Not ready to release upon the world a magical collection of everything from Hello Kitty to Ghostbusters. Her caps, the ones without any dents or tattered edges, were not for play. She used her brother's set when she was playing. But she always used her slammer. Her slammer was blue, a dog with its tongue hanging out imprinted on one side. A paw print on the other.

"He uses that one silver slammer."

"Who?"

"*The Slammer* does." She said it, brows furrowed, as if the boy wasn't listening. "His slammer doesn't have a picture. Does yours?"

"All of them do," the boys said. "Are we playing?"

"*The Slammer's* doesn't."

"I played his sister once." The boy took a stack of Pogs from his tube, checked his Casio wristwatch.

"Really?" The girl asked. "She played?"

"It's why he plays. She taught him how to play. Now, he doesn't even keep the ones he wins."

"But you've seen how hard he throws the slammer?" The girl stood then looked out across the sun-washed playground. "Like he's trying to throw it straight to China."

The boy looked at his watch again. "Recess is almost over. We playing?"

"One time, when I played him, he threw the slammer so hard it bounced off the stack and hit me in the forehead. He didn't take the ones he won, though."

"Did you take the ones you won?"

"Well, duh," she said. "I gave them to my brother. I was playing with his Pogs."

The boy looked at the girl, shook his head. "You shouldn't have. Those were his sister's."

"Who's?"

"*The Slammer's* sister."

"So?"

The boy laughed. "I wish you would play me. You're so dumb, I'd probably take all your Pogs."

The girl stood and shoved her tube of precious Pogs under her arm. "Shut up. I'm not dumb."

"You took those Pogs from his sister."

"No, I won them from him."

The boy turned now and walked past the girl. On his way by he said, "Have you seen his sister lately?"

The girl turned, watched the boy walking away. "No, why?"

"Why do you think he throws the slammer so hard?"

The boy disappeared into the classroom, and the girl wished she hadn't taken *The Slammer's* sister's Pogs.

Justin Hunter is currently working on his MFA at Arcadia University. His work has been published or is forthcoming in Corvus Review, Down in the Dirt Magazine, and Typehouse Magazine, among others.

BLUE SKY

BY
MATTHEW KEELEY

If this isn't Lewis, sorry – this is the only apartment code we had for him. Or you. Whoever you are. It's Thomas, Anna's son. Remember me?

They made us write these things at school, but I don't remember the proper way. Never really had to use one. Just thought it would be safer. I reckon they monitor all Clicks. That's what Dad always thought. You probably did, too. Although I'm sure you weren't allowed to say so.

That's why Mum thinks you left the police right at the Change. And left us. You never told her or dad why you didn't want to be on Day Guard. Just moved away.

Anyway, I still haven't explained why I'm writing. Although explaining it is difficult. Don't know what happened. But I just feel like you might. Dad's obviously not around to talk to and I don't want to freak Mum out.

It was three days ago.

I started at 11 pm at the Sun Screens factory in the East Quadrant. Did you know I work there? We make the sky display screens for apartments. The kind of place where people can afford them, I suppose. I'm two storeys down. Don't know if Mum mentioned any of this in one of her Clicks. Don't know if she's stopped sending them now. You never reply.

My hand is getting sore already. Don't remember the last time I wrote this much. Anyway, I was working with Caleb. Most of the shift went

142

by as usual with the regular checks on all the machines and a couple of jams we fixed – well, mostly I fixed. But around twenty minutes before we were closing up, this huge, hissing sound erupted from up top. An emergency light started flashing and steam shot out from one of the exhaust pipes along the ceiling. It was so loud. Caleb rattled over and we could see something had obviously burst up there. The steam pumped out and whistled, although it started to get thicker, more like smoke. Caleb couldn't see a difference.

He shut off the machine and eventually the steam, or smoke, or whatever, thinned out. I headed to the control room to turn off the siren. I knew neither of us could fix anything in the time we had left. Without even asking, I Clicked through to HQ.

After explaining to the same woman as usual, some other suited guy appeared on screen. He must've been listening in. I'd never spoken to him. He asked if there was still steam coming from the pipes. I told him there was – I could see it from there. I didn't mention my smoke theory, was worried it might make him less likely to send us away before day.

In the end, it didn't make a difference. He didn't even tell me first, just turned and called an order to someone else. "Lockdown – East Quadrant manufacturing site. Now."

I could already hear the day doors clamping into place around me as he explained through the speaker that we'd be in until the next night. They couldn't get anyone out to fix it or to take our place in time. He didn't want the factory left alone with a malfunctioning machine, not during the day when no one could do anything about it. I only thought about it later, but if there was a fire, they'd just locked us in there with it. They didn't care.

I'd never been in for curfew anywhere other than my home. But I guess I didn't have anything to be home for, not living with mom anymore. Caleb had to Click his wife to let her know what was happening.

I don't know if he should've done that. There only was one bed in the control room. I ended up down on Caleb's bench by the conveyor belt.

I didn't sleep much before I noticed.

I saw the glow from a machine bulb or maybe even moonlight. But then I remembered where I was in the middle of the day. Opening my eyes properly, I sat up and couldn't figure out why I was seeing it. But I knew what it was. A little puddle of yellow. Sunlight. I hadn't seen the real thing in the ten years since the Change. The gold colour shone every summer afternoon outside back into my head. Pools. Games at school.

Birthdays. Mum. Dad. You.

Looking up, I traced where it came from. The sun poured in through a hole in the ceiling where the pipe had blown. It was like dripping honey. I knew I should've covered my face from the radiation. But I wasn't scared, not with all those memories now floating down through that gap. I yelled to Caleb and hurried heading toward the ladder to the overhead walkway. I don't know if it was my shout or my boots bashing against the rungs that woke him, but as soon as I reached the top, he had come hopping out, calling up to me. I don't even know what he was saying. I was drawn toward that bright gap in the bricks.

Caleb somehow managed to clamber up the ladders after me. God knows how. He was freaking out about the rays. But all the warnings didn't seem to matter. I was already standing underneath the light. It was warm, but it wasn't burning at all. It was comforting.

And I couldn't just leave it at that. Don't know what the hell I was thinking. But before Caleb could stop me, or I could even think sensibly, I was hauling myself up on top of the burst pipe. And putting my head outside.

Sound opened up. I felt wind blowing at me, but it wasn't cold like I was used to. There wasn't much to look at. Just the flat, dusty roof of the factoryand blue skystretching all around. I couldn't hear Caleb anymore. I think he'd caught a glimpse of it all, too, from down there.

It was only after my eyes adjusted that I saw it. Kind of like seeing the fragment of light on the factory floor. Difference is, I still don't know what was in the sky.

The shiny black cube beside the sun.

But not really square. Jagged. And vibrating. It wasn't right.

I didn't get to look at it much longer, although I don't think anything would be clearer even if I had. Caleb pulled at my leg, yanking me back down, sliding from the pipe. I tried to make him look out, to see it too, but he wouldn't go any nearer, wouldn't even listen to me. He just clamped up, shaking his head, backing away, like the Grim Reaper was sitting up there, waiting for him.

Neither of us slept after that. Back down at the bench I watched that little spotlight on the floor fade away, swallowed by the rest of the shadows. At midnight the mechanics arrived. Neither of us said anything about the hole in the roof. We both just knew it was best. They sent us home straight away.

But Caleb didn't show up today.

I got a Click from HQ saying he'd been assigned retirement. Just like that. Disappeared over a day. They must realise I'll know this seems wrong. And that's why I'm worried. Why I'm writing to you, Uncle Lewis. Is this what happened to you? And am I next? They obviously found the hole – it's all bricked up again and painted over, like nothing ever happened. But they must know we saw. That's why Caleb's gone – he talked about it, sent a Click. I haven't said anything, not even to Mum. You're the first person I'm telling.

Is this nuts? Do people just vanish for looking outside or for saying something wrong? Mum would've been gone long ago, if that was the case.

I probably didn't even see anything that weird. Maybe it's just a satellite. Or just my eyes adjusting to the sun. It was bound to have some bad effect after ten years.

Feel kind of dumb for writing this whole letter thing. Look how paranoid you and Dad made me!

Someone's been banging at the door for a while now. Don't usually answer, but they won't go away. Can't remember how to end these things so… please just contact us, Uncle Lewis. This was Thomas.

Matthew Keeley is an English teacher and writer from Central Scotland, currently looking to publish his first science-fiction novel, 'Turning the Hourglass.'

THE CHEDDAR COAST

BY

E.E. KING

Jean was an academic writer. She spent her days typing out text as arid as her imagination, as dry as the valley between her thighs. She viewed the world through horned rimmed glasses, preferring the safety of code to the complexity of creation. She never took a vacation, or even a day off, favoring the sleek uncompromising lines of her laptop to the infinite variety of sand and shore surging only a block away from her Santa Monica office. She distained even the thought of the bronzed bodies that frolicked in the surf as if there were nothing more important than play or laughter.

But, when the sea wants you, it calls with a roar so powerful, that even if you plug your ears with wax—even if you fasten yourself to figures, you are not secure.

When it was noted that Jean had five years of vacation due, she was given a mandatory two weeks off. Zipping her laptop into her sleek black bag, she left the office and wandered home. The sky was a clear endless blue; it tingled with the tang of salt. Sea breezes tugged at her linen suit and rumbled her bangs. Jean tightened her mouth and marched on.

Once home she turned on her laptop and stared at the pulsing screen. She considered looking for some free-lance writing, but the sites she found seemed too bright and full of promises to be genuine. Jean distrusted promise.

At lunchtime she toasted two pieces of slightly stale white bread. Placing a slice of Kraft cheese thin as a contract between them, she cut them in half. She stared blankly at the plate as she ate, her mind blank. Even though the cheese was barely warm, orange goo began to ooze out of the half sandwich on her plate.

As she watched the toasted bread lengthened, each grain became visible, even though it was white bread. The orange cheese rose up, displaying an underbelly deep and blue as an endless summer. White foam fringed its top and little flecks of moisture, tasting of salt and cheddar wafted toward her.

As Jean glazed up, open mouthed, grilled cheese dribbling from her lips like disbelief, she realized she had shrunk. Either that or the sandwich had grown, because she was now standing, wearing neat black pumps, buried in grains of what had once been bread, but was now unmistakably sand.

She was alone on the beach – for beach it was; streaming in either direction a blinding infinity of sand, white as Wonder bread. The indigo cheddar sea curled above her, drawing back the pebbles and flinging them at her shoes.

She looked around, trying to absorb the metamorphosis of her lunch.

Gliding toward her down the shore coasted a flying saucer. It was an unnatural bright green. But then, nothing about this day was natural.

As it approached, skimming the surface of the sand, she saw that it was being chased by a large, hairy yellowish creature –– a golden retriever, tongue flapping in mindless delight. His paws punched softly into the sand making tiny declivities which shown for a moment in the sun before being damped by the rolling tide.

It was a Frisbee, Jean realized, just a Frisbee. She felt tremendous relief at this minor normality.

Behind the joyful dog, almost keeping pace with, him ran a man, his strong honeyed limbs pumping, white teeth flashing, eyes as blue as dreams.

Cheddar drooled from Jean's mouth, heated by an internal fire. All the dry spaces inside her became moist. The dog leapt up, curving a perfect ellipse in space, as he grabbed the Frisbee and deposited it at Jean's feet.

The man arrived a minute later, breathless and laughing. Jean was breathless too. She had never seen anyone so alive.

"RIIIINNNNGGGG." A sound louder than the ocean's roar, more incongruous than the change of bread into beach shattered the silence.

Jean blinked in the morning light. She was in bed, the alarm clock sounding like a judgment. Jean always set her alarm, although she had never needed it before.

It was just a dream, she thought, *but so real.*

She got up to brush her teeth but as she looked in the mirror – for one brief instance, instead of her normal pale, tight face, it seemed a sun-bronzed goddess looked back. Shaking her head, the image vanished. The flashback of a dream so tangible, even now she could taste the piquant salt air and smell the rich, live sea.

Without letting herself think, she took off her cotton nightgown. Trying not to look at her clam-pale body, she dug through her drawers like a manic puppy. Hidden beneath her underwear she found it. A tiny bikini, striped like a candy cane. It had been a prize won at an office party where Jean had calculated the exact number of pinto beans in a jar. She had meant to throw the suit away, or donate it to Good Will, but instead she had buried it beneath mounds of sensible cotton undergarments.

Squinting at herself in the mirror she could almost see the tanned goddess. Before she could change her mind, she grabbed a towel, slipped on her thongs and ran the three blocks to the waiting beach.

She didn't even notice that surrounding the white plate on her table, tiny bits of sand glittered like promises in the morning light.

E.E. King is a performer, writer, biologist and painter. Ray Bradbury calls her stories "marvelously inventive, wildly funny and deeply thought provoking. I cannot recommend them highly enough." Check out paintings writing and musings at www.elizabetheveking.com

CHRISTMAS PARTY

BY
JACKIE LAYTON

Jessica Hobbs placed the centerpiece on the food table at the community center where she was hosting Kingstown Knitters. Most of the women frequented her hobby shop, and Jessica had wanted to do something special for them. A Christmas celebration seemed like the perfect solution.

The door squeaked open, and she glanced at her watch. Someone was a few minutes early. She turned to greet the first arrival. Instead of an older lady, a handsome man stood on the threshold. Her heart skipped a beat as their eyes met. He looked about her age, early thirties, with thick brown hair and green eyes, and he held a mesh bag full of basketballs. "Um, I reserved this room, and you don't look like you're about to leave."

"My party will start soon."

Frustration lined his forehead as he frowned. "I reserved the center to host a Christmas party for a team of eight-year-old boys."

"There must be a mistake, because I booked the room months ago. You'll need to have your party somewhere else."

His eyes narrowed. "Too late. We're due to start in thirty minutes. The pizza has been ordered and should arrive right after the boys."

Jessica waved her hand toward the food table. "I'm all set up to serve lunch." She looked around the room. Her quiet knitters wouldn't be a match for a group of rambunctious boys if they shared the space.

The man threw his head back and sighed. "These kids are from the poor side of town. I volunteer my time with them twice a week and on Saturdays. I have gifts and the pizza may be the best meal they eat during Christmas break. I can't take their party away. It wouldn't be fair."

"I'm sorry, but I don't see how we can both have parties at the same time. Lively young boys don't mix with elderly ladies."

He spun and exited the multi-purpose room without another word.

Had he given up? Jessica followed him into the building's foyer. A welcome table, water fountain, and two public restrooms filled the small area. "What are you thinking?"

"Is this area big enough for my party?"

"It's too cold out here for your kids." This wasn't going well at all. Time for a different approach. "I'm Jessica Hobbs."

He shook her hand. "Shane Daniels. Your name sounds familiar. As in *Hobbs Hobbies?*"

"Guilty. Some of these ladies don't have family, and this will be their only Christmas celebration. They have huge hearts and give to others. I wanted to do something nice for them."

"Christmas is for kids."

"No, Christmas is for everybody." A twinge of guilt jabbed her. How could she take away a party from kids? Could they combine their events? She didn't want the ladies feel slighted, and she refused to call off her party. Not many options.

The glass doors opened, and a woman entered with two young boys. "Here you go Coach. I can't tell you how excited they are. It's a great thing you're doing." Unshed tears pooled in her eyes.

Shane shook his head. "Well…"

Jessica touched his arm and looked at the young mother. "We're going to have a great party."

"Thanks. See you later."

The boys shoved each other and laughed.

"Settle down guys." Shane turned inquisitive eyes to Jessica. "What's your plan?"

One crazy thought after another chased themselves around her mind, and Shane continued to stare at her. "How about Bingo?"

"I guess it could work." His eyes twinkled. "We can team each boy up with one of your ladies."

"We're going to need more tables and chairs."

"Guys, we need your help setting up." He explained the revised party plan to the boys.

The dark-headed boy shrugged out of a jacket that was too small for him. "Cool. Can we show them some basketball tricks? We can be the entertainment."

Jessica smiled. "Sure you can, honey. Let's get to work."

Fifteen minutes later all ten boys had arrived. Jessica found supplies from the Wednesday night Bingo group, and Shane brought the boys' presents inside and set them under the center's Christmas tree.

"Hello," an elderly lady called out as she entered the room. "Looks like we've got new members to our knitting group."

"Hi, Betty. We have some special guests."

Shane appeared and helped Betty off with her coat. "Jessica is letting us crash your party. Hope that's okay."

Betty laughed. "It'll probably be our liveliest party in years."

Jessica led Betty to a table. "The kids don't have much and the director booked both parties for the same time."

"We always bring mittens, scarves, and gifts to our Christmas party and vote what charity to take them to. Looks like this year the recipients came to us."

She gave Betty a hug. "I told Shane you all had hearts of gold. Thanks." Jessica hurried over to share the news with Shane. "The knitters have scarves and mittens to give the boys. I wouldn't be surprised if there were extras to take home to their families."

His smile stretched across his handsome face. "Maybe it wasn't a mistake we were booked at the same time."

"You could be right." Boys and elderly ladies began filling the room with an air of excitement that couldn't be missed.

"We should follow this up with a New Year's Eve party. What do you think?" He winked at her.

Spend New Year's Eve with an attractive man while helping others? No need to think about it. "I'd love to."

Jackie has written many stories including Christmas Party for Centum and In Focus with Forget Me Not Romances. Jackie will soon live on the coast in South Carolina with her husband of twenty-seven years and their Westie, Heinz.

ALFRED AND ME

BY

TRACY LEE-NEWMAN

My brother Alfred wakes up from a dream.

He says in the dream he was a giant Action Man. All bristle-haired and plastic private parts.

We're in the caravan. I can't see my brother. I get out of bed, lean over him, and my hands feel about for his head. His hair is long and the elves have been tangling it up in their night knots.

I tell him he's fine, but he begs, "Katie, get in bed with me."

We're twins, me and Alfred, and Mum says when we were little we always slept cuddled together. But now we are giants. We are eight years, two months, and thirteen days old. I am older than Alfred by six entire minutes.

Mum says holidays are good for making friends. She says, "Stop being giants and go to the playground and find some new friends." Well, she doesn't say the giants bit, but that's because she doesn't see we're giants now. She has her phone on and she's Facebooking with that man she likes. He makes her laugh. That's because he has this massive orange beard. It's like Mary Poppins' bag – it has everything in it, like hat stands and bluebirds and new patent school shoes and twenty pound notes.

"Come on," I say to Alfred, "let's go to the stupid old playground."

"Okay," he agrees, "but not to make friends."

"No, of course not," I assure. "Just to look at them; look down at them; like they're just little ants we can squish."

Alfred doesn't like Mum's man. He says his beard is scratchy, scratchier than Action Man's head.

"Where's Dad," he keeps asking.

"I've told you," I say. "Dad's gone to the moon in a rocket. Or was it to Mars? I forget."

"You told me he was in Africa," says Alfred. "Or the rainforest."

"The rainforest is in Africa," I say. "He went there before he went up in the rocket."

We're up at the top of the slide and we're not letting anyone else up or down. They're stamping their feet, saying they will get their mums and dads to tell us off.

"Go on," we say. "We'll kill them with our laser eyes."

Mum says if I keep telling fibs I'll get a nose like that puppet-y boy in the book.

"No you won't," Alfred assures. "She's just lying."

She says if I keep telling fibs I won't have any friends.

"Good," Alfred says. "Friends are stupid."

Alfred never tells lies.

There's a girl in my class called Amelia Rose. One day she saw me being a giant white shark in the playground, chasing and eating the fish who were screaming. She asked me if I'd be her friend. I agreed, but only if you're Alfred's friend as well.

"Who's Alfred?" she said.

So I bit her.

In the playground this lady comes up and says, "I don't know what you think you're at, my girl, but you better start letting the other kids use this slide right now, do you hear me? Standing up there like you're some flipping queen or what have you."

"We're giants," I tell her. "And monsters. We are monster-y giants with eyes that shoot lasers."

"You're a pain in the backside," she says. "Where's your parents?"

"Dead," I say.

My teacher says, "Tell the truth, Katie. Amelia Rose said you bit her."

"I didn't," I say.

"She has teeth marks on her arm," my teacher says.

I say, "If you look closely, you'll see those were made by a shark."

"I want to go back to the caravan now," Alfred says.

"Okay," I agree.

I give the lady my full laser eye blasts.

"Now you're dead too," I say.

If you want the truth, I'll tell you. When we were four and a half,

Alfred died. This big tree fell down in a storm. It squashed him, and his Action Man. I found them. They were really flat.

Back at the caravan Mum's still on her Facebook.

"You make any friends?" she asks.

"Oh yes," we say. "Loads and loads of them."

"Brilliant," she says. "See? I knew you could do it."

Alfred didn't get squashed by a tree. He just had a disease. But it's true that he's dead and it's true that he's never been dead and is still here with me all the time. And no, he really doesn't want me making friends.

I do wish I had laser eyes.

Tracy Lee-Newman (@writeatme) lives in the South-East of England and is currently working on her second novel whilst touting her first around agents. Her short story, 'Arthur and Me' was inspired by her work with children who struggle to express their emotions.

THE FLAG

BY

THANH-NU LEROY

Recently, a German friend told me that while visiting California she had seen entire neighborhoods still flying the flag of South Vietnam – a golden background with three horizontal red stripes in its centre. At first I laughed in derision at these overseas Vietnamese who can't give up the past, even forty years later. Then I spoke to my friend with an air of historical detachment, as if many years living in Zurich has made me neutral, allowing me to talk about the Vietnam war like a Wikipedia page. But that night when I looked at the moon, a memory of childhood spoke to me clearly.

In 1969, when I was eight years old, our house in Saigon was one of the rare ones with a television -- a classic model in a wooden case with four pointy legs. There were only two black-and-white channels available, 9 and 11: Channel 9 was national, broadcasting Vietnamese-language shows, news, and announcements, and Channel 11 was the American NWB-TV in English, relaying popular shows for the American troops.

I found the American channel far more attractive, although I didn't understand a word. I remembered watching the "Bewitched" series with regular roars of laughter marking the end of each scene so I learned what was funny. Although the language was a mystery, I guessed the plot through actions, the actors' expressions, and the tone of their voices. I also watched "Wild Wild West", my favorite adventure series because the good guys always won.

Every night after dinner, our family gathered in front of the magnificent device and my father turned on the switch. My parents sat on their two recliner chairs and us seven kids had the bamboo mat on the floor. My parents only watched channel 9, and when they finished the Vietnamese shows, we children were allowed channel 11. That was our family entertainment and sometimes the maids joined us on the bamboo mat. One of them always offered her lap as a cushion, and I often felt asleep feeling her silky black-satin pants under my cheek.

During the day, the screen displayed the test pattern consisting of a big circle decorated with an American Indian head at the top and four little disks in the corners of the screen. Although there was no program to watch, I would stare at the Indian head and imagine horses, arrows, cowboys, and all sorts of adventures exuding from the feather headdress.

One day, my parents did not go off to work, but opened our living room to host friends and relatives who began to arrive mid- morning. Chairs and stools were placed in front of our mighty television for invited guests. Neighbors also stepped inside to stand, their kids hanging at the windows grids like monkeys. The crowd gazed in awe at the television, even when the transmission was poor and all we could see was snow.

It was Monday, July 21, 1969, and Neil Armstrong made his first step onto the surface of the moon. We were told that the entire Earth was watching the same emission. Everyone held their breath, watching these men in bulky white suits against the black sky. Now and then, the snow returned and frustrated grunts rose from the crowd. My father would rush to the TV, hit it a few times, and the images would reappear. We were part of the world-wide audience hearing "one small step for man, one giant leap for mankind." For me, world-wide meant the US and Vietnam. In my childish understanding, the Earth consisted of two nations: the United States, and its favorite buddy, Vietnam. We were the best friends, proven by the fact there were only two TV channels. Plus, at every intermission on Channel 9 the American and the South Vietnamese flags fluttered together like inseparable chums.

This was why, when the astronauts planted the American flag on the moon, I expected our flag would be planted next, but it wasn't. As the live emission ended, our flag still didn't show up. I climbed on my father's lap and asked him, "Why didn't they plant our flag next to theirs?"

My father burst out laughing, and I couldn't understand what was so funny. As he realized that I was waiting for an answer, he replied, "Our country is too poor to have a flag on the moon."

Poor? It was the first time I sought the meaning of this word. I had been born into a rich family, and didn't know that we lived in a "poor" country. Poor meant lack of money. How could we be poor when we lived in a huge house with ten servants? We had a chauffeur, a Mercedes, more than enough food and clothes, we could not be poor!

I wondered how much it would cost to have our flag planted next to the American flag on the moon. Suddenly the small basket of leftover coins beside our TV seemed to be the solution. As the neighbors started to disperse, I took the basket and asked my father if I could collect funds to have our flag on the moon too. I thought if each neighbor gave me a coin, there would be plenty to pay to plant our flag. My father puffed a laugh again, and gave me a gentle pat which meant "go away!"

I was frustrated and angry. For the first time, our flag was not shown side by side with the American flag. I experienced this as my first betrayal – in French, the word deception means disappointment, but I also felt the English sense of having been deceived.

Time went by. Betrayals between these two buddies cumulated until I had to flee Vietnam with my family in a little boat on May 1, 1975. The day before, all of Vietnam had come under communist rule. The last thing I remember seeing as we left port was a little boy with a pot of grey paint, erasing the South Vietnamese flag painted on the roof of a house. Before the fall of Saigon, all the communes still belonging to the South Vietnamese government displayed the yellow and red flag on every roof, so from the air our territory could be distinguished.

As I looked back, the image of the boy painting the roof became smaller. He was not just erasing my flag; he was wiping out who I was.

***

Years later, I told my French husband how the South Vietnam flag missing on the moon still frustrated me and he showed the Wikipedia entry related to "Apollo 11 goodwill messages":

"The Apollo 11 goodwill messages are statements from leaders of 73 countries around the world on a disc about the size of a 50-cent piece made of silicon that was left on the Moon by the Apollo 11 astronauts. [...]"

Indeed, among the goodwill messages from 73 nations, there was one from South Vietnam. The messages were photographed and reduced to 1/200 scale ultra-microfiche. Around the disc rim is the statement "From Planet Earth –July 1969."

I still hold a secret hope that my flag is portrayed on this disc on the moon, where no one will bother erasing this tiny emblem of my childhood and identity.

Thanh-Nu is a computer scientist, living in Zurich with her family. In her free time, she enjoys writing short stories and memoir.

WHAT WE YEARNED

BY

SOPHIA LI

That arid night, you staggered down the moss-cobbled street, rounding the rusted curb, arms shooting out as you stumbled into a mail post. You lay on that road, back slumped over the gutter, broken teeth gnawing on a shriveled apple core, eyes closed to the world. You spit out the black pits, and they rolled down the sidewalk cracks. I leaned against a wall, thinking about whiskey. It was a ghost town. Nothing but ruined copper and scraps of newspaper curdled on concrete. For some reason, the lights still worked. The night was brightened by lamp posts, tanning gold like a panner by the creek side, sloshing murky water with his sieve till he found that brilliant yellow gleam. Water, oh, how we yearned for it. As night grew, we walked past the broken-down brothels and the rotting mansions, towards a greyed motel. There was no clerk at the desk, so I reached into the key cabinet. I noticed something white. A dried-out bone. We didn't touch anything in our room that night. Didn't dare open any of the closets. We feared finding more skeletons.

By morning, we were parched. The sweltering heat climbed in through the chipped window-panes. I craned my neck around, looking for a sink, while you rambled on about an oasis a couple miles west of town. As the sun rose, I acquiesced to your feverish plea, men of bravery, now men of desperation. We walked out of the closed-off ruins and into the open desert. We swam in that sea of sand, searching for a single droplet in the ocean of desolateness.

I kept on seeing fish jumping from the clouds. You had vision of rolling rivers and running hills. Hours passed, and we were reduced to crawling on four limbs. You said, "We are going to die." We both laughed about that.

Alas, when night fell again, there we lied on the desert floor, broken as the day we were birthed.

Sophia Li is a writer from Houston, Texas.

THE CITY THAT FORGOT

BY

PAUL A. LYNCH

There once was a city that grew very poor. The population grew very miserable because there was not enough food, clothes, or even houses. In the same city lived an old wise man who had a dog as his best friend. The grey hairs on the old man's head showed he had surpassed many generations, and he had seen many things in his life. He had seen the good, the bad, and the indifferent. Everyone wondered why the old man and his dog were so happy each day. They wondered why he didn't have enough food, clothes, or even a big house, and yet he was so happy. So, a group of citizens who were very unhappy decided to visit the old man's little shed because they wanted to know why he wasn't unhappy or even sad, as they were. The angry citizens turned up one bright early morning, and the day was beautiful. The sky was blue, the birds gave thanks and sang, however, the people were ungrateful and unhappy.

When they got to the old man's house they saw him busy preparing a little meal of bread and cheese, and a drink of warm milk. The dog too seemed to be at rest in both mind and spirit. The angry citizens looked at each other in bewilderment because the old man and his dog were so happy. The old man saw the angry citizens about twenty - five in number, and he said to them, "Ah, good morning, friends. Isn't it a beautiful day?"

"What's so beautiful about the day, old man? We came here to ask you why you are so happy every day?" Replied the citizens.

The old man smiled. "You see, I am 130 years old. Few have lived to see my age, and generation. The baby that is just born isn't guaranteed years of life, but he or she desires it. You see, I have seen a generation that was unhappy for quite a long time, until anger consumed them and they were destroyed."

The citizens looked good at each other in amazement. The old man didn't look as though he was 130 years old. One man asked, "Old Man, why don't you look 130 years old?"

The old man looked at him. "You see, I have travelled the world on ships, and by foot, and I must say this isn't the worst of towns, neither the best of towns, however, what keeps me going is the hope I have in the world. When you plant an apple seed in the ground and water it, doesn't it grow? Did you by yourself make it grow? I look this young because I smile and hope because life will get better."

The people reflected on his words, wondered if it were true. The old man continued, "You people are unhappy, however, I remember when you were happy with the morsel of bread and cheese you had. You had 1,000 cows, but now you have only 300. Don't the cows produce milk anymore? You had good fertile land to cultivate crops, but now you're unhappy because the land has become a wasteland. Why don't we work together as before to make the land great again?"

The people listened and pondered among themselves for a short time. They remembered when they were young and happy, as the old man had said. They remembered their beloved land and the many herds of cattle. They decided they wanted the old man's help. They told the old man to help them, and he gladly accepted. Each day, the old man instructed the citizens what to do, and they obeyed. Three months passed. The citizens looked at the town and saw it was very beautiful, the wasteland was no more, the cattle increase, the apple trees had ripe fruits, no one was hungry. The old man, however, told them the town wasn't finished as yet, and they did more work. For one year they did hard work on the town, and it became as one of the most popular and beautiful cities in the world. The people were so happy that they partied every night, got drunk, and no one remembered the old man who helped them. Each day the old man looked down on the city from his little shed, and shook his head. None the less, he and his dog were very happy. The citizens of the town, however, allowed greed, gluttony, and pride to deceived them into not thanking the old man. Some time afterwards, the town became poorer than before, and everyone remembered the old man. However, when they arrived atop the mountain, they didn't see him. They looked around, but saw no one, neither the dog. They realized they were wrong in their affairs and minds. The citizens wept bitterly while the old man dwelled in a peaceful forest with his dog, where they were happy. The people learned on that day that wisdom is to be desired more than treasure.

Paul has written many short stories and full length books.

SPROUTING GLASSES:
A TRIPTYCH

BY

JOY MANNÉ

1.   Sprouting Glasses

A crescendo of twinges in the thumb of her bow arm forced Melia to interrupt her practice. Securing the Stradivarius under her chin, she examined her hand in the morning sunlight refracting through the bay window. Blue and red flashes from her thumb refracted back.

Melia gasped with delight.

"How fortunate I am to have been born left-handed," she said.

Impelled by a passion for precision inherited on the paternal side (her father was a forensic scientist), she posed her instrument on the painted Bohemian wedding chest inherited from her maternal grandmother. She tucked her long legs beneath the tapestried stool in front of her husband's *bureau de roi*, and took advantage of a pause between twinges to turn a small bronze clock to face her and place a ruler within reach and then began to write, *staccato*.

8.27.33 –protuberance from tip of thumb

8.33.12 –rosebud?

9.01.02 –pushing upwards on a stem?

As the stem rose and the bud's transparent petals folded open, Melia's fingers too began to sprout in twinges sweet as orgasm.

Grows 0.4 centimetres at each pulse; time between pulses variable

10.15.57 – bud opens into crystal bowl.

Melia shivered as she admired erect stems and voluptuous petals

164

making fractals in the sunlight. *Like a fan set with diamonds*, she thought. In her delight, she picked up her melody where she'd left off and began to hum, *contralto*.

A resonance of overtones swelled out from antique lead crystal glasses in an inlaid maple display cabinet, her maternal grandmother's wedding gift.

The glasses sprouting from her fingers ripened.
thumb: burgundy
index: white wine
middle: champagne
ring: red wine
pinky: sherry
All identical to Granny's

Still humming, she harvested each sparkling glass as it reached maturity and placed it on the overshelf of the *bureau*, rejoicing as they harmonised with overtones of their own. She would have clapped, but feared damaging the new sprouts.

It was her maternal grandmother, a gypsy, who taught her to play the melody the sprouting glasses interrupted. Several years earlier Melia had been obliged to pawn her violin to pay off her husband's student loan and then, that very week, she'd found the Strad in a holdall in the empty cloakroom of Victoria Station (Brighton Line) as if it had been left especially for her. She played her grandmother's melody before handing it in to Lost Property.

The clerk allowed her to take it home, on receipt.

"I'm a violinist too, my dear," he said. "Instruments must be played."

As she hummed and harvested, Melia recalled dancing to that tune, naked with her husband under the recent red moon, leading him in the steps her grandmother had taught her as she worshipped and wished for an easy way to redeem her instrument. The crop of crystal chalices and the Strad were the fruit of her wish. But how would she sleep?

At 17.48 she discovered that the glasses grew only in sunlight, like plants.

That night Melia wished her fingers would grow a decanter.

2. Mom

'Mom.'

'You shouldn't have married her. Didn't I tell you a thousand times you shouldn't marry her? What kind of a wife is she for a *notary*? Didn't we tell you, your father and I, you need someone respectable? Someone who can run a household, give a dinner party. A girl from a family without stories.'

'Mom.'

'What was that you told me? You came home from work yesterday and there she was, sitting in the last sunlight from the bay window where everyone could see her. Your father will be turning in his grave."

'Nobody can see, Mom. The drive is thirty metres long. The house is hidden by trees.'

'—where everyone can see, like I said. A busker! Didn't I tell you that woman had no shame?'

'She busked to pay for her violin lessons.'

'Violin lessons. Since when does the wife of a notary play the violin?'

'Mom. She was the star student."

'The wife of a notary doesn't have a profession. Your father was a notary and I didn't have a profession. I gave dinner parties. Every celebrity in town came. That famous actor – what's his name – flew in from Hollywood. Now that your father's departed, I miss the dinner parties. Who would come just to see me? What is a daughter-in-law for, if not dinner parties? And now you tell me she's growing glasses out of her fingers? Burgundy goblets, white wine glasses, champagne flutes. First she grows her own vegetables and now this."

'Mom. I had the glasses valued at Sotheby's.'

'This is all the fault of your father's great-aunt Natalya who was famous for being a virgin several times over. I knew no good would come of it when she left you that *bureau de roi* that your father expected to inherit.'

'Mom.'

'No need to lie to me, son. I'm your mother. Whatever you've done, whoever you've married, I'll always be your mother. So what did Sotheby's say?'

'Antique lead crystal. They match the set she inherited from her grandmother.'

'And that grandmother inherited from her own grandmother. I know all about her grandmother. That family has stories. I could tell you some of them.'

'She's told me the stories.'

'So what are they worth?'

'The stories? I suppose she could write them down and look for a publisher.'

'The wineglasses.'

'They are Antique Bohemian Moser gold gilt Cabochon Wine Hocks.'

'Her grandmother came from Bohemia. What did I tell you when you married her? Roots will out. She'll be able to give dinner parties.'

'Mom.'

3.   From *The London Morning Herald:*
Antique Bohemian Wine Hocks – Real or Forgery?

At eleven o'clock yesterday morning the Art and Antiques Unit of the Metropolitan Police swooped on Sotheby's, the London auctioneering house, just before the hammer fell on six crates of Antique Bohemian Moser gold gilt Cabochon Wine Hocks. Only last month, this unit, led by Detective Chief Inspector Monika E. Meurse, had uncovered a hoard of eighty-seven imitations of the paintings of Jan Zrzavý by the master forger Libor Prášil. Now, convinced she was on track to break up a glassware forgery ring, DCI Meurse alerted selected newspapers to the raid.

The detective had been contacted by the Glassware Section of the Society of Antiquarians. While it hadn't doubted the authenticity of the glass, the Society became suspicious because each set was in its original crate stamped with the seal of the castle of provenance and nestled in straw from the region. The Glassware Section suspected GM straw.

":GM straw? Phooey! Sir Stanley Brilliant of Brilliant & Blown Fine Glass," the President of the Section, said., 'The crates contained six each of red and white wine glasses, champagne flutes, sherry glasses and brandy goblets.' He drew a long breath. 'Where, I ask you. Where was the decanter?'

The owner of the glasses, Ms M, insisted she'd inherited them with the castle of provenance from her Bohemian grandmother. When the communists took over, the crates were hidden in secret caves leading off the ancient dungeons in which, by custom, enemies were tortured and then starved to death. The glasses only came to light when Ms M took possession of her inheritance and, through staff shortages, personally undertook a full inventory. She could prove they were authentic because they matched a set her grandmother gave her as a wedding present, seven years earlier.

Eventually, under sharp questioning by DCI Meurse, the young heiress confessed that the glasses grew from her fingertips in sunlight and she harvested and packed them into the ancient crates with straw that had been left to age on the stone flags in the dungeon.

DCI Meurse read aloud the report from forensics that the DNA of the glass closely resembled that of the heiress.

Ms M reached into her bag and handed DCI Meurse the notes she had made the first time the glasses sprouted. 'My father was a forensic scientist,' she sobbed: *crescendo,* on DCI Meurse's shoulder. 'I have inherited his passion for precision.'

Ms M raised her head, leaving a shiny wet patch where her nose had been, 'I wanted to buy the violin my granny gave me back from the pawn shop.'

Ms M's husband, a notary, could not personally attest to having witnessed the sprouting because he was at work during daylight when the glasses grew, and on weekends his wife covered her arms to prevent sunlight from instigating growth because the young couple were trying for a baby.

DCI Meurse asked, 'Surely as a man of the law you must have suspected something?'

Mr A replied, 'My great-aunt, who left me a *bureau de roi,* was a virgin seven times over.'

DCI Meurse was obliged to drop her inquiry. She warned Ms M, however, that the police would continue to search for the owner of the Stradivarius.

Joy Manné is group leader and a well-published and much translated author in the personal development field. She has had many Flash Fictions published on the web in Chicago Literati, Pygmy Giant, Café Aphra, Flash Fiction Online, Every Day Fiction, Flash Fiction Magazine and FlashFlood and in Lakeview International Journal of Literature, 100 Voices 2, and The Ham A. Joy has published two children's picture books, No, I Won't Go To Bed Tonight and Stinky Goldfish, and a chapter book, Don't Blame the Dog.

A LITTLE BIT OF HEAVEN

BY

MARY ROSE MCCARTHY

They say I'm special. They think I don't hear them talking but, special as I am, I'm not stupid and undertand what they're saying in whispers and codes.

"E head e no full up".

That's how they say it. One of them was in Africa for a while and claims that's how people talk there. It means there are bits missing in my head. Doesn't everyone have a bit missing from somewhere?

Funny thing is, I thought all people were special, all made by God and precious to him. As far as I understand, God lives in heaven, a place I've not yet been. It seems you can't go there until you die. When you die you're gone for ever. It means not coming back forever and always.

My parents died and went to that heaven place to be with God. When I die, I will meet them there. Without parents it falls to the others to keep an eye on me. Because I'm special, they keep two eyes on me at all times. It's very hard to be ordinary with that amount of supervision.

I went to a special school and now have a special job. You see how that special word is always cropping up? Yet you walk along the street and every second woman has a buggy and is talking nonsense to the mini person in the buggy. More often than not, most of the nonsense has the word special in it.

My mother was a saint. That's what they say. I have no opinion, as I don't really remember her. Also, I don't know any saints personally so I can't make a comparison.

169

Her being a saint has something to do with me and how different I am. According to things overheard 'no one, but no one knows what that poor woman had to endure. A difficult pregnancy, an awful long labour, only to have it result in poor simple Jimmy.'

I am poor simple Jimmy. When they don't know I'm there, they drop all the politically correct stuff and refer to me as poor and simple.

"Would you look at him, poor fellow. He knows no different."

"At least he's happy."

"Sure why wouldn't he be? He knows no better."

These are snippets of things people say. All telling me I know nothing but at least I'm happy.

My job is caring for the garden centre. I think heaven must be like a garden centre. All those trees, beautiful garden ornaments, seeds, small plants, flowers and a coffee shop. The birds love it there, always singing and flying about the place. I love it there too, but can't sing. The smell of the earth delights me, even in the cold wet of winter. The thoughts of tiny little white shoots like the threads that unravel from my jumper, working away down in the deep, dank, darkness fascinates me. A tiny little mound of earth erupts just as the first sign of green appears above the soil, the first shoot of a new plant. Such joy and excitement.

"Jimmy, please stop talking about your plants and the smell of the earth. Who cares? There are more important things to worry about like getting the wash on, dinner on the table and paying the bills at the end of the month. Not that a thought for that ever crosses your mind." My sister is obviously not in a good mood.

"Ah leave him alone. He doesn't have a mind for anything to cross, and no amount of yelling at him will change that." The other sister always has to chime in.

Those are the conversations when I'm foolish enough to stop in the kitchen on my way in from the garden centre. Usually I go straight to my room and play my karaoke machine until called for dinner. But there are days when the excitement of the miracle of nature causes me to stop and share my story with my sisters. It's an ordinary kind of thing, to talk about your day.

Ordinary is denied me. Going to nightclubs to meet girls is out of the question. As is having a drink. There is no such thing allowed. Ever. Not with the medication I take. The two would not go well together.

"What's it you want? To be writhing all over the place in a paroxysm of seizures? Calling even more attention to yourself and to this family. Is that it? That what you want?"

Well, how can I argue with that? Especially when I've no clue what paroxysm means. Being special means so many things, all supposed to be positive. It's just another way of restraining me, keeping me from the life I want to lead. That's why I've asked to move to sheltered accommodation. It will give me freedom, giving them peace from worrying over me. Then I can be with Mandy.

Mandy and I would like to have children of our own someday. Of course, they would be special, they would be ours, but we will never ever tell them that. Instead, we will treat them as ordinary people, living ordinary lives.

I'll not tell the sisters that Mandy's in the group home I want to move to. Mandy and I are friends. Special friends. The whole reason for moving there is to gain independence and privacy. Perhaps Mandy and I can have our own little bit of heaven. But there is no need to tell my sisters any of that.

Having gone round in circles, living in London, Sierra Leone and Dublin, Mary Rose McCarthy is now back where she stared in West Cork Ireland. She writes to make sense of the world.

A DANDELION IN A SEA OF BUBBLES

BY
ELLEN MERRITT

I was updating the website and saw an adorable picture of a little girl blowing bubbles. Somehow, a dandelion got in the sea of bubbles and it started me thinking about things. You know, pictures can say a great deal about life. There are different characteristics of plants, different characteristics of bubbles and different characteristics of people. However, we are not so very different from each other.

Dandelions have gotten a bad rap over the years for being little weeds which creep into nice, green, expensively maintained lawns and announce Spring with joyous yellow dots of color. Many people just sigh and head for the weed killer. I protest. Dandelions provide many benefits. Their pollen nourishes bees, who pollinate flowers, and it helps to produce honey. Its greens make nourishing vegetables, and the plant parts produce many health benefits.

During medieval times, it was common to use dandelion plants in broths, medicines, wines and garnishes. The plant itself gives us lessons in the values of tenacity, perseverance, adaptation and passing values on to the next generation. For generations, kids like me were taught that by blowing dandelion seeds and making a wish, the wish would come true.

Many young people today have lost their hopes, dreams and aspirations. They have been convinced that nothing they can do is going to change anything. Thankfully, many others in the same generation do hold fast to their dreams and are working toward achieving these goals.

These young adults have learned the lessons of the dandelion.

In the movie *The Neverending Story*, the evil Gmork observes, "People without dreams are easy to control." I know I have quoted this before. I intend to keep on quoting it until the message sinks in. There have always been those who seek power through control. They have discovered the most effective means of control is through fear. Dreams, goals, passions and progress itself cannot even live under control, much less thrive.

Bubbles are shiny, magical and numerous when they are first created. They almost create themselves and drift tantalizingly across the breeze. Dandelion seeds are plain and require a good, hard puff of air to send them scattering. It's easy to chase after bubbles. But they cannot last very long before bursting. Dandelions, by contrast, endure the gusts and ride the winds. Once they find ground, they are quick to put down roots and establish a home. They announce the seasons, progress through their life cycle and at the proper time, allow their seeds to scatter far and find new ground in their turn.

Each of us holding dreams has been, in our own way, called a weed; less than worthy, dismissed, rejected. We have a choice. We can choose the way of the bubble: a moment of flimsy, shiny glory before we pop in the wind; or the way of the dandelion: understated, deep-rooted, tough, a survivor. We may perish, but we have a chance to see our dreams live on and take root in the seeds we release.

I am proud to be a dandelion.

Ellen Merritt has been a leading light in the world of spirituality for over two decades. Her piece, "A Dandelion in a Sea of Bubbles", addresses the importance of self acceptance.

THE NEXT BOAT OUT

BY

BILL MICHELMORE

The young poet had changed his name to Stephen Sutcliffe. He took the Stephen from James Joyce's novel, Stephen Dedalus (Portrait of the Artist as a Young Man) and Sutcliffe from Stuart Sutcliffe, the Beatles' original bassist who died of a brain hemorrhage in 1962 at the age of twenty-one.

"It seems weird calling you Stephen," I said as we drove down Highway 101 through Big Sur in a black-over-yellow Cadillac. When he didn't say anything I added, "When you were born I wanted to call you Ringo, but your mother wouldn't have it."

"You should have anyway," he said. He stared out the passenger window as the California coast rushed by. And then he noted, "The Beatles were great, by the way."

"So I heard."

"John Lennon," he said.

"Yeah," I said.

"That fucking madman."

"Chapman?"

He turned toward me. "Don't even say the name. The name we must never mention, as Paul McCartney said."

174

"I understand."

He turned back to the road that lay ahead. After a while he said, "He should have killed himself instead."

The young man now known as Stephen Sutcliffe who was heading down the California coast would have other names, like the Mad Prophet of Ward 3C and Horatio Windsock.

As the latter he planned to start his own nation with the wild horses on Sable Island, an uninhabited slip of sand dunes off the coast of Nova Scotia. He would be the poet laureate. He said he'd appoint me Minister of External Affairs, just in case we had to conduct negotiations with the Canary Islands.

He wrote to me about his plans. I was in L.A. researching a magazine story and he was in Toronto planning to hitch a ride on a Nova Scotia government boat that made the fourteen-hour trip to Sable Island only four times a year to service the two lighthouses on the island, the West Light Main Station and the East Light.

"Where will you live?" I wrote back. He didn't have a phone. He wrote in his next letter that he would doss on one of the bunks in the main lighthouse until he built his own shack out of driftwood. The island is known for its shipwrecks.

And in his letter he added, "I'm taking the next boat. I know you're busy out there right now, so I thought you could come on the boat after that. I'll be settled in by then. I'll send you a timetable."

I was writing a letter in reply when my ex-wife phoned from Toronto and said, "Brace yourself for a shock."

Our son had taken enough barbiturates to kill himself three times over. He wanted to make sure this time. His previous attempt had failed and he had woken up in Intensive Care. From IC he went to Ward 3C and from the psycho ward to a halfway house, halfway between madness and death.

The doctors had their own name for his condition, but he called it a babbling hell of confusing signals from space. They put him on chlorpromazine and a few other mind buckers, but he was determined to have the final say.

At one o'clock in the afternoon, in his room on the second floor of the halfway house in Toronto he lay down on the bed and let the barbiturates do their stuff. He was twenty-three years old.

Spinning toward oblivion he may have thought about the wild horses on Sable Island, ponies really, running free on what is little more than a windswept sandbank, twenty-three miles long and barely a mile wide, with a powerful surf and seals and seabirds; no trees but lush grass and wildflowers in the gullies and wild strawberries.

Bill Michelmore's fiction has been published in the Santa Fe Literary Review; Marco Polo Arts Magazine and the Miami Herald's Tropic Magazine. He lives on the outskirts of New York.

WHEN SHIT GETS TOO REAL

BY

BENNETT MOHLER

Freddie Tempest had a hard voice and soft eyes. His friends adored him for the hot mess he was and could always expect a train-wreck of a good time in his company. Common activities with Freddie included excessive drinking and wrestling. Things often got broken, but Freddie's friends' love for him did not diminish on even the worst of these nights where, as Freddie put it – "Shit just got real."

Women were very attracted to Freddie perhaps because they perceived him as mysterious, a puzzle to be solved. All of Freddie's friends were well aware of all his sexual encounters, from either hearing about them or Freddie speaking of them. Everyone was quite relieved when he decided to get a vasectomy.

The first big step in Freddie's downward spiral was when he got 86ed from Fat Jack's, his and everyone else's favorite bar. Freddie and a few of his very close friends believe he was set up to be 86ed and it is true that the bartender was serving him Long Island Iced Teas, two at a time, which Freddie consumed vigorously as soon as they were handed to him.

He had broken a very expensive light fixture, which seemed like a crime undeserving of such punishment. Other patrons had done much worse and were welcomed back the very next night without even one mention of the transgression.

The staff of Fat Jacks harbored no ill will towards Freddie and remained cordial towards him afterwards. They just didn't want him in the bar anymore lest he do even more damage.

Freddie finally landed a job as a bartender at one of the other favorite local bars, Lunar Lounge. He had no experience, but was such a downtown fixture that Lunar Lounge's owner decided to give him a chance. He and most others believed Freddie had a good heart.

Drunken phone calls and tearful confessions created rumors that spread quickly around town about Freddie's deteriorating mental state. Whether or not these accusations were true, Freddie's family found out and informed the police, who did a wellness check on him at work. This only worsened Freddie's mental state, as he now felt the shame of knowing that his family thought he would commit suicide. None of his family reached out to Freddie directly.

Freddie got fired from Lunar Lounge after not showing up for a shift. When his roommates discovered this, they gave him till the end of the month to move out.

Freddie finally reached out to his family and they invited him to come back to the farm where he grew up. He would work on the farm until he got back on his feet. He quit drinking. After moving back in with this family, his circle of friends in the city lost contact with him and moved on with their lives. Still they remembered him fondly and jovially recited his catch phrase whenever shit indeed got real.

I saw him once in the city, clean-shave, wearing nice clothes. He looked sober and serious, walking somewhere with intent. I tried to make eye contact with him, and for a second it seemed like he returned it, but then he quickly looked away and went about his serious business.

Whenever Freddie comes up in conversation with my friends and we wonder what happened to him, we laugh and say that "shit just got too real."

I haven't spoken to Freddie in years. I learned shortly after seeing him that time that he now works for the church and goes door to door selling bibles. He doesn't stay in contact with any of his old friends, but then again, we didn't stay in contact with him. I often wish to reach out to him, to see if his religious turn was legitimate, since it did not seem like the kind of life decision he would make. Not while we all knew him.

Before I ever got the chance to reconnect with Freddie, I received the news from a mutual friend that Freddie had shot himself. When I asked the mutual friend what had happened, he said that "shit had gotten too real" and we both laughed.

Bennett Mohler was born and raised in San Jose, CA before moving to Portland, OR to pursue a career in the arts. Along with being an avid reader and writer, Bennett enjoys hiking, playing music and drinking scotch.

FABLED CURSES

BY

EDDIE D. MOORE

Dermock rested a hand on his sword hilt and rubbed the stubble on his chin with the other while he studied the vine-covered ruins ahead. The river beside him vanished under a canopy of large trees where the ancient city once stood. He saw a flock of birds take flight from a tall tree inside the ruins as he heard his client stop behind him.

"So, these are the cursed ruins of Kalidan." Milan sighed. "That barkeep was right; I couldn't have hired a better guide."

Dermock barked a short laugh. "It's not hard to follow the river. He meant I was the only guide you could've hired. There is a reason the ruins are called cursed, and don't say I didn't warn you when we get there."

Malin tugged the packhorse forward and took the lead. As they walked, he said with an exasperated tone, "I could never in good conscience deny that I've been warned. Every guide I approached told me a horror story, and you've been a constant source of *encouragement* with your stories of blind treasure hunters and murderously insane adventurers."

"I got those *stories* from a reputable source, and we'd do well to take the curse seriously."

Malin laughed. "That is if you consider the ramblings of patients in an insane asylum reputable source. I'm an archeologist; I don't believe in curses. I do, however, believe that crazy people tell crazy stories. There's nothing to fear here; you'll see."

Malin knelt and inspected a few stones that at one time were part of the city walls. He muttered to himself excitedly when he found markings on them. Dermock followed him closely and watched for any sign of danger as they traveled further into the ruins. The trees became more twisted the deeper they went, and the empty windows on the crumbling buildings left Dermock with an itch between his shoulders.

Dermock squeezed his sword's hilt. "It's getting dark fast under these trees. We should go back to where we came in and make camp for the night."

Malin stopped writing in his notebook and looked around with a confused expression. "I didn't even notice that we were losing the light until you pointed it out." He shrugged and motioned around them. "This looks like as good a place as any to me."

"You want to camp here?"

Malin smiled. "We've already spent the afternoon here. Don't tell me you're still concerned about the legendary curse?"

Dermock's back stiffened, and his eyes narrowed. "Of course not. I'll just unpack our stuff and tie up the horse."

"Good. I'll gather some wood and build a fire."

Dermock pitched the tents and watched Malin stoke the campfire from the corner of his eye. With one smooth motion he pulled out his sword and turned to face a dark patch of trees. "Who's there?" After a few silent moments, he glanced at Malin. "Did you hear that?"

"I didn't hear anything. It was probably just a bird or small animal."

After sheathing his sword, Dermock released a long breath. He sat by the fire. They roasted a few pieces of jerky over the fire and washed it down with a weak tea that Malin favored. Dermock stood when he noticed a thick fog rolling across the ground.

Malin ran his fingers through the fog as it washed over them. "Have you ever..." He fell silent when Dermock held up a forestalling hand. A moment later, the both heard the whispers. Lights moved in the distance, and the whispers grew louder all around them.

Dermock held his sword ready and stood closer to Malin. "Can you tell what they are saying?"

The voices synchronized into a chant, and Malin listened close a moment before he answered. "It's Nayon; it's been a dead language for hundreds of years." The chanting grew louder and picked up speed as a distant drumbeat joined the rhythm. A worried expression crept over Malin's face, and his voice shook. "They're singing a song of death."

The chanting abruptly stopped, and the dark shape of a man

formed in the mist. Dermock dived and pulled Malin to the ground as a small dart thumped into a nearby tree. The packhorse screamed as darts struck his side, instantly falling to the ground in spasms. The chanting resumed as Dermock and Malin scrambled up, running into the woods.

As they ran, they heard the now familiar thump of darts striking the underbrush and ground around them. Silhouetted by an eerie source-less light, the dark form began to take shape again, and Dermock tugged on Malin's arm to run the other direction. Malin held his ground and shook his head. "He's blocking our path out; we must run toward him!"

Dermock opened his mouth to protest, but Malin pulled his arm loose and charged toward the now fully formed man. Hoping to lend his weight to Malin's, he braced his shoulder and ran toward whatever was blocking their path. He stumbled as a chill washed over him, and he passed through the apparition. When he glanced back, there was no sign of their attacker, and the distant lights winked out.

As they passed the crumbled city walls, clear air, twinkling stars and a bright full moon greeted them. They collapsed to the ground a safe distance from the cursed city, and as Dermock caught his breath, he noticed that Malin was holding one of the darts.

Malin studied the dart a moment and then nodded. "Poisoned darts. That explains some of it."

"How's that?"

"Do you hear the tree frogs?"

"Yes."

"They're poisonous. The Kalidan warriors used poison from the frogs to incapacitate and kill their enemies. It can cause muscle spasms, blindness, brain damage or madness, and death."

"What about the lights, voices, and the apparition we ran through?"

Malin swallowed hard and met Dermock's eyes. "What? You don't believe in curses?"

Eddie D. Moore's stories have been published by Jouth Webzine, The Flash Fiction Press, Every Day Fiction, Theme of Absence, Flash Fiction Magazine, Fantasia Divinity Magazine, and others. Find more on his blog: https://eddiedmoore.wordpress.com/.

HOUSE SHOW IN BADGER COUNTY HIGH SCHOOL GYM

BY
SIMON NAGEL

Blood geysered out of Maisy's face and onto her mask. She missed her next spot and flopped onto the canvas, the house lights so bleary that her hand groped she had to grope with her hands out to find the bottom rope. Her outstretched fingers plucked at them several a couple times before catching she got a good hold to pull herself back up, the entire time feeling like she had botched the timing and she'd get knocked on her payout. Her boots scuffed up skid marks from the puddle gathering that had gathered beneath her as she reached her mark. The front few rows had come to life by then, the loss of Maisy's bodily fluids giving them something to believe in. She peeled her mask away from her face to drain it out and keep the blood from pushing up to her eyes. Blood in the eyes was the danger of masks, but to Maisy anonymity beat out a couple blind spots. Rhoda had also slipped in her puddle, but without so much as a nod she was already up and back on Maisy. Rhoda stomped like bush league, but maybe Maisy had it coming. It was her blood after all.

#

It would be a delicate balance removing the mask. If the blood had dried already, that meant the mask would be stuck to her skin. If her nose was broken, ripping the mask off would unsettle it, right after she had crooked it back and she'd be bleeding all over again. What had Maisy worried most about was her eyebrows being ripped . She didn't want to rip them off if the blood had glued them to her mask. She could take the sting. She didn't know how she'd pencil in fake ones.

Someone had sent a doctor into the locker room to tend to her nose. He waited in the hall with a box of jawbreakers while Maisy shimmied the mask off her face. After he had crunched through his second candy he stepped inside before she had finished.

"Buenas noches," he said. "They told me to come in here and take care of Cuerva." Maisy grunted and ripped off the mask, pulling out a stringy patch of blond hair.

"I'm Cuerva. It's a work." The doctor looked at her and leaned over, not wanting to get any closer.

"Your nose is broke."

"Thanks."

The doctor muttered about not being paid enough to stay at the school this late and walked out. Maisy wondered if he was one of the types who that never left high school, if maybe she looked around the gym she'd find some picture of him somewhere. The jock that became school nurse and insisted on being called "Doctor." It made the thought of her approaching ten yearten-year reunion creep back into her head and she decided that now wasn't the best time to worry about such things.

Maisy reached into her bag after she had wiped herself off and pulled out the spray can. The one advantage to doing gym shows was no one cared if she sprayed there. Maybe they did, but no one mentioned it. had said anything yet. She let the spray fly, her skin taking on the initial orange hue that she'd have to even out. It was always good to get out ahead of it before it began to fade. She looked took a look in the gym mirror, where SARAH SUCKS BIG DICK was lovingly etched at the bottom. Her nose would be okay. The spray tan pocked through her T-shirt. It was still wet, but it was warm outside and it felt good.

#

The pay was shit. Shows in gyms always paid shit. Maisy was smart enough to never complain. Bitching never got anyone booked. She asked her booker if she got paid less for bleeding. He said no. Mid cards just go that way. He stopped, wanting to ask her something, but thinking better of it. She made it easy on him and asked for if she could have a flier from the night, just as a keepsake. He planted it in her hand, saying and told her he'd let her know if they'd have anything for her in a few weeks.

Her shirt was stuck to her body by the time she reached her car. She overheard Rhoda talking to a few fans who that stayed behind to get an autograph. They were mostly men who believed that thought if they could convince Rhoda that they were somehow different, gain from the other fans, then they would be accepted into her good graces, and she would let them go home with her.

"You really beat the hell out of that Mexican."

"Thanks. You all drive safe now."

Maisy looked at herself in the car window. The spray had dried already, and she was right. She'd have to even it out. She needed would have to find a way to make her face match her body. a little more. Maybe that was something she could call Mom about that without leading into a wouldn't lead to any kind of dust up. The worst were the big gaps in conversation where Maisy heard everythong could hear all of the things her mother was prohibiting herself from saying, offering and would instead give her some pleasantry about how she's making the yard really come together back home. A closed fist or a missed spot never hurt like whatever Maisy thought her mother really wanted to say. It was always lurking there.

"They all got masks, too," she thought. She glanced at her nose without much thought and looked down at her stomach. It was getting soft. She had been working her arms and chest too much lately.

#

It was a few minutes to one before Maisy's food came out. Some of the veggies had been fried along with her steak, which made her think of her stomach again. Muffin tops don't do shit against boots, Rhoda had made sure of that. She'd do sit-ups before heading out to St. Paul in the morning

Simon Nagel is an award-winning screenwriter and author. He lives in Ventura, California.

BOOK OF THE BLACK MOON

BY
C.H. NEWELL

The book is swathed in purple leather, bound by aged and weary Coptic stitching. At the middle sits a fat black orb with one single star below, a perfect crescent moon enclosing both images. He found it in a section of the library dedicated to the island's history. Completing a doctoral thesis on the folklore of Newfoundland's rural communities, Jacob spent plenty of time seeking out old manuscripts.

Loosely translated from its original French, the title is known as *Book of the Black Moon*. Deeply connected with a little known town named Red Crescent and one of its founders, Abel Blackwood, the book is now written in everything from Latin to English, even dead languages.

Just the title sent cool liquid terror oozing beneath Jacob's skin.

Things written in the book, what he could translate, made his mind wander toward awful places. His thoughts walked headlong into the darkness. Travelling the bleak landscape of its pages he fell under endless despair, as if the bottom of humanity disappeared suddenly, his body cast down into nothingness. In the fog of dreams Jacob even envisioned himself doing unspeakable horror to those he loved.

In the face of this perpetual night he wanted the book gone.

On the Metrobus he felt an omnipresent eye scouring him, dying to find the book. He felt many eyes. They wandered over him the way fingers do on skin, touching lightly but always moving.

When Jacob looked up no one was watching.

At the library no comfort came. Not another soul stirred except for the thin, rake-like man attending the counter, a walking skeleton in a cardigan and black slacks.

"Apologies, sir," said the librarian, "but this does not belong here."

"Nonsense. I checked it out here – I found the damn book *here*!"

The librarian smiled giving Jacob back his card. He folded two gaunt hands in front of him, sinister little curls at the corners of his mouth. "I cannot take this book, Mr. Camden."

Jacob felt the book's black words seep into his skin the longer it remained nearby. "Well I can't keep it."

"Of course you can," replied the librarian in grim exultation. "After all – it *is* yours."

His tone, those stagnant yellow eyes and decaying smile, hypnotized Jacob. The man's face looked ancient and the skin hung heavy like a Dali painting. He wanted to leave the book, to never see it again. Leaving it on the counter he turned to walk away. Only a few feet and the deafening sounds of the book's screams stopped Jacob in his tracks.

Somehow he felt the librarian was right; perhaps it *was* his book. Jacob rushed back, the librarian leering with that wretched smile, tucked the rotten thing in his jacket and left.

Outside the evening air sweltered like the universe boiled, the Earth just a hot blue marble. Yet Jacob felt cold, alone, lost in the urban jungle of St. John's with its ancient structures looming tall, history dripping from cracked and jagged pores in the streets. Looking back the library seemed more a mausoleum than house of books. Jacob walked further into fading evening light until he noticed a tall man amongst the shadows of a nearby street.

"Verus in altari cruor," spoke the man from out of the black.

The words rattled Jacob's skull until they pulsed in rhythm. He recognized them as Latin. Their sound made him shiver like a boy, once again forced to hear dusty Catholic priests delivering their archaic Sunday masses. These words came draped in tenebrous robes.

On the lips of the shadowy tall man they sounded of death.

Jacob's feet began running without any intervention from his brain, the fear immediate. He made off into the coming night, knowing the book must be destroyed, those eerily venerable words nipping at his heels: *verus in altari cruor.*

Having barely slept, just before dawn Jacob made his way to a clearing in the woods near Cape Spear. As a teen, he and his friends dropped acid there, down near the water. They named it Moose Jaw on account of their first visit: one boy found a rotting moose head baked in the sun, flies lining its sockets like eyelashes. He knew this place was best for destroying the book – out of sight, undisturbed by ghouls in the night.

Once a fire was roaring Jacob tried tearing the book into pieces. The hardcover barely bent under Jacob's straining hands, not even a ruffle in the pages. He groaned, hauling fiercely at each side of the hellish book until every finger went numb.

Jacob could've swore he heard the book laugh at him.

In the surrounding deep forest, gathered the tall man and others like him. The flowing cloak of darkness swallowed them all up, yet they looked on in silence.

Jacob raged and tossed the book. It landed amongst flames with a dusty thud sending out a sparky shower. The book sat there in the fire; at rest, peaceful. Not a single page so much as curled. The hardcover glowed, its colour brightened and the words across it beamed onto the night as if replacing the sky itself.

Jacob's anger swelled with no idea what to do next.

From a small cleft of trees came the tall man and his followers. A coiling line of people slithered from the forest's opening towards Jacob. Surrounded on one side by fire and a gushing river, the other a dark, throbbing congregation, he stood frozen.

A low murmur crept from their masses. Voices melted together in dreadful unison: "Verus in altari cruor." They descended upon him.

Screams muffled in Jacob's throat. The tall man's followers all snared a limb, a bit of skin, a finger, a molar; anything to which they might grab hold. Each of them extracted little drops, streams even, of thick, warm blood from cuts they made. The tall man himself collected what he could in a goblet underneath, while the followers lifted Jacob above their heads, faces slick in crimson paint.

Their Latin chant echoed on in the darkness.

The tall man took the book from its fiery seat of ashes, opening it on the ground. He poured the goblet's contents into its pages. Steaming, full of blood, the book sighed in a mix of beautiful agony and pleasure.

Back at the library sat the book with its newly moistened pages, forgotten once again on a dusty shelf. The purple cover more vibrant now than ever, next to musty historical records long filed into obscurity.

And soon some poor soul will hear faint whispers, all but forgotten words in Latin, drifting from within the book's pages. The words beckoning towards an unknown and desperate place. It will ring in their ears like a dark symphony, a rhythm of blood and bones and screams.

C.H. Newell is a BAH graduate of Memorial University of Newfoundland, whose thesis explored the communal aspects of Paradise Lost and its affects on authorship. His first short screenplay – a period piece set in 1888 titled New Woman – is being produced in the spring of 2017.

13-23-13

BY

SUSAN OKE

You can lose yourself there in the grey, in the humming distance. Patterns shift, merge into blocks, lines and lines of blocks. The sun tracks your progress, its bright eye glaring from your wing-mirror, pushing from behind. Gantry after gantry pass overhead—silent gateways, flashing coded cautions. You're moving, making progress, you're sure of that.

Distance is a subjective thing, chomped up by rotation; did you really pass through all of its permutations? Tyres thrum. The vibration is familiar: feet, hands and body in resonance. Tongue and taste: dry, steady, gritty. The ping of a stone against bodywork. The crack of a stone against windscreen. You flinch. Dragged back to the present, to the blur of movement. Lorries lumber behind, grumble past. Headlights flash. What do you think you're doing? Automatic reflexes; autonomic responses.

Still alive. Tick the box.

Habit keeps you on track. There's a rhythm, an exact route. Not just a direction, but visual triggers flagged in memory: the hieroglyphs of gantries and hoardings, the humped leftovers of construction greenery. Repetition hardwires response: Change Lane. So you do. In the same one-hundred-yard stretch, like the changeover in a relay race, handing the baton over to yourself.

Three lanes morph into six and the dance begins. Size and speed set the tempo; watch and wait; signal your intention, time to change partners. Tyres trip over old wounds, gouged and tarmacked, the scars of missed chances. How many times have your wheels thumped over that exact spot? You half expect it, but are still surprised. Every day you wonder what draws you there—a magnet for the miss-timed, for broken connections, the collision of intentions. A portal to another place. And every day you ask yourself: how many died here?

Vehicles transgress, over and over, second by second, building up momentum. It's a numbers game. The matrix of probability tightens with time. Will it be today?

You play the game, but you don't know all the rules. Distance and time make cozy bedfellows, whispering secrets into each other's ears. Heart beat counts out time, splices, delineates, but what if you stop listening? Parse your attention: construct your reality; construct your journey. Go on, look into the shadows—you might be surprised.

Thinking, that's the trick, that's the way through it. Not a road, but a tunnel into the imagination. Unlocking doors—what treasure lies there, waiting to be picked over? Raise a piece into the light, watch it sparkle, watch it take on a life of its own. Reasons unfold; rules apply themselves. The world takes shape. Looking, lurking, lying in wait: snatches of dialogue, of emotions pent and waiting for release. A slice of your attention is all that is required. The flashlight of perception—focus there! Dispel the shadows and reveal a truth. A road trip of revelation. Now all you have to do is remember.

Sentences, you hear them, see them, feel their perfection. Notebook and pen are in your bag at your feet. Temptation. You've done it before, the ten-mile-an-hour scrawl; a couple of words at a time while you try not to collide with the car in front. You grip the steering wheel with both hands and repeat the rule out loud: only if the car comes to a complete stop. Not unusual on the M25. But it never happens when you want it to.

So you fall back on repetition. Scour grooves in your memory to match those of the road. Bullet point: one, two, three. You're trapped in a cycle of knowing and can't move on. Who is the king of the castle? Ideas battle it out, fall silent, rolling, wrapped in sand, lost in the dunes of 'what if'. Vistas open, new layers of complexity present themselves. There's a logic to it all, a stitching together of action and reaction. You revel in the warm glow of being right: you've always known he would do that, and now you know why. It all makes perfect sense.

The gentle harmonic of rubber on concrete weaves and lulls. You feel the harmony through your fingertips. It travels through wrists and elbows; a symphony of micro-damage. Unaware and uncaring, you're lost in the dream of the road. You have to fight to keep your eyes open. It's one temptation that's called too often. You recognise its taste, that signature drawl through your body. Don't go there. Fight the tide. Not long now.

You're treading water, drowning without noticing that you've stopped breathing. A voice screams in the back of your mind and you open your mouth.

A slipstream of time and the sun burns through the windscreen. You felt no discernible shift in direction, you just kept moving, no idea when onwards became backwards. Your journey is an act of faith: in the sun, in its mad trajectory. Start and finish points merge, change places, reflective synchronicity. The only thing you're spending is time.

Susan is primarily a SFF novelist and short story writer, who occasionally dabbles in literary fiction. You can read examples of her work on her website: susanmayoke.com

LAST CHANCE

BY

SUSAN O'REILLY

This retirement lark is killing me. Boredom has settled in big time. Looking up at the sunny blue sky I decide it's a day for a picnic basket for one and a good book. This would have been a big thrill back in the day; just to have the time for it would have been wonderful. Now it is a common occurrence, weather permitting.

Going to the fridge, I cannot wait to see what delights are waiting, I jest. The usual array of cheese and beetroot are hidden in the back, a slice of turkey; a veritable feast. I have asked her, I don't know how many times, to buy things for such occasions. She says she has, but I ate them before they had a chance to be escorted outside by me. Cheeky bitch, I tell her that I have not eaten them all and ask where could they have gone? She claims I have and I'll find them if I go over to the full-length mirror and stand sideways. This turned into one of our all too frequent arguments these days. Ending with her telling me to cop onto myself and that since I'm the one who wants the stuff and she's the one who has to work all day, so go get it my bleeding self. I can still hear the slam of the door, but the realization that she is right hits me harder. I was brought up that women do the shopping and cooking; it is up to the man to provide the money for such things. With a heavy heart, I realise those times and people have changed. I'm going to lose her if I don't buck up my ideas. The money I have certainly provided for us and I have a good, solid pension from time served in the army band, and then

I have retirement income from teaching, before I finally retired for good. Since then, I have wallowed in doing nothing.

I took a test and got a taxi licence, which was all right for a while, but all those years in an enclosed space with trombones and trumpets blasting my eardrums have left me totally deaf in one ear. I had to give up driving as customers and I were getting more annoyed with my predicament with each passing day. I have a case pending under Health & Safety laws, as the right equipment to avoid a long term injury was not provided to us. I heard an old army mate received a tidy little sum, and I expect something on the same line.

I'm not sure when the ennui and despair started to hit, but now this boring nothingness is set on walloping me every day, repeatedly. Today I'm going to wallop right back. I'll have my picnic and read, but be back home in plenty of time to get the bus and go shop for the ingredients for an extra special meal. Roast potatoes, chops and onions. She never was high maintenance, monetary wise, but I believe emotionally lately, I've let her down.

Food prepared and packed, I take my walk to the local park. I am a regular visitor there, so the park warden greets me with a cheery wave. I nod in reply. Settling down under my favourite tree, food laid out, wouldn't you know my luck; a huge rain cloud appears menacingly in the sky. I forgot about our gorgeous Irish weather, three seasons in one day. Sighing, I get ready to pack everything away when a dog bounds over, seeing my picnic treats. He looks like his tail is ready to fall off, he's so excited at his find. Usually I would have shooed him away, but today I decide to let him have it all. He gulps it all in about five minutes flat, barks a "thanks" and is gone. I realize he has shown more gratitude to me than I've shown Siobhán lately and he gave me a better welcome.

Walking briskly home with a new spring in my step I am going to nip all this despondency in the bud. I'm lucky to still have a life to be bored with. My mum, bless her, if she were still here, would have given me a well-deserved kick up the arse a long time ago.

Siobhán's car is in the driveway, unusual. She must have taken some time off work. I start walking faster, a big smile on my face, which is wiped clean the instant I open the door and notice her suitcase in the hall.

"Siobhán, everything okay?" I call out.

I already know it's not, but try to buy myself some time.

"Hi, Tony, no everything is not okay. I'm leaving you. I can't take things as they are any more. You're constantly in a depressive state and dragging me down with you. I'm sorry I'll be back for the rest of my things at some stage during the week."

"Can't we ta …?"

"The time for talking has been and gone. I don't want to hate you Tony."

She walks past me and doesn't turn or hesitate, picks up the suitcase, and is gone.

Devastated, I slide down the wall to sit on the floor and sob like a baby. I have left changing until too late. I realize I've wasted so many months feeling sorry for myself and now I've lost the most important person in the world to me.

For three days I wallow in self-pity, until I even piss myself off. Time to take action. I'm going to get back a life I can enjoy. Then I'm going to get the love of my life back.

First things first, I make an appointment with the local Barnado's to volunteer in the shop for a couple of hours a week. They seem delighted with my interest. I am scheduled to return next week to observe to see if I think I'm suited. Next, I look up the youth band that our son used to play in and that I taught occasionally, when the army and time allowed. I offer them my services. I have a ton of music sheets upstairs boxed. I could never bring myself to get rid of. They will be getting an airing.

It feels good to finally be taken positive steps. Siobhán did the right thing. We both needed a break from each other and our stagnant life. I know in time we will be back together, snuggling and making plans. She loves me, I know it, and she just wanted me back.

Susan O'Reilly from Dublin, Ireland. Writing is a new and much loved hobby. A late bloomer as only started writing at 44 and is now 48.

LEN AND SMITHY

BY

CARL "PAPA" PALMER

Leonard Miller is homebound in the home of Roy Schmidt. Len, as Leonard likes to be called, is seventy-one, dying from leukemia, and in the last two months, drifting deeper daily into dementia.

Len has family in the city, a daughter and son, both married with grown children of their own. They enter his conversations often, but they never visit or even telephone Len at Roy's home.

Mildred, Len's wife known as Millie, passed away six years earlier in her sleep and is still very much alive somewhere at the edge of Len's focus.

Smithy, as Len calls Roy, his lifelong friend, is likewise in his early seventies, a widower with two grown children in town, who also never call or visit. Smithy shows signs of forgetfulness, too, but confides they're his senior memory moments, well earned, and sometimes best forgotten.

"Len won a football scholarship out of high school. He was our quarterback and I was his center. Instead of taking the full ride, he enlisted in the Army," Smithy mused as we three sat eating cereal, back when Len was able to feed himself. "After serving his time in Germany during WWII, he came home to marry Millie, the head cheerleader and his high school honey, before starting back to work beside me in our Dads' boat shop."

"I didn't need college to do what I'd always loved to do as a kid, more of a hobby than a job," Len points out. "My son wanted to do the same when he finished high school, but Millie and I insisted he get a college diploma. His education is in design and Smithy's son got his degree in business. After graduation our boys began to build the original small boat shop into what our company is today, *Schmidt Miller Watercraft*. It's named as one of the best 500 small businesses on the west coast," Len boasts, then chuckles, "Of course, Smithy and I are retired figureheads now, with our pictures on the showroom wall."

"Our families were always close, did most everything together," Smithy maintains. "We have so much in common, Len and me. We even buried our wives the same year."

"That's also when everything changed," Len adds and looks at Smithy who nods for him to continue. "After the wives were gone we spent more and more time together, sometimes not even bothering to go home to an empty house. I'd crash in Smithy's guest room or he'd sleep in mine. It made sense."

"It made sense, too," Smithy agrees, "we should sign over both houses to the kids and move into an apartment together. We invited them over to share our good news. Without letting us finish, all four children and all four spouses start wailing at once. *Are you telling us that you're gay? At your age. I am so ashamed. How could you? How long has this been going on? Who else knows? What will the children say? Do you realize what this will do to our business? Have you given any thought about us?* They allowed us no time to answer and themselves no time to listen."

"Each tried over the next few months to talk us out of our decision, each time ending in another argument," Len discloses. "They stopped communicating with us when I sold my place and moved in here with Smithy four years ago today. Happy Anniversary, Smithy, I love you."

"I love you too, Len", Smithy whispers at the graveside, one year today since Len was buried.

"We call that person who has lost his father, an orphan; and a widower that man who has lost his wife. But that man who has lost a friend, what shall we call him?" ~ Joseph Roux

Carl "Papa" Palmer of Old Mill Road in Ridgeway, VA now lives in University Place, WA. He is retired military, retired FAA and now just plain retired without wristwatch, alarm clock or Facebook friend.

I WISH YOU HAD STAYED

BY

KONSTANTINA PAPADOPOULOU

I was there, holding her hand; I knew it was the end and I needed to inhale as much of her as I could; commit it to my memory for later recollection and repentance. She stared at me with pleading eyes, but all I could do was pray for the misty oblivion of sleep to come sooner. I rearranged her pillows and tried to give her some water. She couldn't swallow it; she started crying. Kneeling beside her, I felt her forehead; she was burning. What could a man like me do to make her peaceful? How could such a creature suffer so much?

Two hours later and I was still standing there. The light was gone from her eyes; her voice only a whisper. I stooped closer trying to absorb the hoarse words.

"All I wanted was to make you happy... I'm sorry"

"You already have," was the answer that died on my lips; I had run out of time. It was four in the morning when I lost her.

I can't remember how I left the hospital or for how long I wandered around. I remember empty streets and it was raining; that I desperately tried to picture her face, guilty for the tears that were clouding my vision and for the unhappy thoughts that overwhelmed me. But I was determined to remember every single second of us. What I am now? I owe it all to her, no matter the broken heart she left behind. I had to remember how I met her, the first smile, the first touch, the first kiss. It was the only way I knew to prove how much I had loved her and how much she took away.

One of the first things she said to me was that she couldn't comprehend when I was serious, when I was joking around or when I was just making fun of her. I am ashamed to know I never made her feel safe around me; that I was swirling in ecstasy, in a myth I built around myself, uncaring and unsatisfied. Every single detail comes to me now. I can remember every little move and it hurts so much more.

When we were apart for the first time, I simply took her hand and asked her to stay, holding her gaze. And she did without asking why, knowing I wasn't ready to say goodbye yet, trusting in the false sense of awareness surrounding me.

The first time I visited her at the hospital she was laying broken. That's when the truth came crushing down, like a wave of lava destroying everything on its path, making souls and minds despair. I was ready to get carried away too, no matter how strong my foothold was. The power of the fire was melting every inch of hope and, slowly but firmly, it burned my own ego and her trust to ashes. The only thing that kept me in touch with reality was her strained smile, creepy yet reassuring; the secret expectation that I hadn't lost her yet. She asked if her scars were ugly now and I said that everything was a part of her. So how could they ever be ugly? She smiled that deceitful smile of hers and went back to sleep. I stared out the window in the quietness of an early autumn knowing soon I would be forced to leave behind the best part of myself. I was so afraid the remnant could never do justice to the person she helped me become.

The only time we made love I had my lips glued to hers, thirsty for love and passion. We were on the beach and she was afraid to get into the water, open scars always burn against salt. I picked her up and laid her on the muddy sand, unaware that it meant so much more for her than an impulsive erotic instinct. She was giving me herself and I didn't deserve it. Afterwards, she slept naked in my arms uncaring for the repercussions. The night had come when I finally got up and left her there, her eyes shining with unshed tears of betrayal.

It's been a month since I lost her, but time cannot fly forward when you so stubbornly think of the past. For days I felt lost and this is not me; I can't stand it. What would happen if I just disappeared? Who would be worried? The only thing keeping me here is her. Her precious smile, her tiny fists that can hold the whole world. I need to pick up the phone and say "I need you" but who would answer? Who would say "I'm here for you, don't be scared"? Everything would be so different if you had stayed…

I look at past photographs and wonder if we had been there together; what was she wearing, had I kissed her, had I made her smile? One year and a half and, finally, I was able to tell myself that I was well. Not because the pain and loneliness subsided but because I learned to live with them. I learned to get up every morning expecting nothing, living each day in vain until the next morning came and everything started again from the beginning.

I need to stop thinking; tear these few pages apart and look forward. But I don't want to, not yet. She once said through the darkness she kept hearing my voice, that it was the only thing keeping her head above the water. I wish I had a similar comfort. But soul and mind are two things incompatible. When the one is ready to take over, something happens at the last moment and takes happiness out of your grasp. The balance is thin and delicate and I had to walk on that tightrope many times since I met her.

No matter how much I try to smile now for my little girl, I know it's in vain. It's fake and she can feel it.

The night we learned she was pregnant she came to my room and curled her body around me, whispering that she was scared, asking for my help. All I did was stroke her back and let her lie there with me, without the words she desperately needed to hear. She started singing an old lullaby and I kissed her forehead, letting myself drift off to sleep.

"What do you fear so much?" I asked the following morning.

"I am afraid of you, that you don't love me anymore, that I'm alone, that I have let you down".

"I promise I will be there for you, but don't ask for more. That's all I allow myself to give." And once again I walked away knowing I was only fooling myself. When the time came and she gave birth, I knew she wasn't going to love the tiny creature who breathed with difficulty, lying in a bed a few rooms down the corridor, simply because part of it was mine. And it only became worse.

The morning I took our little girl home she couldn't stop crying. I begged her to try and hold her, but she screamed to take the baby away and make her quiet. She had lost what few shreds of logic she had left.

I spent days after the funeral alone in her room. I should have seen it coming when she told me that she would leave, but I guess I needed to think that she was stronger than that. After a week I forced myself to go see my daughter again, a strong reminder of what I had lost. I felt hours passing by rearranging her small furniture and folding her colorful clothes. I didn't want to be alone anymore.

So it's time now to end this story and store it away in a box full of memories I never want to lose and never need to disturb. But how can I truly miss you when I never really had you? I close now this notebook in hopes that one day I will meet you again… The girl that I only loved once, but gave me something that I will love forever.

Konstantina Papadopoulou was born in Greece in 1988, has a BSc in Physics, a MSc in Materials Science and currently studies for a PhD. Her previous work consists of four plays which were performed at festivals in Greece while more details can be found on her blog konstantinasays.wordpress. com

PETALS OF MADNESS

BY

BRENDA PATTERSON

I watch. I watch as the petals fall in a cascade of flushed satiny teardrops, creating a rain of dappling shadow. They surround her by the thousands; clinging to her hair, hiding within the folds of her summery dress, creating contrast with the smooth creaminess of her skin. The petals envelop her, hug her, love her as I do.

She leans against the tree with book in hand; legs crossed in front of her and a contemplative look on her face. The grasses and flowers that dot the area around her shiver in the wind, fickle embodiments of her natural influence over nature. She is more at home here than anywhere else, welcomed by the land, caressed by the petals, illuminated by sunshine that spears down through the canopy above her.

She once confessed her belief that she belonged here, rather than in society. Her words were soft and melancholy, her eyes downcast. She stared at her clasped fingers and her lip trembled, but her words were crystalline. There were discussions of her return to life beyond the well-camouflaged institutional walls, and panic flooded her eyes. She did not wish for that. Nor did I, but, I bit my tongue. I feared for her, feared that by staying, she was condemning herself to a life of bleakness here, with me.

We met upon her entry of this place. I had come two weeks prior, having all but abandoned my former life, ready for more docile insanity. I was already enmeshed within it. I knew order here, peace, patience. She shuffled through the door with scars on her arms and the trapped animal glaze in her eyes, and my new existence crumbled.

But I did not mind. Taken aback by it, I became a slave to the pounding within my chest, the roar of my suddenly-alive blood within my ears. It was like a drug to me, the effect unlike the medications prescribed to keep the denizens of this place orderly. While they haunted the halls with blank expressions and empty thoughts, I lit through with an inextinguishable flame. She fed kindling to it with the first ghostly remnants of her smile, something that emerged timidly, but blossomed as the weeks passed. Lately, the smile seemed to find a quiet home on her face, slowly spreading to touch the turmoil in the depths of her eyes. Lately, she hasn't seemed so adamant about staying here.

I hate her smile, almost as much as I love it.

Today she sits beneath the cherry tree. The sense of calm swirling around her is highlighted by those damned petals, stealing from her the tortured beauty that captivated me. The purple lines marking her wrists have faded into a shade of silver that sometimes catches the sunlight; her badge of courage within weakness, the thread weakly binding her to this world. She doesn't notice me. I walk slowly down the crest that obscures the buildings from this haven of hers, careful to not make a sound. I wish to capture this scene of contemplative beauty, to hold it in my heart and my memories forever. But I know no matter how hard I try, it will fade. She will fade; from me, from this life, from her isolation within insanity. She will fade and then she will be reborn; to blaze brighter, to rise toward the heavens as all phoenix do. And I alone will stand in her ashes, my hand outstretched toward a flame I never could possess.

The wind shifts now, carrying the scent of the blossoms to me. Her scent. The essence of her calls to me, knots me up inside, makes me want to double over in pain. Instead, I glance at my hands, paper-thin skin stretched over twisted bone. These hands will never run through her soft, golden hair, nor should they. No, these hands will free her.

I stand beside her now. Although her eyes do not meet mine, greeting comes in the form of a wistful sigh. Together, we watch the birds swoop and dive over the meadow below. The sun sends slanted rays of light across the floor, illuminating floating insect and gossamer dandelion. It is silent, but for the whisper of the leaves above us, and the roaring of my heart in my ears. What I wouldn't give to make it last.

She knows. In this one moment, I can sense her awareness. I can feel her eyes staring up at me, and when I let my gaze fall, hers travels to my hand. There is bewilderment there, but for only a moment.

With a match spark, something ignites within those chestnut orbs, and her expression changes. Her book falls. She faces away once more, toward the meadow and her freedom.

Melodic, her voice catches the wind, carrying with it a hint of fear, a tidal wave of acceptance. I shut my eyes against it, but it washes over me still, a tortured tsunami of a life suffered.

"I'm ready, Dr. Clark."

Kneeling behind her, I lay my cheek against the back of her head, wrap my arms around her. I can feel her heartbeat thrumming wildly within my embrace. My hand grasps her delicate wrist and she stiffens, but only for a moment. With fluid movement the blade passes through, spilling her life in a cascade of metallic crimson. Quiet moments slip by, her head resting upon my chest. Finally, a meek sound escapes her, then nothing more as she falls gracefully upon a bed of petals—so beautiful, so broken.

As always, I am surprised by the sudden warmth on my face. I touch my fingers to my cheeks; tears and blood; life and suffering. I touch them to her lips, sharing with her my own pain, and then I stand. Soon, she will be found, and I will not. A consequence of my calling.

I walk away, into her meadow, touched by the warmth and light that resides there.

Brenda is an artist, writer and lover of all things creative. If she is not in her studio, you can find her enjoying her time with her two awesome kids and new husband, Angelo.

KALEIDOSCOPE

BY
VALERI KATHLEEN PAXTON-STEELE

She stood at the edge of the dappled shade of the forest, watching as the children returned. A brother and sister, just as small as small can be. They held hands as they followed the path into the clearing. Just a few more minutes and they too, would arrive at the rim of the woods. The green and brown earth tones of her dress half hid her against the trees, and her long russet hair reflected the reddish-orange carpet of fallen pine needles. She waited, smiling, holding the kaleidoscope in her gentle hands. A wren bubbled and chirred sweetly in the distance.

She was no ordinary woman. Not a princess, nor one of the fairy folk. She was magic. She was a witch. Many think of old women as witches, hunched and warted hags, if you will. This witch was winsome, and beautiful, with a slight, slender figure and sparkling green eyes. Her eyes were old enough to know the truths of the world, and she kept a small smile to herself.

She was a seer, a scryer, a KNOWER OF TRUTHS. She could use anything with a reflection to see into the future. A small puddle worked as well as a crystal ball. She could read the dew on a rose, a drop of rain on a leaf. She had started her training with this simple kaleidoscope. It shone brightly of gleaming brass. Inside were such jewels. In and among the mix of semi-precious stones were rubies, emeralds, jades, sapphires and topaz. They swirled inside the magical toy. Diamonds sparkled and reflected pattern after lovely pattern. The pictures spoke to her, told her stories.

It all started when she was just a mere slip of a child, a little thing, smaller than small. She had been walking on a path through a field with her brother, heading toward the forest, back toward home. A beautiful woman met her, and gave her a most beloved treasure, a brass kaleidoscope. With it, she learned the secrets of the future.

The witch had waited patiently for this day. She caught a glimpse of time, as fragile as a mote of dust, and put the moment in her pocket. A butterfly floated in the air. Ready, she stepped out, smiling.

*

The little girl was startled, but pleasantly so. A woman daintily stepped out from the forest. She was attired in a richly adorned brocade dress. An embroidered tapestry of vines, leaves and small flowers travelled along the length of the dress in a warm brown and green crewel pattern that fairly danced as she moved. The pleats were gathered and rouched to accent her lovely figure. Her auburn hair hung in long, soft waves, as if it had been recently released from plaited braids.

The girl had been distracted on this warm, perfect day, looking for birds as her brother guided her gently along. The meadow they traversed was very high, and the reeds and grasses swayed calmly in the breeze. The slope of the hill was soft enough, so the walk was easy for them.

The woman held something strange in her hand. It was solid looking, and very shiny. It was somewhat long and made from metal, and the girl had never seen anything like it before. It was true, in fact, that Gytha had never seen very many things of this world, as she had only just turned Five Wheels of The Year this past spring. Her older brother, Anders, had always been the one to watch over her. He had the same strawberry blonde hair and the same green eyes, although her brother was much bigger, perhaps by as many as two whole years.

Gytha smiled back at the woman. Her brother stopped short, protectively. The woman greeted them warmly, "Good day."

"Good day, missus," said Anders.

"Hello, Anders! You are looking fine and fit today!" Turning to his tiny sister, she said, "I have a gift for you, little Gytha." She knelt before Gytha, her hand offering out the spectacular present. She sounded jovial; there was laughter in her voice. "It is very precious. It is made from magic. I have always given it to you, and you have always accepted it. With this, you will learn many things. Here, sweet child. Take this. It is called a kaleidoscope. You look inside it, and turn this rounded piece just so, and you will see pretty colors. Sometimes the colors make pictures, and the pictures will show you many secret things. You are going to be a knower of secrets, and a keeper of time. You will become a woman of profound magic- a witch." She thoughtfully handed the kaleidoscope to the girl. The wren warbled its song again, and the fat, lazy bumblebees droned quietly in the field.

Anders looked at the woman, so vaguely familiar. He had never expected to feel this strong sense of loyalty and attachment to a complete stranger before. He would follow her to the ends of the earth, if she had asked him to. He would protect her and care for her throughout all time, if need be. *A talisman*, he thought. *A magical talisman for Gytha. What a strange and wonderful thing!* He had always known there was something special about his sister. She was delicate and kind, patient and virtuous, soft-spoken and humorous, so calm and loving to everyone she met. Of all his sisters, this littlest one was his favorite.

Gytha took the toy, with awe. Today was not necessarily a special day, not a birth-day nor any other gift-getting day. She followed along as the woman instructed. She held it up to her eye. She turned the rounded piece just so, and the patterns and colors inside rattled and melded together and made the most glorious designs. In it, she saw the small wrens of the field flit against the blue sky and the butterflies flutter and bounce in the wind. In it, she saw waving grasses and dappled shade trees. In it, she saw a beautiful woman wearing the earth tones of the forest. She laughed at the sights, recognizing each moment.

She brought herself to stop looking through it. A great many years from now, she would be holding this glass out to a small child... a younger than young (and smaller than small) little girl. A peace settled over her. She looked up, expecting the magical woman to be still standing before her. Alas, the woman was walking away, her gown swooshing as she began heading back into the depths of the woods. She turned back briefly, to look at Gytha. There was love and a deep knowing, in her eyes. Her eyes smiled as she turned away.

In due course, Gytha would learn many truths from the kaleidoscope. She saw herself grow up, and her strawberry blonde hair turn to a rich, russet auburn. She saw the magic and mystery of timelessness. How to tame it. How to play with it, like teasing a game of cat's cradle out of a length of string. She would come to know the secret of how to snatch a moment out of the air, and to keep bits of time in her pocket. She would learn incantations and spells, and she would become a woman who, although considered a witch, would be held in the highest esteem. She would have the respect and gratitude of all she met.

Anders and Gytha followed where the path led. When they returned home, they would tell their family of their meeting near the forest. They would describe the woman and her lovely smile. They would describe the sun, the blue sky, the birds, the sweet smelling grasses that swayed. Hanging out of Gytha's little satchel was a perfect toy. She passed it back and forth from hand to hand. She showed everyone all of the beautiful colors, although they could not see pictures, as she did. The family helped Gytha clear off a little spot on her shelf, within easy reach, where she could take down the kaleidoscope any time she took a fancy to do so.

The homestead itself grew quiet after twilight. Stars came out against a sky bathed in indigo blue. Tucked safely in her bed after supper, Gytha looked with longing at her special toy on the shelf. Momma blew out her candle, and gave the five year old a small kiss on the cheek, goodnight. The crescent moon glowed brilliantly through the small window. Her momma called it "the kitty cat moon." It was considered a good luck omen, because of the way it smiled sideways at her. She would have such sweet dreams tonight! Tomorrow was going to be a very exciting day. She knew the truth, and the truth was good.

Author and poet Valeri Kathleen Paxton-Steele is a Binghamton, New York native. She primarily writes about such topics as domestic violence, mental illness, rape and childhood sexual abuse in an effort to reach out to fellow victims and survivors with this message: "You are not alone."

CROCODILE COUNTRY

BY

LUCHO PAYNE

"Even if you're completely still in the water, they know you're there. They can sense your heartbeat from a kilometre away."

Billy Gurrawah was back in crocodile country. As he drove towards the Adelaide River, the thought of them made him shudder as did the thought of talking to his ex-wife. She ran the "Spectacular Jumping Crocodile Cruise" and the last of today's customers were leaving.

"Hey Shelley."

"Well, if it isn't the big shot Private Detective. What happened? Did the city chew you up and spit you out?"

"I'm here on a case."

"Not to see your daughter then… *two years* Billy."

"How's Kathy going?"

"Like you care."

"Look, I saw a report of three girls missing from round here. I recognised one of them – I think she's a friend of Kathy's. Can I show you the photos?"

Billy held up photographs of three teenage girls.

"This one, in the middle. Wasn't she at school with Kathy?"

"Yeah – Julie Freeman. Beautiful chick, no wonder *you* remember her. She started to go berko. Too much grog and weed. Kathy stopped hanging around with losers like that. Don't know the other two. And I didn't know any girls were missing."

"I was thinking of asking Kathy..."

"Really? Will you bother to ask her anything about her life first? Or just launch straight into your *inquiries*? Presumably you've been hired by someone. So you're only actually here for money."

"No. I saw the photo of the girl and I thought it best to come."

"Well go and speak to her then. She's started work behind the bar at the Humpty Doo Hotel. She'll be there tonight."

Shelley carried on closing up, chairs clattering together as she stacked them. The rest of the crew kept their distance. Billy got in his car and drove back to the Arnhem Highway, pulling into a lay-by as the sun went down. He saw headlights coming up the track from the Crocodile Cruise, a car travelling fast. It sped out onto the main road, tyres screeching as it turned off down another track towards the river. Billy smiled and carried on towards Humpty Doo.

"A schooner of Carlton Draught, please."

The girl behind the bar looked up.

"Dad. Mum already phoned. She said you'd pretend to be interested, but you're really here about work."

"How are things between you and her? She seemed a little tense."

"She works. He *drinks*. You know how it is."

"Kathy, I've said it before. You can come and stay with me whenever you like."

She handed him the schooner.

"Thanks. I'll be around for a few days so maybe we could catch up again? How about tomorr–"

"Billy? I heard you were back. How ya' going?"

"Detective Reynolds. I'm good thanks. You?"

"Yeah all good. Hope you're not sticking your nose into anything you shouldn't be, Billy?"

"Just catching up with family and friends, Detective."

Billy necked his beer.

"Kathy – I'll call you. Reynolds – see you around."

"Keep that nose clean, Billy."

Outside Billy noticed two men standing by his car. As he approached, one of them spoke.

"Gurrawah isn't it?"

Billy didn't break his stride. Instead he unleashed a vicious right cross and caught the man smack on his chin, knocking him out cold. Then he spun round and lunged towards the other guy, who brought his fists up to protect his chin. Billy landed a thundering left foot right into his groin and the guy bent over in agony as Billy yanked his head up.

"I don't know who you work for or what you want from me. But I want to see those three girls back where they belong – pronto – or people are going to get seriously hurt. Do you hear me?"

The man nodded while moaning.

"Now move this other idiot or I'll drive right over him."

The next morning Billy was woken by a phone call.

"Billy, it's Superintendent Chalmers here. Thanks for coming back so soon after I contacted you."

"No worries."

"Listen. Good news. The three girls re-appeared last night. Not entirely sure, but it seems they were working in a makeshift brothel for truckies, down by the river. Looks like they weren't allowed to leave and were being kept doped up. Something happened and the guys running the joint let them go. Bunch of amateurs, by the sound of it."

"That's great."

"But Billy, you've only just got back. Did you actually do anything? Even for a hot-shot P.I. like you, that's fast work."

"Well, sometimes Superintendent, it's just a question of getting into the water. Somehow, they just know you're there."

Lucho Payne from Bristol, UK. He is the co-author of the book "London in a Lunchtime". His flash fiction has been short-listed for the Bridport Prize (UK), long-listed in the Fish Publishing Flash Fiction competition (Ireland) and selected for a Flash Walk during the UK National Flash Fiction Day.

HORSES FOR COURSES – DINNER AT DICKENS'

BY

RONNIE PEACE

When I received an invitation to a dinner party o'er the wire from Dickens, I had trouble containing my excitement (I eventually tied it to a chain connected to the maple tree near the back porch). It was fair to say I had great expectations of what was to come.

In fact, I was so overcome with eager anticipation of the event that I'll skip straight to that very night (my calves will be sore in the morning!).

On such an auspicious occasion I donned my finest suit and tails. It was a hirsute made from horse tail, and tails made out of the mane, which was the style of the time (7pm).

My hosts had the finest cutlery. In fact, they were so fine that if laid on their sides you couldn't see them at all.

On entry, appetisers were presented on a dumbwaiter, awaiting our consumption. No one was more taken aback than our host when his dumbwaiter spoke. More annoyed, than anything. And quite rightly so. He had outlaid big money for the damn thing.

Dickens quickly calmed down when he found the receipt and instantly made plans for his butler to return the faulty server by noon in the morrow. Upon hearing this (there was no problem with his hearing), the faulty dumbwaiter was taken aback, and all was once again well.

Our host immediately began to talk to Drummle: not at all deterred by his replying in his heavy reticent way, but apparently led on by it to screw discourse out of him. And then he tried to screw the next course out of him as well. Which was fine. My good chap had always been quite the tight arse. Horses for courses really.

And tonight we were having just that:

> Horse d'oeuvre was *Shetland bruschetta on shortbread*;
> *Medium rare mare on a bed of mash potato & horse radish for main, wrapped in fried mane* for the main;
> Dessert was *caramelised stallion with strawberries and horse-whipped cream, served in hoofs*. And hooves.

Though the aftertaste had most throats in the parlour a little hoarse, it was quite tasty nonetheless. Unfortunately, something didn't quite agree with me (this time, I wasn't talking about Drummle). My stomach tried in vain to harness the whinnying meal I had consumed with gumption (regrettably, I had chosen the multi-purpose cleaner to accompany my meal over the informal noun, showing a complete lack of horse sense). It couldn't. And so I was up with the trots all night.

This left my lavatory deterred, very much dissimilarly to Drummle in earlier sentences.

Earlier in the evening, Drummle was heard to remark to the host about the quality of the meat for the main, and inquired as to how he could get his equine to taste so succulent.

"My good man, the trick is all in the tenderising of the beast. And make sure you remove the little man sitting up top on the horse before you pound the meat."

There was a sigh from Drummle. He knew more than anything that there's nothing worse than flogging a dead horse.

'Cept for flogging a live one. That's bestiality.

(Disclaimer: No horses were killed in the creation of this article. They were already dead. And never existed in the first place. But, if we did use real horses in this fictional piece (which would be quite absurd and, therefore, quite suited to this story), we would be sure to take them from the leftovers at Melbourne Cup and other race meets, and dressage)

Ronnie Peace is an Australian attempted Humo(u)rist who enjoys placing mostly old and some new words in random orders for his own amusement.

Shoddy examples of his work can be found at uwannapeaceome.blogspot. com.au and Twits @Ronnie_Peace

THE LITTLE FOLK

BY

ANNIE PERCIK

"Beware," she said. "Beware of the little folk."

But we didn't listen. Of course we didn't listen. It was just Great Aunt Clarissa, muttering away, sitting in her ancient rocking chair by the fire, like she always did. Her dire warnings didn't apply to us; they were just make-believe. Fairies weren't real; our mother always said so. After all, didn't mother know best?

So, we tramped and we stamped through the woods and over the stream, no thought for the signs that lay all around us, there to guide us, if only we had paid attention.

The tiny brushes of disturbed air against our skin were just the wind in the trees, a spring breeze to remind us that winter had only recently left us.

The sudden sharp smell of pepper in the air meant one of us had brushed against a wild bergamot plant without realising it. And, sure enough, there were the distinctive pink flowers, though we could swear they were not there a moment before. Great Aunt Clarissa sometimes made tea from their leaves to ease the ache in her joints, so we gathered some as a gift for her.

The ravens collecting in the branches above our heads, soaring from tree to tree, seeming to keep pace with us, but were really just going about their own business. We wouldn't mind them above, and they wouldn't mind us below.

That circle of mushrooms was just a coincidence; of course plants would grow in clusters, wherever their seeds might fall. We knew which mushrooms were safe, so we plucked them up and filled our pockets to take them back for dinner.

The sound of distant laughter in the air was just our imagination, a reflection of our own joy at being free to run and play outside after a long and tedious week at school. We revelled in our release from lessons, and knew ourselves to be masters of our own fate, immune to any danger.

Those little points of light flickering in the bushes were just a trick; our eyes dazzled by the sun filtering down through the leaves. We made a game of chasing them, following ever deeper into the darkening woods. They led us down a path, surrounded on all sides by thick foliage that grew closer around us as we walked, until we made our way through almost a tunnel of branches. Twigs caught at our clothes, tearing them into tatters and scratching at the skin beneath, but we went on, undeterred.

The sound of tinkling music drew us further, until at last we came out into a beautiful clearing, where magical creatures danced and sang in the golden sunlight. Now, they revealed themselves to us openly for, unknown to us, the trees had closed behind us, blocking off our route back to the mortal realm. But we were happy and carefree, eager to join in the fun and games, our old lives quickly fading to a distant memory of a time that no longer mattered. We belonged to the little folk now.

Annie Percik lives in London, where she is revising her first novel while working as a University Complaints Officer. She publishes short fiction and writing about writing on her website (www.alobear.co.uk).

PROMISES, PROMISES, PROMISES

BY

DAVID PERLMUTTER

....We now come, ladies and gentlemen, to lot #145 in this auction of the holdings of the Belton estate. As is well known, Mr. Belton possessed an extensive collection of alien artifacts, of which his heirs have allowed only a select few to be auctioned off for fear winning bidders would not be able to care for them in the manner which they were accustomed, as it were. This is one of them.

To aid those in the back unable to see the item, this is an election campaign poster. Specifically, a campaign poster from the last election held on the planet of Klopstockia, prior to the advent of the tragic civil war which ensued shortly thereafter, in which the planet itself was destroyed by unknown destructive forces. We do not know the circumstances under which it survived the planet's destruction, nor can we describe the circumstances under which Mr. Belton acquired it, for his will specified that these facts will not be revealed to the public. We can only describe, again for those unable to see the item, some minor elements of its physical provenance.

What?

Yes, I know you're upset about not knowing more about the circumstances, but as I just said a number of other times today, the auction house is not responsible for collecting that information unless the estate provides to us, which they have not. Take it up with them, not us.

Now, as to the item...

It is a rectangular sheet of white paper, attached by pushpins to a sheet of plywood, as it would have been in a number of places in Klopstockia during the 365 day campaign. The ink is black, and the writing is chiefly in capital letters. In the center of the sheet is a cameo portrait of the leader of the party who leaned toward leftist politics. A circle surrounds the portrait and a line goes through it. (This piece was produced by the party leaning to the right, hence the obvious bias.) On the bottom it says clearly: "PROMISES, PROMISES, PROMISES! WE DON'T NEED MORE OF HIS (expletive deleted) PROMISES" in the native language. Some unknown hand has, in pencil, scratched this message out and written above it: "We don't need more of *you* idiots, either!" We can ascertain that this piece was placed in a left-leaning neighborhood in an attempt to convert the natives to the other side, an attempt that failed.

As mentioned, this is an artifact of the last Klopstockian election, in which the left-leaning side won overwhelmingly, but caused the party leaning to the right to contest the results, leading ultimately to first the civil war noted in many recent history textbooks, and finally to the tragic nuclear explosion visible even from here on Earth a couple of years afterward. So keep this in mind as you consider your bids.

We will begin the bidding at $100. Do I hear $100?

$95?

$90?

$80?

$70?

$50?

$25?

$20?

$10?

$5?

Yes, a bid for $5. Any other bids?

$5 going once, twice, *sold*....to the man, who, for some reason, bears a very strong resemblance to the natives of the late planet of Klopstockia.

Now, to item #146....

David Perlmutter is a freelance writer of history and fiction, sometimes at the same time. He lives and works in Winnipeg, Manitoba, Canada

NEW BEGINNINGS

BY

SALLY RAMSEY

"I think this is the longest we've ever been out of our closet," Mop observed.

"There was Clarissa's sixth birthday party," Broom reminded him.

Mop swayed on his tendrils. "Oh yeah. Once they realized how much stuff those kids dropped on the floor, they left us in the corner. It took months for the pink from the sticky stuff on the cake to soak out of my fibers."

"And I had crumbs stuck in my bristles for weeks," Broom recalled. "Still, this was something different. After Melody used us to clean up the glass she broke, Jim got very quiet. Then they both started talking to each other more than I can ever remember them doing before."

"That's true," Mop agreed. "Usually Melody will ask Jim a question and he'll answer with one word. Then he leaves the room as soon as he can." He waved his tendrils wistfully. "Wish I could do that, leave whenever I want to."

"That makes two of us," Broom commiserated. "When sugar hits the floor, I don't want to be anywhere around."

"Same goes for me with jelly," Mop offered. "But this time it didn't look like Jim wanted to get away. Melody had water running down her face and it looked like it scared him. He tried to use his finger to wipe it off, but it just kept coming out of her eyes. She said something about a divorce. What is that?"

217

"I don't know," Broom answered, "but it sounded like Melody was leaving. And Jim didn't want her to."

"That was pretty obvious," Mop observed. "He was trying to hold her hand. We've never seen him do that before, but it seemed to make her feel better. I don't know why. I sure don't enjoy having hands around my handle."

Broom scratched his bristles against the floor. "I don't mind. It's not as if we can move by ourselves. At least when they hold us, we get somewhere, even if I do get crumbs in my bristles.

"I suppose you have a point," Mop considered, "but Jim didn't take Melody anywhere, at least not at that moment. They just talked."

"Could you hear what they were saying?" Broom asked.

"I heard it, but I didn't understand it. Melody said she was pregnant. I don't know that word. Do you? She said she thought it happened on Superbowl Sunday when Jim was so excited his team won --- whatever that means. Can you understand any of that?"

"Pregnant, I've heard that word before," Broom recalled. "It means she is going to have another little one like Clarissa. I don't know what she meant by it happened, though. Whatever it was, she didn't look happy about it."

"She wasn't," Mop confirmed. "She said they barely talked anymore; that Jim is always at work or in front of the TV. She didn't know how they could stay together. That's when her face got really wet."

"I saw that," Broom recalled. "His eyes were wet too, but the water didn't roll down his cheeks."

"Yes, and he promised he'd try harder," Mop added. "Then they put their arms around each other and went to that room with the thing they close their eyes and lie on. They just left us here leaning against the wall. Do you think they'll come back?"

Broom flipped a straw. "I wouldn't count on it, at least not until morning."

Sally Ramsey is a chemist and and an author, who enjoys invention both in the lab and on the page. She likes creating quirky characters, including inanimate ones.

SHIRELLE

BY

STEPHEN RABURN

When Shirelle was a little girl she liked to look at maps. She spent hours contemplating the various shapes and sizes of states and small countries, studying the straight and winding blue and red lines that connect cities to one another inside the covers of a road atlas her mother bought for her at Dollar General. One would think by this early fascination Shirelle might one day end up a cartographer or navigator, perhaps at least a travel agent or truck driver.

Shirelle didn't end up doing anything, in fact. By the time she reached womanhood she had long since dropped out of school, her drug addiction left her depleted of any ray of hope that young children instinctively possess and the string of pregnancies (two abortions, one miscarriage, one stillborn), random beatings and other acts of violence inflicted upon her left her body and spirit worn out and ugly.

You hear stories about how some people find the resolve to escape their fates in life, to overcome life's obstacles and succeed against seemingly impossible odds. This is not one of them. Like her mother before her, Shirelle fell victim to the horrors that sometimes entangle the poor, disempowered, disenfranchised, downtrodden residents of US inner-city slums.

Shirelle also liked to play with coins. Her grandfather, already old and dilapidated by the time of Shirelle's first memory of him, often came to stay with her for long periods of time. Her grandfather had an impressive collection of old and foreign coins and one shiny silver dollar for every year of his life. He started collecting when he was in the Navy during World War II and kept them in a White Owl cigar box. Come January every year he took the city bus to First Union and swapped out a paper dollar for a newly minted silver one. He instructed Shirelle, his only grandchild, that she would someday own the coins if she promised to continue the tradition and vowed to hand down the collection to one of her grandchildren. Shirelle spent hours at a time cleaning and polishing the coins, fantasizing of the day they would all be hers. Her favorites were the ones from faraway lands.

Shirelle's grandfather died on his birthday and she used the coins to buy crack on the street corner that same afternoon.

As a young woman, Shirelle moved out of her mother's house and into an apartment in the same housing project. She and her mother had a falling out and rarely talked. Shirelle was always being evicted for one reason or another. When she exhausted all other resources she ended up spending most of her days walking around town, most nights sleeping on park benches.

She sometimes stayed at the various shelters, didn't like their rules and chose the streets instead. One bitterly cold January day as she walked about town she glanced up and became startled and saddened by the reflection she saw of herself in a storefront window on Tryon Street. She looked terrible: thin as a rail, her clothes and hair tattered and in disarray, her two front teeth missing, both arms pocked with needle marks and swollen with infection.

She pondered how things came to this point, this far out of hand. Then a gentleman in a fine navy pinstriped suit walked out of the downtown library and noticed Shirelle sitting on the sidewalk with tears streaming down her face. With great disgust he mumbled something rude to her while avoiding eye contact, emptied his pockets into the paper cup she held out. She noticed a shiny new silver dollar. She picked up the coin and held it between her thumb and fore finger, fondling the edges and admiring the way the silver sparkled when the sun's rays caught it just right. She noted the date and realized it was brand new.

Perhaps Shirelle saw the coin as symbolic of an opportunity to fulfill the promise she made to her grandfather years before, to start anew. Perhaps it somehow, in some strange way, proved to be the impetus she needed to kick the drug habit and get her life together. Maybe she saved some money, bought a new road map, and took a grey hound bus to a faraway place where she could start a new life. Or, perhaps she used the dollar coin as down payment on her next binge. Who knows? No one has seen her since that day.

Stephen Raburn is a writer, editor, publisher, daydreamer, coffee snob and entrepreneur who lives in Durham, NC with his two amazing little girls.

A MOMMA FOR HALLOWEEN

BY
NEYSHA REEVES

Halloween - I used to think it was scary. The one time of the year when the thin veil separating the living and the dead is cast aside, so all can mingle together as one.

It was Halloween night. I got into my pyjamas early and sat in our living room reading one of my favourite books waiting for Momma.

The hallway doors suddenly flung open. I held my breath as strangers walked in. They didn't seem to notice me as I shrunk into the corner of my lounge chair and held my breath. Who were they, why were they in my house, and where was my Momma?

They dragged in a round table from the kitchen, then chairs. Four strangers entered the room, one an old lady assisted by another younger lady and two men. All four strangers sat facing each other, holding hands in silence. Then one man dressed in black with a Bible in his hand spoke. His voice reverberated around the room.

I was frozen to the spot, but I couldn't look away from them.

"Tonight on All Hallows we call on the departed, the lost souls, the forgotten. We call on Suzanne Sprigg, to come forward and make contact."

"Where is my Momma?" I ask them.

Placing my book beside me, I inched off of my chair and stood beside the old lady at the table. She swung around quickly and looks right at me with grey-white eyes that didn't seem capable of seeing anything, except me.

"Suzie, is that you," she asked in a croaky voice.

Her scary eyes bore deep into me. I screamed and ran away, slamming the door behind me.

Momma always told me the closet was a safe place to hide when strangers come into the house. I remember her putting me in the closet once before and making me promise not to come out until she came and got me.

I shouldn't have come out. Look what's happened now. "I'm sorry I wasn't a good girl, Momma," I cry out, wiping away tears. "Please Momma. I need you to come back now."

Footsteps entered my bedroom, then voices waft into the closet.

The man who called my name spoke, "The most common activity is here, in this room?"

The younger lady answered, "Yes, this is where we heard the footsteps, and that closet opens all by itself."

"Step aside," said the old lady as the closet door opens.

The old lady sat on the edge of the closet door. This time she didn't look right at me, but I knew that she saw me.

"You have been waiting for your Mother for a long time, haven't you."

I watched her closely and shuffled a tiny bit closer to her.

"Momma?"

"It's ok," whispers the old lady. "Come," she said holding out her arm for me to come to her.

I climbed onto her knee and held back tears. I finally feel safe.

"Do you remember what happened to you, Suzie?" she asks.

I shook my head and nestled closer to the old lady.

"Robbers came to your house. Your Mother hid you in the closet... you would have been safe if they hadn't burned down the house with your Momma and you in it."

I hid my face. I remembered. The smoke was so thick that it took away my breath. When I opened the closet door, it was too hot that I had to close it quickly. I was so scared as I cried out to Momma with my last breaths, but she didn't come for me, not then, not ever.

"You died that night in the fire, Suzie, but your Momma didn't. That's why nobody came for you."

I sat up and looked at the lady, "Momma?"

That's right Suzie, I am your Momma. I've come to set you free. You don't have to hide anymore". She let out a ragged breath, "50 years and I never stopped looking for you, Suzie."

She pointed a melted looking wrinkled finger above her head. I looked up and saw a golden light, just like sunlight. As I looked into the light I was sure that I could see the park in the distance. I wanted to go and play, but I waited so long to get Momma back. I couldn't leave her now.

"No Momma."

"It's ok. We can go together," she whispered.

She stood up, leaving me in the closet. The man in black took her arm. "Are you ok?"

"Yes, it's time to go. I'm tired."

The man paused. "Are you sure?"

Momma kept shuffling, pulling him along until he followed and lead her out of the room. I followed them back to the living room and watched the man lay Momma on the lounge. He held her hand and patted it gently, before asking the other two people to leave the room. They nodded and closed the door behind them.

Rifling in his pocket, he produced a shiny silver tin. He opened it, took out a syringe, flicked it with his finger twice and then pushed the bottom, making a tiny bit of the liquid inside squirt out.

"Please Lord, take care of your faithful servant. Help her find the peace in death that she couldn't in life."

The man inserted the needle into Momma's arm. She let out a long breath and closed her eyes.

"God bless you, holy man."

The room was lit up by the same golden light. I looked toward it still wanting to go into it when I felt a hand in mine. I turned to see my Momma as beautiful as she was the day I last saw her – before the robbers came.

"Momma!" I cry out happily.

"It's time to go play at the park, baby," she says with a big smile and lead me toward the light.

I used to think Halloween was scary, but it turned out that this Halloween was the best one ever because I got my Momma back.

Neysha Reeves is a mother, Journalist and Author. She lives beside a Pink Lake with her husband, 5 children and tiny Chihuahua.

SCHWINN VOYAGEUR

BY

JON ROBINSON

"Charlie," my mom yelled.

 She was calling my younger brother. He was upstairs, not far in our house, and wasn't coming down. I was on my way to the garage.

"Sullivan, what's your brother doing?" she asked.

I didn't really answer.

"Sull, did you hear me? Go get your brother," she repeated, "please."

"But," I said.

She looked at me. And, I turned towards the stairs.

"Thank you," she said.

Our steps are creaky and loud. Just walking up the stairs was like a little warning siren for Charlie, letting him know mom was serious. I heard him in our room, listening to nineties hip-hop. He's twelve, but loves my music. I hate that he thinks we "share" it, though. I pushed open our bedroom door. The music got louder and the artificial cheese smell of Cheetos hit my face.

"Hey, Mom wants you," I said.

He didn't reply, but just combed through his bangs with his hand.

"Charlie," I said, "mom wants you. Stop being an idiot."

"I'll be down in a minute," said Charlie, not looking at me.

"Dude, just go see Mom. Stop being so difficult all the time."

"Shut up," he said, getting off his bed and heading downstairs.

I walked to my dresser and grabbed a pen and my notebook. My grandma gave me the notebook after her trip to Japan. It was navy blue with red Japanese characters on its bottom left corner. "Voyageur," is how it translates to English. I take it on all my rides.

I turned off the speaker, walking back down our aching stairs. Mom was talking with Charlie, asking him what "the rappers" were saying and why he didn't come down at first. I tried to steer clear.

"Wait, Sull, now where are you going?" she said.

"The garage for a sec," I said, barely stopping.

"Why?" she said.

"I'll just be really quick," I said.

"We're leaving soon. At 7:30," she said.

"Okay," I said.

I left through the side door in our kitchen. It was quiet and not near-ly as hot from summer. The sun had started to go down. I booked it and finally made it to the dang garage.

"Hey Sull," my dad said, "you have a second?"

He was going to change the oil in our truck before we left. And, yeah, I had a second, but didn't want to give it. I looked towards my bike. He saw me.

"You know we're leaving in about twenty minutes?" he said.

"I know, I'll be quick," I said.

"You might want to pass on riding the bike tonight," he said.

"I'm not gonna go far," I said, looking at my bike again.

"Okay, but we're not waiting up, Sull. And, tomorrow I want to show you how to do this, okay?" he said, raising a jug of motor oil.

"Okay," I nodded, already reaching towards my Schwinn.

I shoved my pen behind my ear and rolled my notebook so it would fit in my back pocket. It wasn't as stiff as it used to be when my grand-ma first gave it to me. I wheeled my bike out of the garage, jumping on as soon as I hit the driveway. I didn't sit, I just pressed the pedals and started rolling.

I live in a pretty rural area, but I like it. Like it reminds me of ancient Tokyo or something. And this bike. My parents got me this thing when I was thirteen. I've probably ridden it every day since. Well, when I can. I got about a half-mile down in and turned right.

Carlisle Road. It's an older, unfinished path of dirt, rock, and gravel. A few houses speckle the land surrounding it. The sun was getting lower, oranger, and shining through the trees. I hooked a left off Carlisle and onto Jefferson Ave. The road is paved about a quarter mile in. Makes for smoother, faster rides.

I hit the pavement and rode just a bit further. I like the way the trees line Jefferson. They're a whole mix. Tall and skinny with barely any branches. Or, some look like Christmas trees, those are spruces. All of them looked orange from the setting sun. I heard birds chirping and squirrels shuffling from tree to tree. Occasionally I saw a deer on one of my rides. My grandma said she saw a bear on Jefferson once. I'm not sure I believe that. I turned left, back onto a dirt road. It doesn't have a street sign, but pretty much everyone calls it Creek Street.

I took the path fast, bumps and all. It dumps out at a man-made boat launch. The name comes from this river. It's my favorite spot. I set my bike against one of the tall, skinny trees, and pulled out my notebook. I flipped to the first page, like I always do, and sat cross-legged next to the water. The river was a pink-orange with the last rays of sunlight.

My grandma had written across the top: "Life's a voyage. Around every turn, another adventure. For Sullivan. 2011." I said her words in my mind, turning the pages until I came to the next blank entry, and I wrote:

> *September 26th, 2015*
>> *Went on a ride today. Made it to Creek St. pretty quickly.*
>> *Oh, and Charlie's being an idiot. What's new?*
>> *Dad's gonna show me how to change the oil tomorrow . . .*
>> *Missing grandma today.*

I finished writing the day's "voyage," and looked back at my grandma's words. Then, closing the notebook, I stared at the Japanese characters. I decided I should get back home before my family left. I began refolding the notebook, and stood up to stretch. I don't know what happened, though. I started to slide the journal into my back pocket, but dropped it. It fell right out of my hand and into the river.

I swallowed hard. The current was already moving the notebook downstream, and I knew I shouldn't have gone on this ride when I only had twenty minutes. Now it would take even longer to get home because I had to get this dumb notebook. Okay, well, it's not dumb.

I ran ahead of where the journal was floating, and waded into the first few inches of water. This part of the river was narrow and not too deep. The current was slowing too, so the book floated about ten feet away. A branch was to my left, sticking off a dying tree. I ripped it off, and tried reaching for the book. My shoes and ankles were soaked. I was getting hot. The branch kept grazing and tapping the side of the notebook as I reached for it, nudging it millimeters further away. I growled out of frustration.

Finally. The branch caught the binding's ridge. Slowly, carefully, I drug the notebook closer until I could snatch it out of the river. But by then, it was really dark. I sloshed my way back to the bike and shook my legs, trying to dry them. I stared at the notebook. The cover was soaked and the inside pages were bleeding ink. I closed my eyes, breathing through my nose. I whipped a rock at the river.

I rolled the book, slipping it in my back pocket. I wrenched my bike from the tree and jumped on. I zipped back to Jefferson and curved right, then sped to Carlisle. It was dark, and I didn't know how long I'd been gone, but I thought maybe my family hadn't left. I turned onto my street and stopped pedaling, coasting into my driveway. I got off and opened my garage. Our car was gone.

I shoved the bike against the wall. The oil jug fell off the work table, but didn't spill. I left it there. I went back into the house. Empty. I went to my room, and saw the time on my clock. 8:15 p.m. I pulled out my notebook, which was practically molded into a fold now because of the water. I threw it on the ground. I turned on my music and sat on my bed.

After about three songs had played, I heard the doors open downstairs. Everyone was talking. I turned up the music. The stairs creaked. I closed my eyes. My door started sneaking open, and I sighed, waiting to be scolded for being gone for way too long.

"Why! That how you treat my notebook these days?" she said.

I darted my eyes to where I'd thrown the notebook, and then back to the voice at the door.

"Wha-" I said, smiling, teeth and all.

"I was surprised not to see you at the airport, Sullivan," she said, raising her eyebrows.

"I went for a ride, Grandma," I told her, "I was seizing the day, ya know?"

"I bet you were," she said, smiling, "now come downstairs, I've got something for you."

I knew she'd understand.

"Okay," I said.

Jonathon Robinson is a freelance writer, editor, and creative living near Detroit, MI. He loves exploring life on this good, good earth with his family and friends.

GOODBYE GRANDPA

BY

MARK ROBYN

Today we shot and killed Grandpa. I know that really sounds cruel and like not a very nice thing to do, but believe me, it really was for the best.

You see, Grandpa just wasn't very happy, though he tried his best not to show it.

It wasn't that Grandpa didn't enjoy being a werewolf; he loved it. He always had the loudest howl on nights of the full moon and led the pack when we chased people through the moors.

In fact, Grandpa said being werewolves was an important part of our cultural heritage. Our history dates back to the 1800s when Grandpa's great-great grandfather, Claus Zuckerman, was bitten while hunting deer in the Black Forest. Grandpa was the one who said we should move back to Germany so that we could feast on our own type and keep the bloodline pure. Grandpa loved being a member of the pack; it was a source of great pride for him. He even kept the heads and hands of some of the more prominent people he'd eaten in his study mounted on the wall, and all you had to do was ask and he'd gladly tell you all about them.

So, what's the problem, you ask? What would make us think that we needed to put poor Grandpa out of his misery? Just this: Grandpa was just getting a little long in the fang.

It wasn't that his spirit wasn't willing or that he didn't feel the howl deep down inside; it was simply that his worn out old body just couldn't keep up with the pack anymore. The call of the wild for Grandpa had turned into the whimper of the tired and worn out.

I'll give you some examples of what I'm talking about. Lately when we all gathered for howling sessions, Grandpa would be right there at the head of the choir, howling at the top of his lungs and having a great time. After a few minutes though, his voice would start to crack and he would run out of breath. He'd start to sound like an empty bagpipe, and his face would turn red from the effort. I felt so embarrassed for him, especially the one time he fell to the ground gasping and out of breath. When it would happen, we'd all try to look the other way and act as if we hadn't noticed, but it really was beginning to ruin it for everybody else.

Then there was the whole eating thing. Ever since Grandpa got false fangs, when he would gnaw on an arm or a leg, he would have real, serious problems. We'd all be munching away happily, and he'd start complaining that his was too tough or old, even when we gave him the juiciest and softest villagers. Finally, they gave me the job of cutting up his meat for him, because I was only ten and they still called me a pup. It was humiliating for both of us. It was even worse later, when I had to put the body parts in a blender so he could drink them with a straw. I could tell how much it hurt Grandpa to watch the others chomp and chew with relish while he slurped. And the time he left his false fangs at home and didn't realize it until he tried to maul the local priest and ended up only giving him a nice gum massage! It would have been hilarious, if it wasn't so downright embarrassing.

It was even worse on the nightly hunt. When we'd start, Grandpa would be right in front, teeth bared and snarling, eager as a young pup full of fire and brimstone. He'd look just like he did in the old days when he was the terror of the village. But after an hour or so, he'd start to fall behind. Soon he'd be holding his side and walking. We'd try to slow down so he could catch up, but it was beginning to be a real downer.

He'd swear that he'd be right behind us, just go ahead and don't worry about him, so, we'd reluctantly leave him. I always hung back and waited for him. Sometimes it would be hours before he would catch up, and often he wouldn't come at all. We'd find him on our way back, on his back snoring, oblivious to the World. I was always worried that he was going to be shot by a villager, snagged in a steel trap or caught by some traveling Gypsy and end up as a sideshow act in a circus; until he grew too old even for that, and they made a wolf skin rug out of him.

The next day after a hunt, poor Grandpa would be so sore that he couldn't even get out of bed. It was left to me, of course, to feed him, and change him and empty his bedpan, and he'd be cranky as old Frankenstein's monster the whole time. It was at least three days after a hunt before Grandpa started feeling chipper again, and then all he'd do was complain about how cold and drafty it was in the house or ask why the house had to have so many stairs. It got to where we'd all avoid him so we wouldn't have to hear about how his gout was acting up or his stomach acid was eating him alive.

One day when we were all out hunting, we couldn't find Grandpa at all. I searched and searched, and finally located him. He was cowering in a corner of the bakery. Fat, old Mrs. Frankfurter stood over him, threatening him with a rolling pin. I was able to convince her to let him go, but only after buying a dozen sweet rolls and a Bundt cake.

I had to keep an eye on him all the time lately, especially after I caught him once curled up in the corner of Mr. Fuchs's study next to the fireplace, snoring away; and sitting in his lap, purring, was Mr. Fuchs's cat!

Then there was the time he got lost on Baalsdorfer Street and had to ask directions of the local constable. You see, Grandpa's eyesight wasn't what it used to be, either. Once I caught him ripping the stuffing out of a pillow in Mrs. Biermann's bedroom, and all the while she was taking a shower in the bathroom ten feet away, singing an awful tune at the top of her lungs. After I finally convinced him it wasn't her, I helped him make a meal out of her, but it took him three whole days to stop spitting goose feathers out of his mouth.

Grandpa used to be the leader of the pack, the Alpha male. He was the fiercest wolf of all, big, mean and fast, with fangs that glistened in the moonlight and brought terror, not just to the villagers, but to most of us too. When Grandpa came around, tails tucked between legs and werewolves laid down, their heads between their paws. No one would dare cross him, unless they wanted to be nursing a nipped ear or sore bite on the behind. I was so proud of him; I wanted to be just like my Grandpa. Villagers used to be scared of Grandpa too. When he would show even a tip of his tail, out would come the torches, Wolf bane and silver bullets.

But lately things have begun to change; werewolves laugh at him behind his back, and even worse, they challenge him to his face. It's just downright heartbreaking to see him slink off and then to see them chuckle, with smug looks on their muzzles. I want to bite their faces off, but I'm still too young. I'll remember though, and someday they will pay.

The bad thing is, the villagers have changed their attitudes to

Grandpa too. Now when they see him, they point and say, 'there goes that big, shaggy dog again'. One night I saw little Amy Krause patting Grandpa on the head. And he was licking her hand!

Dad was the one who first suggested that we put poor Grandpa out of his misery. At first, we all howled bloody murder and Dad let the subject die. But then there came the nail that sealed the vampire's coffin lid. Grandpa was even later than usual one night, so Dad sent me back to check on him. What I saw, well, I'll never forget it, though I sure wish I could. I found Grandpa all right; he was using a cane and being helped across the street by a little, old, white haired Mrs. Fassbinder!

When I told Dad, he sat us down in a circle and convinced us that putting Grandpa down was really for the best.

Poor Grandpa; we'll miss him. He'll always have a special place in our hearts. Or I should really say, in our stomachs. Grandpa sure tasted good.

Mark Robyn lives in Tacoma, Washington in the shadow of Mt. Rainier. He is currently working on many projects, including a young adult novel, a play and screenplay.

AN UNEXPECTED DEMON

BY
ZACH ROGERS

"Perhaps you wish to make a deal, hmmm?" The demon leered down at Tren, who peered curiously at it over her third cup of coffee this morning. When Tren frowned slightly, the demon cheerfully continued. "Ah, sorry, but that won't be happening. Your father promised me his firstborn, and that is you. I will have many uses for you, don't worry."

"Fascinating," Tren muttered, taking a sip.

"What?" said the demon, slightly put off. There was usually more weeping and screaming at this point.

"Hmm? Oh, yeah, not happening. You have no rights to me."

"Denial will get you nowhere," it said.

"Not denial. An understanding of modern custody laws and historical precedents."

"What?" said the demon again, even more off balance.

"People sold their children off ages ago because they could," said Tren. "Until they came of age, children were legally their parent's property. Females often remained their parents property until married, and then they were the husband's. Which is seven kinds of fucked up, personally. Modern law is different. Parents have a duty of care, and cannot legally violate it. Even though that does give them a fair number of options, selling your child is not legally supported anymore."

"I care not for your petty mortal laws!" screamed the demon.

Tren shook her head, and placed her mug down on her kitchen counter. "Of course you do. You're a manifestation of human consciousness, initiated when laws allowed certain things. The laws now do not, humans don't really think that way, and you're out of your time."

"Silence! I am ageless, immortal! Beyond time and life and light!" roared the demon, raising its arms in the air as a cloud of darkness swelled behind it.

"No," said an unimpressed Tren. "We know how the universe began. Demons not included. We know how humanity evolved. We know how big the universe is, and how insignificant we are. Do you involve yourself with other species? Other planets or cultures in other galaxies?"

"...What's a galaxy?" said the now terminally confused demon, lowering its arms.

"Yeah, I thought so."

She took a deep breath, and grabbed a choc-chip cookie from the jar on the counter.

"The visible stars we see are suns, and they are barely a fraction of the stars in our own galaxy, one of billions of galaxies. The majority have planets. While they may not be anywhere near enough to talk to, there are almost certainly other intelligent races out there. The idea that the universe was created just for humanity, that more matter and energy than we can conceive by a dozen orders of magnitude was spent just to give us a pretty back-drop when looking up is ludicrous."

"You know none of this," she continued, gesturing with the cookie, "because you are a product of a time when this was not known or understood. And I use product literally. You're a manifestation of human thought, entirely created by us. Which has fascinating implications. None of them good for you though. I wonder if you have a persistent existence, or are only called into being for encounters like this?"

The demon said nothing. The mortal's words were nonsense, yet hit like jagged blades.

"Do you remember all of your existence?" Tren continued, taking a bite of cookie. "All the times you are not here? Or is it sort of an assumption, a memory in your head of where you come from? Both are intriguing possibilities. You either only exist here and now, but potentially maintain some sort of externally-stored persistent memory, or you are not the only manifestation of human belief, but an entire additional sub-layer of reality is too. Thought that may be giving us too much credit."

The demon opened its fanged mouth, and paused. What did it remember of its home? Flames, screams, the red light. But...nothing concrete. No real details. Just a place in its mind that was an assumption, a "Of course Hell is real, now don't think of it anymore".

It shuddered. The mortal's madness was infecting it. It snarled, and raised its claws.

"Don't be rude," said Tren, pointing at it with the cookie.

Something shivered over the demon. An icy fist clamped onto its arm.

"What?" it stammered.

"You are a manifestation of human will. But I don't think many people know that. You turn up, they think "Oh no, demons are real" and bam. Of course you are. But if I say you only exist here and now because I'm thinking of it, then I own you. Or at least I think I do, which is much the same in the end."

The demon's glowing eyes swelled, and swivelled in their sockets. It couldn't move.

"Hey, can you grant wishes? I mean, you must have the ability to do something to get people to offer you souls." said Tren, nibbling a chocolate piece out of the cookie's edge.

She froze suddenly.

"Hey... What the hell did my dad trade his firstborn for?"

The demon glared at her, hatred and fear filling its face.

She stared at it, unamused and unimpressed.

"Answer," she said, in a voice of bored certainty.

Something twisted within the demon's mind, and its mouth opened.

"A 1984 Kawasaki Ninja!" it gasped.

"That bike he trashed when I was 5?!" Tren shouted. "Ugh. Way to go, dad."

She finished her cookie, and was about to reach for a second when she stopped.

"Get me a cookie," she said. "One of those really awesome ones that the cafe down the street makes."

The demon blurred and vanished. A second later, it returned, the jar of cookies that usually adorned the cafe's front counter in its claws.

Distantly, Tren heard someone screaming.

"Huh. Ok, this may take some getting used to. But don't worry!" she said, smiling widely. "I see a loooong, bright future ahead for us."

There may have been a tear glowing hotly in the corner of the demon's eye. This was the worst attempt at soul collecting since it had tried to claim Theodore Roosevelt.

Zach Rogers is a science fiction and fantasy writer living in Brisbane, Australia. He lives with their partner Meredith, and their dog Axton.

TEN YEARS GONE

BY

PHIL ROSSI

I already told Snapper I wasn't making any pickups at the Holiday Inn. Protocol in the cab business states the dispatcher is the boss, and he tells the drivers where to go. Not tonight. In one of the hotel ballrooms, my high school class was holding our ten-year reunion.

On work-release and driving a cab for Comet Taxi, I wasn't in the mood to advertise my flunked-out life. My classmates would be left wondering how far I'd fallen as we collided at the taxi stand, in lieu of the open bar. Thanks, but no thanks.

Decades have habits of grinding out and showing up early drove me. My ten-year goal was to spit through this night like a missile, and make a big shot splash. Just like Janis Joplin, blasting into hers as a rock star.

The Facebook page posted the reunion from seven to eleven. Once I got into my shift with the cab, Snapper did right, feeding me calls nowhere near the Holiday Inn. The anxiety eased and I forgot all about the reunion. It was already past midnight when I returned from an out of town fare.

"Pick up at Lionel's Cafe. They gotta lady goin' down to the train station," Snapper said over the tablet.

Rolling up to Lionel's Cafe, I spotted a huddle of smokers in the parking lot. Ten years in the tank, and despite the bald heads and husky frames, I fingered my old schoolmates. The reunion wrapped up at the ballroom and splintered off to Lionel's. *Great.* I let Snapper know I arrived.

"I'm a little busy right now. Go inside and announce yourself," he said.

Yeah, right--when hell freezes over. I used my cell to tip Lionel's management to tell my fare the bird they ordered was at the curb. I then watched Juanita Martinez leave the cafe, stir up my butterflies and approach the cab.

An old crush and classmate, Juanita didn't give a duck's ass I skipped the reunion to drive a taxi. She told me what a snooze I missed. Gossip, hookups, and bloated fables. The rest remained inside Lionel's, playing power ballads over the jukebox.

I didn't get into my *since we left high school* story. The liftoff, crash, and shame. How I siphoned capital gains, snarfed Doctor Feelgood's stash, and burned down the fast lane. Once the high life spit me out, I was fried to pieces, strung-out, and buzzed in to face fraud charges.

The hearing showed a heart full of soul and commuted my sentence to a halfway house. I followed a curfew and scored a job washing dishes. A square deal compared to prison, where the boy scouts are known to bite your ears off.

"I wish you would have called. I wanted to help," Juanita said.

She was a big time lawyer in the city. Married, junior partner, then divorced, Juanita tumbled through the rocks herself. What the reunion taught me, is beneath the working man's sun, the picks and shovels get heavy for everybody.

I told Juanita I appreciated her concern and asked her to let it go. I'm done with drugs and running scams out of boiler rooms. Driving a taxi on overnights forces you to think a bit. Mainly about how you got here, and the downtime you need to plot your escape.

"Call me, or e-mail. We could meet for drinks, coffee, whatever," Juanita said while passing me her business card. I told her I would as we reached the train station.

I anchored the cab and watched Juanita slip into the terminal. I wasn't too concerned about what might happen between us, or might not.

More determined to do something with myself, no matter the caseload and price. All on the straight, with no shortcuts or monkey business. I punched the gas, lighting off for the promise of the near future, and a fresh start for the next ten years.

A fiction writer and short filmmaker from northern New Jersey. Phil's fiction has appeared in various e-zines and anthologies.

A MEDITATION ON MEDITATION

BY

SCOTT RUBENSTEIN

Someone once said, there's no such thing as quiet.

But there's something called, quieter. One eliminates the detritus of sound. The cars going to and from work. The neighbors arguing about arguing. The electronic world strutting its stuff.

And then I listen to myself breathing. The breeze softly playing nature's xylophone.

Ever so softly, my breath begins to harmonize with the breeze. Not an ohm. I've never been that deep. But a soft genetic sound. Suddenly I hear my dead's parent's sound.

They must have had this moment, too. We harmonize.
Each of us with a different voice but the same
sound. And then other voices join in. I don't know who they are.
But they seem to know me. And the sounds become louder
And louder.

And for a brief moment I know what quiet is.

Scott Rubenstein is a comedy writer/accountant who's been writing poetry all his life. His poem is A Meditation on Meditation. Using neither comedy nor numbers.

SCHOOLGIRL DREAD

BY

ROB SANTANA

"I'll turn his face into a Jackson Pollock painting!" I howled at the HD screen. The TV newscaster had launched into telling the Breaking News. My eight year-old daughter's kidnapper, John Roach, was free. I gazed at his pock marks, his thinning hair and downcast eyes, the cameras clicking away like a photo frenzy in Cannes.

The bastard was free.

"Eddie, calm down." My wife Jackie said. But the way her fingers gripped the sofa's arms betrayed her composure. If looks could kill, indeed. The timing could not have been worse, the way it happened six months ago.

And the way it happened went against everything I believed a solid gang and drug-free neighborhood, a community where you could walk the streets safely at night, should be. How naïve.

Sabrina, our daughter, had been snatched like a ring in a merry-go-round by Roach and was pulled into his damaged Chevy. It happened so quickly the school's bus driver hadn't noticed. Right there on the curb, just ten yards from the school. Amazing. Just like that. Little Girl Gone. *My* little girl. The only witness, a crossing guard, managed a glimpse of the horror, but her mind registered 'kidnap' and she dialed nine-one-one.

What were the odds of a midday kidnapping taking place the *exact* moment the victim's father is waylaid by a drunk driver? The souse who ran the red light had ground my hips into oatmeal. Meantime, the scumbag who took my little girl had parked his car into a wooded area unfit for insects. This had all taken place the same day. It astonishes me still.

The police were at Jackie's doorstep a half-hour after the swipe. Ten minutes later she had called the emergency room where I lay clueless and traumatized.

She gave me the bad news first: Our little girl has been kidnapped by an "alleged" pedophile.

Good news: the 'pedophile' dropped off Sabrina at a street nearest our home, then turned himself in. How strange. But 'Saby' was alive and well.

Months passed after the arrest.

During that time all I could think about was my daughter's brief encounter with Roach. I became obsessed by it. Before the incident, our only child displayed exuberance, curiosity, and affection. Since that harrowing day, she would come home from school and dodge Jackie's touchy-feely salutations. My arrivals from work were met with broody silence.

Despite Roach's claim that he never laid a hand on Saby, and the police report that confirmed it, I knew, I somehow *knew*, that something went down in that car; something so mind-bending it caused Saby to refuse my pleas for a sit-down.

"Ed, the tests came out negative. Stop this." Jackie implored. Sure, no traces of semen or bodily trauma. Let the bastard sweat it out in jail while his suck-ass lawyer finds a loophole.

And sure enough he did.

And now the man who ruined my daughter's life was free on a technicality. A dumb rookie cop had forgotten to read the creep his rights.

That, coupled with lack of 'real' evidence, sent Roach home. I shot to my feet, turned off the TV, and pulled on my leather jacket. I knew where Roach lived.

"Where are you going, Eddie?"

She blocked my path to the door. "Ed, you need to get over this. The man gave himself up.

He never touched her! What do you plan to do, beat his brains in?"

How could I make her understand? This was *retribution*.

Perhaps my forgiving wife didn't catch what I thought to be a subtle smirk on Roach's face. She planted her skinny frame against the door like a soccer goalie.

"Eddie, please! You have a family and a job to think about."

I thought about it and made no move to shove her aside. I called out my daughter's name instead. Later for protocol. "Sabrina? Come out here! Now!"

In moments Sabrina stood before us wearing her pink pajamas. I wondered if she would ever smile again. I cleared my throat.

"From your own lips, baby. Tell me what happened in that car. Don't avoid me this time." She glanced at her mother, who nodded.

"He…"

"He what…"

"Showed me a picture of Amy."

"Who's Amy?"

"His daughter. She's dead."

Jackie covered her mouth.

"He said I looked just like her. And I did! He showed me her photo. She was seven. He told me how much he missed Amy and pretended I was her, how last year he forgot to tell her to buckle up before the truck driver hit his car.

He saw me come out of the school one day and parked in front of it for a week, watching me. His wife left him. He was so ashamed he didn't tell the police about it. Only that he never touched me, which he didn't."

"Sweetie, why didn't you tell us this before?" I asked, forming a mental image of Sabrina and Amy side by side.

"He made me promise never to tell anyone how Amy died. He looked so sad."

I felt a twinge of disappointment. It would've felt so damn good hammering Roach's face.

Rob's work has been published by, The Story Shack, HP Lovecraft Lunatic Asylum, StreetWrite.com, Creativity Webzine, Short Story Me, Centum Press. His two feature films have screened at various festivals.

THURSDAY AFTERNOON

BY

LAURA SCHEINER

Jimmy hated broccoli, he hated spinach and homework and baths. But he loved TV, especially series like *The Rifleman* and *Gunsmoke*. He could sit for hours watching those old shows about the old west.

Which is what he was doing on Thursday afternoon when he should've been watching his sister, Carrie, who was doing something (probably with dolls), somewhere (probably someplace she shouldn't be like their parent's closet).

"Jimmy! Come here!" Carrie shrieked.

Damn! It was at the best part – right when the Rifleman and the bad guy were having a showdown. And Jimmy refused to miss it, not just to get Carrie's doll out of the toilet or whatever dumb thing she needed him to do. She couldn't do anything by herself. She needed help opening and closing things, reaching things, turning things on and off, getting on and off things. He wasn't that helpless when he was four.

"Jimmmmmmy! I need you!"

"Not now, Carrie."

On the screen the men faced each other. The music grew more ominous. The time had come. Jimmy jumped off the couch determined to outdraw them both. He got in his showdown stance – hand hovering inches above his holster, eyes trained on the hands of the two men on TV. Carrie continued to call him, but he was too focused to respond. He wished he had a rifle like Lucas McCain, he wished his toy pistols

243

shot real bullets. He wished there still was a "wild west" where he could be sheriff. He wanted to be a policeman when he grew up so he'd get to carry a gun and if he was lucky, he'd shoot a bad guy one day. Most of the cops in town seemed to spend all their time giving out speeding tickets. That wouldn't do for Jimmy. He wanted real action, real danger, real blood and gore.

The gunshot was so loud Jimmy's heart practically leapt out of his chest. He grabbed his guns from the holster and shot at the screen. *Bang! Bang! Bang! Bang!* When he stopped shooting he noticed that the Rifleman and the bad guy were still staring each other down.

Jimmy looked around confused. Carrie was no longer calling. He wondered what she had broken this time. It must have been something pretty big to make a noise that loud. And he knew from experience he'd get in more trouble than she would – because she was only four and he was supposed to be keeping her out of trouble. He couldn't wait until he wouldn't have to watch her anymore.

"What did ya do this time, Dummy?" he asked as he climbed the stairs.

She was on the landing in a pool of blood. It looked almost black against the beige carpet. Somehow, without any help she had unlocked the cabinet, got their father's gun, inserted the bullets. Somehow the gun had gone off. Jimmy finally had the real blood and gore he craved. It was the worst wish that ever came true.

Laura Scheiner is a screenwriter and story consultant. Her credits include the award-winning "Janie Charismanic".

FOUL AND FAIR

BY

TIM SHERF

One fairly foul morning, Drab Street was somewhat busier than usual. This wasn't difficult to accomplish, since Drab Street was usually as empty as a miser's heart. Truth to tell, Drab Street was little more than a half-sized alleyway putting on pretenses by way of calling itself a street. Amidst the muck and broken bits of odds and ends piled on either side of the lane, a few tufts of foxglove had somehow managed to bloom. The blood red flowers hung limply in the weak light and poor soil, a garish choice for the only color to be seen in such a dismal scene. It was the kind of place one ended up in only by accident or through some arcane knowledge passed down by those in need of a dark, dingy, and--well--drab little street.

The crowd trudging down the street this morning consisted of one individual shrouded in an enormous raincoat and wheeling a squeaking grocery cart. Midway down the block, the cart rattled to a stop, and the figure peered intently into the gloom to her left and right. Apparently satisfied by the bits of rubbish and heaps of trash strewn about, she reached up and pulled back the hood of her raincoat, revealing her identity to the shadows and boarded up windows. The foxgloves' poisonous red blooms added a lurid touch, she thought. The flowers had other names, too—"dead men's bells" and "bloody fingers" amongst them. Fitting, she thought. No sense in getting morbid though. Plenty of time for that later.

Amphiba, as she was known to the few vagrants who occasionally and quickly crossed her path, let out a deep, weary sigh. She was almost finished. It had taken weeks to get this far, or maybe months, she realized. Time was a bit more blurry now than it once had been. Years of spells and tricks and blood. But that would change soon enough. Now that the three were almost ready.

The inventory then, and quick about it. No sense in squandering what time she did have. She scrunched her eyebrows in thought, rehearsing lines of a spell last used lifetimes ago. Lifetimes, she thought, and paused again without realizing it. The thought dazed her, lulling and pulling her away from her own urgency like an insistent undertow. Distracted, she scratched her head and absently patted at her wiry hair which was sticking out belligerently.

Amphiba was proud of her hair's greenish hue. She nurtured it and encouraged the strange color through her own personally developed regimen of natural oils and assorted mineral agents. Negligent about most other things regarding her appearance, Amphiba had carefully cultivated her hair's coloring until achieving its current patina somewhere between moldy and mossy.

Below this verdant halo, her potato sack of a dress was wrinkled and soiled and rather lumpy, like she had forgotten to remove the potatoes before donning it. What had appeared to be a raincoat at first glance was really a witch's cloak of sorts, with a multitude of inner pockets that Amphiba had begun rifling through while talking to herself.

"Fillet of a fenny snake,
In the cauldron boil and bake."

She patted one pocket which squelched loudly and then sighed balefully. "Sorry, my dear. Had to be done. Nothing for it." Her bulging green eyes rolled upward in a sorrowful look, but soon shifted into a squinting look of determination. "We'll see you served justice soon enough."

"Eye of newt and toe of frog."

Two more pockets checked and secured, then a soft whisper into two others.

"Wool of bat and tongue of dog."

A crafty glint shined in her eye as she thought of the merry chase those particular ingredients had led her on. And the look on that hound's face! Grinning, she reached in two more pockets to pull out two small vials.

"Adder's fork and blind-worm's sting."

Maybe a trouble for some to get these particulars, but not for Amphiba, she thought with a smirk, slipping them carefully back into their pockets.

But her smirk turned quickly to a scowl as she reached simultaneously in two pockets. One hand pulled out something soft and warm, though not alive. The other hand held something cool, slimy, and squirming. Her fingers dropped the owl's wing back into her pocket and went automatically to soothe the writhing creature held delicately in her other hand. It was a salamander, shiny black with bright orange spots about its ribcage. It moved about on her hand restlessly as she tried in vain to calm its agitation. The cause was obvious enough. An open, raw wound ran along the front side of the creature, pink and fresh. She still felt its pain. She had put it off as long as she could, but in the end, she could find no way around it.

Over the years, Amphiba had learned not to name the creatures. That only made it harder to face the inevitable, which was what brought her here, today, to this forsaken alley in a tangle of back streets and broken lives. One more ingredient for the cauldron. One more item off the list.

As much as she didn't want to admit it, this would be a hard one to see through. She didn't lose sleep over the crying, not yet. But it unsettled her, that look in their eye. The knowledge that such a thing could not be undone. Somewhere deep within, Amphiba could feel not so much a change, but maybe a shift. She couldn't quite identify it. Couldn't pin it down like the owl she had so swiftly dispatched or the bat she had snatched from the sky. But it was there, just as sure as those swift heartbeats she had snuffed out without a second's pause.

And now this. She shook her head in the darkness, a shapeless figure in the gloom waging a silent war.

And then a bell. Chiming somewhere in the distance. Three times. Followed by the sound of slow, shuffling footsteps.

Amphiba lifted the salamander to her lips, murmuring comforting sounds to both of them as a shape emerged at the other end of the alley. A woman, pregnant and clearly in pain. Arriving just as expected.

Examining the shift that was occurring inside her, Amphiba wondered if she would be able to follow through with what she had been sent here to do. The iron pit of resolve within her left little doubt as to the outcome; yet there was a glimmer. Faint, but undeniable.

One hand slipped the dark wounded creature back into a deep pocket. Its sacrifice was already made, though more was required from her this day. Her eyebrows furrowed, betraying the hesitation she felt, even as her other hand dipped into a different pocket and emerged slowly, gripping a knife, small but sharp enough for its edge to catch a gleam even in the dusky half-light of the alley.

The woman was slumped against the wall now, her strength all but failing. Amphiba knew what needed to be done. The words came out murmured, unbidden, as she took the next steps toward her destiny.

"Finger of birth-strangled babe,
Ditch-deliver'd by a drab."

"Who's there?" the woman barely managed to get the words out as Amphiba slowly covered the distance between them. "Can you help me? Please."

"The child. Whose?" Bluntness, she had learned, was best in these matters. Quick and over. Not easy. Never easy. But done.

"Mine," the woman whispered fiercely. She was sweating profusely, sickly pale in the wan yellow light. But her protectiveness touched something in Amphiba. Something she had thought long gone.

"Yours and whose?" A name didn't matter, but the answer did. She had to be sure or the mission would be unsuccessful, the ingredients unfit.

"Mine," the woman answered.

No husband, then. Confirmation enough that the babe fit the description of the spell. Of course it did. Her sisters were never wrong.

She took another step toward the woman, who was beginning to realize no help would come from this strange cloak figure in the dark alley of Drab Street. She scrambled and kicked further back into the ditch she was half slumped in, churning up the soil and uprooting the foxgloves in the process. The effort was too much for her. Her eyes glazed over and darkness took her.

Later, the woman awoke to the sound of her baby's cries. The child was wrapped in a warm cloth, tucked safely in her arms, with only slight bruising from where the mother's cord had wrapped around its neck during delivery. The woman wept quietly while humming a soft lullaby to her child.

Down in the shadows at the end of Drab Street, a stem of the uprooted foxgloves was tucked deep inside a cloak. Amphiba smiled a small smile and whispered in the darkness, *"Finger of birth-strangled babe, Ditch-deliver'd by a drab."* Not exactly what the spell called for, but it was a shift she was willing to accept.

Tim C. Sherf is a high school English teacher and play director in downriver Detroit, MI where he lives with his incredible wife and wonderful children. He is currently working on the first book of a YA fantasy adventure series.

TWO TOYS

BY

NEHA SHRIVASTAVA

The cliché *boys will be boys* worked little to calm me. The noise, the tugging and pulling for attention became so suffocating I walked out of the house to catch a breath. Closed my eyes and my whole system looked like a red light shown in movies, as a symbol of danger or explosion. I was going to explode. Must not do it near my house! I peered into the doorway, the noise was still on.... "Leaving for some grocery shopping." I was gone before anybody could follow me.

The jeep's wheel showed I was still in control of some things in life! I wheeled it slowly and rested back, shut off the music, wanting no noise. I pulled into the mall parking, slowly backing up, oblivious to the car honking madly behind me. Tuned off as I was, I glared at the young teenager and shouted, "Aren't you going to park too, or is it your first drive? You know it takes those two minutes." The poor boy just looked down; he had encountered another mom in the mall. One in the house was enough.

Just like a zombie I waded aimlessly in the malls brightly lighted shops, walked in a coffee shop. I waited for the attendant to finish his job explaining the infinite options offered, then asked ordered a plain coffee. The tone in my voice didn't allow discussion of any more of his unbeatable offers. Where had all my happiness gone, why was I so grumpy all the time?

The strong smell of coffee reminded me of items I needed to buy for the kitchen, home. Determined not to hurry, I prolonged the coffee. Closing my eyes, my mind went from a blank to a vision of my son's naughty smile. Some minutes of my 'own' space and coffee did the magic. I jumped up, paid the boy a little tip with a smile. I purposefully walked towards a toy shop, bought a game for two. Then walked towards the electronic gizmo shop and looked about helplessly. A familiar face came up to me, "Aunty! You look lost, can I help you?" It was the boy I screamed at in the parking, "Sorry I was honking so much, but I wanted to be first in the movie ticket line." I saw his point. I too apologized.

Drove back home. Entered our house to see a glass broken, scrabble game pieces scrambled all over the place. This time I didn't lose my cool. Even the blaring music didn't break my cool, "I've got toys for whoever cleans up this mess," I negotiated. The statement had an electrifying effect on the two. Both boys made the house look like a 5 star home in minutes.

Gave our son the game he had been asking for a long time, I had avoided getting it as I would have to play with him. He jumped up and looked up as if questioning, "Mamma will play?" My nod was the key to his happiness. It wasn't the toy my son wanted, but my time. He had got both now.

My husband also got his toy, he had wanted for a long time and we had avoided buying such an expensive phone. My husband is a man of small needs with no other wants or indulgence. He looked up and his eyes gleamed, "So you bought it? Isn't it a little out of our budget?" It was, but why budget our happiness all the time?

The toys had a cost difference of about twenty thousand! But there was no difference in the smile and happiness on the face of both my boys when they got their respective toys. Each one of us has a key to the world of happiness; it may be a movie ticket, music, a house, a little bit of 'own' space, intellectual reading, a very expensive gizmo or of course a toy! I learned each one has the right to go ahead and live life to the fullest without any 'but' and 'why'.

The toys broke sooner or later, but the memory of those smiles will never break from my mind. And I learned happiness on the face of my boys and two minutes of 'my own space' was my toy.

Creative Consultant. Full time Mom. Author of many short stories. Advertised for over 20 brands over 17 years. Finalist for the prestigious International Museo de Palabra Award. Volunteer to teach underprivileged children.

HELL HATH NO FURY

BY

CHRISTIAN MIKE SIMMONS

Walking down Bourbon Street, Terry Samuels and Selene Roberts held hands. Selene loved Terry in spite of all the rough patches they had endured. Terry knew that Selene would never leave him and decided it was time to talk about a future together. Suddenly, the twosome became hungry and decided to stop at a local restaurant for a bite to eat.

When they entered the restaurant, they noticed the dimly lit lights, the disco ball spinning over the center of the dining area, and the staff dressed in Victorian style clothing. Moments later, the waiter walked up to them in clothing reminiscent of Clark Gable's suit from *Gone with the Wind*. He smiled, greeted them, and then showed them to a table. The woman politely excused herself to freshen up in the restroom. Once inside, Selene pulled out her cell phone and made a call.

"Mom. Terry took me to this beautiful restaurant and we have been talking about our future together. I think he's going to propose. I'm so excited!" Selene's mother clearly heard the anticipation in her voice.

Minutes later, she hung up her cell phone and with a smile from ear to ear, she walked back to her table. She sat down and stared intently into Terry's eyes. The moment seemed to last for hours. Finally, she decided to break the silence.

"Are you going to say something or are we just going to sit here and stare at each other all afternoon?" She asked Terry.

Terry remained silent and still. Not sure how to handle it, Selene reached for his hand and shook it to get his attention. She stared in horror as Terry's head rolled off his shoulders and onto the floor. Blood shot out of his neck like a geyser. The sight rendered her speechless.

Immediately, the restaurant erupted in pure panic. Customers screamed as they ran out. Frightened employees stayed cowering in the back of the restaurant while the manager dialed 911.

An hour later, the police arrived and began questioning the patrons. No one saw or had heard anything out of the ordinary. Puzzled at the lack of eyewitnesses they turned to Selene who was shaken and crying.

"Did you witness anything strange? Do you have any idea who could have done this?" The young officer asked her.

"No. Neither of us had any enemies." The woman cried frantically.

The police instructed everyone to leave the restaurant when the coroner arrived. Once he determined the time and manner of death, he motioned for his assistants to place the body onto the gurney and put it into the ambulance parked outside.

Selene sat across the street from the restaurant. She stared at the officers as they placed Terry's body into the back of the ambulance. The slamming of the doors startled her out of her trance.

"Who would do such a thing and why?" She struggled to imagine how this could happen, with tears running down her face. "When I find that person he or she will know the *true meaning of pain!*"

She returned home to a two-story home on Chipman Street, plopped down in her easy chair, and turned on the news. Frustration began to invade her body as she listened to the several reports of police ineptitude. At the end of the newscast, the reporter told of a tip line for anyone who possessed information related to this grizzly attack.

"Grizzly attack?" She thought to herself. "Is that what you call it?"

Rage filled inside of her like a violent tsunami. "If they won't catch whoever did this, THEN I WILL!!!"

#

She decided to go out for a while to clear her mind. She noticed a family orientated restaurant called the *Peekaboo* and chose to dine there.

Once inside, Selene noticed the childish artwork, paint-splattered floors, and a huge jungle gym located in the center of the dining area.

As she sat down at her table to watch the children play, she began to recollect the memories of her own childhood. All the fun she had with her friends. She didn't have a care in the world.

Suddenly, she felt a tug on her arm. Snapping out of her trance, she looked to see a little girl in pigtails. The little girl wore a flowered white dress and had a smile that seemed to stretch for miles.

Moments later, a tall and obese man made his way behind a little girl. Without warning, he grabbed one of her arms and began to violently tug upon her. Selene saw the once happy little girl was now crying in pain.

"Let the nice young lady enjoy her food and you go play with the other kids, or we will leave now!" The large man demanded.

Selene saw that the obese man wore a green t shirt and blue jeans that were faded so badly they were anything but blue. She felt sorry for the little girl as she cried with each harsh tug by the obese man. Suddenly, Selene felt angry and knew she had to leave.

The next morning Selene woke up and turned on the news. She was shocked to learn that the obese man's death appeared to be in the same manner as the other victims in the other restaurants. Again, no one saw or heard anything out of the ordinary. The killer had struck again.

Without delay, she took a cab to the restaurant and saw an old familiar scene. The yellow tape that edged the crime scene, the patrons inside being questioned by police and a curious crowd outside looking in.

Once again the waitress recognized Selene, pointed at her. The police turn to see, but once again Selene had vanished.

On her way home from the restaurant, she picked up a newspaper. She read the front page where the killer was immortalized as the "Dine-In Killer".

Upon returning home, Selene searched for a pattern, clues, or anything that would help her catch this killer. Every theory she came up with led to a dead end. Then, just as she began to give up, paranoia rushed in and she was hit with an answer.

"The killer is stalking me." She thought to herself.

Armed with her new found knowledge, Selene devised a plan, one she felt confident would help her catch the killer. With a list of local restaurants, she look for a location to implement her plan. Toward the bottom of the list, she found the perfect one.

The next morning, Selene woke up and prepared herself for the trip to the "C-Me" restaurant located on the outskirts of town. With her plan thought out to the last detail, she was confident today she would have her revenge.

Little did she know, the police also devised a plan to catch the killer.

As she entered the restaurant, Selene's confidence rose as she noticed that the entire dining area was surrounded by mirrored walls with a romantic view of Paris overhead. Satisfied with the scenery, she sat down to eat.

At a far corner booth, Selene saw a young couple about to be seated. The woman wore a beautiful blue sequin dress while the man wore what was clearly an Armani knock-off. The woman excused herself to go to the bathroom, leaving her date seated alone.

Knowing in her heart what was unfolding in front of her eyes, her mind drifted back to recall her special night with her beloved Terry. Each scene played in her mind so vividly as if it happened only yesterday. Suddenly, she recalled how her special night turned into a night of horror. Her body tensed up, sweat rolled down her body like tiny waterfalls, as she remembered his head rolling on the floor.

Moments later, she heard a shriek. She instantly turn to the nearest mirrored wall in the hopes that she would discover the killer.

She stared at the image of herself holding the knife that dripped with blood. Not believing what she had seen, she quickly turned to another mirrored wall to find herself standing in front of the decapitated body holding the murder weapon. Quickly turning to the last two walls, she finally realized that the killer she wanted revenge on, the one she had stalked all those weeks, the one she made a trap for, was HERSELF!

Weeks later at the Delsym Institution for the Criminally Insane, Selene looked around her padded cell. Struggling to get out of her straight jacket, she found herself alone. Alone with her thoughts.

All of a sudden, she remembered Terry and the way he was before her special night. She remembered the torture and the abuse she suffered while remaining true to him. Night after night of not knowing which Terry she would see. As she relived each terrifying moment, she bore a sinister smile and whispered:

"NEVER AGAIN!"

Christian is a forty two year old writer of serial killer short stories. His ultimate goal is to become a full time freelance writer.

HAPPY HOURS

BY

FIONA SKEPPER

At the end of days there was table service. You could sit and watch at bars as the wind grew stronger, and the surroundings, slowly, blew away. There were so many cheap cocktails that the customers didn't notice the dust growing around their shoes and the waiters quietly kicked it into the corners.

We started with frozen daiquiris while the freezers still worked. Then mojitos, piled high with the ice that was left. This was followed by Pina coladas, while cows at the back of the bar gave milk until their grass turned to dust, then the earth beneath, then their hooves. They managed a few plaintive moos, before they disappeared.

We arrived there on the last boat, or at least I heard no further horns in the bay. Rob somehow managed to get tickets, I didn't ask how. When the word finally got around, we had already unhooked ourselves from the jetty. Some tried to swim after us but we didn't stop. Some even followed in makeshift rafts but were doomed when they reached the turbulence of the adult ocean.

We didn't look back.

The ferry glided in. There was no panic, no one to challenge us. Cobwebs and rot had already begun to form in the terminal, but the squares were still sundrenched and pretty.

Rob held my hand as he helped me ashore. We followed the crowd to the bar in the ancient Plaza de Arms, where previous governors had ruled while imprisoned on top of a tall fortified tower. I wondered if the current ruler made it to the bar for Happy Last Hour.

A five-piece band played songs in an unknown language and shook maracas.

Rob steered me toward a corner table. He pretended he could protect me and I pretended to believe he could. He couldn't hold back the dust, so we pretended we didn't see it. This had worked well for us in the past. He managed to blurt out his standard question, 'What would you like?'

By the seventh round there was only a four piece band, the bongos had disintegrated. Then the bass went, then the guitar, as the empty glasses piled up around us. The maracas kept shaking until the end, even after the last musician had disappeared. The final sounds at the end of the world were seeds awash in a rumba rhythm.

Rob raised his head with difficulty, and managed to swing it to the left and then the right. A dust cloud had enveloped the sky, turning it mud brown. Squinting, he looked at me.

'Should I say I love you?" he asked.

'Do you?' I had to be a little difficult, even then.

'Ah,' he opened his mouth, and fine grains of sand escaped from under his tongue. Then his tongue became the grains and his jaw fell away, before the rest of him collapsed into a level plain.

I sipped the final dregs of my warm Bahama Mama. The ice had run out several rounds ago.

Fiona Skepper is a criminal lawyer in Melbourne Australia. She has been writing short stories and travel articles for years. She has published in the Queen of Crime Anthology, That's Life, The Age Newspaper, Inflight Magazines The Stockholm Review and the Jane Austen Anthology.

THE VICTIM

BY
CHARLES SMITH

Josh Cooper hurriedly descends the stairs to the basement, taking the last three with an effortless jump. He lands steadily on the ground but puts his hand to his stomach before turning to face the other figure standing in the room.

"A'right, Mike," he says. "Wish I didn't finish all that pizza on my own now."

"You're probably going to be wishing that even more once you see this victim, Detective," Mike replies. "It'll make you even sicker."

Footsteps can be heard above their heads in the main body of the house, but neither pay it any mind. Instead, Josh walks over to Mike, hand still resting on his stomach. His overcoat drapes along the floor as he walks; because of its length he treads on it once but he doesn't stumble, instead he keeps going on determinedly. His trilby, like his coat, is a little too big for him but that doesn't distract him, either.

He reaches Mike and looks up. Josh is six inches shorter than his companion even with the hat on and is very slim in comparison. This doesn't seem to matter as he stands there with an air of confidence not matched by Mike.

After a few seconds of quietly standing side by side the silence is broken by the sound of a door opening and closing above their heads; using that noise as a signal to begin, they both look down and survey the victim on the floor.

The body is laying face up, eyes closed, with one arm outstretched towards the stairs of the basement, with the other resting peacefully on the chest. The legs lay straight as arrows. The body is wearing loose jeans with holes in them at the knees and upper leg; black Nike trainers are at one end and a scruffy black t-shirt is at the other.

"Yikes!" Josh exclaims. "Urghh! Look at his face. What's wrong with it?" Josh puts his hand to his mouth and mumbles from behind it, "I think I'm going to hurl just from looking at it."

A grumbling noise follows this announcement.

"What did you say?" Josh asks.

"Nothing," Mike replies in a flat tone. "But he has had a knife driven into his face at force about a hundred times."

"Really? Are you *sure* he doesn't look like that all the time? Like, his mugshot in his driver's licence actually looks like that." Josh begins to chuckle to himself before he glances to Mike, sees he is steely faced and quietens down ready to hear the breakdown of the scene with the waving of his hand in the universal 'wrap it up' circular motion.

"No. It is definitely the stab wounds," Mike begins with no hint of emotion in his voice. "I can't give you the exact number of how many he's received until we get him back to the lab, but I wouldn't be surprised if it really does number in the hundreds."

"ID?"

"Nothing. No wallet and his phone is locked so I haven't been able to get into tha—" Mike holds out his hand with the victim's phone in it and Josh quickly snatches it off him, halting him mid-sentence.

"Fuckin' old phone isn't it?" Josh scoffs. He tries entering a few pin numbers but gets no luck in managing to unlock the phone. He quickly gives up and begins twirling the phone around in his hands. "Even five year olds have iPhones now. What is he: a bum or somethin'?"

"As I was saying," Mike ignores the question and carries on with his breakdown of the scene but his once steady tone is now tinged with mild annoyance. "We have no ID. The murder weapon isn't here and there are no footprints in the blood that's pooled all around the body."

"Who called the crime in?" Josh's tone has finally shifted from jovial to serious as he kneels down to look closer at the body, starting with its head.

"No-one. Or at least, we don't know. It was an untraceable number and the only information on the call was the address."

Josh continues his inspection of the victim's face, now leaning in to within an inch of it and sniffing loudly. He goes to flick a finger across the victim's nose, but seems to think better of it and withdraws his hand.

He then motions to start padding down the body, but also thinks better of that and finally stands with a puzzling look etched across his face.

"Does look like a puzzler, eh?" Josh begins. "There was no forced entry into the house from what I saw, so if we assume this guy lives here – and given the state of his face we can't tell if the pics upstairs are of him – then the murderer must know the victim. Surely he wouldn't just let a stranger in and come down to the basement with them. So we should start there once we hack the phone"

"Anything else? Possible motive?"

"Motive, could be anything. He smells pretty bad so maybe he just farted in the murderer's direction, plus there's the fact he's fucking ugly, so that as well." This time Josh cannot control his own laughter from breaking out fully.

A sudden scratching of movement is heard which brings Josh back to his senses. Once he manages to control himself he continues: "But given the number of wounds it's clearly a hate crime. One out of passion? Unlikely."

"Why not?" Mike catches himself and holds his hand up to Josh before he can reply, before continuing in a tone imitating Josh: "No wait, let me guess, because with his face he won't get a girl, right?"

Josh chuckles again, "You said it, not me."

"So I am going with maybe he was part of a bust and he stashes the goods down here. The baddies he's done this job with come-a-calling and they come down here and kill him once he shows them where it is."

"But why would they call in the murder? Surely that would tip them off. Wouldn't they want to keep this under wraps?" Mike queries.

"I don't know why. What am I, a detective?"

"Yes!"

"Oh, yeah. Sorry I forgot."

The sound of a car pulls up to the house and the two look towards the stairs as the front door to the house is opened and keys are heard rattling and chiming against a ceramic object close to the basement door.

"Anyway," Josh shakes his head and continues, "I would say it is more than one person that did this as I remember in school we once learnt that Caesar was stabbed 23 times and there were a lot of them doing that, so if there's more than a hundred stab wounds here, imagine how long you'd be here doing all of them on your own."

Once he finished speaking he had clearly rushed that sentence and was out of breath and panting.

"So we're looking for more than one murder weapon then?"

Once again, keys begin to rattle near the entrance to the basement as more footsteps are heard.

"Michael! Josh!" The cacophonous cry comes from up the stairs and freezes the two of them to the spot.

"Shit!" They both exclaim at the same time as Josh adds a "*Not now*" in for good measure.

"Time to go to your Granny's," the voice booms again. "Say goodbye to John and shift your butts. You can finish playing when you get back. Does John want dropping off back at his?"

"OK Mum!" Josh yells back.

"And have you seen your dad's hat and coat? He can't find them anywhere," the voice cries one more time.

The victim suddenly jumps up and grabs at Josh, knocking the hat off and placing him in a headlock; he then begins to rub his knuckles into Josh's scalp repeatedly. "This'll teach you fuckin' little cock. Not *sooooo* smart and funny now are ya, eh, eh, eh?"

"Arghhh! Get off!" Josh grumbles, struggles to free himself and drops the victim's phone to the floor.

At the phone hitting the floor the victim eases his grip and Josh manages to free himself from it. He quickly runs and scrambles up the basement stairs, taking two at a time and aiding his escape with his hands, but in his haste he keeps tripping over his Dad's coat he's still wearing. He makes it to the top of the stairs leaving the two others behind standing still, having not moved a muscle since he began his mad dash for freedom.

Mike bends over picking up the hat and phone before shrugging to the victim, handing the phone back and heading up the stairs himself without saying a word.

The victim takes a final look at the scene of his death and begins to ascend the stairs of the basement. "Next time I'll make you the victim," he mutters to himself.

Carl Smith is an experienced publishing professional based in London. As well as working for Allegiant Publishing Group, he has worked with various other leading publishers such as Penguin Random House and Egmont UK. He possesses three degrees in English.

A TWISTED TAIL

BY

ROBERT SMITH

A quick glance to the corner of the screen quickened his pulse. It was 4:45 AM. He had fifteen minutes left.

The thump in his chest, throb in his throat and pounding inside his head had to be nerves. Dan also dismissed the prickling in his fingertips and kept typing. With wide eyes, he reviewed his last paragraph. He pressed forefinger and thumb together. The prickling in his left hand did not subside, it grew. Dan suppressed an urge to lick his itchy hand and shook it instead.

With the clock ticking, concentration on the task was vital. He refocused. His fingers danced on the keyboard and letters formed words streaming across his screen. The sensation in his fingers spread through his hand as he worked. Finally, Dan paused, his hand cramping. Three times he made a fist, squeezing harder each time. When the feeling only intensified, he looked down with brow furrowed. Expecting to see a rationale for the sensation, he saw none.

Air escaped his lips like the last gasp of a whoopee cushion. He moistened them with his tongue and tasted copper. Chewing the inside of his cheek was a habit Dan did during anxious moments.

His wristwatch rattled as he shook the offending hand at his side. Dan looked back to the monitor. It was 4:52 AM. Dread washed over him. A bead of perspiration rolled from his hairline to his eyebrow, the cool liquid tickled his fevered forehead. He dragged the back of his right hand across his brow and continued typing.

Dan laid into his keyboard and it erupted clacking like dice rattling in a cup. Around him, an expansive cubicle farm lay empty. His shallow breaths and the hurried click of his keyboard were all that occupied the cavernous space.

His frantic eyes followed speedy letters across the screen as his tongue traced the chewed flesh on the inside of his pasty mouth.

The digital clock changed to 4:58.

The nerve endings in Dan's hand lit up, pain radiated up his arm. He screamed out and slid forward off his chair until his knees hit the floor with a thump. He squeezed his left bicep in a vain attempt to keep the pain from spreading further.

A noise from the far side of the room drew him. The door's groan was unmistakable, its sound carried across the vacant space. Dan's eyes snapped to his monitor. It was 5:00 o'clock, his time had run out.

"*It's him,*" Dan thought. "*He's here to take me.*"

Another wave of fire ripped inside his arm and he fell back onto the floor. He tried to get up, grimacing with eyes clenched. He wanted to run, but the pain was disabling.

Dan squeezed his throbbing left arm with his right hand, the pain radiated to it. He pulled it away, opened his eyes and looked.

The arm throbbed and bubbled before his eyes. His skin grew dark and the veins darker. Cramps gripped him. There was a deep aching in his legs.

He tried to bear the pain and rise. The right elbow gave leverage while the left arm pushed. Onto his side he rolled, gathered himself and opened his eyes. A pair of feet were at the cubicle's entrance. Someone stood over him.

Jeff, a maintenance man around the office, stood looking down at him.

Dan peered back, face dripping with sweat. Feeling an urge, a feverish blood lust, he seethed, "Get away from me."

The maintenance worker's face slackened and his brow furrowed. His eyes darted about Dan's decumbent body as he knelt.

"*Get out!*" Dan screamed.

His demand only intensified the man's concern. After a brief hesitation, Jeff put his hand on Dan's shoulder. The touch ignited something within the fallen man. Something flickered in his eyes and the slack body grew taut. The maintenance man drew his head back on its axis, his brow elevated. Dan felt a current flow to his throbbing arm. Blood—*or lava*—coursed through it. The burn was intense, and sharp electrical tingling lit his fingertips. With a mind of its own, Dan's left arm drew back. He knew its intention. He felt what was coming but could not stop it. The speed with which it shot out was blinding. The black mitt brandished razor-sharp claws. One swipe lay Jeff silent.

The large dark space had again grown quiet. There was still time. Maybe not enough to convey everything he needed to say. There was too much. He had to leave a lifetime worth. His unborn child and his wife needed to hear why. They deserved to know.

Sompelled to finish the words to his wife, Dan pulled away from the prone body and returned to his chair. With one hand he tapped away trying to capture a few more sentiments. His eyes burned, his blood was on fire and heart ached. His one-handed efforts were much slower. They sounded more like a lazy wind-chime of bones than dice in a cup.

His good hand shook. Blisters formed on his skin and the veins darkened. The smell of sulfur burned his nose. Dan reached for the mouse to click send while he still could. The pain in his arms ripped into his shoulders and from his neck down his spine. He arched his back and grimaced as red-hot razor blades tore down the center of his back.

Resolve forced his eyes to open again. Focus willed his unsteady hand. When the quivering cursor reached the send button, Dan clicked and sighed with relief.

At least his wife and child would know, it was not his will to abandon them.

A message popped up in the bottom-right-hand corner.

"*Sending reported an error. Cannot connect to the network. Verify your network connection.*"

Dan's heart dropped. Nausea gripped, a severe stomach cramp pitched him forward. He dropped to the floor and vomited.

Through the retching and moaning, a noise stole his attention. The door groaned. Someone or something disturbed the room's dark sanctity once more. A fluorescent light in his workspace flickered. Dan felt the oxygen being sucked from the surrounding air.

He wanted to get up and run, but his body failed him. An all-consuming pain gripped his lower back. He writhed and screamed until his coccyx erupted. He reached back and felt his spine protruding. Trying to hold it in, compress the pain and hold himself together did not matter. It kept coming. It tore through his pants, twisted its way up and then arched down over him. From his side, Dan looked up and saw it there dangling, swaying, as if reveling in its own splendor.

"*Magnificent,*" a voice boomed.

Dan turned his head. He recognized the demon who stood at the entrance to his cubicle. The devil motioned for one of his two henchmen to remove the maintenance man's body.

The blood coursing through Dan's throbbing veins still burned like molten lava yet a chill ran down his spine.

"Stevens, take care of Daniel's computer, would you?"

In horror, Dan watched over his shoulder as Stevens unceremoniously deleted the message.

"Daniel," the demon grinned. "You promised to disappear without a trace, remember?"

Dan looked back toward his escort.

"That was your part of the bargain. When the trial was over, you agreed to come back quietly and we'd take care of your family." The devil pulled a long breath and smiled again. "If we hadn't severed the network in time, we would have been forced to kill your family."

The two minions who had carried off Jeff's body returned. They were lab technicians from the basement. Dan had seen them before, always at the director's heel.

They rolled a large cage to the mouth of Dan's cubicle and opened the door.

A third man wearing scrubs arrived. His badge read,

Chris Evans
Genetic Modifications Analyst
Ledyard-Roberts Genetics

"Director, lab three is ready," he said.

"Thank you, Evans."

"Crate him up boys," he said to his two minions.

He looked back toward Dan.

"Let's get you settled into your new home, shall we?"

The pain had subsided. Dan glanced from the cage, and then back to what had been his body. Short black fur covered large feline haunches and torso.

As they wheeled Dan away he heard Stevens ask, "Will the panther remember his time as a human?"

"That's what we aim to learn," replied the director. A smile played on his lips.

Robert Smith draws on his experiences and from his time supporting investigations to develop characters based on the strange human behaviours he has observed. He writes thrillers. The areas of the genre that interest him most are; Psychological, Suspense, and Horror.

CAST INTO DARKNESS

BY
MARTIN SNEE

Up on the estuary, when the night is falling and the tide is low, the light leaches away one colour at a time. First the pale green of the far shoreline fades, then the umber and sienna of the river itself disappear, and finally the hint of purple casually painted across the sky is the last to remain. On either side the beach stretches away, cobbles flung against the sea wall by a wild winter storm. Soon it will be covered by the advancing tide, while I retreat, yard by yard, but for now I stand by the water's edge and fish.

The great beach rod stands in its rest in front of me, white banded tip nodding gently in time with the waves. I watch it carefully, waiting for that break in the rhythm, that insistent jagging pull that says 'Fish!'

Is that a twitch? Maybe. I step forward and reach for the rod. It's time to re- bait anyway. I lift it high and step backwards, winding hard. The rod hoops forward as I feel a moment's stubborn resistance, but that's just the grip wires. Another heave pulls them free and I step back again, spinning the reel handle to keep the hooks from snagging the sea bed in front of me.

"Anything?"

"Not this time." I glance over my shoulder to see an old man silhouetted against the sky.

"Still early though," the stranger offers.

I catch the line and squat down to rebait, stringing the worms on

266

the hooks, their sandy skin squirming against my fingers. I hear the strike of a match and a moment later, catch a whiff of tobacco. In silence he watches me cast, sending the lead in a big, lazy arc to splash down seventy yards from the shore. I wait for the lead to hit bottom and the line to tighten before placing the rod carefully in the rest and turning to examine my visitor.

Well-worn is my overriding impression, from his faded rubber boots to his weather beaten face. He's hunched into a red padded jacket with a long rip over one shoulder. The spill of white fibres is matched almost exactly by the unkempt hair that escapes from beneath a patched woollen hat. His eyes though, they sparkle blue with a shrewd intelligence.

"Fishing the tide in?" He asks between drags of his cigarette.

I nod in reply. "And out again probably."

"You got a lamp?" He lifts his hand and I realise he's holding a hurricane lamp, one of those old fashioned ones.

"Are you selling that?"

"Course. It's what I do. I buy old ones and restore them."

"New lamps for old, eh?" I joke.

Those bright eyes hold me in a stare and a slow smile spreads across his face.

"So does it work?" I ask, slightly flustered.

"I'll show you." He sets it down and after a few sharp pumps there is a crackle and a hiss as a soft glow brightens the gloom around us.

"See!" He says proudly, "Beauty, ain't she?"

"How much?"

"Call it fifty quid?"

I shake my head slowly. "I haven't got that kind of money. I wish I did!"

"Is that your wish?" Again that unnerving stare. "Do you wish for fifty pounds?"

"Yes," I reply and at that precise moment there is nothing I want more. Suddenly an odd noise intrudes on our conversation, a fluttering slither and scrape. I look up just as something whirls towards me on the wind, tumbling over the beach to rest against my foot. It's a white paper envelope. My hand trembles as I reach to pick it up, I feel its weight and I realise there is something inside. I glance at the stranger who nods encouragingly. Quickly I slit the envelope with my thumb and pull out five crisp ten pound notes. Wordlessly I hold them out.

"Cheers mate!" He chirps as he folds them before shoving them deep into a greasy pocket.

"That's amazing!" I finally find my voice. "How the hell did you do it?"

"Do what?" He asks with a sly smile.

"You know, I don't care!" I lift up the lamp, admiring the way it casts its light "I've got my lamp." I smile at the stranger, "Maybe I should have wished for ten thousand pounds!"

"Is that your wish?" Once again I am trapped by those blue eyes. "Do you wish for ten thousand pounds?"

"Oh come off it," I force a laugh but it dies in my throat. "Yes," I hear myself say.

I don't know what I expect to happen. I look up and down the beach and even glance up into the sky where the first stars struggle through the clouds. I look back at my strange companion but he just takes another drag on his cigarette.

"Wh..?" The noise behind me cuts my question short. I whip round to see my rod bending, the tip pulling down and round. I've never seen anything like it.

"What the hell's this?" I ask as I pull the rod from the resting stand and try to gain some control. It feels like I've hooked a train, no, more like an oil tanker. All I can feel is this huge solid weight gripped in the indefatigable pull of the tide. I try to reel in, but I can't get the handle turning so I strain to lift the rod higher in a desperate attempt to gain line. It is too much. With a painful crunch the carbon fibre splinters six inches below the rod tip which hangs there for a moment before breaking off completely and disappearing down the line into the sea. All the strain comes to bear on the second ring and before I can react that breaks too, pinging away from the rod and following the rod tip down the line. My beautiful rod is now a lifeless stick in my hands and I know I'm losing this battle. Swearing loudly I take the only action I can and run to the water's edge, pointing what's left of my rod directly down the beach. The slack line loops round in the tide and the force of the current pulls towards the land. Moments later something wallows in the shallow water, indistinct in the gathering gloom. I walk closer as a wave lifts and turns it over. Something rises from the foam and to my horror I see the unmistakeable silhouette of a hand.

Throwing my rod up the beach I run to the body and then immediately wish I hadn't. The stench hits me first, then a brief glimpse of yellow waterproofs before my eyes are drawn to the face and I feel the bile rising in my throat. He's been in the water for some time and the crabs have done their work. For a moment all I can do is gag, but I swallow it down and reach for my phone.

"What are you doing?" He lifts the lamp, illuminating all the gory detail.

"Phoning the police."

"Wait, let's just have a look first" He squats down and tugs at the zip of the waterproof jacket, feeling inside with one gnarled hand.

"No!" I put a hand on his shoulder, but he shoves it away and then stands and holds out a plastic wrapped package.

"Yours, I reckon," He leers at me as, despite myself, I reach out and take it. Through the clear plastic I can see money, lots of money.

"Drugs money probably," the stranger says. "Or illegals. He's probably come off a trawler, there's quite a few who do more'n just fish"

"I can't keep this!"

"You wished for it!"

"So do all my wishes come true now?" I ask sarcastically.

"Not all," the blue eyes cut like lasers.

"How many then?"

"Guess?" His smile is cold, my stare incredulous.

"So I've got one left then?" He nods and for a moment we just stand face to face on the shore. I can feel the weight of the money in my hand. It's my move but I don't know what to do.

"What's it going to be then?" There is just a hint of impatience in his voice. Suddenly I make up my mind.

"Here!" I toss him the money. "Take it, and take the lamp. I'm done."

"Is that your wish?"

"No. I'm not wishing, in fact I'm not playing your game anymore." I turn and start to walk away.

"But you could have anything!" He shouts from behind me. "Money! Power! Your heart's desire." I stop where the fishing line is singing in the wind, reach down and cut it. There is a shout of rage from behind me. The wind slaps my face as I walk on and retrieve my rod. Further along the shore, lights appear on the towers of the oil refinery, briefly illuminating the gulls that skim the surface of the sea. But the lamp has gone and the beach is cast into darkness.

Martin Snee lives in Lincolnshire, England where he writes, paints, reads and walks the dog, but not necessarily all at once. He is currently working on a series of the Fantasy books with the first due for release in 2017.

THE SOUL OF A DANCER

BY

NADA ADEL SOBHI

Leaving her apartment early Saturday, Haya was greeted by a gentle but slightly cold breeze as she stepped on the pavement. She inhaled, enjoying the quiet and sleepy world.

She walked past the shops, some still closed, some just opening and starting for the day.

"Hello Mr. Ibrahim," she told the Egyptian fruits and vegetables vendor.

"Hey Asil," she greeted the Turkish boy of a trinkets and sweets seller.

"Drop in at midday; we're getting some Turkish delight I promise you'll love!" Asil said as she passed. He waved to her then continued sweeping the entrance to the family shop.

She smiled. Asil knew her weaknesses for Turkish delight and chocolate. The former, he could provide, the latter he would buy her sometimes before or after exams.

She strolled past several other shops. Gary and Lina hadn't opened their bookshop yet. She felt sure if they added a small café to go with the books, they'd make far more money, but they worried it would become simply a café rather than a place for bookworms and intellectuals.

She stopped by the local coffee shop.

"Morning Amir. My usual, please."

"My pleasure. Mint or raspberry?"

"Mmm…"

But before she could decide, Amir said "I am feeling raspberry today."

"Spot on."

A few minutes later she left with a large plastic cup of raspberry-flavoured hot chocolate. The sweet scent tickled her nostrils and put a smile on her face. The rich favourite sent filled the air bringing memories of a dark chocolate bar her uncle bought whenever they met. It was filled with the tastiest raspberry juice with a tinge of sourness. Her taste buds suddenly yearned for it.

Haya continued to wander the empty streets, her body feeling alive and excited. She passed by the metro station, the pianist who usually sat there playing her tunes was nowhere to be seen. *Most likely resting on a Saturday morning.* The pianist's music was often sad but always beautiful. Alya was her name and they were fairly good friends. An unlikely friendship, but Haya never said no to decent people or music.

She walked onwards. Then, she heard it. Strange music caught her ears, enchanting her heart.

It reverberated within. She stood almost transfixed, trying to locate the tune. The shops nearby were closed with no one to ask where the music came from.

Following the sound Haya started on a path but the music seemed to die away, so she returned to the starting place and listened. The music did fade away and nearly stopped. Then, a new but similar tune began. It sounded like Celtic war music. It was breathtaking and more beautiful than the previous tune.

Listening attentively, she moved in a different direction, the music thrilled her ears, enlightening her heart and body. She wanted to dance. Her inner vision imagined dancing and sword fighting scenes from movies and books. Haya felt her spirit soar like an eagle to the magical tune.

She felt herself coming closer to the music, which grew louder. She crossed a small street. Deeper and stronger the music played and faster and nearer she walked, almost running to find it, hold it if she could.

She came to a large public space, one with a beautiful garden like London's Trafalgar Square but smaller and without fountains. On the other side, she found a band playing. They were so immersed in their music they did not notice her arrive and sit on a bench beneath an ancient tree.

She closed her eyes and listened. But then the music suddenly stopped. She opened her eyes, almost in agony. Several members of the band were looking at her.

"Why did you stop?" She pleaded. "Please go on!"

The bass guitarist took off his headphones and said in surprise, "You could hear it?"

"Of course! I've followed the sound for several streets till I found you. Please don't let me interrupt."

"But Miss, you couldn't possibly heard. We're still practicing using headphones. We weren't playing out loud or using the amplifiers," said the bassist.

She was confused. "I'm not sure I understand you correctly. I heard it. You were playing a sort of Celtic instrumental piece just now. The kind played in movies with wars and stuff, right?"

"Yes," the boy said. Another man approached with long hair, like the metal bands on YouTube.

"Is there a problem?" He asked.

"No. Look, I just want you to keep playing the music. It's beautiful and I can feel my body responding to it." Her tone was frustrated and pleading.

The newcomer looked curiously at each band member, then at her. He shrugged then clearly decided he'd entertain her. After all, they were practicing to play later in the day. Having an early and happy audience couldn't hurt, even if what she was saying was impossible.

As the two musicians walked backed to the band, the first said "I don't understand how she can hear the music. We weren't playing loud, were we?"

"No, we weren't," a third member said, the lead guitarist. A thought came to him, something he had heard long ago from his father or grandfather.

Music spoke to some people. It reached out, calling to their hearts and souls.

Although he never believed the legend this girl was living proof. She heard from blocks away, what people in nearby buildings could not, sounds it was theoretically impossible to hear without the headsets. She heard what only the band could hear through special gear.

The band adjusted their gear and resumed their rehearsal.

She closed her eyes as the beat and pace picked up. A smile spread across her face. The weight of the world began lifting from her shoulders.

Her heart and mind were in the sky again. Every drum beat, a beat of her wings as she soared above. Somehow, she could see the band playing below, and herself seated on the bench. The trees and flowers seemed to enjoy the music as much as she did.

She wasn't sure how it happened, but her presence was spreading to the world around her. The music was strong and powerful, engulfing her being.

The lead guitarist watched her, as he played. He could feel a strange but soothing presence amidst the music, as though she was with them, not just seated on a bench nearby. Her eyes were closed but the happiness painted across her face was as clear as the sun on a summer's day.

The band continued to play a Celtic tune. The music reverberated within each of them, musicians and woman; a magic flowing and connecting all who believed in it.

The song was long and hard, a journey of music and she was on it with them. And each of them felt it. Her soul transcended as theirs did.

When they were done playing, sweat covered their faces and bodies. She was still seated, her eyes closed, calm and smiling. The wind ruffled a few strands of her dark hair.

When she opened her eyes, they were looking at her again. Some had confusion etched on their faces, others recognition. The lead guitarist smiled.

"Thank you!" She said. For some reason she was as out of breath as they were.

"I wish I could have that last piece you played."

"We'll be playing here later today. Why don't you come again and listen to it?" The one with the long hair invited. She bowed her head slightly. She didn't feel the music well in the presence of crowds. It was stronger when it was intimate, when people played because they wanted to not when they had to.

Seeming to read her thoughts, the lead guitarist gave her a CD.

"We'll make you an exception. The track you want is number three."

Her eyes spoke volumes as she whispered, "Thank you."

"But…" the first one who approached her began. The guitarist shot him a look and the other quieted.

She thanked them all and walked home to truly dance to the music, no limitations, no onlookers, no boundaries.

"I still don't understand how she could hear our music or why you gave her the CD," the first one said after Haya left.

"She is unique. She has the heart and soul of a dancer," the guitarist said, his eyes following her.

"What are you talking about?" the bassist asked, confused.

"One day, you'll understand," The guitarist said, then added, "until then, let's leave her to the music."

Nada Adel Sobhi earned her BA in English Language and Literature from Cairo University in 2009. She is a poet, writer, translator, book reviewer and blogger. Her poetry and short stories have been published in various anthologies. She regularly blogs at Nadaness In Motion: http:// nadanessinmotion.blogspot.com/

A SWEET AVERSION

BY
AMY SOSCIA

Our relationship was fraught with conflict from the outset, but lately things have turned red hot.

***

After spying me from a few aisles away, the tall brunette made eye contact. Then, with obvious determination, she headed straight for me. With the exception of one long moment when the rhythm of her walking faltered, her nonchalance was impressive. A round shouldered middle-aged man stood along the outer wall, between the escarole and the bib lettuce, lecturing new employees about the importance of rotating the stock. No one else paid attention as she approached.

She flipped her long, espresso colored hair away from her face and tilted her head. Her eyes moved over me, seducing as well as examining, until my every vulnerability was exposed. She whispered something about hoping I was as firm as I looked, while sizing me up and squeezing my bottom. I had no idea where this was headed, but I was ripe for the picking. She pinched and caressed and ogled me. I felt cheap, yet so excited when she said, "I need to get out of here."

She held me tightly on the walk to her place. Fantasies of being nibbled on and savored by her distracted me from the silence. I hoped whatever was about to happen would be positively wicked.

Once inside her apartment, she pushed and shoved me around, moving things out of the way, as she searched for the perfect location.

Her hot breath sliced the air between us. When she spoke I became so excited, my eyes nearly fell out of my head in anticipation. Then, in the midst of all of this groping and grabbing, I became wedged into a corner. I was now immobilized, slightly bruised, and thoroughly confused. What kind of game was she playing? I never saw the rest coming. She slammed the door shut and left me alone in the dark.

Imprisoned in a tomb-like shelter that lacked both warmth and light, she held me captive for almost an eternity. Her indifference provoked my curiosity and bewilderment. Feelings of dejection and abandonment covered me like a fungus. Nothing had ever prepared me for such coldness.

As I awaited my release, I speculated about our future, if there was to be a future. I assumed she meant to keep me for a time when her interest matched her desire. She had, after all, sought me out.

My spirit and firmness began to shrivel at an alarming rate. Her neglect produced feelings of terror that enveloped me like a cellophane wrapper. Chilled to the core and despondent from her promised, yet unfulfilled solicitations, I began to pray for a swift ending to my tortured existence.

Freedom passed by when she opened the door and stared at me with a well-starched facade of intention. A bright light emanated from behind her dark shadow and slapped me out of my vegetative stupor. She dropped all pretenses of tenderness or affection as she grabbed me and shoved me under the stinging needles of a cold shower.

Her long seductive fingers, had been transformed into clumsy paws, handled me roughly as she scrubbed my skin raw. I tried to scream, but nothing came out. She whistled and smiled as I choked and sputtered.

Her viciousness effervesced as she lunged at me with a shiny metal weapon, her face twisting into a copy of Munch's *Scream*.

"I can do this," she cried as she stabbed me over and over. Her expression contracted as she plunged the fork, with psychotic abandon, into my weakened flesh and her crushing grasp threatened to squeeze the life out of me.

"They say you're supposed to be good for me, but they weren't there when you made me sick, week after week. I need to know if you're as awful as I remember, or if things have changed."

Minutes later, a slow sinister laugh erupted, mutating into squeals of delight as she tossed me into a brightly lit cell, slammed the door, and punched some secret code.

The heat was stifling as I spun, around and around, clinging for dear life. Her eyes peered through the window, tracking my every movement in anticipation of my demise. Droplets of sweat and fear oozed from my pores while the timer ticked away precious moments. As the strength was zapped out of me, and my form wilted and collapsed, I gave up my struggle.

As I moved toward the light, the noxious burning smell of my skin produced immediate and violent results. A low rumbling sound came from deep within her, forcing her body into quick, jerky spasms. She danced and retched and cursed. With one hand, she covered her mouth, with the other she reached in and pulled me from the fires of hell. My once desirable form was now reduced to a charred, stinking, oozing mess.

She tossed me back and forth, from hand to hand, as if playing a child's game of hot potato, not knowing what she wanted, unable to either love me or discard me. For this, I loved her all the more.

© Amy Soscia 2016

Amy Soscia, an MFA recipient from Albertus Magnus College, is working on her first novel "The Frozen Game." She has been published in "Chicken Soup For The Soul: Recovering From Brain Injuries", "898," "The Westie Imprint", and online in "Down In The Dirt Magazine."

SHEEP

BY

ELIZABETH STOKKEBYE

Sitting by the window, her gaze through the glass, landing among the sheep in the meadow. "I wish I could be down there among the sheep. Don't they look peaceful lying there under the oak tree? So many of them with their thick cuddly fur."

I look at my mom as she enters her dream. Her dream of being protected and taken care of without a care in the world.

"I think I have counted around forty sheep, but they move about, so not quite sure," she continues.

We are having brunch at Mission Ranch restaurant in Carmel, just the two of us. My children live in other cities far away and today they sent texts and videos to wish me Happy Mother's Day. One got through on FaceTime. With families of their own, they are busy celebrating Mother's Day. I'm happy for them.

I don't think my mother ever thought that way: that her children were busy with their own families. Always, she expected our attention, whether from her husband or from her children. And we all complied. Like now, sitting with her, looking at sheep.

She talks about the sheep but also about my father, who died thirteen years ago of cancer after too much booze and too many smokes. Lately, she tears up talking about him and wishes to join him.

I see the association now, between the sheep and my father: the island of safety, either among the sheep or with my father. Being straight-forward, he practiced what he knew. He lived hard. My mother, cuddled and free to look pretty and perfect, was naive. She hated competition and did not want to live in the city among peer girlfriends and moved us to the country among farmers, where her status remained unchallenged. I understand her life-long strategy now: always placing herself where she felt superior.

We toast our glasses of sparkling wine and smile. And I see it: with me she's back with my dad, enjoying life, admired and carefree. Right now, her reality, real reality, are her memories and when she lives her memories, she's happy. Everything that takes place now, around us, is not her reality; that is a dream to her. I feel dizzy. We don't share the same reality. I look out the window at the sheep. They do have long hair, so long that it's hard to see their feet. Must be time for shearing.

I bring my mother her plate of salmon. And I get an omelet with mushrooms, bell peppers, onions and cheese for myself. I'm hungry. Afterward, I get some salmon, too.

"So, when are we leaving tomorrow?" my mother asks.

"You are not leaving tomorrow, mom, you are not leaving until a couple of weeks from now," I smile.

The plan is for her to visit my brother in North Carolina for a month, and he will be in California on a business trip and able to escort her to North Carolina. She was there at this time last year, too. But he will deal with yet another mom this time. More frail, sadder, more afraid.

I let her drink. All her life she's been drinking with my dad. Martinis and wine for her, bourbon and ginger ale primarily for him but also, wine, beer, cognac, Bloody Mary's and Manhattans. She likes to have wine when I have wine. I let her because she asks me and craves the liquid like me.

The next day she can't get out of bed. Hangover. Migraine.

She calls me. She's wondering about her sister-in-law who died of a brain tumor last year.

"But when they scanned my brain, it was okay," she says.

"Yes, mom, you don't have a brain tumor, you have a hangover!"

During the last ten years with my dad, she complained of migraines but I'm sure she had hangovers. With my mom inching closer to the grave I discover her and must absorb who she is and was. The Alzheimer reveals her true self. I don't like her. Her wishes surface uninhibited, her cravings and her needs. My father had his hands full. I had my hands full. He as the provider of luxury and I as the caretaker of all her kids. No, I cannot engage in her suffering, that is my challenge. After all these years I see through her, behind her mask of make-up, behind her dreams, behind her lies, and behind her fear.

I see our relationship as superficial and 'pretty' and not authentic or real, as I understand real. She fits into a box and she sees me fit into a box. I have exhausted all compassion and that is cruel but I feel it deeply. Hurt, I only want to protect myself.

"Let's go outside and sit in the Adirondacks to be with the sheep. I'll take pictures of them," I suggest.

"Yes, good idea," she smiles.

I collect her sweater and her purse and escort her outside.

Elizabeth Stokkebye is American–Scandinavian with a master degree in Scandinavian Languages and Literature from University of Washington. She is also a painter of large figurative work, oil and mixed media.

TIME SEEMED TO STAND STILL

BY

JUDY SULLENS

Her breathing was shallow. We sat by her bed watching. She had been like this for days. Would she ever wake again? Time seemed to stand still.

I was at my house when I got that first call. My life was pretty normal. I was drinking coffee, reading, and doing laundry. Just having a quiet morning at home.

The phone played my family/friends tune. I picked up, expecting my sister's icon. It was my mother calling. That wasn't unusual except it was early. Mom isn't keen on mornings.

"Jim, Sandy's been in an accident. They don't know if she will make it. You need to get here right away."

"What sort of an accident? Where are you? What's happened?" The questions poured out of me as I tried to wrap my mind around my mother's words.

My little sister, Sandy, our athlete, our healthy eater! She was our brightest light; the only family member loved by all. She is the kind one. She even thinks before she speaks. What's going on?

Mom's voice broke through my reverie, "We're at the hospital. She was riding her bike to work. A man in a pickup ran the light. I don't know anything more right now. I just got here. Please come!"

Those were my last sane moments. Since Mom's call I spent a short frantic time dressing, tossing laundry in the dryer, looking for my keys

281

then driving to the hospital as safely as one can while crying. I found Mom in the waiting room of the surgery floor.

Mom looked like death warmed over. It suddenly hit me again, this was real. My little sister was in the operating room. My little sister; I might not ever see her alive again...

Sandy's in her early thirties. She is a pediatrician, loves her patients and her work. She even has her life in order. She recently bought a house near her office so she could safely walk or bike to work. She has been seeing another doctor, who we all like and hope will be Sandy's choice too.

Now we are all in a state of suspended animation, waiting...waiting for her next breath...waiting for any change. Hoping she will open her eyes. Hoping she will still be there; still be Sandy if—No, *when* she wakes.

After surgery, her doctor wasn't willing to offer us much hope, except to say that her EEG showed activity and it was now up to Sandy.

If she were awake I would tell her how much I love her, how much we all love her. I'd also say I really hate waiting and beg her please, wake up already!

"Sandy, please, wake up! You know I don't use the 'please' word very often so you know I'm serious now. Please just give us a little sign that you are just kidding us here...just enjoying the attention...Okay? Please wake up!" I whispered in my best big brother manner. I've always been able to get a smile from her with my *best big brother in the world* act. Of course, I am also her only big brother. This time though I leaned back and saw only her sleeping form. No change. No answering smile. No flickering eyelid. Nothing.

What to do? I can't just sit here for hours doing nothing to help while watching her unresponsive expression. What would she do if our positions were reversed? Then it dawns on me! Sandy is a music lover. She almost always had her music playing in her home or when she was driving.

"Mom, I'll be right back." I whisper as I head out the door. My poor mother only has time to nod.

I run over to Sandy's house and there I pick up her earphones, player and charger. While I am there I draw a deep breath and offered a quiet, "Please!" to the universe and maybe to Sandy, since I was standing in her personal space.

When I walk back into the hospital room I feel hopeful and hook everything up. Starting to place the headphones in Sandy's ears, I glance over at Mom who is looking dubiously at me. "It's her music, Mom. I'm hoping it will stimulate her brain." I say.

Mom shrugs with a lifted eyebrow but doesn't stop me. At this point we're willing to try anything. I turn the device on and we wait.

Nothing.

We wait, still holding our breath. Not sure what I am looking for, I scan her face.

I still see nothing but Mom suddenly shouts, "Jim, call the nurses' station! Sandy just squeezed my hand!"

I stare at my mother with shock. Even though I wanted it to be true, for a moment I couldn't believe it. Then I grabbed the call button and pressed it hard, as if my own life depended on it.

Within minutes a nurse appeared at the door. She asked if there was something we needed. Then she clearly realized our expressions were both shocked and hopeful. At that moment Mom and I both started talking, "Sandy's awake!" Mom exclaimed while I was saying, "She's responding to her music!"

The nurse quickly but efficiently moved to Sandy's bedside. She raised her eyelid and flashed her penlight on and off above Sandy's eye. Then the other eye. Next, she checks Sandy's pulse. She smiles very slightly and says, "I'll be right back," as she moves quickly toward the door.

I realized I was holding my breath as I watched Sandy's face and whispered, "Breathe!" to myself.

Mom whispered, "How did you know I wasn't?" I heard her inhale a deep breath.

Then we heard another whisper, "I am breathing, you dolt."

Judy Sullens recently had work accepted for an in-progress anthology, "More Than a Dream: Stories about what matters most" edited by Lorna Lee. Judy lives in Vancouver, Washington.

THE WIDOWER

BY

MARQUIS SYLER

"This is better than sittin' home all by yourself, isn't it? It keeps Sam company and me, I'm concerned 'bout ya, Jared," Edgar said. I kept my feelings inside.

"It's a fine April day to be outside, isn't that right, Sam?" Edgar asked.

"Yep," Sam said.

Edgar turned to me, "I know you haven't been yourself. Ever since Marge died you hold up in your house in front of the boob-tube drinkin' all day, and that don't do you any good."

His assumptions irked me, "One: yes the house feels empty, and I feel empty. Marge and I were married for fifty years. I always thought I'd be the first to go. Secondly: I don't drink all day."

"You smell like alcohol," Edgar said.

"One glass of wine."

"Not even noon yet. Not good to take alcohol before noon, ain't that right, Sam?"

"Yep."

"Look at that hot shot," Edgar's tone dripped with sarcasm. An olive green Mustang, a 69 Mach I, a classic, had stopped for the red light.

"They don't make them like that anymore," I said.

"He thinks he's special."

"What makes you say that?"

"The way he sits behind the steerin' wheel, smug. He's a punk."

"That's harsh."

"I'm a good judge of people, ain't that right, Sam?"

"Yep."

"You always agree with Edgar, Sam?"

"Yep."

Over the years, Edgar had been a good friend to Marge and me. I don't know anything about Sam. I turned to Edgar, "Why does he agree with everything you say?"

"Sam's a smart man." Edgar tapped his index finger on the side of his head, indicating Sam wasn't all there.

"I agreed to come down here. By the way, you know people call this the dead pecker bench. Old guys with nothing better to do than hanging out and gossip, Edgar."

"And now you too," Edgar made a good show of laughing it off. "You're funny, but what the talk around town is you're losing it. You don't have Marge to look out for you. It's 'bout your report of a murder that never happened."

"I saw a man killed. It doesn't matter to me what the gossipers say. Yes, of course, I reported it to the police, Edgar." His insinuations made my anger boil.

"What did the police say?"

Regaining my composer, I replied. "They took my statement and said they'd investigate. The police didn't find the body."

"Exactly where were you when you witnessed this supposed murder?"

Edgar's smug tone struck a nerve and my muscles tensed. It was getting harder to remain polite. "In the sunroom, at my desk, reading emails. As you know, the room has nine windows where Marge and I spent many a morning watching the sunrise. Behind my house is a new subdivision. That's where the man was shot. He ran from a house in his underwear waving his arms."

Edgar laughed. "You sure know how to spin a yarn."

"It's not a yarn," I said.

"Okay, the man ran out the front door. Carry on."

"From the back of my house, I can see the side of the dead man's house. I can see the front yard, the backdoor, and backyard."

"I get the picture."

"The man fell down on the grass. That's when I grabbed my hat and fast-walked to the edge of my backyard. I saw blood on his back."

Edgar listened. Sam sat still as a post staring at the Victory Temple across the street. This man was a strange old bird.

Edgar snatched my attention, "What 'bout neighbors?"

"A family lives in a new home on the other side. The police questioned them, but they didn't see anything."

"Not surprised," Edgar mumbled.

"I froze for a second staring at the body, and then the back door opened. A person dressed in black clothing and a ball cap stepped outside. I squatted; the person spotted me, raised an arm, and aimed a gun. I threw myself to the ground and flattened my body. I feared getting killed." My hands shook, my heart raced, and a bead of sweat rolled over my brow.

"So, the person leaving by the back door had a gun. Did you hear gunshots when the man ran from the house?"

"No, the shooter must have used a silencer," I exclaimed.

"Sure, why didn't I think of that?" Edgar's sarcasm is a sharp blade. "You said the man waved his arms. Did he yell?"

"Yes, as a matter of fact, he did, but I couldn't comprehend the words. I laid there for a while, and then the shooter left. I ran into my house and phoned the police."

"Was the body still lying in the front yard?"

"I believe so."

"Could you identify the suspect if you saw him or her again?"

"The ball cap was pulled down to shield most of the face. I was close enough to see the mouth and chin. I'd guess it was a man about 5'10" tall. Now that I remember, he had a limp. I'd forgotten that when I spoke to the police. I need to call them and give them an update."

"Nothing good will come of that! The police did not find the body. There's no crime. I'm concerned you're losing your mind, getting that old-timers disease."

"You mean dementia," I replied.

"Yeah, but with the Alltimers," Edgar said.

"You meant Alzheimer's."

"That's it, where a person sees things that aren't real."

"No one believes me. If Marge were here, she would. I have no one on my side. There was a body, but I don't know what happened to it. The police went to the house, but it looked like the owner hadn't moved in yet. They didn't find bloodstains or an impression in the grass to show someone had fallen there. Edgar, we've been friends a long time."

"'Bout thirty-five years, I reckon."

"Yes, when Marge and I moved to Lenoir City. We were outsiders from the North, and you gave us your friendship when others wouldn't."

"I remember," Edgar said.

"You were concerned for our welfare, and we always appreciated your kindness. I realize you don't believe I witnessed a murder, you are a rigid-minded man, but please have faith in me. I know what I saw. It was real."

When I returned home, I was exhausted. Having to recount that stressful event to satisfy Edgar's self-importance in my life left me bewildered. I poured a glass of Red Moscato, walked into the sunroom, and settled down on the couch with an *Alex Cross* tale. I hoped the book would take my mind in a different direction. As hard as I tried, I couldn't concentrate on the book. The image of that man murdered just beyond my backyard, was seared into my brain. Edgar's belief I have Alzheimer's scared me.

The click startled me. The empty wine glass sat on the end table. The book lay on the floor, it was dark outside. I sat up and heard it again. It was a distinctive clicking sound. My hearing was as sharp as it had been in the Army. I stood and waited, listening. A door opened and then shut. An intruder had entered the house. My breathing quickened. I didn't have a weapon to defend myself. Paralyzed by fear, I stood still. Footfalls in the hallway told me the intruder was walking toward the bedrooms. I pushed fear aside and reasoned that I had an opportunity. I could get through the kitchen and living room and out the front door before the intruder caught me.

I hastened my escape and then bumped into the kitchen table. The noise alerted the intruder. The hall light flipped on. I stood motionless, a death grip on the top rail of a chair, holding my breath. The prowler dressed in black garb and the ball cap limped from the hall to stand between me and freedom. With his head lowered, he held a handgun at his side.

My voice quivered. "Are you going to kill me?"

"Yep," Sam said.

M.E. Syler lives in East Tennessee with his wife. He is an author of short stories and novels.

OL' BLUE EYES

BY

LAURIE THEURER

They say life is a song. If this is true, your life has been accompanied by the honey, wood-smoked baritone of Sinatra. You love his music even though you are a bass, which adds a depth to Frank's songs that even he probably would have loved. I can still hear your rock bottom bass rendition of Old Man River, begging you to sing it before bedtime just one more time. Just one more time. You always obliged. Frank himself couldn't have done it better, although he tried.

1932 - "It was a Very Good Year"
You were the fifth child of an auto mechanic, a man forever angry. Your birth coincided exactly with the death of his wife. Your mother. You were raised in an atmosphere of aggression and neglect, learning early in life the lessons that would inspire you to become the opposite; to become a better man than he was. A better husband. A warmer father. A nobler person. You succeeded. Your philosophy is not to degrade or belittle or dictate. You've led your life, and your family, with love, compassion, and above all, security. You made it your task from the start to protect your loved ones.

"Love and Marriage"
You never were able to meet your mother, or to know anything about her except her name. When you married, you chose a motherly woman, albeit nearly 14 years your junior. You've cherished and safeguarded this

woman for over 52 years.

"Strangers in the Night"
You found love in the most unlikely of places... a bowling alley. Grouped together into a team by mutual friends, you noticed a shy young woman and casually asked her for a ride home after the match, conveniently forgetting your bowling ball in the trunk of her car. One phone call later won you a date, and then two more weeks of dates before you decided to propose. Two weeks after that you were married, despite the protests of her mother; a woman who, over the years, came to love you as a son.

"Fly Me to the Moon"
Twice you sped your wife to the hospital in the middle of the night, careful to go gently over the pregnant bump on the freeway that made her belly pulse and the contractions increase. Those were the days when fathers waited outside in the waiting room until it was cigar time, their wives dipped into twilight sleep for the duration of the delivery. Twice you paced the hospital corridors, driving home reeking of cigar, adding to your household another female to love and cherish.

"That's Life"
You spent the remainder of the 1960s (and 70s and 80s) devising ways to pad the house and the world for your daughters so they would never experience a moment's pain, misfortune, or unhappiness. You gave us everything you could, working long thankless hours at the Department of Water and Power, traversing the congested freeways for hours each day, returning every evening to a scotch-on-the-rocks and your girls. You decompressed by sharing the idiosyncrasies of your day around the dinner table, making us all laugh at your stories of eccentric customers, even more eccentric coworkers, and then listened intently to the stories of our days.

"I've Got You Under My Skin"
You stacked your trademark white Hanes t-shirts carefully in your bottom dresser drawer where we could borrow them, back in the days when they reached down past our knees. Your laugh echoed as we twirled, whipping endless cartwheels, splashes of soft white cotton circling the living room on hot summer nights. You'd caress our backs or tickle our feet while listening to Vin Scully announce the Dodger game on the old Zenith. Better pictures than TV, you say, even though the Zenith has

long been replaced with a flat screen.

"Come Fly With Me"
There was never anything you couldn't do. You gave us Louisville Sluggers, taught us to grip them like Steve Garvey, to lean back and wait for the pitch; and the importance of follow through. A good swing is nothing without follow through.

You and I stayed out front together long after the street lights had gone on, throwing baseballs from mitt to mitt, aiming high so we could see the ball against the half-light of a dimming sky. When called in for dinner, we'd call out to Mom in unison "just a few more… just a few more". It was always more than just a few.

"Me and My Shadow"
You volunteered for every Girl Scout activity and pinned each badge onto our uniforms. You waited on the sidewalk as we sold Peppermint Pinwheels and Marshmallow Meltaways door-to-door, ever patient, always watching. You jammed your tall frame into tents during camping trips, cleaned up my wounds after I fell down that hillside during that hike, and taught me to speak up for myself to receive the hiking badge, even though I had fallen from the trail.

"Night and Day"
When horseback riding called to me, you drove me to countless lessons and weekend training sessions, sat front and center at the arena while I competed, and scooped me up to safety when I fell and couldn't get back up on my own.

"All the Way"
When the love of springboard diving outweighed my love of horses, you drove me to school before dawn for practice, running laps around the track until I was finished, making sure I was safe before you would dream of going to work. You volunteered to serve as treasurer for the entire swimming/diving teams, putting in long hours on top of everything else you did for our family.

"Mack The Knife"
Manipulative boyfriends, abusive coaches, false friends came and went. You were watching, teaching us when it was time to "choose our battles" and when it was time to "battle our battles". Some of the battles you fought for us, righting the wrongs, easing our paths, without even

letting us know. The others found you staunchly by our sides, guiding us through the minefields of life.

"I Get a Kick Out of You"

There was never anything you couldn't fix. I'd perch in the garage for hours, watching you saw, drill, screw and glue. By the age of eight, I knew the difference between a Philips and a slot head screwdriver; between a ball pein and a claw hammer; between garnet, emery, and diamond sandpaper; and was hopelessly addicted to the smell of fresh sawdust. While my friends played Barbies and styled their hair, you showed me how to build furniture for my room, tape off and paint the walls, and locate wall studs with my knuckles.

"My Funny Valentine"

Unlike your father, you have always been able to enjoy the lighter side of life, to laugh at the ridiculous aspects of what makes us fundamentally human, to laugh at others, but more importantly, at yourself. We spent countless Saturday mornings perched on the carpet in front of the TV, laughing ourselves silly at Peanuts, Garfield, Bugs Bunny, Elmer Fudd, Daffy Duck, and Yosemite Sam. We would swap sections of the Sunday morning comics until we had both read them all, and then show them to each other once again so we could laugh together.

"High Hopes"

You retired at the age of sixty, filling your days with Honey-Do's while mom still worked, and setting up an artist's studio in the spare bedroom, the one with the best light. You'd waited your entire life for the chance to indulge your natural talents in drawing and painting, and you made the decision not to lose one more bit of time. Your skills improved quickly with practice, your colors blending and deepening, and the clarity of your images sharpening with every piece. Commissions followed, as did exhibitions, and entreaties from family and friends. You obliged us each time, producing copy after copy of well-loved creations for those you cherished.

"My Way"

For a boy with a precarious start in life, raised in a tumultuous home largely void of any emotion besides anger and fear, you rose above. You educated yourself in the best way possible for your situation. You grounded a family of your own and ensured that your household was ruled by love, light, and laughter. Above all, laughter. Some of my first memories are of your cerulean blue eyes twinkling and your rumbling deep bass laugh. You have done it your way.

And what a fine way it has been.

Laurie Theurer's writing adventure began in 2012 at a writer's conference in Geneva, Switzerland, and she hasn't been able to stop since. Her stories draw on her childhood in California, Peace Corps Thailand, and the past 20 years living in Zurich, Switzerland. A freelance project manager, mother, ranch manager and emerging author, she's addicted to flash fiction and short stories, but especially the moment where mere words flow and meld into something magical. Ol' Blue Eyes is dedicated to her father, Chuck.

SHOUT OUT LOUD

BY

SARAH TINSLEY

It's scratchy in here. I ease one foot back, then the other, my breaths are little clouds. Still light enough to see the house, perched like a promise on the hill. The leaves poke up under my skirt, like little fingers. Crouch down, let the scramble of twigs hide my face. If I keep still, it will be ok. Half an hour at most. Delay this coming thing, gathering like pools of syrup in porridge.

So still. It should come soon, a sound that will tell me I have been missed. My arm slips, shouldn't have leaned so hard against that tree, still shiny with frost. One hand to the ground, baked hard by the cold. Concentrate on picking the brown lumps off, tangled in between the grey wool of my gloves. Practical, she said.

There it is, the call. A voice hanging over the field. Still time to shuffle back, lose my legs among the branches. A step, one more. Something under my feet: a chunk of rock. Stumbling, a flurry of crackles around me. Two birds lift out of the tumble, grating the sky. So loud. A signpost to my hiding place.

It's closer now, the sound shaping into words. A tilt of anger in it. I close my mouth, pressing down my chest so there's only tiny puffs coming out. A bit dizzy. It will be worth it.

Keep still, very still. Steady my arms against the trunks, wet moss creeping into my gloves. There's movement, feet stamping. She must be down past the gate, the bit where the hedge cuts off, withered. Can't be far away.

The sound takes shape. Click of the tongue, rounded out, then squeezing, stretching wide the mouth. Louder now, a screech at the end. Delicious panic. Again and again it comes, the repetition like a fanfare.

The shape of her appears through the trees. Shoes half on, feet fumbling out of the back. She didn't even go out the back door for her wellies. That's what she always does, when we play this game.

There's something in the voice that's unfamiliar. Higher pitched. It tugs somewhere, down underneath the toast and jam I had for breakfast. I could run out, pretend I didn't hear. Her feet are close now, right at the edge. Then she'd put me upstairs, make me sit in silence, like the time I ambushed her when she fell asleep on the sofa and I curled in next to her. Better to wait.

She stops. Her head waves from one side to the other; a balloon on a stick. A pause, the seconds dripping from the twig in front; the water making holes in the snow. Could be a catch in her breath, clearing of her throat. Or was it my name? Sighed this time, like an apology. She must see me, crouched here. There will be a snap, the moment this game is broken.

Another bird clatters up, right next to me. Her head catches it, following it out towards the river. She calls me again, an imitation of the bird, cawing my name , heavy steps taking her back up to the house. My name rises and falls, lifting away from me. I scramble out, follow the source before it moves beyond hearing. It feels different. As if I don't have much time. Must catch her, before she gets to the door, or something will break.

Legs bending, straightening, knees up, knees down. The hill is steep, the grass wrapping around my ankles. There's no time. Her back retreats, further, almost at the door. Air burning out of my lungs, gasping, forcing. The green space between us is not great. She could turn now. A pause, she feels the possibility too. Something propels her. She steps away from it, feet scraping up the steps. It's so slow, impossible I won't get there first.

When I reach the door, she's at the kitchen counter, back stiffened. The prepared shout gets caught, comes out like a cough. She turns, there's something on her cheek. I check the sideboard–no onions. Her face creases, eyes hidden. This is not the face she usually presents me with. I step back, a flinch in my shoulders. She's too quick, coming forward and taking my arms.

"Chloe." It's flat, stripped of the emotion from earlier. My mouth opens, the thing I was going to say, how I didn't hear her, how sorry I was that it had happened again. Then she'd hug me, another glimpse of contact I could hold onto. The only time I was allowed to feel her arms around me. More than once a month and she got suspicious.

She drops down; on her knees she's lower than me. Arms around my waist, the top of her head just under my nose, the three white hairs tickling it. I concentrate on not moving. Stay really still, then she won't move away too quickly. Her mouth is moving, sending warm syllables into my chest. They get caught in my coat. I want to unzip it, send the air into my jumper, where it would heat me, leave a scent, something I could keep. But then she might move.

It's me. The same sound I heard in the field, the clipped beginning and stretched out ending, squeaking at the last bit, up into a siren, a panic. I'm right here, I want to say. Keeping my arms stiff, careful not to let my hands touch her , so she won't move away.

It doesn't sound the same, up close. I want to shake her, make it stop. It was the usual game, the one we play. I don't tell and neither do you, we both get to be close to someone. It gives us that excuse.

When she stands, she leaves a hand on my head. Flat, open. Pushing down, like she wants to leave something there. It's only then I notice the suitcase.

Of course, maybe it didn't happen like that. It's easy to widen an afternoon in your memory, clip bits onto it, the things you wish had been there.

Social Services had been investigating us for months. My mother hid the letters at the back of the food cupboard, so when they took them out they were sticky with spilled jam. I think now they would call it autism, the way she stayed away from me, how she couldn't understand I needed feeding at the same time each day. How can you imagine another person's hunger? Perhaps now she would be given some pills, or we would have gone to a home together. Instead, I was discarded in a house where kisses at bedtime made me cringe. They thought I would be like her when I grew up.

That was the last time I saw my mother. I carry the print of her palm on my skull.

Sarah is a writer, teacher, runner and drummer who lives in London, musing over gendered issues and finding the words to express them. Currently working on the second novel and polishing the first, her short fiction has won prizes and her reviews and blogs have been published on a variety of platforms, so if you want to connect you can @sarahertinsley or on her blog at http://sarahtinsley.com.

LITTLE HOPE

BY

ROBERT B. R. VERHAGEN

David Christmas dipped his face toward his beer and hovered there while Archie read his Greek.

"One must not tether a ship to a single anchor, nor life to a single hope," the boy translated.

David afforded a quick and polite grin. He never finished school with Greek, and after school he never started work with hope. He wondered if those two things went together. Do you learn hope like you learn a language? Archie went on reading and David went on drinking.

'The new university in Melbourne has invited me to study,' the boy remarked after a while, closing the pages of his volume softly.

'Why don't you go then?'

'I was thinkin'. What about the station?'

'Ah, you're too bright to be wasted out here.' David's voice was spiced with bitterness. 'What was that you were readin'?'

'Epictetus,' Archie stated with giddy esotericism.

David threw up a hand. 'Long dead philosophers. Whatever happened to Macbeth and the Good Word?'

'The university is a bigger place than any state school. We wouldn't grow our minds too much if we kept on with the same books they read to children. Doing the same makes a man like a bullock.'

'But this is a bullock life, Archie! Least it was on the track. Ah, your type wouldn't survive on the trail to Sydney. There's too little to hope about, and the bush speaks in a tongue more confounding than Greek.'

'Why do men choose that life, then?' Archie asked in an ingenuous voice.

'Men go chasin' a cheque, lad, and sometimes they won't find it. We're not all born governors. I don't know what a silver spoon tastes like. You go out to Bishop's Creek and I bet you'll find three hundred men panning and sluicing for *the colour*, all of them hard up. Their only hope is that the creek bed pays them a little for ale and thread, and maybe some tobacco. Melbourne's no use to them, and sometimes even the digging life gets too much. They take off into the scrub looking for silence because there are no answers.' He paused, considering his amber reflection in between the islands of foam in his glass. 'Naw, hope doesn't buy much here. So you should get on. Let Melbourne make you a learned man.'

At that minute David's daughter, Faith, came rushing in, dusty and pink in the cheeks. David's eyes came aglow. She ran into his arms and he pressed her little head to his chest.

'What you been up to, sweetie?'

'Playing with Watson's dog!' she squeaked then turned and ran outside.

David Christmas chuckled. He took out his pipe, stuffed the bowl with nailrod, and broke a match. He was still smiling as it came up in smoke.

Archie looked on with a curious eye. 'Hope doesn't buy much here, eh?'

* * *

'Don't you think Faith could do with a school such as the town of Japheth has?' Archie suggested gingerly the next day as they yarned in the afternoon. 'A little girl like her shouldn't grow up on a stead such as this.' He looked around the station, every fence and chair chalked with dust. The parched eucalypts rustled, whispering over a tired day.

David was bitter. 'You think I don't know that? When her mother died, and Faith had to come out here 'cause of this job, I was worried sick. Still am. But what can I do about the bush? I can't move, and without me she doesn't eat.' He slipped into a trance that Archie determined was a souvenir of his time on the track. 'I'm all she's got.'

For all his hard words, any man who worked on Watson's Station knew that they were nullified by Faith's chubby smile. For Archie, it was his most cherished lesson from the station days, watching how a little girl softened the crude look of a man as weary as David Christmas.

* * *

The days got on, and Archie made ready to leave, giving his farewells to Watson and all his cattle hands. When he went to farewell Christmas he couldn't find him. He had just finished searching the shearing sheds when a young lad came tearing up the cart-track.

'He's out at the Old Hill,' he panted. 'Little Faith ran off after one of Watson's dogs. She hasn't been seen all afternoon.'

Without a thought, Archie delayed his coach to Melbourne and took up the track with a few other blokes. They came before twilight upon the Hill. Voices echoed *Faith! Faith!* about the brush.

Christmas was darting frantically at the head of half a dozen fellows. His shirt was drenched and dirty, his face pale. Archie and his companions joined the search awhile, before night sucked all light from the world and forced them to bed down on the grass.

Archie lit a fire and threw a billy on for tea.

'If I lose her,' David said through the steam off his brew, 'that'll be *it* for me.'

Two letters never rung so fatally together as the letters that made the word *it* in such a sentence. Only the firelight danced in his dark eyes. They had no candle of their own.

'Where's your heart, mate?' Archie said, slapping David's shoulder.

'She's out there.' David fought back the urge to weep. His gestured across the cloth of darkness that spread beyond the dim glow of their fire, percussing with the mockery of crickets.

Archie wanted to say, 'We'll find her,' but the hope so common to him had somehow slipped his grasp. It was like the bush under night would not permit wan-hope. There was everything hopeless about it, and no shine, not even in the moon. Yet, Archie looked around the ruddy faces at camp, silent blokes fanning their tins of tea, and saw the means for great hope. He saw men, and in the hearts of men there has always lived a capacity for triumph against the direst days, or so he thought. David's face didn't seem to agree.

Perhaps hope had to saddle its own horse sometimes, when men couldn't possibly picture a bright day? Maybe that's what God was: the movement of hope throughout the mortal world.

Archie whispered the name of God and turned in.

The next morning, considering the creases on his face, Archie deemed that David hadn't slept. His face was a sketch of grief, but that did not drain the energy from his bones. He drew off draughts of striving from an undisclosed well and led the surge, up and down the sliding hills, calling Faith's name always.

He cried her name until he became hoarse. The bush threw back the call of *Faith!* for the thousandth time and Archie became certain that hope would not find them so far away from the civilised world.

David fell into the dust and began to sob. His moaning echoed in the gums. It was almost disregarded when David's own cries, repeating in the gullies, turned to a different kind of yelp.

David's ears pricked. The barking grew louder and he rose to his feet. He began to run. The beating tail of a dog appeared on the brink of the next gully, and behind it, rubbing her eyes, a little dusty girl.

David ran until he fell down where she was. Faith collapsed in his arms, and he pressed his tear-stained face upon hers. Sobbing beyond control, but smiling against the dirty streaks on his face, he whispered in a stuttering voice, 'You came back to me, Faith. You're not lost no more. We're not lost no more.'

R.B.R. Verhagen is a Melbourne-based author who released his debut publication Murder at he Mountain Rush *in October 2016, a work of historical fiction. He is the contributing author of* Little Hope *to* One Hundred Voices.

SOUNDS OF THE SOUL

BY

GAURAV VERMA

It starts with the morning *beep* when fingers touch the fingerprint scanner marking the attendance and ends with the *tap-tap* of footsteps of my partners on the corridor leaving. I call them partners and not my employees, because *ha ha ha* I laugh with them at jokes anyone cracks; *shout* or *whisper* while discussing important matters; sip tea with a *slurping* sound together; and at lunch time our plates *clank* in unison.

A *knock* on my door was followed by the *rumbling* of the wheels of the chair, while my fingers *clack* on the keyboard. I heard a *rustle* of papers being put on my desk, I turned around and asked "How are you doing Smith and what are these papers?"

He hesitated and I heard *silence* in his hesitation, "My resignation," he stumbled.

"What? But why?" I asked surprised.

He didn't reply, instead he started scribbling on paper, *screeching* sound the pen nib made against the paper made me a little uncomfortable. I sat at the helm of this company for the last eight years, after my father declared me his successor upon his retirement, and this was the first resignation in all these years.

"Smith, why are you resigning?" I repeated my question while I heard his knees *clicking* with nervousness.

I was waiting, he was silent, the *tick-tick* of the clock hit my head hard.

301

There were times when the company didn't make a profit, days when a bullish market company was bearish, occasions when competitors fared better than us. But today I was losing my nerves for the first time in these last eight years. I shouted again, "Smith, are you going to tell me why you want to resign; and is there anything I could do to make you change your mind?"

"There is nothing you could do. I have already left this company. Now I want to leave it formally. I'm sorry," he spoke gravely while I could hear my teeth *grinding* with anger.

"No, I won't accept your resignation, until you tell me the reason." I clenched my fists.

"There is no reason really, it is just I'm so happy here that I find myself bound here, I want to be free. Please don't stop me," he urged. While his face said he loved this place, and I didn't understand the reason, I had no right to stop him. I picked up the pen and immediately signed his resignation letter.

"Thank you," he said while I heard a *sob* with the lump in his throat and opening the door with a *creaking* sound, he left.

I looked out of the window at the kids playing in a park opposite our office. Trying to imagine their *sounds* is a self-soothing thing I often do. On any other day it calms me, but today it wasn't helping. Suddenly a *trin-trin* of the phone on my table gained my attraction. With heavy steps I move to reach for it, but on listening to the first sentence, it fell off my hands, with the faint sound from the receiver still telling.

'Smith met with a car accident last night. He kept on saying your name in his unconsciousness, as if bound by something. He was in pain, but still alive. Then a few minutes ago he suddenly he took his last breath and "thank you" were his final words. I felt maybe those were for you.'

Gaurav Verma, author of "Sounds of the Soul" is a native of Dehradun, India and earned his MBA degree from IIT-Delhi. He started writing accidentally when a few of his school assignments turned out to be so good that teachers started to believe he was either copying or someone in his family was a writer.

FIFTY-ONE

BY
DOUG WALLACE

Teri Greensburg coughed deeply, the stinging in her chest lingering longer than before. Her face must have conveyed the her pain.

"Are you alright, Ms. Greensburg," asked Professor Kariya.

Teri had been feeling ill the past several days. So like most busy people on Jupiter Station, she put off going to the infirmary.

I just don't have time to be sick. , she thought.

Last week marked her fiftieth jump through the new Teleporter. It was a record. The most successful jumps by a civilian. Not that she really cared to hold a record like that, but it garnered her the attention from many of her colleagues in the Media. Some even wrote stories about her in widely-circulated publications. Not those backwater presses, but publications with readership in the millions. The notoriety would be a boon to her career. And somewhere along the way a clever wit had done her the favor of dubbing Teri the "Teleporter Reporter". Despite the pain in her lungs, she managed a smile at that thought.

It was true, though. The Teleporter had enabled her to publish more first-hand accounts of mankind's expansion into the solar system than anyone else. And she was determined it would help her win the Pulitzer Prize someday. But most people still had an irrational fear of teleportation. So what if your matter gets atomized and converted to energy? So what if it gets blasted across the solar system to be reassembled as matter again at your destination? Conventional spaceflight wasn't exactly risk free, so why not give teleportation a try? At least that's how she responded to questions regarding those who asked her if she had ever been bothered by the "what-ifs" of teleportation travel. But she hadn't been bothered. by them. And now, here she was on Jupiter Station getting an exclusive interview with Professor Kariya and Dr. Johnson, the award-winning physicists who had made nearly-instantaneous travel a reality.

Teri coughed deeply again before responding.

"The cough? I'm sure it's nothing. I probably picked something up on Mars before making the jump here."

Professor Kariya shot a seemingly worried glance to Dr. Johnson, who tilted her head slightly and raised an eyebrow.

"Ms. Greensburg," replied Kariya, "the Teleporter removes all unwanted pathogens from your system before reassembling you. I highly doubt you have been infected."

"Then what is it? I just had a pretty thorough medical exam last month. The magazine execs insist on keeping close tabs on my health for insurance purposes. Especially with all the Teleporter jumps I make."

Professor Kariya breathed a lengthy sigh.

"Right now we're calling it Teleportation Syndrome. It affects some people deeper more than others. Symptoms don't seem to show until someone has made at least twenty jumps."

Teri's heart began pounding hard in her chest.

"What symptoms?"

Dr. Johnson answered.

"Well, the coughing and chest pain like yours. Some people have reported blurry vision, heart palpitations, diarrhea, dry mouth, the shakes, and general achiness and lethargy."

Teri's head was spinning. She had more than one of those.

"How serious is it," she calmly managed, though her mind was racing wildly. "Are the effects permanent?"

Kariya shook his head.

"No, we don't think so. But we do have to scale back the frequency of your jumps. In fact, we probably should revoke your license until we get a better handle on things."

"Better handle on things? Revoke my jump license?"

Dr. Johnson tapped several commands on the capacitive surface of her personal comm unit. One of the cards on Teri's lanyard vibrated and chimed at her. She thumbed through them and found her jump license flashing. It's screen flashed the word "Revoked" in bright red letters. Then it said "Emergency Medical Transit Only".

"I've scheduled you one final jump to Earth. Your health is a major concern to everyone on the project. We have some colleagues at the Mayo Clinic helping us with treatments and research into the Syndrome. They will treat you well."

Teri's head was pounding, she was hyperventilating. Were the naysayers right all along? Is something wrong with the technology? What weren't they telling her? What about those who jumped after her? Would they also get sick? She turned to Professor Kariya.

"How will you prevent others from developing the same condition?"

Professor Kariya responded matter-of-factly, and without the emotion she would have expected from someone whose life's work was in jeopardy.

"It's simple really. We'll shut down the system, fix any problems, and reboot it. It's scheduled to be done a couple hours after you jump back to Earth."

#

Teri knew that jumping didn't hurt. It really didn't feel like anything for that matter. One minute you were in one place, you closed your eyes, there was a slight rush of air, the next minute you opened were opening your eyes in a different place. But this time, Teri opened them to something entirely unexpected. Instead of a teleportation facility, she found herself in a vast and seemingly shapeless room. And she wasn't alone. There were hundreds of people milling about, conversing. The din of the crowd echoing in the chamber was loud in her ears.

The people around her looked strange. They seemed fuzzy and had a metallic sheen to them. Some even appeared to be glowing. Just as her confusion began to give rise to fear, Teri recognized a woman in the crowd. She could have been looking in a mirror. The woman had noticed Teri too.

"Hey everyone," the woman yelled back to the crowd, "we got another Teri here."

A hundred set of eyes gazed in Teri's direction. Some of them merely noted her arrival with a nod, but others took greater interest. Within seconds, a group of forty-nine other Teri's had joined the first. As they gathered around her, Teri noticed they were all wearing her clothes, her jewelry, and more importantly, her expressions.

"Oh, dear, look at her face! She's frightened," noted one of them.

Another replied, "We just need to explain the situation to her. Knowing what's happening in here seemed to calm the rest of you when you first appeared."

The original 'other Teri' nodded her head. "I was the first to notice her so I will explain everything."

Teri half expected to wake up. Surely this was all a dream.

Wake up. Wake up!

She closed her eyes, but when she opened them again, Other Teri was still there, waiting expectantly.

"How many times have you jumped through the Teleporter, Teri?"

It was an easy answer. She'd set the record.

"Including today, fifty-one."

Other Teri gestured with her hand at the group around them.

"You can count them, but you'll find there are fifty of us in here. Fifty-one including you." She let that sink in for a moment, then continued. "We're in the Teleporter memory buffer."

Teri's face wore a look of consternation.

"But...that's not how it's supposed to work!"

Other Teri gently touched her arm.

"We know. They told us the machine rips us apart, shoots us to the new location and puts us back together. It does rip us apart. But we never make it out of the Buffer."

"Then who comes out of the other side? I've done this dozens of times."

"Fifty-one," replied Other Teri. "And each time a fresh copy is created on the other end, complete with your memories right up to the point of teleportation."

Teri's bottom lip quivered with realization.

"So I'm a...copy?"

"Copy of a copy of a copy. Fifty-one times."

That would explain the Teleportation Syndrome, thought Teri. The loss of fidelity each time a copy is made. But am I stuck here? Will my copy, now back on Earth, win the Pulitzer and finish living out my life?

"There's no going back, is there?"

Other Teri shook her head in the negative. By now a copy of Professor Kariya had approached. He looked just like the man Teri had spoke been talking with less than an hour ago on Jupiter Station.

"You knew about this?" she asked him, a hint of accusation in her voice.

"No. We had no idea. We've been trying for years to get a message out to my copies. To warn them."

Teri tried but couldn't hold back her tears. Were they really tears?

"We understand," consoled Other Teri. "We all experienced loss when we came to terms with our new existence."

"No, you don't understand," responded Teri between sobs. "We're all going to die."

Professor Kariya waved his hand dismissively.

"As long as the machine is running, we exist. We've been here for ages."

"Not anymore, Professor. You're copy is going to shut down the system in a few hours. Doesn't that mean the Buffer will be purged and we'll cease to exist?"

Kariya rubbed his chin as he thought for a moment.

"Yes, I suppose it does. But that won't be for a while. You see, an hour on the outside is like a year inside the Buffer. We have quite a bit of time." He put his arm around her shoulder. "Now, what shall we call you?"

Teri responded in a somewhat shaky voice.

"I guess you can call me Fifty-one."

When not dreaming up and writing crazy sci-fi and fantasy stories, Doug Wallace hikes the rocky mountains, during which he dreams up more crazy sci-fi and fantasy stores. His work can be found in various print anthologies and online journals, as well as at his website jamesdouglaswallace.com.

THE GIFT SHE NEVER WANTED

BY

LYLE WELDON

Katherine was furious. Three hundred dollars was no small amount, no matter what Darren thought. She could stretch three hundred dollars an impressive distance. If that much money dropped in her lap, she'd put two-thirds of it toward their rent, fifty dollars would go into their savings account and the last fifty would buy several days worth of food. Darren was a good, industrious cook which was the only positive thing she could say about him right now.

Katherine sat in the kitchen shooting angry, vengeful daggers at the monstrosity Darren brought home last night. It was bright red and took up way too much space on the countertop of their tiny apartment kitchen.

She could still hear his voice echoing in her brain from the previous evening.

"Honey," he said excitedly. "They gave us a credit of three hundred dollars. It's like free money!"

She wanted to hit him with the cast iron skillet she was cleaning in the sink after dinner.

"Darren," she said patiently, as if she were speaking to a child. Not that she'd ever have a child with him. Not now. Not after he revealed after two months of marriage, to be the most irresponsible man in the world. "That credit was meant to cover the charge that appeared on last month's bill, the charge that we never made. It corrected a mistake." She considered the soapy skillet in her hands. One smack would do the job for sure. But then Darren would be dead, she'd be a widow in jail and that red atrocity would still be in her kitchen. Worse, it'd still be on their credit card statement.

"Honey," he cooed, "look at it this way. We have this amazing thing. We can pay it off over time, but we'll have it forever." He said *forever* like it was free. Like forever only lasted two months.

Katherine lifted the heavy skillet from one side of the sink to the other, where she allowed it to rest on the plastic drying rack. She'd let him live another day. Maybe.

Now, the morning after, the skillet was still in the sink, completely dry. Katherine considered putting it away but she didn't want to move. She wanted to sit and shoot laser beams out of her eyes toward the horror in the corner of her kitchen.

Darren entered, saw his wife and almost smiled… but then he saw the glacial stare on Katherine's face and followed her gaze to the thing in the corner. Had he forgotten how mad she was at him? Before she could muster any new anger, Darren surprised her. He knelt down and took her cold hands into his, which were surprisingly warm.

It was the exact same position they'd been in when he'd proposed. He's tricky, Katherine thought to herself. Keep up your guard, girl.

"Honey, I'm sorry for buying it without discussing it first. But my parents had one, my grandparents had one, and I really wanted us to have one, too. If we really can't afford it, let's return it. But know this, we're getting one sooner or later. You're the best. You deserve the best. And I'm the luckiest guy in the world. There's no way my wife and I should make biscuits or meatloaf with a knock-off mixer."

Damn him. Katherine wiped a tear from her eye. He was sweet, handsome, and smart. He loved her like no one ever had. She was going to have to tell him the truth. It wouldn't be easy. She had dreaded this moment for months.

"I don't know how to make any of those things, Darren! I can't make biscuits unless I pop them into the microwave. I can't cook anything!"

Darren smiled, rose to his full height and moved toward the monster, and pulled something from behind it, something Katherine hadn't noticed before.

It looked like a homemade book, maybe thirty ratty pages bound together. Darren gently placed the pages in Katherine's lap.

"These are recipes my mom put together for us. Family recipes. Honey biscuits, pumpkin cake, my grandma's sticky lemon rolls. These recipes have been in my family forever and now they're ours, too. We'll add to them and make them our own. And we'll do it with this." He looked over his shoulder at the machine in the corner.

And that's when Katherine knew she was stuck. She was stuck with the KitchenAid mixer, stuck with the three-hundred-dollar statement on their credit card, stuck with these recipes which terrified her and she was stuck with the beautiful man standing over her in their ridiculously tiny kitchen. She couldn't have been happier.

Lyle has written for multiple Emmy-winning primetime television series as well as both live action and animated children's series. He lives in Los Angeles with his beautiful wife and their two equally-lovely daughters.

AND THE COURTLY TONGUE DID LASH

BY
NICK JOHN WHITTLE

And so came Arthur, King Born of all England, and with his brethren seated thus said, "Right, it has come to my attention that the toilets in the East Wing of the castle have been vandalized."

A noble gasp did rippleth about the Round Table and it befell by misfortune a good knight and archer named Tristan choked on his apple, and there fell down suddenly dead among them.

"That's right!" the King said standing afore them. "The ones at the end of the corridor leading to your dormitory." And with this he did wave a regal finger thus about each of his eleven sires. "The damage is as follows," Arthur continued, "a cracked loo seat, a smashed mirror and urine on a door."

Then as the book saith, each of the knights did look at each other, ever his thoughts privily on each other's guilt.

"I'm assuming none of you will own up to this pretty mammoth breach of misconduct, so we'll do this the hard way." And when he had all said, the King did walk slow around the table staring at each of his glorious knights until he heard some manner of tidings.

"Sir Lancelot. Dear, dear Sir Lancelot," saith the King slowly. "Didn't you get a surprise visit from Gwen last night?"

Those in the noble court didst snigger at thither rebuke.

"No, my Lord," saith the knight, yet did he turneth bright crimson and hunched over, hoping his liege would leave him alone.

"Sir Gawain, how about you?"

"Sorry, I don't know anything about it. I went to bed early."

"Hmmm," mused Arthur. "What about you, Geraint," saith the King, and he did kneel beside his third brethren as if to do great worship. "Who are you anyway, Sir Geraint? I don't know anything about you and nor does anyone else," spake he with his eyes looking about his court. "How does that make you feel?" The King stood tall above the knight. "Does it make you want to break things?!"

"No, sir! Please! I think I'm in the wrong group anyway. I should be at jousting practice."

The noble King from thenst arose and made haste about the table, stepping upon the poor Sir Tristan and descending on Sir Percival, and those brethren about him who skewed their faces.

"Those garden gnomes again, was it, Percy?" the King tarried.

"I – I'm not entirely sure, mine Lord."

"Fail!" said the King, then blew he onward to his next knight. "Ah-ha! Bors the Younger, always a slippery customer."

"It wasn't me, Sir. I stopped at the nunnery. There have been reports of dragons in the area."

"Fail!" the King cried aloud again, now assailing the empty Siege Perilous and thenst Sir Lamorak. "Hmm, perhaps you vandalized the toilets, Lamorak," mused the King, "the one with all the strength and the fiery temper and the chagrin; the one always doing the press-ups."

Sir Lamorak swooned pale and did bow his head, unable to cast his eyes to his King. "No, my Lord, I was," saith he...

"Yes?" urged the King.

"...Pressing flowers with Sir Pinel le Savage."

A great cheer and merriment did arise from the court, but then Sir Gaheris leapt mightily to the table and saith, "Have mercy on Lamorak, my Lord, it was me!" Thus shrieked the most valiant, agile and handsome of all the nobles: "I did it!"

Yet good and wise King Arthur, all-knowing of Gaheris's afflicted right arm, which was six-times longer than his left, upheld not the brethren's plea and spake harshly: "Get down, Gaheris, you're covering for someone."

"No, I am not!"

"Another word from you and you'll stay behind!" Spake the King, bending Sir Gaheris to lose his countenance and so to sit most heavily back upon his seat.

"Then again," the King mused, "perhaps it was Sir Kay or Sir Gareth, both of whom have been sitting so quietly throughout and who are as we all know quite, quite inseparable!"

For shame the two nobles did at once flood crimson at the King's words.

Then finally did the King of England, having walked about the whole Round Table, kneel betwixt the last of the brethren, the noble Sirs Bedivere and Galahad and spake he gently, "Seems it all boils down to Dumb and Dumber."

Sir Galahad did shuffle uneasy and cast his eyes downwards to the floor.

"What are you going to pull out of the bag this time, Galahad?"

The knight who would one day achieve greatness uttered tidings which the great Arthur couldn't quite make out.

"What did you say?" the King asked.

"S-s-Sir Bedivere was the last one to use the toilet last night!" hurried the noblest of knights.

"Ah-ha!"

"OK, OK, I admit it," spake Sir Bedivere, who more than any of the others was most repenteth. "I was last to go to the toilet, but it's not my fault. While I was in the cubicle a woman's arm, clad in white silk that was interwoven with gold and silver thread, rose up out of the toilet and mugged me."

"Mugged you?" the King saith with contempt.

"Yes, it pushed me against the door then shook me harshly thrice before slipping beneath the surface of the water again. It was freaky," saith the last and greatest of the knights.

Arthur Pendragon espied his court with fury and did fast slam his fist upon the table. "Bollocks!" saith he, having a countenance most tired of mirth. "Putting sugar on shit does not make it a brownie!"

"You lot know exactly who it was, but don't have the gumption to spill the beans. So, you can all stay behind this evening and write me a book review for Beowulf."

HOW DID THE KING KNOW WHO IT WAS?

Despite his lengthy interrogation, King Arthur suspected Sir Tristan was the culprit, but the archer knight's trick of choking on the apple sealed the deal. Sometime after Tristan had returned from the Holy

Land apparently empty-handed, it was brought to the King's attention that unlike the other knight's beds, Tristan's had a large lump under the mattress. Further inspection revealed the lump to be the Holy Grail. Assuming Tristan had – at some point since returning – drunk from the Grail, it was now impossible for him to die. Thus, his act at the table was merely a ruse for avoiding any further questioning. As for the reasons for vandalizing the toilet, he later admitted covering up for the wizard Merlin who had caused the damage while trialing a new type of magic toilet brush.

Case closed.

Award-winning screenwriter, independent film producer and director, and film festival director based in Birmingham, UK. Born in Manchester in 1972 and attended The Glasgow Academy, afterwards Napier University and finally the University of Gloucestershire (1998-2000) receiving an honours degree in Education.

THE VICTIM

BY

EUGENE WILLIAMS

I'll not cry for the fear of dying but I'll shed a tear for all the things I'll never know. The grand wormwood ran through the cracks of my broken glass and I could not look away. I watched them slowly put the needle back under the straw bed, in an instant rage the filthy ragged wool blanket was in the air, like a fool I could not look away. The smell of Absinthe filled the little room, blood! Whose blood, it was warm. I could not look away. I just want to sleep forever never to awake, I just want to sleep. Can I sleep just for a little while?

Will it ever stop raining, Father? So much pain, I do not remember when they came for me as I was asleep. Like pennies in a murky glass of wine, so were the days of my life, like pennies unspent collecting, collecting, piling, piling, I do not remember when they came for me.

Wake up! I can't wake up, I want to sleep, sleep yes sleep. Eyes wide open I could see a shadow standing over me. They were doing something to my chest, putting something over my face, calling out a name. Was it my name? Why can't I speak? Are they calling me? All I want to do is sleep.

Will it ever stop raining, Father? Can I dream? It's so quiet right now I can hear the wind blowing, it's so quiet in here. I heard someone say he is dead. My eyes are wide open, yet I cannot see anything. I smell burnt almonds, little bells fill the air. I smell burnt almonds. I heard them say he is dead. EW

Born in Waterloo, IA, Eugene Williams loves to study ancient history and write about everyday people and places.

HOMECOMING

BY

TINA WILLIAMS

She still has that pretty face, although I'd forgotten just how dark her features were. My heart thunders against my chest at the first glimpse of her passing by her father's rose bush. The scarlet flowers catch her attention and I imagine seeing their striking colour reflected upon her soft pale skin. Her wide almond eyes are as familiar as if I'd seen them only yesterday, but the brunette curls that had barely touched her shoulders back then are tumbling halfway to her waist now. 'You sure she's mine?' Thomas used to tease. He was blue-eyed and fair.

I've waited so long to see her again, but now that she's here I can barely catch my breath. Unsure whether I might laugh or cry, I press my fingers to my lips to stop myself from doing something silly. But as she nears the garden, I sense something unsettling. A look, maybe; the one I'd hoped would be gone by now.

I hover in the doorway, not knowing where to put myself. Half past, Mr. Collins had said they would get here from the station, but they're well over ten minutes late. I wipe my hands in my apron for the umpteenth time, still smelling the bleach on my trembling fingers.

He unlatches the garden gate for her and she smiles a little as he makes a grand gesture of letting her pass through. She's grown tall. The top of her head is already to Mr. Collins' shoulder and she has more growing yet to do. I suppose I'd expected to see the same girl who left six years ago. She was only seven then, almost a young woman now.

She hadn't wanted to leave, of course she hadn't. What child would want to be torn from her home and everything she knew and loved? We had filled her head with such made-up nonsense; saying she'd be the next Nancy Drew, for goodness sake, going on some wonderfully grand adventure. But she would have none of it anyway, not when we were disowning her like that, sending her away without a second thought as if we didn't want her anymore. Because we didn't, not here, not then.

She stops when she sees me come out from the shadow of the doorway. The fixed smile she's been wearing for the benefit of Mr. Collins abruptly falls, robbing her features of any hint of radiance. I remind myself this was never going to be easy. She was always a stubborn one. 'Oh yes, Thomas,' I used to say. 'She's definitely yours.'

Despite my fears, old feelings threaten to overwhelm me. I squeeze my hands together to stop from rushing forward and pulling her close because, as much as I want to, I can see she wants nothing of the sort. Mr. Collins sees it too.

'Right you are,' he says, loud enough to wake the dead. 'Here she is again. Back where she belongs, safe and sound.'

He hands me the box he's been carrying beneath his right arm.

'Thank you, Mr Collins,' I say. 'It was very good of you.'

He touches the edge of his cap in reply and retreats back down the path. I watch him go and give a small wave, half wondering if I should call him back, ask him in for tea, anything to delay what will happen now that she and I are being left alone together. But I dither for too long and he's already halfway out of the garden. When he's latched the gate and gone, I step forward to take her suitcase. She pulls away.

'I can manage,' she steps past me into the house. They are the first words she's spoken to me in six years.

'Right,' I say.

Inside, she stops at the foot of the stairs, looking all around; to see what's changed, I imagine, or maybe to remember. We once knew each other better than anyone else possibly could have, better even than Thomas and I knew one another, but I struggle to read her expression now. If I were to guess, I might say it was disappointment.

'Your room's still there, in the same place,' I say, and I could kick myself. Of course her room is still there. We weren't trying to erase her altogether, were we?

She doesn't move and I'm stuck where I am in the doorway, the box Mr Collins gave me digging into my arm.

'I wrote to you. Well, we both did, until Daddy had to—'

'Yes,' she cuts me off.

'After that, I tried to write often, when I could. Did you get the letters?'

She looks at me as if there's plenty to be said but now isn't the time. Not yet, at least. I ask if she's hungry or thirsty, maybe tired, but she shakes her head at all three, so instead I reach out my hand. She looks at it blankly.

'Your coat,' I say. 'Let me take your coat.'

She puts down the case, slides her arms from the sleeves and hands it to me. It's heavy. A beautiful emerald green. Made entirely of wool.

'Expensive coat,' I say, looking it over. There's no point pretending. I'm not sure what she's gotten used to, but I couldn't buy her a coat like this, not then, and certainly not now.

Ignoring me, she picks up the suitcase. She turns and I watch as she climbs the bare wooden staircase, her dainty, shining black shoes tapping upon each step. I place her coat on the peg beside mine. A loose thread trails from the hem of my old mackintosh, and I wind it round my fingers and snap it off. I stand still, listening, wondering what she might be doing up there in her old room. Looking out of the window, perhaps, at our garden she had so adored playing in. Gazing maybe upon the rope swing Thomas had strung up for her which still hangs from the aged oak. Or is she unpacking the case, carefully placing the clothes they bought her into her old wooden chest? Is she pausing with her hands upon the skirts, jumpers, underwear – thinking of her other home? Missing them?

But she makes no sound. I can't hear anything but the ticking of the mantelpiece clock in the front room. It almost seems as though the house is more silent than ever.

I take a deep breath, shake myself. Yes, it's going to take some time, that's to be expected. Especially now it's just the two of us.

I walk through the pantry to the cupboard doors beneath the sink. Pushing aside the Vim and tins of Brasso, I slide the cardboard box toward the back, out of sight. Though I try hard not to look, I am drawn to the large black letters printed across the side: GAS MASK OF JENNIFER CLARKE.

Memories return – happier ones – of all three of us before the war began.

'She's back, Thomas, darling,' I whisper, closing the cupboard doors softly. 'They've let our little girl come home at last.'

It's all over now. So they say. A new life awaits us all – thanks to our brave boys. But what sort of life that will be for the two of us, I can't be entirely sure.

Tina Williams lives in South Wales, UK, and is self-employed as Tina Williams Editorial Support, proofreading and copy-editing fiction and creative non-fiction literature for independent authors.

VACUUM RIGHT UP TO OUR WINDSHIELD

BY

OLIN WISH

At a time when others were preparing to go to college, I was preparing to disappear into the mountains. I had an old pickup truck and a twenty-one foot fifth-wheel with a leaky roof and threadbare tires. It sat in the vacant lot behind my girlfriend, Evelyn's house for a month while I made preparations. Colorado is cold in the high country, even during the summer. The furnace needed attention, as did the roof, which had the bad habit of turning every overhead 12-volt light fixture into a small aquarium whenever it rained.

The truck needed an overhaul. Bleeding rust spots needed beaten out and replaced with new metal. The driver side floorboard was completely rusted through. Without a repair, my feet would touch asphalt, Fred Flintstone style, going down the highway. There was also the frightening prospect of becoming tangled up in an exposed drive shaft.

I'd buried Evelyn's dog in the backyard a few weeks prior. As payment, her mom allowed me to use all her dead husband's tools and garage space. Included as payment, I promised to pull all her weeds; some with stalks as big around as my forearm. The job was sneezy work. But I got it done.

I salvaged metal from the tailgate to repair the holes. Spot welded, sanded, spray painted everything to prevent naked metal rusting again. For the roof I used caulking until the roof was more gelatinous goop than not. Evelyn acquired a heavy quilt sewn from upcycled jeans her mother made. She packed it and a wedding dress that had been handed down to her.

She showed me the dress, cheeks rosy with embarrassment and I smiled. Whatever plans she made prior to this trip, I wasn't privy to, which was fine. Grinding, spot welding, and terrified of the future; that was me. I knew others were going away and leaving me behind. Strangers my age, going about their lives. Going off to war, leaving home for the first time. Some with a safety net beneath them as wide and forgiving as mine was moth eaten and nonexistent. Others, with a tangled parachute and a swift kick to the ass. Those were going off to avenge 9/11.

While I fled, they moved forward towards something. They would return better and stronger men and women. Or they wouldn't. This didn't seem to bother Evelyn the way it did me. To her mind, we were going off on an adventure together. Nothing yet had happened in her life to convince her otherwise. Nothing broken for which there could never be an adequate repair job. All was still redeemable, fresh and new, like ocean glass. It's all in how you look at things, she tried explaining.

My friend whose father got us the job working at the campground told me I might want to consider letting my hair grow out. "They don't have shaved heads in Colorado?" I asked.

"No," he said, choosing his words with care. "They do. You just don't see it very often."

To reduce towing weight on the poor, decrepit truck, we brought only things we immediately needed. Birth control pills, a bedside novel, a knife, a gun, and tools. Clothes were kept to a minimum.

With all moving parts greased and the roof sealed, we linked up. Even with the grey and black tanks purged and the freshwater reservoir empty, the old engine labored in granny gear to exhume bald tires from where they had sank into clay. Every traffic light became a test to see if we could stop, and then once we did, to see if we could get going again when the light changed.

The engine pinged incessantly in high RPM's and the tangy aroma of hot ozone as the brakes gnashed made my hair stand on end. There came a point when traffic thinned and the stoplights ended; where the asphalt narrowed to two lanes and streetlights disappeared like dead children during war. On the interstate, we played chicken with gravity. Every sweeping curve became an asshole clenching experience. The name of the game was momentum conservation. At dips in the rolling hills I'd mash the accelerator, speeding maddeningly towards bottom, trailer lashing like an agitated cat's tail.

Immediately upon entering the incline we would begin to decelerate.

By thetime we reached the top of a gentle, desert foothill we were barely doing fifteen mph. People behind us honked, took unnecessary risks to pass us, slowing just long enough to see their middle finger register in our glassy eyes. Two scared-shitless kids in the early dusk fleeing invisible enemies.

A hundred miles from our starting point we discovered the second gas tank was leaking.

We stopped at a mostly empty Indian casino parking lot and there it was, drip, drip, dripping. In full dark with the emptiness of the desert, the flashing marquee was dazzling. There it was, drip, drip, dripping. There we slept in a puddle of highly combustible fluid. At dawn the tank was dry, the puddle evaporated, and it was once again safe to travel. By the light of day pink sandstone baking for all eternity reminded me of that raw, hard, abrupt stop that comes with every fall. Where others had fashioned parachutes, where tight rope walkers usually kept safety nets, I kept concrete. A great wide slab of it.

The engine overheated before noon. At a rest area reserved for the act, in the middle of nowhere, we waited for it to cool. Sitting inside the fifth-wheel without air conditioning, we sweat through our clothes and tasted what all the sweat lodge fuss was about. On the road again, well after dark the vacuum of space extended right up to our windshield. With microcosms beyond measure in the sky as bold as bioluminescent bugs, we had front row seats for the unfolding of the universe.

A day later, we were stuck again. This time on the side of I-70 with a frozen wheel bearing. It happened in the night, about 1 o'clock. Black smoke billowed out from the rear driver side hub. I thought for sure the trailer would catch fire before we pulled off the road. I remembered the leaking gasoline. The thin steel membrane separating us from oblivion. In the cold, parked on a soft shoulder, there was no chance that we could do anything about it. Instead, we waited till the smoke cleared, then climbed up into the fifth wheel.

Inside, it was dark except for whenever the semis passed creating headlight supernovas. Thunderous concussion waves from passing trucks in the next lane with blasting air horns pummeled the tiny space, rocking it back and forth over the axle. We lit candles and tried making macaroni and cheese on the stove with bottled water. But the noodles came out tough as trout bones. The cheese, runny and tasteless as snot. In the tall, flickering shadows with eighteen wheelers in the next lane passing by us at eighty miles per hour like close encounters or explosive decompressions, we felt like war orphans crouched inside a bombed out church.

Sucked into the vortex, cupboards slammed open and shut, as if possessed by evil spirits. Had we any real cutlery or plates we would have been cut to pieces. Instead, plastic ware tumbled and bounced around like popcorn kernels. It was decided our only hope for sleep was to curl up in a dry culvert beside the highway. Protected from the road by a steep decline, we pitched our tent right up against the cattle wire adjacent to some prairie land.

As I laid my head down on the water resistant nylon, I became convinced one of two things would happen while we slept. Either the hurricane force winds of the semis would tip the fifth wheel over onto its side, or in the pitch blackness a distracted driver would drift too close to the edge and slam into the home where our things were, turning our few possessions into road confetti. I stayed up, like a kid on Christmas Eve, awaiting that awful sound. The end of all things. At some point it never came and I drifted off.

We made it eventually to the safety of the mountains. We scrubbed camp latrines and helped siphon vaults full of shit and piss a thousand gallons deep. We stirred camp ashes and ate rainbow trout. Drank bourbon by firelight from the bottle and made love the way only twenty year olds can.

Once a week we paid for a shower at a hot springs down the road. Communal showers. I carried a ceramic knife in the pocket of my swim trunks, just in case. We stayed till the snow evicted us. Till the mountain herself shed us from her womb, down and out the steep path, momentum and its conservation always a consideration, even for those of us with youth in our rearview.

Olin is a husband, father of three young children, student and full time bread winner. He currently resides in a small, mid-western town in the United States.

THE OPENED DOOR

BY

JANNA WONG

It was Saturday morning and just like every other spring day in Los Angeles, it dawned gloriously. But, when she woke, she knew instantly that her mood was not going to match the beautiful day. This was the day her husband was moving out.

As she wandered around the two-bedroom apartment they shared during the nine months of their marriage, she took pains to look at everything carefully. All the pictures lining the hallway between the first and second floors were memories of their life together. As she walked past each frame, she thought they looked so happy, not a frown or look of dissatisfaction in any of them. She stepped into their living room, which was filled with furniture they bought as newlyweds. She remembered the first day they moved in – they had a party and their hulkingly big friend Leon sat down on their brand new couch and instantly broke two of the springs. What gales of laughter they shared! She looked out the window to their small patio and there sat the yellow Weber BBQ she bought him as a wedding present. She bought it because it was on sale and it was on sale because it was yellow and no one else would have it. How many impromptu grill sessions did they enjoy using that ugly yellow BBQ?

As she looked around, she realized the home they shared, the home they painstakingly put together with their meager earnings – he as a bank teller, she as an office worker at a film school – was breaking apart.

Today.

How did this happen? Why did this happen? It was love at first sight when they were introduced by a mutual friend. From that moment, that Friday night, when they got to know each other over margaritas and nachos at that bustling Mexican restaurant in Westwood, they were inseparable. Even though the date of their first meeting was Friday, October 13, it had no significance for her then. She was not experiencing bad luck that night. On the contrary, she knew immediately that she was falling in love.

Their courtship was stuffed full of fun, adventure and romance. Although both were young and neither made much money, they didn't need fancy trips or expensive cars to prove their love. There were afternoons at Farmer's Market, sitting by Bob's Donuts like the old folks and watching tourists all day. There were long days spent roller skating along Venice Beach, giggling at the odd people along the boardwalk and vowing that they would always be a normal, loving couple. There were nights when they were happy to stay at home, cuddled in each other's arms, watching mindless television in a fierce display of togetherness.

But then it was over.

Only weeks ago, when they were still a happy couple, they had enjoyed another great day at the beach, their two closest friends in tow. They went back to their apartment and the foursome had dinner together. Then, in the middle of everything, the phone rang.

He answered it pleasantly enough before a grim look came over his face. "I'll take this upstairs," he whispered to her. "It's my mom. There's something wrong with my dad."

After a few minutes, she followed him upstairs and listened quietly while he spoke to his mother. Except, the things he said were not those a son would say to his mother. She heard him whisper, "It won't be long now." And, "You have to be patient."

When he hung up, she asked him point blank, who was on the phone.

He looked at her. She froze because she could see something in his face. She tried not to focus on those features of his that made him so damn good-looking – strong jaw, crystal blue eyes, blonde hair. Instead, she tried to remember why he had fallen in love with her in the first place. She was smart, he said, and nice. He never said anything about her looks. They both knew he was the pretty one, not her. Still, he made her believe they belonged together.

Her attention was pulled back to him. He was talking but she wasn't hearing. Then he told her that he was unhappy. He added that the woman on the phone – Debbie was her name, was a friend whose opinion he respected. He was talking to her only because she was helping him through his crisis.

She realized at that moment that she was being thrown over for another woman. He said no, that wasn't true. But she didn't believe him. He said everything wrong with their marriage had nothing to do with anyone but him and her. She still didn't believe him.

Though she suddenly felt like she was drowning, she made a decision that night that she was going to hold on – like one of those kids who hangs on for dear life when a buddy is biking furiously and he's being pulled along on his skateboard. She wasn't about to let go and be sent spinning out of control. This was her marriage, her romance, her happy ending. So, she would hold on and would not let go. She would try everything she could to keep him safe within the walls of their marriage. She would be more loving than before and she would change for him.

For a few weeks, she did try. Whenever possible, she reminded him of their vows: What about his responsibilities? What about his commitment? What about the sanctity of their marriage?

At that point, he plied her with hope. He said maybe they could work things out. But for now, he felt he should move out. He had decisions to make and needed to make them on his own. She told him she would wait. She would cling to that sliver of hope she thought she saw in his expression.

And then one day it all changed for her. She called to talk to him about something that upset her that day and she got nothing – nothing from him. Angrily, she hung up the phone. She started to cry.

Her boss, a man 30 years her senior named Jim, looked up and shook his head. "You don't know how lucky you are," Jim said. "You found out early what an idiot you married."

She argued that her marriage was now an utter failure, that she was now young and a failure. Jim looked at her carefully and asked her if she would be happier if she were old and a failure? "Be thankful," he said. "Learn from this." This experience would amount to nothing if she learned zero from it.

She cried that her world was crumbling and it felt god-awful.

Jim then said Yes, she had a few rocks at her feet. She should sweep them away and be grateful it's not a whole building. Jim told her to trust him, that she would see this experience was a good one. He said she should take a deep breath and move on. That she, of all people, could do it. Because she was young, smart, nice and beautiful. She didn't believe him but he repeated those words to her. Then he said the door was open for her and she should walk through it and be happy the door was there.

The door was important. It's not always opened for people in her position but he knew it was opened for her. Her husband was a louse and the opened door allowed her to see that. She should walk through it and not look back. She would be happier for it. It was a guarantee he could promise her. Jim also said that if her husband didn't want her, she didn't want him. It was just that simple.

So, she decided at that very moment – 2:12 pm, to be exact, that she had had enough. She thanked her boss for his words of wisdom. He said he had plenty of doors opened for him when things looked bleak and that's how he knew about the doors. She said she didn't think he would have any doors opened because he was so wise and so smart and he said that the only reason he was wise and smart was because of the doors.

Jim believed she would have options. At his urging, she called a couple friends and made plans for that night and the next night and the night after that. Nothing rowdy; just dinner with friends. As he instructed, she kept her attitude up and her mood happy because he advised there was nothing worse than an embittered woman. He had met bitter women and whatever beauty they had was washed from their souls. She must never become bitter. Also, she mustn't let her friends offer any sympathy or pity for her situation. He reminded her to tell herself she was fine a million times a day, until she finally began to mean it.

By the end of her second week of independence, Jim assured she was going to be fine. At first, just like he warned, she committed to things to force herself to believe that she could survive. Soon enough, she was convinced that she could.

And then, the day came. This day. Saturday. The day her husband chose to move out. She was worried she would fall back to that simpering little thing she had been when he first broke the news to her. In fact, she was certain that's what he was expected. So, he gently requested that he ought to move out without her there.

She told him she wanted to see him and at least say good-bye. He thought she would cry and cling; she knew she wouldn't. She wanted to say good-bye so she could end it with dignity. But he told her he didn't want her there because it would be too hard on *him*. He still loved her and seeing her there would make him change his mind. And, he had thinking to do, decisions to make, he reiterated.

She agreed; she wouldn't be there. She went to work before he arrived to pack his things.

At the film school, there was always activity abounding. True enough, there was a film screening scheduled for that Saturday. She walked into the darkened screening room and sat down to watch a film she had already seen three times, the last time with him. She couldn't focus. She couldn't concentrate. Her marriage was ending and she could not sit placidly by in the dark, letting it die there without saying something about it.

And then she had a moment of insecurity. Maybe her newfound independence was all a ruse. Maybe it was stupid to let their commitment to each other break so quickly, so easily. Maybe she was just fooling herself.

She left the screening room and raced back to their apartment. She figured she had one last chance to keep things the way they were. But, did she really want things to remain as they were?

She put her key in the lock and pushed open the door. Oddly, the door opened too easily; she realized it was being opened from the other side. She found herself standing face-to-face with a woman. A tall, thin brunette. A woman she recognized as Debbie, his "friend." To her, that woman would always be known as Debbie Homewrecker.

At that moment, standing at the same threshold, their hands on the same doorknob, her life – her future – came into focus. She realized right then that she was not merely standing on the threshold of her front door; she was standing on the threshold of a new life.

That man who, months ago, promised to love, honor and cherish her, was not doing any of those things anymore. Her hanging on, her desire to keep her marriage whole and the sadness she felt at this failing were absurd. That part of her life was now over. Completely and utterly over. The thinking he had to do? The decisions he had to make? Inconsequential.

It wasn't about the two of them. It was about the two of *them*.

At that moment, she also realized she should not be sad. She should be happy that she was letting this jackass move on and out. How dare he thoughtlessly bring his new girlfriend to their apartment and boldly lie to her about the reasons for their marriage's demise. She should be happy that he was walking out the door with things she would never have to look at again, including Debbie The Homewrecker.

On that glorious Saturday morning, when she opened the door and found herself looking straight into the eyes of the other woman, she grew up in an instant. She was no longer the young, passionate bride or the naïve, foolish girl. In that instant, she became a woman who comprehended the complex machinations of two lives coming apart at the seams. And she realized she was coming out of this as the winner.

She thought about a future without him and she smiled. She thought about the ability to live on her own, independently, and she smiled. She wasn't afraid. She was excited about the possibility.

She wouldn't have been able to get to this place without first opening that blessed door...

Janna Wong grew up in Los Angeles, earning both her BA (English) and Master's (Professional Writing) from the University of Southern California. In addition to teaching Business Communication at USC's Marshall School of Business, she writes creatively and two of her novels, Mariana Wong's Summer of Love and Let's Get Lost, are currently available on Kindle.

THE INVERTED CROSS

BY
JOHN PAUL XAVIER

"Today's message is one to myself just as much as it is one to all of you, brothers and sisters," said Cardinal Dolan as he began his sermon that fateful morn in Saint Patrick's Cathedral. "As many of you know, I was named 'The Person of the Year' by Time Magazine last week. For that reason, I would like to speak on the subject of humility this Lord's Day."

Orbitus laughed to himself with much scorn as he heard the opening of Cardinal Dolan's sermon. The Archbishop of New York was in no way a humble man. He was after glory, Lucifer's glory. Lucifer, Orbitus' god and fellow demon, was not one to share his glory.

For two years in a row, Time Magazine had honored Catholic prelates rather than pawns of Lucifer, celebrities who worshipped him subtly in the signs they made, the symbols they chose for themselves, and the causes they supported. Orbitus' name was the Latin word for death, and death he would bring to Cardinal Dolan for his offense by the direct order of Lucifer himself, who was known to the world as the Devil.

Orbitus shuddered at the thought of his first meeting with Lucifer. Orbitus was not a curial demon, one who was among Lucifer's inner circle, but he was romantically interested in a female demon who was one of Lucifer's cronies. Therefore, he had agreed to assassinate Cardinal Dolan in hopes that such a feat would impress Adelia, on whom he had rested his eye for over a thousand years.

Killing Cardinal Dolan would not be difficult. He was a mere mortal, and his life could be snuffed out in an instant by any demon worth his salt. What would be difficult was the defeating of Cardinal Dolan's guardian angel who would prevent the Archbishop of New York from being harmed while he himself was still capable of fighting. His stomach crept into his throat as he thought of what Lucifer would do to him should he fail.

He and Adelia already had quite a good relationship as friends and allies, and Orbitus was sure that she would be willing to pursue a romantic relationship with him should he prove his worthiness by slaughtering Cardinal Dolan after defeating his guardian angel. Should he fail Lucifer, however, he would be burned. Demons could not be killed even by Lucifer, but they could be tormented until the end of the Great Tribulation by him.

Orbitus trembled like the ground during an earthquake at this thought and quickly decided to distract himself from it by taking action. There was no point in procrastinating, after all. He stood up in his pew at the back of the auditorium of Saint Patrick's Cathedral and pulled out a small thirty eight caliber revolver. It wouldn't be his murder weapon, but he would definitely make use of it. He shouted at Cardinal Dolan, "Alright, that's more than enough, you old hypocrite. You've spoken enough to condemn yourself a dozen times over."

Cardinal Dolan looked at Orbitus with confusion but little fear and said, "I wasn't aware that I was on trial. Please put your gun away, and we can forget that this whole thing took place."

Orbitus scoffed with a chuckle, "Rebellion cannot be pardoned or swept under the rug. You are going to die this day. Lucifer numbered your days the moment you were selected to be Time Magazine's 'Person of the Year.' Your time has run out. You will die now. You think that you are a righteous man, but you are an abomination who will either be instantly damned upon his death or who will burn in Purgatory for billions of years. Popes have been cast into eternal damnation and many more have suffered for their unpurged sins in Purgatory. Dozens still burn as I speak to you. What hope do you have of seeing Heaven?"

Cardinal Dolan said to Orbitus with his voice shaking, "I trust that the God and Father of Our Most Holy Savior will do what is just. Our Lady of Fatima will have mercy on the souls of Her children. I am a sinful man just like you and everyone else assembled here. You needn't remind me. I may very well experience the fires of Purgatory, but I put my faith in Jesus Christ and His Work on the Cross."

Orbitus felt as though he had been shot in the gut by a flaming arrow upon hearing the Holy Name of Jesus, but he quickly regained his composure and shocked everyone in the cathedral by putting his gun to his head. He squeezed the trigger and painted the cathedral's floors, pews, and occupants with his brain. The Faithful screamed in horror. He, in spite of the fact that he was missing the top half of his head, said as he pointed his revolver at Cardinal Dolan once more, "I am not a man. You are going to burn in Purgatory." He quickly shot a child next to him who was whimpering softly in the shoulder and relished the child's screams.

Orbitus said cruelly as he stepped on the maimed shoulder of the fallen child whom he had shot, "Your screams will be thousands of times more intense than those of this little whelp." He shot the child in the head, killing him instantly and further dousing the interior of Saint Patrick's Cathedral with brains then said, "And unlike his screams, yours will not be mercifully ended in just a few seconds. Your screams will haunt your fellow sufferers in Purgatory for billions of years." He raised his revolver and aimed it at Cardinal Dolan's chest whilst saying, "Prepare to die!" He fired.

To everyone but Orbitus' surprise, the shot didn't result in the Archbishop falling to the floor in a puddle of blood. Instead, a young man with red hair, a tall stature, and imposing musculature dove in front of the elderly cardinal with a supernatural jump and took the bullet for him. Orbitus grinned. Timothy Dolan's guardian angel had made himself known.

Orbitus instantly began hurling huge balls of fire at random members of the Faithful who were assembled in Saint Patrick's Cathedral. He watched with sadistic amusement as His Eminence's guardian angel leapt about to deflect the balls of fire with a great shield that he had created using ice. Unfortunately, however, the angel was able to handle all of Orbitus' attacks.

With a smug grin at first Cardinal Dolan then his guardian angel, Orbitus lit every last one of the pews contained within Saint Patrick's Cathedral aflame. His Eminence's guardian angel began rushing about even more rapidly in an attempt to cover over the fires Orbitus had started with snow that he generated from his hands. He was now far too busy to defend the Archbishop of New York. The lives of hundreds of the Faithful were at stake. It wasn't possible for him to save Cardinal Dolan too. Orbitus could now kill the prelate at his pleasure.

Orbitus tossed his revolver to the ground with disgust. It would not be his murder weapon. This mission was not about simply killing Cardinal Dolan. It was about sending a message of terror, a message that glory was to be given to Lucifer alone. He looked about the auditorium for a moment then found his murder weapon. He telekinetically ripped a massive crucifix from the wall and sent it flying at Cardinal Dolan's back. Even he cringed as the cross' base, the part below the Feet of Jesus, impaled the elderly prelate through the back, pierced through his front, and deposited his internal organs onto the ground in front of him.

Orbitus flipped the crucifix upside down, placing Jesus' Head in a position that made it seem as though the Most Holy Savior were looking up at the ceiling. He ripped off the rendition of Jesus, creating a simple inverted cross, a sign of Lucifer, on which Cardinal Dolan had been impaled.

Satisfied with his work, Orbitus teleported himself into the presence of Lucifer, healing the incredible self-inflicted wound to his head as he did so and leaving the late Cardinal Dolan's guardian angel to attempt to save the Faithful whose lives he had endangered. Arriving in Lucifer's presence about ten minutes later due to how great a distance it was between New York City and the Devil's lair, he knelt before the Devil and rose only after he had been invited to do so. He met Adelia's eyes and could easily see that she was both impressed and pleased.

Orbitus said, "I have done His All Lordship's bidding."

Lucifer said, "You have done well. I congratulate you, yet I now wonder if simply killing Cardinal Dolan wasn't enough. Perhaps a less subtle approach is needed." He picked up an iron paper weight from his desk that had been fashioned into the shape of an inverted cross and stroked his chin thoughtfully.

John Paul Xavier is an aspiring author interested in the arcane and mysterious. Particular genres of interest to him include fantasy and history.

BALDASSAR AND HANNO

BY

CHRISTIAN LEE

Baldassar squinted across the crowd to see Pope Leo X, who was being carried behind his pet elephant in a procession that was moving towards them. He instantly felt shabby in his own fine garments. His clothes were nothing compared to Leo X's heavily jeweled tiara and intricately embroidered mantum. That was saying a lot given that he wore the garb of a relatively successful artist from Medici coin ladened Florence.

Baldassar turned to a friend of his, a sculptor taught at the same school as he was, and pointed out the elephant that lumbered in front of the Holy Father. "Is the elephant a baby? It looks as though his shoulder is just four feet tall. I recall reading that the elephants brought to Rome by the caesars were much taller."

Niccolo replied, "No, Hanno is full grown from what I understand. He's been kept in a small enclosure since he was captured. I believe that he comes from India."

"Didn't the King of Portugal have him captured and sent him as a gift for the Holy Father's coronation?"

"Yes, that sounds right", Niccolo said slowly as though he wasn't quite sure.

"I don't particularly understand how he's so small. You said that he was kept in a small enclosure, but what does that have to do with anything?"

"Many animals can only grow as large as their environment will allow. Hanno doesn't have access to as much food as a wild elephant in India. He isn't able to move around nearly as much, making it difficult for him to build out his frame."

Baldassar mused, "I wonder if the same would happen to a human."

"Yes, of course it would. If you were only given a small amount of food and were unable to exercise, you would be a skeleton. If a cobbler was only able to sell twenty shoes a year for less than he could get elsewhere because he lives in a small, poor village, his business would be small compared to others just as Hanno is small compared to other elephants that have access to vaster resources."

"Interesting." Baldassar looked away from Niccolo and realized that the Holy Father was almost upon them. What a powerful man. The streets of one of the largest cities on earth were lined with people wanting to catch a glimpse of him.

"Did you hear of the Holy Father's commission to Raphael? He's to paint a fresco based on the deliverance of Saint Peter. I'm sure you could only imagine being given a commission so large and valuable back home in Florence."

Baldassar nodded thoughtfully and then looked up at the Pope who was now upon them. Before him was a man who had the money to pay twelve other men to carry him through a city that he virtually owned. He wore more jewels on his tiara than all of the kings and queens, prince and princesses, and dukes and duchesses of Europe combined.

After the Holy Father had passed them along with his cardinals and attendants, Niccolo inquired, "Should we begin preparations for the return journey? We've been gone long enough and have seen much of what the Eternal City has to offer."

Baldassar said with a bit of trepidation, "I won't be returning to Florence with you, friend."

"Baldassar, you must be joking. Don't you have a half dozens patrons waiting to give you commissions? We've been gone weeks and weeks. You can't keep them waiting."

"I've managed to scrape by on their money like Hanno has managed to scrape by on the food afforded to him by his enclosure. It's time for me to break free of Florence, which is my enclosure. It's time for me to operate in a city of unlimited resources. Here I can grow."

"I didn't mean to give you this idea with my talk of Hanno, but when you paint the Pope's apartments or a chapel in the new basilica, remember me."

Baldassar said with a smile as he embraced his friend, "I certainly will."

Christian Lee is the Founder and Publisher of Centum Press and Executive Chairman of its holding company, Allegiant Publishing Group, Inc. In his spare time, Christian enjoys working on writing projects that include historical or magical elements.